Wild Oats

Veronica Henry

An Orion paperback

First published in Great Britain in 2004
by Pengiun Books Ltd
This paperback edition published in 2014
by Orion Books,
an imprint of the Orion Publishing Group Ltd,
Carmelite House, 50 Victoria Embankment,
London EC4Y ODZ

An Hachette UK company

5 7 9 10 8 6 4

A CIP catalogue record for this book
is available from the British Library.

ISBN 978-1-4091-4691-9

Veronica Henry worked as a scriptwriter for *The Archers*, *Heartbeat* and *Holby City*, amongst many others, before turning to fiction. She lives with her family on the coast in North Devon. Visit her website at www.veronicahenry.co.uk or follow her on Twitter @veronica_henry

Also by Veronica Henry

Wild Oats
An Eligible Bachelor
Love on the Rocks
Marriage and Other Games
The Beach Hut
The Birthday Party
The Long Weekend
A Night on the Orient Express
The Beach Hut Next Door
High Tide
How to Find Love in a Book Shop
The Forever House

THE HONEYCOTE NOVELS
A Country Christmas (*previously published as* Honeycote)
A Country Life (*previously published as* Making Hay)
A Country Wedding (*previously published as*
Just a Family Affair)

For Jacob, Sam and Paddy

Acknowledgements

With huge thanks to Louise Treutlein of the Bugatti Owners Club for her kindness and patience in answering all my questions, and for taking me up the famous hill at Prescott. Any mistakes or technical gaffes are entirely mine ...

Thanks also to Julia Simonds for her insight into running an estate agency, and Dr Alisha Kaliciak for medical advice.

I

Jamie Wilding thought it ironic that, of her somewhat epic journey from South America, the final leg from Paddington to Ludlow had been the most traumatic. She'd missed her connection at Hereford, and the next train had come to an agonizing standstill in the wilds of the Shropshire countryside for no apparent reason – at least, none was given. By then she'd been travelling for over twenty-four hours. Now, with judicious use of her elbows and a certain ruthlessness, she finally managed to push her way through a dithering gaggle of American tourists, extricate herself from the train carriage and alight on the platform. She was tired, dirty, hungry and thirsty. As she struggled out of the station with her rucksack, she prayed there would be a taxi. There was. 'Bucklebury Farm, Upper Faviell,' she told the driver, and flopped into the back seat wearily. The smell of the driver's cigarette combined with the sickly smell from his Wallace and Gromit air freshener turned her empty stomach, but she didn't care. She was nearly there.

The cab nudged its way slowly through the midday traffic and up the hill to the town centre. Jamie feasted her eyes on the familiar buildings: the black-and-white timbered edifices bowed down with age juxtaposed with the more gracious red-brick frontages introduced in Georgian times. She wondered which she preferred, then decided it was the contrast that was so charming.

As they pulled into the town square, the farmers' market was in full swing. Stalls with gaily-coloured awnings to protect them from the summer sun were crammed with vegetables: rows of cauliflowers, creamy white, luminous green and purple, enormous pods bulging with broad beans, punnets of voluptuous red strawberries. Other stalls were selling delicious-looking pies and jams and cakes; local honey; pots of herbs to take home and plant; handmade ice cream thick with raspberries or ginger or chunks of bittersweet chocolate. Someone was cooking free-range sausages on a portable barbecue to entice customers: the smell drifted in through the cab window and made Jamie's mouth water. She was ravenous. There'd been no buffet car on the train. Her last meal had been an unedifying airline breakfast in another time zone. She was tempted to ask the driver to stop, but knew that would just be prolonging the agony. It was something she could look forward to after months of meagre and monotonous rations: coming to the market, chatting to the stallholders, trying their samples, coming home with a basket groaning with fresh produce. As the traffic nudged along, she caught sight of Leo the cheesemonger, with his mop of unruly black curls, deep in conversation with a customer, talking her through his mouthwatering selection of wares, paring off slivers for her to try. You could have a full-blown meal just by sampling what was on offer at Ludlow market, starting with marinated olives, moving on to cured meats and home-baked breads, finishing with a sliver of lemon tart or apple cake.

2

At the far end of the square the castle overlooked the bustling scene with an air of benevolent superiority. It had, after all, been there the longest, long before Ludlow became renowned as a gastronomic and epicurean mecca. Tourists swarmed over its ancient ramparts, armed with lurid ice creams and guidebooks, spilling out of its magnificent gates to discover the rest of the town's treasures.

At last the cab was free of the traffic. It crossed over the river and on to the road that led to the Faviells. As they sped along the winding lanes, hedgerows thick with emerald greenery, Jamie felt the faint drumming of butterfly wings against the wall of her stomach. Why was she nervous? She was coming home, that's all. She had no need to be nervous.

Yes, she did. After all, she had no idea what to expect on her return – what she was going to find, how she was going to be received. Or what she would do and say. Jamie always feared the unknown, because her imagination worked overtime and presented her with the worst-case scenario. Give her a rope bridge to cross or an unbroken horse to ride and she had nerves of steel. But when she wasn't sure what to expect, her courage seemed to fail her.

Only too soon they arrived in Upper Faviell. The village hadn't changed, which was hardly surprising, as it hadn't changed for as long as Jamie could remember. The hanging baskets at the Royal Oak were sporting a blue and white colour scheme this year, compared to yellow and red the year before, and there was a new 'Please Drive Carefully Through Our Village' sign, but otherwise it was the same as it had been when she'd left, almost a year ago now.

Half a mile outside the village, on Jamie's instruction, the driver pulled into a gateway. Weeds and grass poked through the cattle grid; the sign that would have told passers-by that this was Bucklebury Farm was overgrown with brambles.

'I'll walk from here,' Jamie told the driver, and thrust a crumpled tenner at him. Heaving her rucksack back on to her shoulder, she stood for a moment, heart thumping, knowing that by walking this last quarter of a mile she was delaying the moment of reckoning yet again.

She trudged down the drive, a simple track flanked on one side by orchards and on the other by pastures dotted with grazing sheep. Her feet kicked up the dust of earth dried by the midday sun, but the heat was nothing compared to what she had endured over the past few months. Instead, she relished the gentle breeze that swished through the boughs of the trees and set the buttercups, sprinkled like gold dust over the fields, nodding furiously. Eventually, two stone gateposts and another cattle grid pronounced the entrance to the farmyard, whereupon the track became tarmac and led past a decrepit hay-wain and a magnificent Victorian stable yard, before coming to a halt in front of the house itself.

Bucklebury Farm embraced the two styles of architecture that typified Ludlow. The oldest section was seventeenth-century black-and-white timber, irregularly shaped and peppered with leaded windows. The floors inside were wooden and leaned at alarming angles, the rooms were predominantly wood-panelled, the ceilings low, the staircases winding and narrow and crooked. Upstairs, one frequently had to bend to avoid concussion on a beam or a sloping roofline. Overall, it gave one the

4

impression of being on board a rather cosy ship. In the late nineteenth century someone had obviously found its confines claustrophobic rather than charming, and had made a red-brick addition to the house that was stout and square and perfectly proportioned, allowing a rather grand staircase, a large dining room, a study and some sensibly sized and shaped bedrooms. Jamie infinitely preferred the older part, where her bedroom was tucked into the eaves up its own little staircase. The windows were tiny but gave a magnificent view of the rolling countryside, and in the distance she could see the ramparts of Ludlow Castle standing guard over the town.

Ignoring the imposing front door, with its arched fanlight, that was only ever opened to people who didn't know any better, she made her way around the side of the house. She couldn't help noticing a general air of neglect about the place: the lawns and hedges were badly in need of attention, and the vegetable patch, once immaculate with its regimented rows of carrots and cabbages and lettuces all neatly netted to protect them from the rabbits, had become rampant and choked with weeds. But then, her father had never taken any great interest in gardening. Never mind; she could bring things back into order soon enough.

As she walked past the kitchen garden to the back door, a brace of Jack Russells came tearing round the side of the house with a volley of barks, leaping up at her with muddy paws, stumpy tails wagging furiously.

'Parsnip! Gumdrop!' She dropped to her knees and embraced the pair of them as they sniffed at her in disbelieving delight. Overwhelmed by their greeting, she was struck by the absence of a further presence. Their vanguard would once have been followed by her mother vainly calling them off; the little dogs were the one thing over which Louisa seemed to have no control. They were notoriously quite the worst behaved dogs in the county, over-indulged and under-disciplined, saved from being thoroughly dislikeable by their ebullient mischief and effusive welcomes. Now, Jamie noticed, they could both do with a good bath and needed their nails clipping. If she needed any further reminder that her mother was no longer here, then this was it ...

She'd been working in California when it happened. An American family who had hired her to look after their first child when they'd lived in London had her flown over to San Francisco when number two arrived. It had been a very happy few weeks; the baby was an angel, Marin County was heaven and the Knights treated Jamie like one of their own. For the first time, she was seriously tempted when they begged her to stay on. It was one of her golden rules, why she'd chosen maternity nursing over nannying, that she never got attached to a child or a family, that she only stayed eight weeks maximum, and that once the mother had recovered from the birth and the baby had settled into a routine, she was gone. That way, she could be sure of her freedom. She could pick and choose her jobs, and never be at anyone else's beck and call.

Her father Jack had phoned on a Sunday morning, when they were all about to set off for brunch at a harbour-side restaurant in Sausalito.

'It's your mother.'

6

Jamie could tell by the strain in his voice that something was badly wrong.

'What is it?'

'She ...'

'What?' Jamie couldn't keep the irritation out of her voice. It was one of her father's more annoying habits, not being able to get to the point when there was something unpleasant that needed saying.

'The doctors say she probably won't make it through the night.'

Jamie was stunned into silence for a moment, then delivered a barrage of questions.

'What do you mean? Why? What's the matter? Has she had an accident?'

Jack gave a heavy sigh in response.

'She's got cancer, Jamie.'

To say Jamie was shocked was an understatement. Her mother couldn't have cancer. She was never ill. At first she told herself there'd been some mistake, that the phone would ring and Jack would tell her to relax, Louisa had made a recovery, her notes had been mixed up with someone else's. But when kindly Dr Roper, their GP, had called ten minutes later, Jamie could tell from the tone of his voice that the situation was as grave as Jack had outlined. Louisa had been diagnosed with secondary cancer six weeks ago. It had reached her lymph nodes. There was nothing on God's earth to be done.

Jamie had tried valiantly not to become hysterical, but the harsh reality of being thousands of miles away with her mother on the brink of death made it hard. The Knights booked her a flight, repeatedly reassured her that she wasn't letting them down, helped her pack and

7

drove her to the airport. Mrs Knight slipped her a couple of Valium for the journey. Jamie didn't dare take them. She wasn't sure what effect they'd have. And if she got there, and her mother was still alive, she wanted to be fully aware.

As hard as Jamie had willed the plane to go faster, the hours had slipped through her fingers. As she waited for her connection at JFK, she called home. Dr Roper broke the news as gently as he could: Louisa had passed away during the night. She sat on the final eight-hour flight numb with shock. Someone, she couldn't remember who even now, had met her at Heathrow and driven her home on what had become the most pointless journey of her life.

Even worse than her mother dying had been what she perceived as her father's betrayal. Perhaps that had been the easiest way to deal with her grief, to displace her anger on to Jack. She was incandescent with rage, and vented her fury upon him with little or no thought for his own feelings. Why on earth hadn't he warned her? Phoned her? Called her back home as soon as they knew the awful truth, the moment her mother had been diagnosed? He put up a weary defence.

'It was what she wanted, Jamie. She wanted you to remember her as she was. She didn't want you to see her sick.'

Jamie couldn't accept his justification.

'What do you respect?' she'd stormed. 'The wishes of someone who's about to die? Or the feelings of the person who's got to live with it afterwards?'

'Don't think it was easy for me, Jamie.'

'I don't understand. I *don't understand.*'

8

'You wouldn't have wanted to see her. There was no point, believe me. It was harrowing. She wasn't your mother ...'

'I'd like to have been given the choice.'

There was no point in railing at him. He stared catatonically into the middle of the room, eyes red-rimmed, the beginnings of a beard that Jamie had been shocked to see was white. Jack the dandy shaved twice a day, and smelled of spicy, woody aftershave. Now he was beginning to have the waft of an old man who hadn't bathed for several days.

She tried to remember the last time she'd seen Louisa. She'd spent a weekend at the farm just before she went to California. Had her mother known she was dying then? She tried to recall her mood, whether she'd said anything significant, whether she'd held on to her a fraction too long when she'd kissed her goodbye. But as far as she could remember the weekend had been the usual glorious whirl of dogs, horses, people, music and endless food and drink that was Bucklebury Farm, just the tonic Jamie always needed after a gruelling few weeks looking after a newborn.

The funeral was hideous. The church was packed, the vicar effusive in his eulogizing, the profusion of flowers giving off a sickly scent. Jamie took the Valium Mrs Knight had given her for the plane journey. She didn't want to sit next to Jack, but how could she not? She didn't want people surmising, conjecturing. Her mother deserved a gracious send-off, not to be a source of gossip. Back at the house, she supervised the funeral tea like an automaton, desperate to snarl at people for their sympathy and platitudes. Nobody, thank God, said it had been a shame that she hadn't made it back in time to say goodbye. Nobody was that insensitive. But Jamie couldn't help wondering if perhaps they were all thinking it.

She'd barely spoken to her father, and when she did it was only to consult him on practicalities. They'd operated as islands, moving like ghosts around the farmhouse, praying for each day to end as soon as it began. A week after the funeral, when she'd replied to all the letters of condolence, chosen the gravestone and tidied away the most evident of Louisa's possessions – the gumboots by the back door, the Agatha Christie on the coffee table, the few of her garments in the washing basket – she bought the *Rough Guide to South America*, spent a couple of hundred quid in Millets on sturdy outdoor wear and a rucksack, and booked a one-way flight to Peru.

Perhaps it had been irresponsible. It was certainly running away. But she couldn't stay at home, burning with resentment at Jack, expecting her mother to walk in through the door at any moment. And she couldn't work. Numb with grief, she didn't trust herself to be in charge of a newborn baby and a hormonal mother. Hers was a job that took patience and tact and a strong constitution for what could be weeks of interrupted sleep.

More than anything, she was angry. With whoever it was who'd taken her mother away – God, presumably, though Jamie wasn't a great believer. With her mother, for not having the will to fight. But most of all with Jack, for not having the strength and the foresight to go against Louisa's wishes. It was typical of him, to go with whoever shouted the loudest and not stand up to them. Out of sight, out of mind. Anything for an easy life. That was Jack.

She phoned the agency to say she would be indefinitely unavailable. They were sympathetic, but keen to get her working again as soon as possible. She was one of the best maternity nurses on their books. With her youth and energy, new mothers found her sympathetic rather than intimidating, and looked upon her as a friend rather than someone to be in awe of. But Jamie couldn't give them an idea of when she would be back.

Over the ensuing months, Jamie toured her way round Mexico, Peru, Ecuador and Nicaragua in search of peace. Once every few weeks, she steeled herself to phone home and check up on Jack. They would have a stilted, awkward conversation, not helped by the time delay on the line. Jamie would hang up hastily, her conscience salved for another couple of weeks.

But over the past month, as the shards of grief in her heart had gradually started to melt and the pain began to fade, Jamie had a sudden feeling that the time was right to come home. She'd climbed to the top of Machu Picchu and there, on top of the world, standing amongst the clouds, she could almost believe she was in heaven itself. She'd never been a very spiritual or fanciful person, but somehow she'd felt as if her mother was there beside her; as if Louisa was telling her that it was all right, that she was all right, and that it was time for Jamie to go and make her peace with Jack. And Jamie had climbed back down feeling stronger, convinced that ten months was long enough to stay away from someone you knew you had to forgive in the end ...

And now here she was. The back door was slightly ajar, suggesting that her father was in, though they had never been tight on security. Locks and keys weren't part of the Wilding lifestyle. Jamie breathed in as she pushed open the door and stepped over the threshold, almost expecting the smell of freshly baked soda bread or one of Louisa's casseroles to rise up and greet her. Instead, there was the odour of cigarette smoke and bacon fat. She frowned – her father only ever smoked cigars. Then she stopped short.

The kitchen was undoubtedly Bucklebury Farm's greatest selling point. Nearly thirty foot long and fifteen wide, it had a high vaulted ceiling, crisscrossed with beams, and a limestone floor. The walls were painted a dusky pink, and were smothered in ancient farming implements. An antediluvian range lurked in an inglenook fireplace at one end, and a huge moose head reigned over the scene in regal bemusement – he was a relic from someone's past, though no one knew quite whose. In the centre was a hefty oak table, usually bearing a pile of unanswered post, car keys and a battalion of jars containing jam, honey, Marmite, pickles, mustards and chutneys. For as long as Jamie could remember there had always been people sitting at this table, enjoying a morning coffee, a midday beer or an early evening glass of wine, sharing wit, wisdom and salacious gossip.

Today was no exception. Bent over the newspaper, deep in concentration, a cup of tea at his elbow, was a bare-torsoed man. His hair was somewhere between long and short, whether by design or because he couldn't be bothered to get it cut, Jamie couldn't be sure, but he'd tied it back with a bandanna. He was stripped to the waist, his body tanned and sinewy, not an ounce of spare flesh upon him. As he looked up, a pair of brilliant aquamarine eyes met hers.

'Who the hell are you?' She knew she sounded incredibly rude, but she'd been taken unawares. She'd been steeling herself for a confrontation with Jack. She hadn't been prepared for a half-naked stranger in the kitchen. For some reason – his exotic bone structure, the colour of his skin – she expected him to reply in a foreign accent. Who was he? Some asylum-seeking Eastern European her father was employing at slave wages to maintain the place? Because if so, he wasn't doing a very good job of it.

But the voice that answered her was unmistakably English. A laconic, lazy drawl with the insouciance that only public school could provide.

'I could ask you the same question.' He tipped back in his chair, revealing cut-off jeans and long, bare legs. He'd clearly been doing some sort of menial task: Jamie noticed his hands were filthy, and as he pushed his fringe back from his forehead with the back of his hand he left a streak of dirt across his skin. Then he took a drag from a Disque Bleu smouldering in the ashtray, surveying her through laughing eyes. Jamie scowled.

'For your information—' she began, but he cut her off with a wave of his hand.

'I know. It's obvious. You're Jamie.' He grinned. 'My, how you've grown.'

Jamie stared at him, a memory battling its way into her consciousness, like a poor swimmer struggling to the surface of the sea. In her mind's eye was a boy – well, a youth, perhaps sixteen or seventeen – with the same laughing eyes as the man before her now, but with shorter hair and a lighter physique, sitting on a floating pontoon in red bathing trunks, confident in the knowledge that every female over fifteen and under fifty was gazing at him with longing. Everyone except her, of course.

'Olivier?'

She was rewarded with a smile of acknowledgement as Olivier stubbed out his cigarette and got to his feet. He was going to hug her, Jamie realized, and she dropped her rucksack just in time to reciprocate. His embrace was easy, familiar, and despite herself Jamie relaxed; it could have been yesterday that they last met, instead of fifteen years ago.

'I'm sorry,' he was saying. 'I shouldn't have teased you like that, but I couldn't resist.'

'You never could,' countered Jamie, wondering if perhaps lack of sleep and food was making her hallucinate. Olivier Templeton, here, in their kitchen?

Their fathers had been best friends – inseparable soulmates, until they'd fallen out all those years ago. Yet here was Olivier, holding court as if he owned the place. Even Parsnip and Gumdrop had settled themselves under his chair, clearly quite comfortable with his presence.

Jamie composed herself as best she could, wriggled out of Olivier's grasp and smiled.

'So … what are you doing here?'

'I came to give your father my condolences. He … wasn't in very good shape. I stayed around for a while to make sure he was all right.' He grinned ruefully. 'I keep forgetting to leave.'

Jamie blinked. This was certainly a turn-up for the books. How on earth had the hatchet come to be buried between the Wildings and the Templetons? She didn't want to ask, as she wasn't sure she was ready for the answers. And she had a feeling, judging by the lightness of his tone, that Olivier didn't really want her to probe. They both shared a history that was forbidden territory, for the time being at least.

'Let me make you a cup of tea. You must be shattered.' Olivier moved over to the sink, grabbing the kettle en route. Jamie felt totally bemused – he was offering her tea in her own house, as if she was a visitor and he the host. She accepted, despite herself, and watched in amazement as he filled the kettle, produced two clean cups from the cupboard and emptied the pot of its last brew in preparation for the next.

'Your father will be pleased to see you,' remarked Olivier easily. 'He's missed you.'

He made it a statement, not a reproach, but nevertheless Jamie felt on the defensive. Had they talked about her? What had been said? Paranoia crept up and tickled the back of her neck.

'Where is he?'

'At the races.'

That figured. Some things didn't change. Olivier handed her a cup of steaming tea.

'So. How was South America?'

'Amazing.'

He raised an amused eyebrow.

'That's it? Just … amazing?'

Jamie managed a smile despite herself.

'I could go on for hours. Trust me, once I've started, you'll wish you'd never asked. If you're really unlucky, I'll show you my slides.' She took a slurp of tea. It was heaven. 'This is divine. It's the first proper cup of tea I've had for nearly a year.'

'Is that what made you come home? Tea deprivation?'

The fact that his query was masked with a joke made her feel uncomfortable. Those piercing eyes were very perspicacious. And she didn't know whether she could trust him, or quite what his game was. There were too many pieces of the puzzle missing for her to confide in him just yet. Instead, she made a rueful face.

'Ran out of money. Thought I'd better come back and do some work.'

'Bloody money. Always gets in the way. Stops you from doing what you really want to do.'

'Spoken from the heart?'

Olivier spooned three sugars into his tea and stirred.

'Dad wants me to take over his car dealership in the New Year. This is my last-ditch attempt at having some fun. I've spent the last five years being a ski instructor in the winter and a tennis coach in the summer. He says it's about time I had some responsibility.'

Responsibility? Jamie couldn't imagine that Eric Templeton knew the meaning of the word. When had he ever been responsible? She raised a dubious eyebrow.

'That doesn't sound like your dad.'

'I know. Bit of a cheek, considering what he used to be like. But he's changed a lot. Keeps going on at me to settle down. Keeps asking me if I've got a pension plan.' Olivier rolled his eyes. 'As if.'

There was an awkward silence, as the conversation seemed to run out of steam. Olivier cleared his throat.

'I'm … I'm really sorry about your mother, by the way.'

He obviously felt uncomfortable talking about it, as he couldn't meet Jamie's eye. But Jamie didn't want to dwell on it either.

'Thanks,' she said, then changed the subject quickly as

16

she put her tea cup back in the sink. 'I think I'll go and have a bath.'

For some reason, she suddenly felt horribly self-conscious about her appearance. She was keenly aware that her legs hadn't been shaved for weeks, and though the hairs on them were fine and fair, they were still evident. The shower she'd had at the hotel before catching the plane had been nearly twenty-four hours ago. She knew the combat shorts she was wearing looked butch and unflattering, and the plaits that were most practical for travelling made her look about twelve.

'There should be enough hot water. If not I'll flick on the immersion for you.'

Jamie frowned. Yet again Olivier was making her feel as if he were the host and she the intruder. He must have his feet well under the table, if he knew where the immersion was. She wondered exactly how long he'd been here.

'I know where it is. Thank you.' She couldn't quite keep the coolness out of her tone as she left the room.

The final indignity was when Parsnip and Gumdrop made no move to follow her, but stayed resolutely under Olivier's feet.

Feeling slightly disgruntled, Jamie lugged her rucksack into the utility room, emptied almost all of its unsavoury contents into the washing machine, then went up the two flights of winding stairs to her bedroom. It was just as she had left it. She'd stripped it of most of her childhood detritus several years ago: pony-club rosettes, pop-star collages, postcards, dead pot plants – and tried to make it more sophisticated, with photos in proper frames and candles. But it was still definitely the bedroom of a single girl, with its high brass bed and rose-covered eiderdown, and the patchwork nightdress case she'd made in needlework at school and hadn't been able to bring herself to throw away.

She wondered where Olivier was sleeping. There was another bedroom on her floor, cosy and crooked but with barely any headroom – surely he would be too tall? Or there were three large, well-appointed rooms in the later wing of the house, each with an en-suite bathroom. No doubt he was in one of those.

She sat on the bed, suddenly exhausted, and debated whether food or a bath was the more important. Neither of them had featured prominently on the shoestring budget she'd set for herself on her South American tour. Finally she decided that, for the sake of public interest, she'd make herself presentable first. There was nothing but an ancient box of Radox in the bathroom on her floor, but somehow she felt inhibited about prowling round the house in search of something more exotic, in case Olivier appeared miraculously with an assortment of luxury toiletries. She wanted time alone to gather her thoughts – if there was one thing Jamie hated it was being wrongfooted – so she made do, emptying the remnants of the box under the taps.

She dropped her dusty, sweaty clothes on to the bathroom floor and climbed into the blissfully hot water. She'd been lucky to get a tepid shower in most of the places she had dossed, and the water had often been suspiciously murky in colour. She slid down until she was submerged up to her neck, closed her eyes and began to try and make sense of the strange turn of events. Of all the scenarios she had envisaged on her homeward journey, finding Olivier Templeton in her kitchen had not been one of them.

Jack Wilding and Eric Templeton had met as boys, while incarcerated together at a minor public school. There they'd run scams and wheezes for the benefit of their pockets rather than their fellow pupils, and had narrowly avoided expulsion on several occasions. From then on they'd been partners in crime, terrorizing the streets of Chelsea in the Swinging Sixties with their contrasting good looks and charm: Eric dark and swarthy and dangerous, Jack golden-haired and smooth and suave, both dressed to kill and ready to pounce. They were bad boys together, heads filled with dreams and schemes that, because of their boldness and daring, often came to profitable fruition. Their flat off the King's Road was a notorious sin bin, where a stream of glamorous girls came to lose their virginity and their hearts.

Eventually, they grew up. Jack had fallen in love with the bohemian and almost-aristocratic Louisa, a student at Chelsea Art School. He'd found her sketching passers-by in a coffee bar on the King's Road. He'd demanded she do his portrait, and she'd willingly agreed. The sitting had blossomed into a full-blown love affair, and before he knew it he was married. Five years later they'd taken up residence at Bucklebury Farm in Shropshire, handed over to Louisa by her parents, who insisted they were far too old to manage the place any longer.

To his surprise, Jack found he didn't miss London and took to country life like a duck to water, rather enjoying being something of a squire in the village, with his own silver tankard in the pub. Big fish, small pond, Eric had teased, with his cosmopolitan lifestyle dealing in second-hand sports cars. Then he'd settled down too: on one of his trips abroad he'd come back with Isabelle, allegedly the daughter of a French count. They'd married, and lived in a luxury penthouse in St John's Wood, all mirrored ceilings and leather and glass and chrome, a million miles from Bucklebury Farm.

Louisa and Jack stayed with Eric and Isabelle whenever they went to London, which was often. Isabelle neither understood nor liked the countryside, so the visits were rarely reciprocated, but the four of them went on an annual holiday to the south of France for a fortnight of sybaritic sunbathing and drinking. This ritual had a hiatus when children arrived: first the Templetons had Emile, Delphine and Olivier in quick succession, then Jamie had come along – and they all agreed the French Riviera lost some of its charm when one had screaming infants in tow. But one summer, when Olivier was seventeen and Jamie fifteen, Eric was given the use of a huge luxury villa near Cap Ferrat, and reinstated the tradition.

Jamie remembered the holiday being a frightening mixture of heaven and hell. The setting was divine, the food out of this world, the weather perfect. But she found she couldn't relax with the Templetons. Isabelle was so frighteningly chic, with her Parisian clothes, her twelve swimsuits, her high heels on the beach, her menthol cigarettes. Eric was gregarious and boisterous, and brought out the worst in her father: they were bad boys together again, with their constant calls for champagne. Her mother seemed amused by it all, but kept her cool reserve, as beautiful as Isabelle in her own way, but without the need for constant reapplication of Dior lipstick. But Jamie couldn't help feeling as if an air of forced jollity kept the momentum of the holiday going; a desperation to have fun before time ran out. How true that turned out to be …

While the grown-ups dozed and read by the pool, and Emile and Delphine disappeared off each day on mopeds, Jamie and Olivier found themselves thrown together and expected to get on. They'd played happily enough together when they were little, when their parents had got together for weekends. But no one seemed to have taken into account the excruciating torture of adolescence. At first, Jamie was tongue-tied and embarrassed in Olivier's company. As a self-conscious fifteen-year-old from the sticks, she was a little in awe of his extrovert London sophistication, and longed to crawl away and read books in her bedroom. But Olivier wasn't having any of it: he was friendly, with an enormous sense of fun, and it wasn't long before he managed to bring her out of herself. Soon she was hanging out with the other young people he'd met on the beach, drinking beer in the bars and sneaking off to the boîtes de nuit when they'd managed to ditch the parents after dinner. Occasionally they'd bump into Emile and Delphine, who studiously ignored them. Olivier, meanwhile, treated her with a certain chivalry that made her feel safe, but teased her mercilessly, almost as if she was a younger sister. But not quite. Once or twice she'd caught him looking at her in a way that made her cheeks go pink – though if he caught her looking he'd turn away, make a joke, start playing the fool.

One afternoon, she'd been asleep on the pontoon on her front. She was half aware that her fair skin was in danger of burning, but the holiday had turned her a golden brown for the first time in her life and she wanted

21

to prolong her tan. It made her look so different; when she tied up her hair in the evenings and applied mascara and lip gloss, she felt incredible. She became aware of admiring glances, and aware of Delphine's hostility at having competition. Despite herself, Jamie found she rather liked the sense of power it gave her.

Suddenly from the shore there came an urgent whistle. It was their signal to go back, to start getting ready to go out for dinner, but surely it wasn't that time yet? Jamie sat up sharply, then realized with horror that her bikini top had stayed on the pontoon. She was topless. Olivier fell about laughing as she tried to cover herself.

'You pig. You undid it ...' As she put her arms up in a desperate attempt to retie the strings behind her neck, her breasts betrayed her again, revealing themselves from behind the triangles of gingham. Tears of humiliation stung her eyes. 'Help me, for God's sake ...'

Olivier stopped laughing when he saw how distressed she was. Gently he came over to help her.

'I'm sorry. It was only supposed to be a joke. I didn't mean to upset you.'

Jamie brushed away her tears with the back of her hand, too angry to reply or even acknowledge his apology. She stood as tense as a racehorse in the starting gate as he did up the ties on her back. When he'd finished, his hands slid down to her waist.

'I really am sorry,' he said softly, and Jamie felt the brush of his lips on the back of her neck. Then he turned away and dived into the water.

Jamie stood stock-still. One moment she had been rigid with fury and humiliation, then the next ... His kiss should have filled her with further indignation, but it hadn't. Her anger had melted, to be replaced by a feeling of swirling bliss.

Her father's second whistle from the shore brought her back to reality. She plunged into the cool water. Within seconds the moment was lost, and the feeling washed away.

When they got back to shore, it seemed the holiday had come to an impromptu close. The Wildings' car had been packed up hastily, ready for the journey home. Someone had shoved Jamie's things back into her suitcase hurriedly; nothing had been folded. Jack ushered her into the car, muttering about a misunderstanding between 'the girls', as he always called Isabelle and Louisa. Louisa was waiting in the front seat, inscrutable behind her sunglasses.

As Jack jumped in and started up the engine, driving away without so much as a backwards glance, Jamie was baffled. It was obvious she wasn't going to get a proper explanation for their hasty departure, but she suspected it might have something to do with Olivier's mother. She'd seen Isabelle giving Jack the come-on over the past week, her manicured hands on his knee, her demands for him to top up her champagne and rub in her suntan lotion. And the way Jack kept chirruping into cheerful conversation on the way home, only to be met with if not a stony, then a resigned, silence from Louisa, merely confirmed Jamie's suspicions that her father had overstepped the mark. Not that she was bothered about finding out the truth. She was too busy reliving the agonizing memory of Olivier and that kiss. What might have happened between them if the holiday had been allowed to continue? She tortured herself as only a fifteen-year-old can, imagining all sorts of scenarios. Her fantasies sustained her on the interminable ferry crossing all the way back to Bucklebury Farm.

Now, as her bathwater went from scalding to lukewarm to cold, Jamie recalled the last moment she'd seen Olivier. They'd exchanged bewildered glances through the car window as Jack accelerated out of the drive, and he'd given her a helpless shrug as if to say he hadn't a clue what was going on either. No one had actually said as much, but it was pretty clear that, whatever had gone on between the grown-ups, they were now sworn enemies and she was unlikely to see Olivier ever again ...

Yet here he was, evidently her father's new best friend and with the upper hand to boot – while she'd been caught unawares, looking like the Wild Woman of Borneo. Grabbing the rusty old razor she'd found in the medicine cabinet, she was determined that the next time they met she'd be better equipped to do battle and regain her position as mistress of the house.

Half an hour later, she felt like a different person. She'd managed to shave her legs and underarms, only nicking herself twice. Her hair was washed if not conditioned, and her nails were neatly trimmed and scrubbed. She promised herself a splurge in Boots the next day – the only beauty items she had left were a stick of deodorant, some Vaseline and a bottle of sun cream. In some ways, it had been liberating not to worry about her appearance for months on end, but now she was back on English soil she felt the need to be somewhat more groomed. She was, after all, getting a little old to rely on her natural beauty. At just short of thirty, the youthful sparkle was beginning to fade. Or was she being hard on herself? She pulled on a faded pink T-shirt dress and realized that she'd lost weight – it had once clung snugly to her hips but now hung quite freely. Not that she'd ever been fat, but a combination of unreliable food sources and having to walk and climb long distances over the past months meant she was lean and toned. Or did she look haggard? There was nothing like massive weight loss for ageing you. She surveyed herself critically from all angles, deciding that her golden tan and the freckles like a dusting of cinnamon over her nose saved her from gauntness. Her hair was a disaster though, falling in a tangled mass of unkempt copper to well past her shoulders, her fringe long grown out but yet to catch up with the rest. She tugged a comb through it, then twisted it up in a butterfly clip. She dug round in her drawer for some make-up, finding some old mascara and a millimetre of pink lipstick, and was pleased to see they brought some life to her face. She tutted at herself for being so vain all of a sudden, when she hadn't given a second thought to how she looked for ages.

She wondered if she would have been so anxious if Olivier hadn't been around. She remembered how he'd made her feel all those years ago; how she'd repeatedly checked her appearance on that fateful holiday, wondering if she was too fat, too thin, too flat-chested, too pale, too frumpy, too freckly. Not that she'd cared what he thought then, or now, of course…

She went downstairs. The kitchen was empty and she felt a tiny prick of disappointment. The tea things had gone from the table and the ashtray had been cleared away. There was no sign of Olivier.

Her stomach rumbled and she went in search of sustenance, but there was absolutely nothing to eat. Plenty of bottles of Budweiser in the fridge, half a pint of milk, a packet of curling bacon and some Flora. No eggs. No bread. Typical blokes. Never mind. One of the advantages of living near Ludlow was that the once gastronomically challenged post office was now an epicurean paradise.

She was fishing about for the keys to her old Ford Fiesta when the early afternoon peace was shattered by an almighty roar that made her jump out of her skin. She peered through the window at the sky: sometimes fighter planes went overhead on exercise. But the sky was empty. And the noise was coming nearer. It seemed to be coming from the stable yard. With her heart in her mouth, she hurried outside to investigate.

2

Parsnip and Gumdrop shot out of the door behind Jamie, barking frantically and nearly tripping her up as she raced round to the front of the house, her heart hammering. What she saw made her stop in her tracks.

The impossibly long bonnet of a car was nosing its way through the archway that led from the stables, its blue and silver paintwork glittering in the afternoon sun. It glided across the cobbles, as purposeful and predatory as a shark cruising shallow waters, before coming to a halt in front of Jamie, resplendent in all its glory.

It was a Bugatti, the ultimate in vintage racing cars: a welding of nostalgia, glamour, sex appeal and horsepower. Sleek, streamlined and understated, its perfection lay in its simplicity. Each line, each contour, had a purpose. There was no unnecessary embellishment. It was a design classic. And, like the most ravishing Italian film star, it took centre stage quietly confident that nothing could compete with its beauty, knowing that all eyes were feasting upon its curves with longing and wonder.

At the steering wheel was Olivier. Dressed in a white polo shirt that showed off his tan, a cigarette smouldering in his mouth, he looked for all the world like a thirties playboy on the hunt for his next conquest. He dropped the revs, letting the engine idle. It now sounded like a gentle purr, but Jamie could still feel the power of the car reverberate through her body. It was having a disturbing effect on her, combined with the heat of the sun, the noise and the overpowering smell of the fumes. She told herself it was lack of food and sleep that was making her feel faint, rather than the disarming grin Olivier was giving her as he gauged her reaction, narrow-eyed, through the plume of smoke from his cigarette.

'Is this ... Dad's car?' she managed to stammer. 'The one he used to share with your father?'

Olivier nodded happily.

'They still do share it, technically. Jack and I have been restoring it.'

Jamie gazed at the car as the memories came flooding back. Some twenty years ago, Olivier's father Eric had stumbled across the Bugatti on his travels, had phoned Jack in excitement, and the two of them had gone halves, getting it for a ridiculous price as it was in a shocking state of neglect. As gleeful as two schoolboys, they'd brought the car back to Bucklebury Farm, where Jack had spent a long winter restoring it to its former glory. Everyone had assumed they were going to sell it on, make a quick, easy buck. Perhaps that had been their initial intention. But when they'd taken it to a vintage race meeting at Donington Park to put it through its paces, they'd both been bitten by the bug.

From then on, every weekend during the racing season, from April to October, Eric and Jack would dash off all over the country to take part in death-defying races and rallies and hill climbs, leaving their wives to wonder if they would come back alive. Jamie remembered their jubilant celebrations if they returned with a trophy; the hours discussing tactics if they were defeated; the evenings her father spent in the barn, fine-tuning the engine – the roar that sometimes frightened the horses as he turned it over and over. It had been their joint obsession, and how it had suited them: two devil-may-care jack-the-lads at the wheel of half a ton of precision engineering, competing for nothing but the glory of winning. There was certainly no money in it. On the contrary, it proved a most effective way of burning a hole in both their pockets.

Of course, after they'd fallen out that summer, the partnership had come to an end. As far as Jamie knew, the car had been shoved under a tarpaulin in the barn and forgotten. But here it was, a phoenix risen from the ashes.

'Hop in,' said Olivier. 'I need to get some petrol. I'll take you for a spin.'

Jamie hesitated. It wasn't so much the car as the sight of Olivier's long, brown legs disappearing under the dashboard that made her uncertain. Then a rumble in her stomach reminded her that she was on the brink of starvation.

'I was about to go into the village anyway,' she said, climbing in. There was no door; she had to scramble over the side and slide on to the leather bench seat next to him. There was only just room, and for a moment she felt disconcerted by their proximity, then realized Olivier was far more interested in the car than the fact that her dress was riding up her legs. Nevertheless, as he flung his arm carelessly over the back of her seat in order to reverse, she leaned forwards slightly, anxious to avoid physical contact.

'Don't you men ever do any grocery shopping?' she babbled, feeling the need to bring the conversation round to the mundane in order to bring herself down to earth. 'There's absolutely nothing to eat!'

'We tend to go to the pub,' admitted Olivier sheepishly. 'It saves washing up. Hold tight!'

The next moment Jamie found her breath quite literally taken away as he roared out of the courtyard and up the drive before turning out on to the road that led to the village. The seat was so low to the ground, her legs straight out in front of her, that the tarmac seemed to rush by only inches from her elbow. She could feel every manoeuvre, every bump, every gear change, filling her with a mixture of terror and excitement, and had to bite on her lip to stop herself begging him to slow down. When she dared to look at the speedo, she was amazed to find that they were only just nudging sixty miles an hour. Nevertheless, she felt herself pushing her feet on an imaginary brake as they took each corner, feeling sure they'd never make it, that they would leave the road and be found in a tangled mass of flesh and steel. She prayed that Olivier wasn't showing off for her benefit; that he knew what he was doing and that he respected the Bugatti's capabilities. It was like being on a racehorse: you could feel the power, you knew that it could give you much, much more if you only dared to ask, but at the same time you were only in control for as long as it wanted you to be. No wonder its slogan had been '*le pur sang des automobiles*': the thoroughbred amongst cars.

In record time they were passing the sign she had noticed on her way in, the one that entreated visitors to drive carefully through the village, and to her relief Olivier obediently dropped his speed before finally dawdling to a halt by the village green.

'Better than sex, eh?' Olivier grinned at her.

'I don't know about that,' said Jamie carefully. 'But it was fun.'

And when she got out of the car, she found that her heart was beating ten to the dozen, she could barely walk from pressing her foot on the floor, and she couldn't wait to get in again. As comparisons went, it wasn't a bad one, she mused, as she watched Olivier whizz off through the village. She couldn't help notice the longing glances he got as he tanked past the pub: the men clearly lusting after the car, the women, no doubt, after him as his tousled locks blew in the breeze.

Of Lower and Upper Faviell, the latter was the smart address, where rows of black-and-white terraced cottages formed two sides of a triangle round the village green, with a tiny pond and ducks and a thatched bus stop. The bus stopped there dutifully en route to Ludlow twice a week, but it was rare that anyone got on as everyone in Upper Faviell had their own transport. The church and adjoining idyllic vicarage – no longer lived in by the vicar, but where the village fête was still held – made up the third side. At the bottom right-hand corner stood the Royal Oak, from where a road led off to Lower Faviell half a mile away. Here clustered a semicircle of council houses, the village school and the ancient garage where Olivier was heading that, as well as petrol, sold string, dog biscuits and the *Daily Mirror*. With two working farms, the road through was generally caked with mud and the smell of silage and muck often hung heavy in the air.

Jamie made her way up the top end of the green towards the post office. It was easy to miss, as it blended in perfectly with the houses on either side, only the red pillar box outside giving its presence away. Inside, Hilly the postmistress greeted her effusively. Hilly was broader than she was tall, with a severe iron-grey bob that detracted from the kindness in her round face. She'd taken over the post office five years ago when her husband had died, rescuing it from the brink of closure and turning it from a purveyor of dented tins of soup and faded cereal packets into a destination post office with a daily delivery of organic bread, free-range eggs, a trencherman's cheese counter and a selection of decent wine, not nasty, dubiously labelled gutrot that wasn't even fit to cook with. She'd also pioneered an organic vegetable box scheme, and spent much of her time dividing up leafy green brassicas and rhubarb and beetroot into boxes for collection by her flavour-conscious customers. People from far afield went there to top up on their weekly shop if they couldn't be bothered to go into town. The villagers found it a double-edged sword – it was wonderful to have it on your doorstep, but it could make parking a nightmare.

Jamie wandered round the shop, revelling in the produce on offer that was like manna from heaven after the scanty and somewhat repetitive fare of the last few months. She filled her basket with a squidgy white bloomer, farmhouse butter and a selection from the deli counter – Parma ham, anchovies, a craggy wedge of cheddar. And a big, round, toffee-encrusted lardy cake. She'd soon put back on all the weight she'd lost at this rate. She took her basket to the counter.

'I've been keeping an eye on your father,' Hilly informed her. 'I knew he'd turned the corner when he came in to ask for the *Racing Post* to be kept for him.'

Hilly omitted to mention that a further clue had been

when he stopped buying a bottle of Jack Daniel's every other day, and started buying milk instead. And Jamie was grateful that there was no hint of recrimination in her voice – she'd been anxious that people would regard her as the prodigal daughter, and hint that it was about time that she'd put in a reappearance.

Hilly started totting up her purchases.

'I see you've met your lodger, then?'

Jamie smiled warily.

'Briefly. He's the son of some old friends of ours.'

'Fit as a butcher's dog.' Hilly had a comical way of delivering working-class aphorisms in cut-glass Roedean vowels.

Jamie tried to look non-committal, but it was hard to deny that Olivier was an attractive proposition, no matter how you looked at him.

'It's the one thing that pisses me off about being old.' Hilly pronounced 'off' to rhyme with 'dwarf'. 'He wouldn't look twice at an old boiler like me. Anyway, he probably thinks I'm a lez.'

Jamie didn't like to say that it wasn't surprising, given her penchant for wearing her deceased husband's clothes. Hilly argued that they were perfectly good, far too good for the charity shop, so she might as well get some wear out of them. Most days she was seen sporting his cavalry twills and a dark green oiled sweater with leather patches on the elbows, and more often than not his tweed fishing cap too.

She bid Hilly farewell, promising to bring the photos of her trip next time she came in. Hilly lived her life vicariously through her customers, as running a post office was a huge commitment and she rarely liked to leave it in the hands of a relief manager, who wouldn't understand the foibles of her clientele.

As Jamie loitered on the pavement waiting for Olivier's return, she was assailed by the Reverend Huxtable, whose face lit up when he saw her.

'Jamie!'

'Vicar.'

She smiled warmly. The Reverend was a popular figure in the village. At her mother's funeral, he'd done his very best to make a good job of what must have been an awful task. Jamie felt guilty that she hadn't been more grateful to him at the time for his support, but then he must be used to it. People didn't always behave terribly well when they were grieving.

He pumped her hand enthusiastically.

'I'm so glad you're back. Your father's missed you.' There was no hint of rebuke in his tone either. 'Is he well? I keep meaning to call in, but with three parishes to run ...'

'I haven't seen him yet. I've only just got back. He's out for the day, apparently.' At the races, thought Jamie. So he can't be that miserable.

'Well, he'll have a lovely surprise when he gets back.'

'Yes ...' Jamie was still doubtful that she was going to be welcomed back with open arms.

'And you? How are you?' The Reverend peered at her anxiously. 'You know where I am if you need to talk. I know it's not fashionable to speak to a vicar in times of need these days, but I won't spout at you, I promise.'

Jamie hesitated. She'd been wary about going into the village, convinced the entire population had considered her flight to be uncaring and irresponsible, abandoning her grieving father in his hour of need. And she could never tell them the truth: how cruelly and wickedly he had failed to consider *her* needs, depriving her of her final farewell. So far, no one had judged her, and for that she was grateful. But for a moment she wanted to ask if it was normal to feel so angry with someone you loved, if she'd been right to blame Jack when surely Louisa had been as much at fault, if not more. But then Louisa hadn't been there to take the brunt of Jamie's fury, and Jack had. She was on the brink of asking the Reverend's opinion, for she thought it might give her the strength to face her father with a clear conscience if she had the reassurance of a man of the cloth, when a rumble from the other end of the street announced Olivier's return.

'I'm sorry – here's my lift.' Jamie smiled apologetically, and watched in amazement as the vicar's eyes glazed over in admiration.

'Wow,' he breathed. 'You certainly know how to travel in style.'

Olivier drew up beside them. Curtains twitched and heads peered out of windows in annoyance, convinced that some hideous motorbike was responsible for the ungodly noise. But when they saw the Bugatti, their annoyance evaporated. Noise pollution from such a gracious and noble beast was, apparently, acceptable.

Jamie scrambled in as elegantly as she could beside Olivier, trying hard not to give the vicar an unexpected flash of her knickers, then gave him a jaunty wave of farewell as they accelerated away. Reverend Huxtable struggled to suppress a momentary stab of envy for Olivier – young, handsome, with a beautiful car and a beautiful woman – then reasoned that it was his susceptibility to the uglier human emotions that made him a compassionate man and a successful vicar.

Of course, what he didn't know is that everything isn't always what it seems, that Jamie didn't belong to Olivier any more than the Bugatti did, and that this particular car was going to cause more trouble than anyone could have imagined.

When they got back, Olivier disappeared off to the barn to put the car away and Jamie took a plate of food out on to the little patch of lawn adjoining the kitchen garden, where a hammock was strung between two apple trees. She clambered in, devoured every last crumb then lay back, finally allowing the waves of exhaustion to wash over her.

It was heaven to be home. She had been filled with trepidation on the journey, wondering if she would regret her return. South America had been so detached from reality that she had been able to pretend she was someone else for ten months. Mere survival had taken over her preoccupations. She'd worried that reality would hit her in the face like a brick as soon as she got back, that all the sick anxiety and pain and grief and resentment would take her breath away. But instead she felt a pleasant calm – not joy; without her mother there she could never feel that – but certainly a feeling that she could cope, and that she'd done the right thing.

The hammock swung gently as she basked in her unexpected but welcome relief. All her senses were assaulted with sensations that had been part of her life for so many years: the smell of the honeysuckle, the gentle sun on her skin, the buzz of a bumblebee. Exhausted from her travels, her eyes grew heavy and soon she dozed off, thinking that she might have seen some of the most wondrous sights in the world over the past few months, but she was a true Shropshire lass at heart.

3

Zoe Drace, conversely, didn't get the Shropshire thing at all. When she'd told people she was moving from London to Ludlow, they'd all exclaimed in delight and envy, gushing on about blue remembered hills and Michelin-starred restaurants, which Zoe didn't give a fig for. She wasn't one to coo over *jus*. Give her a crowded wine bar and a plate of pasta and she was happy as long as she was amongst friends. Food had never been elevated to art or science in her book. Sure, it was something to be enjoyed, but not hallowed and revered. Dinner parries in her book meant a couple of cartons of Covent Garden soup sloshed into a saucepan and spritzed up with a swirl of crème fraîche, followed by Delia's tart's spaghetti and shop-bought profiteroles or cheesecake. She didn't need adulation for her culinary prowess. Why spend hours sweating over a hot stove and panicking about whether the filo parcels were crispy or the souffles were rising while everyone else sat around getting sloshed and having fun? Not that she didn't make an effort – she made sure the table looked nice and that there were flowers. And she particularly made an effort with her appearance. While some of her friends were neurotic about never serving the same dish twice and made careful records, she was obsessive about never being seen in the same outfit twice. You weren't what you ate, in Zoe's book. You were what you wore.

This morning she was dressed down in vintage Levi's and a black Joseph T-shirt. She examined her short, choppy bob gloomily. There were chunky streaks of marmalade and apricot amongst the natural dark brown: she could, just about, get away with another fortnight before her roots needed doing. But who the hell was she going to trust with it? She'd loitered outside most of the hairdressers in Ludlow, scrutinizing the fruits of their labour, but none of them came up to scratch. She'd have to wangle a trip to London out of Christopher.

Christopher. The very thought of him made her heart flump down to her JP Tods. Try as she might, she couldn't fathom the change in him. Almost chameleon-like, he had taken on the mantle of his surroundings. In just a few months, he'd gone from city slicker to country gent. A year ago he wouldn't have been seen dead in baggy green cords and a sports jacket. Zoe wouldn't have minded, but he wasn't even wearing them ironically…

When Christopher's father Hamilton had had a stroke eight months before, none of the Draces had realized what an effect it would have on their lives. The initial prognosis had been very optimistic: they had been assured that with time and physio, he should make an almost full recovery. But for some reason, the will to recuperate wasn't in him, and he had slid further and further into an inexplicable decline. Christopher's mother Rosemary had been beside herself with guilt and worry.

Christopher had looked very serious the last time he had come back from visiting his parents. He waited till the children were in bed, then opened a bottle of red wine, urging Zoe to sit down.

'It's pretty grim, Zo. My mother isn't coping at all. I think we're going to have to put Dad in a nursing home,' he'd admitted, and her heart had gone out to him. He looked so woebegone. It must be horrid to realize suddenly that your parents weren't going to live for ever, that they were frail and fragile. She'd hugged him, and offered to come and help him look for homes. Sometimes you needed an objective eye when you were very emotionally involved.

'Thanks, but that's not really the problem. It's the firm.' The way he said it, and the way he didn't quite meet her eye, made Zoe instantly suspicious. Hamilton Drace ran an estate agency and auctioneers, one of the oldest and most respected agencies on the Welsh borders, an outfit that had barely entered the twentieth, let alone the twenty-first, century. It traded solely on its reputation rather than what it had to offer. And there was no doubt that its driving force was Hamilton, with his connections, his local knowledge, his personal service, his charm. Without him at the helm, it would fade into oblivion, sidelined by the sharper young agencies who had more aggressive tactics and competitive fees.

Zoe swallowed. She thought she knew what was coming.

'Well,' she said brightly. 'He would have been retiring soon anyway. All good things must come to an end.'

Christopher shook his head.

'I've got to go and take over.'

'What will you do? Live at your mother's during the

week, and come back here at weekends? I suppose it's doable.'

Christopher met Zoe squarely in the eye. There was no point in beating about the bush.

'We're going to have to move.'

Zoe blinked. Once, twice. Then laughed.

'Don't be silly. How can we?'

'It was always on the cards for me to take over. You know that.'

This was true. But, like death itself, to Zoe this prospect had been something rather unimaginable that was going to happen in the far-distant future. Not now, for God's sake.

She tried very, very hard to be good about it. Christopher was being so brave about his father, whom he adored, and she didn't have the heart to put him through any more stress. And when her friends saw photographs of Lydbrook House, set on a tributary of the River Teme between the villages of Upper and Lower Faviell, they were all green with envy. After all, it looked pretty impressive: huge, built of grey stone, with gables and pointy windows and a terraced balcony that looked over the lawns right down to the babbling rivulet, garages and outhouses and garden rooms and summer houses and even the remnants of what had been a grass tennis court. Zoe managed to persuade herself that a large country house was a natural progression at her time of life, and she'd never have to scour the roads for a parking space outside her own home again.

The reality was different. Lydbrook House would have been described by Drace's as 'a country home in need of some updating' – understatement of the century.

Rosemary and Hamilton were not into interior decoration, being resolutely outdoor people. Acres of worn carpet, reams of faded curtains, threadbare upholstery and large, ugly furniture abounded. The kitchen was hell, fitted with fifties Formica units, with sliding frosted doors that jammed when you tried to open them and nasty metal handles. There was an Aga, but it was in a hideous shade of light blue that Zoe could not begin to persuade herself was fashionable. And every available work surface was covered in orange and brown flowered sticky-back plastic. The wallpaper was almost retro, covered in line drawings of root vegetables – leeks and beetroot and parsnips; she'd seen something similar in *House and Garden* that was over fifty pounds a metre. But this was yellowing and peeling off in great chunks.

Her lovely furniture from Elmdon Road was swallowed up by the house and didn't go remotely. Her sage-green Conran sofa hovered apologetically by the French windows in the drawing room, looking decidedly out of place next to the faded chintz and worn tapestry of the Draces' battalions of mismatched chairs and sofas. Her beautiful light beech table and matching chairs looked utterly ridiculous in the enormous, gloomy dining room, so she'd stored them away in one of the outhouses until the day when the heavy wallpaper and curtains and carpet could be stripped away and replaced with something light and airy.

The boys, of course, loved Lydbrook. As well as their father's old bedroom in the attic, they had a huge room over the top of the garages with a ping-pong table and enough space for Christopher's old Hornby train set, for the days when it was raining and they weren't able to venture out into the paradise of their garden. They were in absolute heaven. Zoe, by contrast, was in absolute agony every time they went out to play. She would hover anxiously by the French windows, tucked out of sight so they couldn't see her, convinced that they would be tempted down to the river and into the water and immediately be sucked under by an angry current and swept away for ever. Christopher told her she was being overanxious. The boys were old enough to understand the dangers, and sensible enough not to venture riverwards without adult supervision. After all, Christopher and his two sisters had grown up at Lydbrook with no fluvial mishaps.

And then there was Christopher's mother, Rosemary – or Ro, as she was known, though Zoe could never quite bring herself to use this term of endearment as that would somehow be accepting Rosemary's presence. For Rosemary was part of the Lydbrook package. Not that she was intrusive: she hovered apologetically; spoke in a tiny voice; scuttled off to her own quarters thereby racking Zoe with alternate guilt and irritation. She would almost have preferred Rosemary to be overbearing and bossy – at least then she could have fought back, snapped at her. But how could you complain about someone who was no trouble at all? Someone who was enormously helpful, in fact. Someone who'd uncomplainingly sewn all the name tapes on the boys' new uniform – a thankless task if ever there was one – and ploughed through mountains of ironing when you weren't looking, leaving baskets of crisp clothing in the airing cupboard. Who would happily babysit at the drop of a hat. Who would play snap and twenty-one and pontoon with the boys on wet Sunday afternoons. Saint fucking Rosemary. Zoe didn't feel as if the house was her own while Rosemary was hovering in it. Which, of course, it wasn't.

She thought longingly of their old house in Shepherd's Bush. It was hardly palatial, and once the swing and slide had been put up in the garden there was only just room for a picnic table for barbecues. But she'd had neighbours – like-minded couples who were in the same situation. There was always someone to leave the kids with, someone to have a coffee with, a moan and a gossip with, a much-needed glass of wine at six o'clock. It was secure, cosy, whereas Zoe felt as if she'd been set adrift on a vast ocean at Lydbrook House. As soon as she'd dropped the children off at school there were six long hours to fill with no one for company.

The biggest problem was, of course, they had no bloody money. Christopher had sat her down very seriously. He had their bank and credit-card statements and some buff-covered files. He'd explained their situation to her carefully, patiently and apologetically.

They'd sold well at Elmdon Road. But once they'd paid off the mortgage – which had swollen considerably by the time they'd extended it to put in a Shaker kitchen and a conservatory and converted the attic rooms to include a new bathroom – and taken into account that Christopher was going to lose his company car (they'd need at least thirty grand for a decent new estate), there was only a couple of hundred grand left. Zoe couldn't see the problem, until Christopher pointed out that he was going to have to take a drop in salary, that there were the fees at his father's home and the boys' school fees to take into consideration.

Zoe swallowed.

'So – there won't be much left over to do up the house?'

'Um … no. I've worked out that you can have two hundred pounds a week housekeeping. And that's got to include petrol.'

'So why are we having to pay your father's fees?'

Christopher put it straight on the line. His parents were broke. Drace's was in danger of going under. He was going to have to spend at least fifty thousand of the profit from Elmdon Road in order to salvage it. A revamp, a relaunch, Internet presence – and he was going to have to subsidize a drastic cut in their agency fees in order to attract some new custom.

'I know it's going to be hard. But if you think about it, life's much cheaper here. The boys entertain themselves, there's no parking to pay, no tube fares. The garden's full of fresh vegetables …'

He trailed off a trifle lamely at this, not quite able to meet Zoe's eye. Fresh vegetables? she wanted to scream. Fresh vegetables that I've got to pick and bloody wash the mud off? Zoe was the type who bought her green beans already topped and tailed, her carrots cut into batons, her jacket potatoes scrubbed and gleaming …

Today was Wednesday. She thought she hated Wednesdays the most. On Mondays she always had hope. Each Monday morning, with the zeal of one embarking on a diet, she convinced herself that this week was going to be different, this week she would find a kindred spirit at the school gates, a decent gym, a decent dress shop, and an exciting whizzy new social life full of people who didn't come to school covered in dog hairs, wearing jodhpurs that made their arses look five times the size they already were.

By Wednesday that dream had always been shattered, and she had reached screaming pitch. By Wednesday she had picked up the phone to her friends back in London and turned green with envy at what they were doing. This particular Wednesday, her friend Natalie was hosting a birthday lunch at the Bush Bar and Grill. Everyone had put their children into aftercare so they wouldn't have to rush off at three with Sancerre and cigarettes on their breath. She'd been tempted to get on the train and surprise them by walking in – but by the time she'd thought of it, only a helicopter would have got her there in time. She'd spent the morning sulking in front of the telly. At lunchtime, she tortured herself imagining what all her friends would be wearing, what they would have bought Natalie, the juicy gossip they'd be imparting, the champagne they'd order…

Fucking Shropshire.

Zoe got up, went into the kitchen, wrenched open the door of the ancient fridge that, like the wallpaper, was almost but not quite retro, and pulled out the remains of last night's white wine. She poured herself a glass.

'Happy birthday, Natalie,' she toasted her friend, from what felt like sixty million light years away.

Tiona Tutton-Price stepped over the threshold of the red-brick terraced cottage, her heart beating wildly in excitement as it always did when she stumbled across a gem. It had all the ticks in all the boxes. Walking distance to the town centre (although Tiona, who never walked anywhere if she could help it, had driven) but far enough off the tourist trail to have plenty of street parking. All the original features untouched; nothing modernized. And a pretty walled garden. She let Mrs Turner show her round, though she didn't need to look. Nevertheless, she made polite cooing noises.

'I think...' She tilted her head to one side and pursed her lips, as if thinking hard, though she'd decided on a figure before she'd even walked through the door. 'Do you know, I think we could ask a hundred and forty.'

Mrs Turner's face dropped.

'But... but next door but one went for one sixty-five. Only a month ago.'

Tiona smiled a sympathetic smile.

'They were *asking* one sixty-five. What they actually *got* was one fifty. I've done my research. And our philosophy at Drace's is to put a slightly lower asking price in order to attract viewers. That way you get more competitive bidding – people come and view and set their heart on your property, and end up determined to have it at any cost.' She demonstrated round her. 'I mean, who wouldn't fall in love with this house? What you want is to get three or four prospective buyers over the threshold, all desperate to outdo each other.'

Mrs Turner smiled fondly. 'I've been very happy here. Even since Arthur—'

Tiona forged on, not wanting to hear the old bat's reminiscences. 'If you put too high an asking price, people won't even come and view. And what you've also got to remember is the market is slowing down. I know you read in the paper about prices shooting up, but actually not at this end of the market.'

'Oh.' This was obviously news to Mrs Turner.

47

'Now, obviously you'll be asking other agents to come and view—'

'Oh no. I don't think so. Arthur always said you could trust Hamilton Drace.'

'Well, that's very kind. But perhaps for peace of mind you should get another opinion?'

'I don't think there's any need.'

Stupid old cow, thought Tiona.

'In that case,' she smiled her most syrupy smile, 'I might as well measure up while I'm here. It would save disturbing you again.'

'Why not? Shall I make you a cup of tea in the meantime?'

'Lovely.'

Tiona let Mrs Turner make her a cup of tea, though she had no intention of drinking it – she'd seen the dark-brown stains in the cups on the draining board – while she pretended to flick round with a tape measure and write important things down on her clipboard. She would pop back into the kitchen occasionally, to ask technical questions about heating and wiring and cavity-wall insulation, at times nodding approval, at others feigning concern. By the time Tiona left they were the best of friends, and Mrs Turner got out the details of the warden-controlled home she was hoping to put an offer on, heartened by Tiona's reassurances that she would be in there by the autumn.

A hundred yards up the hill, Tiona scrambled back into her Golf and got out her mobile phone. The curt 'What?' on the other end made her shiver with delight.

'I've got a dead cert for you. One forty. You could

make two twenty on it no problem, with an Ikea kitchen and some laminate flooring—'

'Go for it,' he cut her off crisply.

'Usual terms?' she purred into the mouthpiece.

'For fuck's sake, just get on with it.'

Her insides quivered. She loved it when he talked to her like that. She glanced round to check for passers-by, then lowered her voice suggestively.

'I'm not wearing any knickers.'

She slid her hand up inside her skirt, just to make sure she wasn't lying.

'Of course you're not. You never do.'

There was a hint of amusement in his voice. Good. He was thawing.

'Where are you?'

'On a building site.'

'Find somewhere ...' Her breath was short. Her meaning was clear.

'Have you ever been on a building site? There's nowhere to have a wank. Only the Portaloo. And I'm not going in there. Not even for you, toffee-drawers.'

Tiona stared at her tiny little Ericsson in disbelief. He'd hung up on her. He'd never done that before. Usually by now they'd be indulging in the filthiest of exchanges, him issuing her with instructions that made her blush even now to think of them. She must be losing her touch. Well, stuff Simon Lomax. That was the last time she was going to give him a tip-off in return for a wad of his dirty bank notes. If he did but know it, she'd got bigger fish to fry than a low-rent property dealer. A fish that was already dangling on the end of her hook, if she wasn't mistaken.

She tossed her phone back into her bag, trying to

ignore the fact that she was squirming with lust, turned on by the brief exchange. She wouldn't be able to concentrate now for the rest of the day. It was hard work being oversexed ... but at least she could hide it. Tiona often thanked God she wasn't a man. How awful it must be to walk around all day with a raging hard-on and nowhere to put it.

4

At half past five, Jamie was woken from her nap by a mad tooting heralding the arrival of a navy-blue Bentley being driven with total disregard. It screeched to a halt and out of it spilled her father Jack, in a cream linen suit and panama hat. And Lettice Harkaway in twenty-five yards of salmon-pink chiffon.

Jamie's heart sank. If there was one person on the planet she couldn't abide, it was Lettice. Her husband had disappeared in a scuba-diving incident twenty years before, leaving Lettice with a whopping inheritance and rumours of foul play that she never attempted to deny. With her flamboyant clothing designed for someone twenty years younger, her false eyelashes and her imperious manner, she'd been the queen bee of the local social scene for as long as Jamie could remember, and she'd always found her intolerably self-centred and superficial. Lettice had been brought up in Kenya, where she was used to lolling about the country club all day and coming home to a ream of servants. To this day she found it hard to remember that everyone around her wasn't there to serve her as she waved a pudgy, bejewelled paw at whoever was nearest to do her bidding.

Jamie slid out of the hammock, suddenly feeling

ridiculously shy as her father bounded up the path with Lettice in tow. At the same moment, Olivier appeared from the stable yard. Bugger. She hadn't wanted an audience. This was an intensely private moment. She stepped out on to the path, wishing she could have given him some warning.

'Hello, Dad.'

Jack stopped in his tracks, unable to believe his eyes.

'Jamie?'

'I got back a couple of hours ago.'

Olivier moved in to explain.

'She found me in the kitchen. Bit of a shock.'

Lettice intervened, her husky growl setting Jamie's teeth on edge. Someone had once misguidedly compared her to Honor Blackman, and it had given her carte blanche to purr like a Bond heroine at every opportunity.

'Lucky thing. I'd love to find you in my kitchen.'

Jack was still looking totally flummoxed. Jamie was surprised that his reactions were so slow. Her father was usually so reactive and spontaneous. It was, she supposed, his age. But to her relief, he finally smiled and held out his arms.

'Jamie, darling. How wonderful.'

Jamie slid into his clasp and hugged him to her, not knowing what to say. Lettice clapped her hands like a little girl.

'What are we waiting for, everyone? This is a champagne moment if ever I saw one. There should still be some chilled in the boot. Olivier!'

She barked his name and to Jamie's amazement Olivier obeyed without demur. Then she turned to Jamie with a dazzling smile. She'd definitely had a face-lift since the last time she'd seen her.

'Why ever didn't you tell us you were coming home? There's a marvellous invention called the telephone, darling. We could have met you at the airport.'

We? Us? thought Jamie wildly. She wondered what else she didn't know about, as everyone trooped inside to the drawing room. Jack threw open the French windows that led out on to a little camomile lawn, and the early evening sun streamed in. The dogs took up their position on the kilim rug in front of the fireplace. Jamie flopped on to the sofa and looked around.

The room still held so much of her mother's personality. The wood-panelled walls were covered in paintings Louisa had accumulated over the years: not the usual hunting prints favoured by so many country homes, but a collection that reflected her artistic background and her wide-ranging tastes. Modern, vivid splashes of abstract colour were positioned next to more traditional portraits and wild, rugged landscapes. Mixed amongst them were Louisa's own works: charcoal sketches of animals whose very essence was captured in just a few skilful lines; vibrant and impressionistic still lifes; thoughtful, brooding studies of the Shropshire countryside in bruised purples and indigos. Each of her many and varied styles reflected a different facet of her character, ranging from lively and gregarious to inward and reflective.

She had been, thought Jamie, so many different people. There was the tortured artist, who would retreat into the old shed she used as a studio, battling with her work with everything else fading into unimportance – no meals, no washing done, the animals neglected – until she was happy with her masterpiece. Or not, as was sometimes the case, in which event it went on the fire. Then there was the nurturing gardener. Louisa would spend all day in the greenhouse, in a tattered old pair of cords, hair tied back with baler twine and hands engrained with earth, pricking out and propagating and fertilizing and repotting. And the country gentlewoman, bastion of the local hunt, upholding the tradition of riding side-saddle, exquisite on her prancing grey steed.

But Jamie's favourite incarnation was Louisa the party girl, the sparkling hostess, forever throwing spontaneous drinks parties, impromptu barbecues, spur of the moment Sunday lunches that went on well into the night. A mere half an hour could see a total transformation from one of the above personae, and Louisa would descend the stairs looking for all the world like a film star in a fitted silk dress that would show off her tiny waist, her rich chestnut hair piled on top of her head, the merest hint of eye-liner and lipstick enhancing her fragile, translucent beauty. Her dark brown velvet eyes spoke volumes and held everyone in their thrall. Under her gaze, you felt like the only person in the world. For somehow, Louisa always made everyone and everything feel special.

Jamie remembered when she was a child. There'd been Easter egg hunts with ingenious clues hidden all over the farm, long cross-country rides with picnics in some magical spot Louisa had discovered, a puppet show for her birthday with fairy-tale puppets Louisa had been sewing all day and all night for weeks. And she carried that magic across all the generations – there'd been pensioners in the surrounding villages who lived for her day on the Meals on Wheels rota, when she'd help them with the crossword, join them in a quick sneaky sherry, listen to their moans and groans without looking as if she wished she was somewhere else. She made them feel as if they mattered for a golden half-hour in their grey, dreary lives.

She had her faults, of course. She was hopelessly impractical when it came to anything boring. Both Jamie's parents were. Anything that involved making a decision, or filling out a form, or hitting a deadline, and they were infuriatingly ostrich-like, the pair of them. As she grew older, Jamie often found herself having to chivvy them into confronting day-to-day realities – they seemed to think they had immunity from the mundane. It could be immensely frustrating.

And Louisa had her dark moments: times when she was distracted; when she would hide herself away and take little interest in her surroundings or other people. Sometimes she would take off somewhere for a few days at a time, declaring that she needed 'space'. But that was because she was an artist. Eventually, she would emerge from the gloom with a renewed vigour and energy, throwing herself into some new project or social engagement with such enthusiasm that you soon forgot the dark side. It was like the sun appearing from behind a cloud; when you were enjoying its warmth, you couldn't imagine it ever raining again.

She'd been such a strong presence that Jamie couldn't believe even now that she wasn't going to walk into the room with a plate of cheese straws fresh from the oven, face smudged with flour or paint or earth, depending on what she had been doing, then curl up in her big, old, battered leather chair by the fire, feet bare and her hair in a knot skewered with a paintbrush.

Instead, bloody Lettice was in that very chair now, unwinding herself from several yards of chiffon scarf and kicking off her stilettos, which were a ridiculous height for a woman of sixty plus. Jamie prayed fiercely that her father wasn't thinking of marrying the old witch. She'd heard plenty of horror stories about widowers marrying on the rebound...

In the sanctuary of the drinks cupboard that was tucked away in the corner of the room, Jack counted down four champagne glasses with a trembling hand and put them on a tray, then quickly uncorked a decanter of whisky and poured himself a slug. He hoped he'd hidden it well, but he'd had a terrible shock. Seeing Jamie like that on the path, like a ghost, an apparition... for one moment, a moment both glorious and dreadful, he'd thought it was Louisa. Jamie looked more like her than ever, now her hair had grown and she'd lost so much weight. Jack felt a bit of a fool, then told himself it was a mistake anyone could have made, with her appearing from nowhere like that with no warning.

And it wasn't the first time he'd thought he'd seen Louisa. In the first dreadful months after her death, she'd appeared to him many times, usually courtesy of a bottle of his namesake, Jack Daniel's. He drank it to blot out her memory, but sometimes she came to him before he'd managed to drink enough to slink into oblivion. She would smile at him through his alcoholic haze, unreachable, untouchable, only disappearing when his consciousness slipped finally away from him in a drunken stupor. There had been nothing for it but to drink harder and faster, to keep her apparition at bay.

Thank God the boy had appeared like that, and given him something else to think about, or Jack was sure he would, eventually, have gone quite, quite mad.

Olivier came back in with a bottle of cold Bollinger as Jack appeared with the glasses. The champagne was poured ceremoniously and Jack proposed a toast to Jamie's return. As she sipped her bubbles, she reflected that this was far from the homecoming she'd expected, to be knocking back the Bolly with Olivier Templeton and Lettice Harkaway, each of whose presence made her wary. She longed to be alone with Jack. He was obviously delighted to see her home, skitting about like a frisky kitten, thoroughly overexcited by the occasion, performing for his guests as usual.

At long last, Lettice drained her glass with an air of finality.

'Righty-ho, darlings. I must toddle off, I'm afraid.'

Thank God, thought Jamie.

'Not staying for supper?' Jack asked.

'No, no – the last thing I want to do is intrude. You've got such a lot to catch up on.'

Jamie let out an audible sigh of relief as Lettice poked her feet back into her shoes and stood up. As she walked past Olivier, she pinched his bottom.

'You gorgeous thing!' she rasped. Jamie was nearly sick, but Olivier just grinned. He was obviously used to it. As the Bentley roared off down the drive, all that was left of Lettice was the overwhelming smell of Trésor and the bright pink lipstick on her champagne glass.

'Well,' said Jack.

'Well,' said Jamie.

They looked at each other for a moment, then Jack held out his arms.

'Come here,' he said gruffly, and Jamie buried herself in his embrace, trying very, very hard not to cry.

'I think I'll go and have a bath,' said Olivier hastily, and made himself scarce.

5

Tiona was in the little boxroom she had commandeered as her private office as soon as it became clear that Hamilton Drace wasn't coming back to work after his funny turn and that she was, for the time being, in charge. Hamilton had never had his own office. He always said he couldn't get a feel for what was going on if he was locked away. But Tiona needed privacy. She didn't want anybody earwigging on her transactions, even though she thought most of the staff at Drace's were too thick to cotton on to what she was up to. She insisted she needed complete peace and quiet to discuss terms with clients, blaming her own lack of concentration, implying that a fluffy little creature like her couldn't possibly walk and chew gum at the same time, and everyone seemed to accept it.

She had one last call to make before clocking off for the day. She stabbed out Mrs Turner's number, then twizzled the cord round her finger, batted her eyelashes and smiled her sweetest smile, knowing they would transfer themselves down the telephone line.

'Mrs Turner? Tiona Tutton-Price here. I've got some fantastic news.' She sounded breathy and excited, as if she could barely contain herself. 'I was just about to type up your particulars, when a man came in to register his details. He was after just what you've got to offer. He's prepared to give you the asking price. Cash, no strings. He doesn't even want to view.'

Mrs Turner hesitated.

'But I thought what we wanted was two or three people interested—'

Shut up, thought Tiona. You weren't supposed to actually pay attention to what I was telling you.

'Let me put it into perspective for you. You'll be saving yourself a fortune. No advertising, no board up, no photography. And I'm sure we can come to some arrangement over our fees. After all, I won't have had to work terribly hard.'

She gave a tinkling laugh, but there was no reply. Tiona knew from experience that Mrs Turner was struggling to take the information in. It took the old so bloody long to cotton on.

'Peace of mind, Mrs Turner. If we move very quickly you will be safe in the knowledge that you've got a definite sale. He's happy to exchange ASAP. Whereas it could be weeks before we get a firm offer ...'

Tiona also knew that the old liked nothing better than certainty, that they hated taking risks, waiting on decisions. It would just take one quick turn of the thumbscrews.

'And the market's very volatile, don't forget. It could take a plunge any moment. We only need an increase in the interest rate.'

'So you think I should accept his offer?'

Tiona feigned hesitation.

'Strictly speaking, I'm not supposed to influence your

decision. It's entirely up to you.' She lowered her tone confidentially. 'Let's just say if it was me ...'

Outside in the main office, Christopher Drace heard the town clock strike six and put down his pen with a sigh that was part satisfaction, part frustration. He thought, at last, that the office was running smoothly. The last three months had been fraught. He'd lost count of how many houses they'd let slip through their fingers while they sorted things out, but that had been fine by him. Better not to handle a sale at all than handle it badly. Once he'd been satisfied they could do the job properly, he'd allowed Tiona out of the door to do valuations again, and now a satisfying rash of Drace's boards were popping up around Ludlow.

But marring this triumph were three pressing problems that he couldn't ignore. And he had to admit he didn't have a clue what to do about any of them. Sorting out the agency had certainly been a challenge, but it was largely a question of assessing the damage, then limiting it. There were practical solutions that could be immediately implemented. His other conundrums were more ethereal, more complicated.

His biggest concern was Zoe. For a start, he knew he wasn't spending enough time with her. He was working a six-day week, Saturdays being the busiest for any estate agent, and occasionally he had to work Sundays too. He tried very hard to be home by seven o'clock each night, if only to have twenty minutes with Hugo and Sebastian, who were already in their pyjamas and slippers and liked to have their bedtime drinks with him, one on each of his knees, even though Hugo was really too big. By then, Zoe would be in the kitchen, three-quarters of the way down a bottle of Jacob's Creek. 'We couldn't wait!' she would chirrup cheerfully, as if Rosemary had somehow been instrumental in its opening and subsequent consumption. Christopher knew his mother had probably had an inch in the bottom of her glass, while Zoe, judging by her glazed expression and the roses in her cheeks, had golloped the lion's share and would rush to open another bottle for, apparently, Christopher's benefit.

She was obviously desperately unhappy, and Christopher felt helpless. If only there had been money to do up the house, she would have been occupied. She had a good eye. But she wasn't one for making do. Christopher didn't like to suggest gardening. Zoe couldn't even keep a pot of Sainsbury's flat-leaf parsley alive. The problem was she'd been in London too long. Noise and fumes and traffic jams and crowds were the stuff of life to her. The silence at Lydbrook House unnerved her – she kept the television on all day if only for the background chatter. The unrelenting darkness at night totally freaked her. Christopher adored its comforting velvety cloak, dark as Guinness. Zoe had to have the landing light on. She would stay awake for hours, longing for the familiar background noises of traffic, sirens, car alarms and revellers on their way home to lull her into the land of nod. Eventually, she would drop off, then sit bolt upright, heart racing, when the hoot of an owl ripping her from unconsciousness would mean another two hours of agonizing insomnia.

It was such a contrast to the Zoe of only six months ago; the Zoe with the rackety social life, who rushed from the gym (twenty minutes cardio; two hours cappuccino) to girlie lunches to crucial shopping trips involving the quest for the perfect pair of boots. Then there would be hordes of small boys back for tea – as she didn't work she was often an unpaid childminder for her career-orientated friends, but this never fazed her; she never bitched or complained that she was being used. It was this generosity of spirit that made Christopher love her so much. He'd had no idea that the gloriously happy muddle she lived in could not be transplanted. She'd been uprooted – more unwillingly than she'd let on, he suspected – and now she was wilting before his very eyes.

Equally as worrying as his wife's state of mind was his father's. Christopher had to force himself to go and visit Hamilton in the home, because he found his condition so depressing. The doctors had insisted there was nothing physically wrong with him. But he rarely spoke, rarely ate, didn't take part in any of the activities laid on by the home, wouldn't have bothered washing or dressing if the nurses didn't chivvy him ruthlessly, day in, day out. Something, some light, some vital component, had gone out in him, and there seemed to be nothing anyone could do. His life, to all intents and purposes, seemed to be over. And he was only sixty-seven.

Christopher had made the mistake of thinking the boys might bring him back to life, but Hamilton had merely given them the flicker of a benevolent smile, lifted his hand to touch each of them on the head and turned back to gaze at the wall. The experience had upset both of the children, who had fond memories of their grandpa taking them down to the river to tickle trout, or to pick raspberries or light a satisfying bonfire. And it had cut

Christopher to the quick, making him realize he was powerless to help.

Lastly, there was his mother. Brave, uncomplaining, but deep-down bewildered Rosemary, who drifted unhappily about the house in the clothes that were starting to hang off her. She wouldn't have looked out of place in the home next to Hamilton. But then, when your husband of over forty years was cruelly snatched away from you, and you didn't have the closure of death, but a cadaverous reminder you were duty-bound to visit every day – well, the most ebullient of personalities would be affected.

He did a quick straw poll of the members of his family. He himself was relatively happy, which of course only added to his guilt. It wasn't until they were back at Lydbrook that he realized how much he had missed the country and how much he loathed London. Here, at lunchtime, he could wander out of his office, buy a crusty cob and stroll down to the river, rather than sit in some smoky hostelry chewing on a soggy, over-refrigerated baguette. And in retrospect Elmdon Road had been suffocating, so claustrophobic; you were under scrutiny twenty-four hours a day. Everyone knew your business – when you had a row, where you bought your groceries, if you were late for work, if you were home early. Everything was shared: babysitters, school runs, pints of milk, secrets, gossip – and, if the latter was to be believed, sometimes partners. Christopher, who was an intensely private person, found it liberating to be able to walk out into his own garden without people checking to see if you'd changed your boxer shorts.

The boys were in their element. They'd lost their city pallor, spending most of their time outdoors, whereas in

London they'd spent most of it glued to the telly or the PlayStation. At Lydbrook, they'd already built their own cycle track, with jumps, coming back triumphantly with muddy knees, bruises and tales of their achievements.

So he and the boys were content, while Hamilton, Rosemary and Zoe were not. Was it in his power to redress the balance? Did any one of them deserve happiness more than the other? Sebastian and Hugo were the most important, of course, but being five and seven respectively they would probably be happy anywhere.

Moving back to London would certainly make Zoe happy. Christopher had no doubt he would learn to live with it just as he had before. Rosemary would carry on wandering round Lydbrook wringing her hands like a wraith. Hamilton, unaware as he was of his surroundings, would presumably be unaffected.

But how could they go back? They'd sold their house; he'd given up his job. And the agency needed him – he couldn't just abandon it now it was up and running again. They would jolly well have to stick it out. He would just have to find a way of bringing Zoe round.

He looked up with a sigh as Tiona came out of her office. The sight of her brought a smile to his lips. He didn't know what he'd have done without her. She was an angel in disguise; his saving grace. She'd held the office together when Hamilton had got ill but, as she explained to Christopher, there was only so much she could do without access to money. She was an absolute trouper, tirelessly pounding the streets of Ludlow and its environs doing viewings and valuations, leaving him free to shore up the agency's infrastructure and work on strategic alliances. She seemed to have boundless reserves of energy and enthusiasm for her job, typing up particulars late into the night as she didn't trust anyone else who worked there not to contravene the Property Misdescriptions Act. Anyway, Tiona was proud of her particulars. She had a well-thumbed *Roget's Thesaurus* on her desk. Delightful, breathtaking, charming, enchanting: she never used the same adjective twice.

He didn't know how to thank her. Of course, what she really needed was a whopping great pay rise, but he couldn't promise her that yet, not until things were more stable. They were just starting to get some fees in again, but there were a lot of below-the-line costs to cover before he could start dishing out bonuses.

He watched her cross the room towards him, in a pale pink V-necked cardigan that gave just a hint of cleavage, a flowery skirt and ballet pumps. Her face was like a china doll, with long eyelashes and rosebud lips that were curved up into a sweet smile.

'Guess what? I've got a sale on Silver Street already. Mrs Turner's very keen to push it through as quickly as possible.'

'Fantastic. Well done.'

Tiona dimpled at him modestly.

'I didn't really have to do anything. It sold itself.'

Christopher put the lid on his fountain pen defiantly.

'Let's go for a drink.'

Her eyes widened like saucers.

'Why?'

Christopher searched round for a reason, then snapped his fingers as inspiration struck.

'Because we can?'

Tiona wrinkled her nose and laughed.

66

'Why not?'

She walked past him to get her coat, and Christopher breathed in the scent of old roses. It made him feel quite giddy as he slipped on his jacket, then placed a chivalrous hand in the small of Tiona's back to escort her out of the door. As the big brass latch clicked shut behind them, he felt a tiny thrill, as if he was about to do something illicit. But that was ridiculous – if he couldn't take one of his workforce out for a congratulatory drink, then what was the point? And the Royal Oak in Upper Faviell was on the way home, so he wouldn't be too late.

6

When Jack and Jamie finally found themselves alone, they took the dregs of the champagne into the kitchen while Jamie cooked supper. Jack had protested that she shouldn't be doing it, but she insisted that it wasn't a chore but a pleasure. It seemed natural for her to step into her mother's shoes. Besides, Jack couldn't cook for toffee. So she sent him out to the greenhouse for courgettes and tomatoes, and while she chopped them she told him of her journey, her adventures, her narrow escapes – edited highlights that didn't include the occasional irresponsible one-night stand or three-day romance that she'd felt inclined to indulge in with other travellers she'd met on the way. The need for someone to hold her had been overwhelming at times; the comfort of another body. Then Jack filled her in on local gossip.

Neither of them touched on the painful subject of Louisa, or their subsequent rift. But every now and then Jamie felt that Jack was holding something back, that she too was only getting edited highlights and there was some important piece of information that she wasn't party to. She was about to probe, see if she could winkle something out of him, when he turned to her gravely.

'There is one sad piece of news. Hamilton's had some sort of stroke. He's had to go into a home.'

'My God, that's terrible.'

Jamie looked stricken. The Draces were their nearest neighbours. Their house, Lydbrook, lay three fields away sandwiched between Upper and Lower Faviell, and she'd grown up with the Drace children – Kate and Emma, a year either side of her own age, and Christopher, three years her senior (who was always called Kif, because that's what Emma had called him when she'd found Christopher too much of a mouthful). Kif had been like a big brother to Jamie. They'd been the family that, being an only child, she'd never had.

'Have you been to see him?'

'No.' Jack looked uncomfortable. 'Apparently there isn't much point. He barely recognizes anyone.'

'You don't know, though, do you?' Jamie persisted. 'It might help. It must be better than sitting there all on your own day after day.'

'Anyway,' Jack seemed keen to change the subject, 'one good thing's come out of it. Christopher's come back to take over the agency. They're all living at Lydbrook.'

Jamie suddenly felt unbearably sad. It wasn't all that long ago that she and the Draces had torn round the countryside together, first on their ponies, with their parents ferrying them to gymkhanas and Pony Club camp. Then later in their teens Kif had got his first old banger, and had taken over the transportation, driving them to discos and parties. He'd been a wonderful escort, keeping an eye out for Emma and Kate and Jamie, making sure they didn't drink too much or snog anyone unsuitable, but without ever being stuffy or boring. They'd all been

69

so close. Tennis matches at Lydbrook, croquet tournaments at Bucklebury, bicycle polo. Jamie remembered her mother setting up show-jumping circuits for her and Kate and Emma to pop over on their ponies, patiently replacing the poles time and time again ...

Now Louisa was dead and Hamilton, to all intents and purposes, might as well be. It was the end of an era, with Christopher taking over at Lydbrook. Jamie shivered, realizing the truth behind two of the most well-worn clichés. Life was too short. And you never knew what was round the corner.

At seven o'clock, Olivier put his head politely round the door. He was washed and gleaming. His hair was still wet and swept back, showing off his bone structure to even greater effect. He had on a clean pair of jeans, Docksiders and a teal-blue sweatshirt that a colour consultant could have told him brought out the brilliance of his eyes. He smelled of Imperial Leather.

'I'm just going down the Oak for a swift pint,' he said casually to Jack.

'I was going to do supper at about eight,' Jamie said, and Olivier hesitated for a moment before nodding.

'See you later,' said Jack, a tinge of regret in his farewell as his eyes followed Olivier enviously out of the door. Jamie was once again left feeling that she was intruding on some sort of male ritual. A smidgeon of resentment bubbled inside her. Her father hadn't seen her for ten months – was it that much of a hardship to miss out on his evening pint?

At quarter past seven, Christopher and Tiona were still happily ensconced in the snug of the Royal Oak.

Christopher was nursing his second full-bodied pint of Honeycote Ale; Tiona clasped an ice-cold glass of Chablis. It was great to be away from the office, away from the chirrup of the telephone and the baleful glare of the bespectacled Norma, his father's loyal and long-serving secretary, whose eyes he had felt boring into his back disapprovingly as he left.

Christopher tried to ignore the fact that the boys would be heading for bed any minute; he really didn't fancy going home yet. Zoe would definitely be on the second bottle by the time he got there, and he'd have to pretend to himself that she wasn't slurring her words. By bedtime she would be tearful, apologetically tearful, and he couldn't bear that. He'd prefer aggressive, because at least then he wouldn't feel so awful. What could he say to her? Get a job? A hobby? A life? He wouldn't feel so guilty if he didn't feel so right himself.

'Penny for them.' Tiona nudged him gently with her elbow.

'I was just thinking how pleased I am to be back. If I was still in London I'd be battling my way home on the tube, stuck in a tunnel, probably, with a drunk on one side of me and a beggar on the other. This is definitely the life.'

Tiona smiled sweetly, taking that as a compliment. As she sipped at her drink, her eyes wandered over to the bar, where an absolute vision had just entered and was chatting up the barmaid. Tall, tanned, a little bit scruffy but probably deliberately so. Perfect peach of a bum in faded jeans. Amazing eyes, blue as a bottle of Bombay Sapphire gin. She looked for his watch. You could tell a lot about a man by his watch. Interestingly, he wasn't wearing one, and there was no telltale white stripe, which could only mean time didn't matter to him. So he was either absolutely loaded or unemployed. Tiona's eyes wandered over him lazily. Wouldn't mind a bit of that, she thought to herself. Then she dragged herself back to what Christopher was saying, chiding herself for taking her mind off the job in hand. Christopher's watch was plain gold, with no-nonsense Roman numerals and a crocodile strap. Discreet, probably a couple of grand's worth if you bought it today, but he definitely didn't have that kind of money to spend on a watch, so it was probably handed down.

Christopher was looking at her strangely and she realized she was staring at it. She apologized hastily.

'I was just thinking ... what a nice watch.'

'My grandfather's. I couldn't afford to buy myself one like this.' He looked at it, and in doing so noticed that another half an hour had slipped by rather pleasantly since he'd last looked. 'I really ought to be going. Supper will be ...'

Beyond hope. Beyond repair. Beyond even the dogs. Tiona smiled her thanks at him. The Chablis had brought a dainty little flush to her cheeks and put a sparkle in her eye.

'Thank you for the drink. It made a lovely change. I'd usually be watching *Coronation Street* with the cat on my lap.'

Christopher drained his pint, and they walked out to the car park, where Tiona reached up on her tippy-toes to give him a peck on the cheek, just so he could be sure how very tiny and vulnerable she was, then slid into her Golf and drove off. Christopher watched her go, then sat in his car for a moment before switching on the ignition, steeling himself for what he might find when he got home. Not that Zoe was a nag who would have a whinge at him for being late, not at all. No – she'd probably welcomed the chance to get another half-bottle of Jacob's Creek down her neck without his watchful eye upon her.

Perched on a highly polished wooden stool with his elbows on the bar, Olivier decided that this was definitely his favourite time of the day. The pub always had a pleasant flow of traffic between six and half-seven as people dropped in for a quick drink after work on their way home, so there was usually someone to pass the time of day with and get the local chitchat. A lot of business was done at the bar on a handshake and the purchase of a pint. If you wanted something doing, there would always be someone who knew someone, and Toby the landlord acted as a facilitator-cum-messenger service. The pub had been bought recently by a small Cotswold-based brewery, Honeycote Ales, who were looking to expand their portfolio of country hostelries. Toby was young to be in charge of a pub, but he'd served his apprenticeship in the Cotswolds and the Royal Oak was flourishing under his watchful eye – superficially, nothing had been changed, but the food had been improved beyond measure. It didn't try to compete with the gourmet establishments that had made the area so renowned, but concentrated on a simple menu perfectly executed: the Aberdeen Angus steak and chips were legendary, making it incredibly popular for a midweek meal out amongst the locals. Added to which, the staff were exemplary and Honeycote Ale itself was acknowledged to taste like nectar.

Jack and Olivier habitually wandered down the road just after six to prop up the bar for an hour or so, but today Olivier was quite happy to nurse a pint on his own and contemplate the latest turn of events.

Just as he'd told Jamie, he'd spent the past few years alternating winter and summer as a skiing instructor and tennis coach. And it had been an idyllic existence for a young, free and single bloke who loved the outdoors. But it was starting to lose its charm. Olivier had been to several weddings in the past couple of years; close friends of his with whom he'd enjoyed many wild nights. At first he'd thought it was strange they'd gone down the marriage route, and had exchanged much elbow-nudging and muffled guffaws with the other single male guests. But by the third one, he was starting to feel like the freak. Everyone seemed to be tying the knot, even the most committed bachelors. On their stag nights, they claimed to envy Olivier his freedom and independence, and made out they were heading for the gallows. He knew that was just window-dressing. They wouldn't be walking up the aisle if they didn't want to be. At the most recent nuptials he had actually felt like a bit of a sad bastard. Everyone had if not a wife then a 'partner'; some of them even had kids. At the evening do, there was no question of copping off with someone; everyone was spoken for, even the bridesmaids.

The problem was that his lifestyle didn't leave room for a great amount of commitment. Every few months or so he would move on: he didn't like to stay in the same resort two seasons running. He wanted to explore as many countries as he could. His references were always good, so he had his pick of the best resorts. There weren't many girls who would be willing to trail round after him, bunking up in the single room hotel accommodation that usually went with the job. And he certainly wasn't prepared to settle down in one place just for the sake of a committed relationship.

He'd felt a little tide of panic rise when he turned thirty. Realistically, in five years' time, would he be such an attractive proposition? A ski or tennis instructor hurtling towards forty didn't have quite the same cachet as one ten years younger. It was part of the job to be young and gorgeous. Old and gorgeous didn't quite cut it in the same way.

And he didn't seem to have the stamina for partying any more. The slopes didn't look as inviting after a night on the tiles as they once had. He needed his lie-in. He *wanted* his lie-in, which was more worrying. Olivier Templeton was feeling his age and realizing that perhaps his existence was bordering on the shallow and self-indulgent.

Then, eighteen months ago, a knee injury had intervened. It hadn't even been a dramatic accident, involving black runs and avalanches and mountain rescue teams. He'd quite simply turned too quickly and ripped a cruciate ligament. Three operations later his specialist told him that if he didn't want to end up a cripple he would have to stop skiing. Of course, he hadn't been insured. Medical insurance, yes, to cover the cost of the hospital bills, but nothing that would compensate him for loss of earnings. He had no rights, as his contracts were always casual.

Totally broke and feeling utterly useless, he'd gone back to his parents to contemplate his future, and had almost been driven mad by his father. Advancing old age and a dicky hip were making Eric irascible and cantankerous, and what was even worse, smug and 'I told you so' about Olivier's lack of prospects. Their values were poles apart. The older Eric got, the more he became driven by the pursuit of money and the subsequent spending that proved to the world how successful he was. Everything had to be the best, from his Jermyn Street haircut down to his silk socks and handmade shoes.

Olivier, on the other hand, had never had the urge to earn money, as long as he had enough to eat and a few quid left over for a pint, he was happy. It wasn't that he was work-shy, for he'd always worked hard, but he made sure he did things that he enjoyed so he could live for his work. He would happily have taught skiing and tennis for nothing.

And he loathed London. There was nothing there to unleash his boundless energy on to. He reluctantly helped his father out at the dealership, a huge emporium of 'previously enjoyed' prestige cars that attracted the sort of clientele Olivier particularly abhorred – aspirational and eager to show off their success. Eric was horrified that he preferred washing and polishing the cars to serving customers. But sitting behind a desk dishing out bullshit and brown-nosing potential purchasers was anathema to Olivier. He was a physical being; London and the dealership and his parents were caging him in.

Eric was frustrated with his son's attitude. Time and again he sat him down and tried to fire him with some ambition.

'By the time I was your age,' he was particularly fond of saying, 'I'd made my first million. Only on paper, admittedly. But a million was—'

'Worth a lot more in those days,' Olivier would finish

the sentence for him wearily. 'I know. So you keep telling me. I'm sorry I'm such a disappointment.'

'I'm only telling you for your own good. You can't bum around the world for ever.'

His father obviously had no admiration for what he'd been doing. And no sympathy for the fact that his injury meant he could never go back to what he loved so much. Olivier grew weary of the nagging and the taunting and being constantly put down. And being compared to his older brother and sister, who were a hot-shot lawyer and head of PR for a Parisian fashion house respectively. His parents positively worshipped the ground they walked on.

'Of course, neither Emile nor Delphine will want to take over the dealership, as they're both so successful in their own right,' Eric said one day, and Olivier's blood froze. Didn't his father understand? He had no interest in it whatsoever. He'd probably run it into the ground within months. He had no head for figures, no head for doing a deal. OK, the cars were beautiful, he appreciated that. But Eric might as well be selling lawnmowers or tractor parts for all the interest he actually took in his commodity. All he cared about was the profit. Olivier didn't find his mother any more supportive or sympathetic. She spent most of her time travelling over to her native Paris to stay in Delphine's apartment. She'd become thinner and more chic and more brittle than Olivier could ever remember.

Eventually, however, he became resigned to the fact that he had no choice but to step into his father's shoes as he was little qualified to do anything else and Eric, annoyingly, did have a point about him not being able to bum around for ever. He couldn't live on fresh air, after all, and his savings weren't going to last long. So he tried to take a more positive approach to the business, get his head around sales figures and targets and selling techniques. He consoled himself with the fact that there probably were worse ways of earning a living.

One November afternoon, he was sitting in his father's office at the showroom going through yet more tedious paperwork when a tiny newspaper cutting fell out of a folder. It was a death announcement from *The Times*. A cold chill ran down Olivier's neck as he read the details: Louisa Wilding had died two months before, after a short illness.

Impulse made him pick up the phone and call Jack. To Olivier, scrawling a few lines of well-meaning condolence was worse than doing nothing – a meaningless piece of middle-class etiquette. And so what if he was encroaching on dangerous territory? Death was a great leveller. Death made you forgive and forget. And Jack had sounded delighted to hear from him – though Olivier suspected that his effusiveness was a result of quite clearly being drunk at three o'clock in the afternoon.

Olivier had always seen Jack as the father he would have liked, for Jack had taken more notice of him than Eric had ever done. On the occasions Olivier had been allowed to accompany his father when they went racing, Eric had expected the boy to keep quiet and out of sight. Jack, on the other hand, had insisted on getting him involved, giving him simple tasks that wouldn't jeopardize the car's performance. And once he'd even allowed him behind the wheel, had patiently steered him through the first rudiments of driving, and Olivier had felt a rush of exhilaration that he'd never forgotten. As soon as his father got back, however, he'd been turfed out of the driving seat and sent to fetch bacon sandwiches and coffee. Jack had smiled sympathetically at him. 'Never mind,' he'd said conspiratorially. 'You can come up and stay on your own one day. I'll teach you how to drive then.' But after the aborted holiday, that day had never arrived ...

So when Jack implored Olivier to come and visit, Olivier needed no second telling. He'd left the showroom, jumped in his car and driven straight up to Shropshire, to be welcomed by Jack with open arms and a full glass; the two of them had spent the weekend getting drunk. Olivier had intended, albeit reluctantly, to head back to London on the Sunday afternoon. But over a very late breakfast of bacon sandwiches and brown sauce, Jack had started reminiscing about their racing exploits. Olivier wondered about the whereabouts of the car, and was staggered when Jack admitted it was still sitting in the barn.

It had only taken half an hour of adjustments, a change of oil and a new tank of petrol to bring about the car's resurrection. Jack became very emotional, as the car for him held so many memories. And Olivier knew he had reached a turning point: that he had stumbled upon something that was going to provide the thrills and excitement he'd been lacking. He never went back to London. He rang his father and told him he was going into business with an old friend, only lying by omission, and Eric's sneering implication that he would be back soon with his tail between his legs told Olivier he was doing the right thing keeping quiet about his rekindled friendship.

There was a tacit acknowledgement between Jack and Olivier that their relationship was on an entirely fresh footing, that the history between the Templetons and the Wildings should be forgotten as much water had flowed under the bridge. And together they had forged a friendship based on a mutual obsession. Jack insisted he was too old to race the car – his reactions were too slow, the fear he felt was inhibiting rather than motivating. But he nurtured Olivier, taught him everything he knew. And Olivier took to the sport like a natural. Although it wasn't as physically testing as skiing, many of the skills needed were the same. You had to be fit and alert, with the courage to take risks and the sense to make those risks calculated ones. There was no place for caution, but no place for foolhardiness either.

Olivier had taken his advanced motor-racing licence and passed with flying colours, which meant he could now compete. He took the car out into the hills on a daily basis to practise, and never tired of the rush it gave him. Such simplicity, such perfection, whittled down to the barest minimum for maximum performance. When he let her go, he and the car felt as one, as if his flesh and bones had become her steel. She gave everything he asked of her.

When the car was entered into its first race for over twenty years at Donington Park that April, Jack felt choked with pride. And although he'd only come seventh in a class of eleven, Olivier knew he had found his *métier*.

A few days later, he found a photograph of his father amongst the paperwork and manuals in the barn. Eric was holding a trophy aloft, a wreath of laurels round his neck, a smile of genuine happiness on his face. Olivier wondered where that carefree young man had gone – he looked so handsome, his hair blowing back in the breeze, his eyes laughing. It seemed impossible that he could have turned into such an embittered and cynical old man. Olivier couldn't remember the last time he'd seen his father really laugh.

Jack found him looking at the photo.

'That's the Richard Corrigan Memorial Trophy,' he said. 'Your dad won it the first summer we got the car going. He was like a dog with two tails...'

Jack trailed off, in memory of happier times. And now, Olivier was determined to win the trophy for himself. The race was being run in two weeks' time, at Sapersley Park, and he really thought he was in with a chance. Perhaps that would be an achievement his father could relate to; something he would be proud of. Because although Olivier told himself repeatedly he didn't care what his father thought of him, and despised Eric's values, deep down he wanted to prove himself to him, prove that he was as good as he was. And maybe, just maybe, winning the Corrigan Trophy was the way to do that.

In the meantime, however, he felt as settled and contented as he ever had in his life. He loved Bucklebury Farm. He loved Shropshire. Everyone seemed unpretentious; no one had anything to prove. Of course, you got the odd nightmare, like Lettice. But once you got used to her, she was all right really. He'd grown quite fond of her over the past couple of months. At least she had a bit of spirit.

As he sipped his pint, he wondered if the return of Jamie would mean the end of his idyllic existence. He doubted things would stay the same: the arrival of a new person on the scene always changed the dynamics. As it was he knew time had been running out, not to mention money – he'd been living on his meagre savings. A few grand, but not enough to last indefinitely. And not enough to finance a cripplingly expensive sport. A new tyre alone was two hundred quid, and a single race could make mincemeat of a complete set if you didn't know what you were doing.

He glanced up at the clock behind the bar. Just gone quarter to eight. He'd better make a move – Jamie had mentioned supper at eight. Not that Olivier usually paid any attention to deadlines given to him by women. But he couldn't help but wonder how Jamie's impromptu arrival was going to affect things at Bucklebury Farm.

7

It was quarter to nine before the three of them sat down to supper in the little paved courtyard adjoining the kitchen garden. Jamie had found some salmon fillets in the freezer and wrapped them in Parma ham, roasting them on top of the tomatoes and courgettes from the garden. While they ate, Jack and Olivier regaled her with tales of their exploits with the Bugatti, and Jamie was relieved that the conversation was kept light – she was too tired for anything else.

They'd spent the week preparing the car for a vintage hill climb that coming weekend, Jamie looked baffled.

'What's a hill climb?'

'Just what it sounds like. Basically, you go from the bottom to the top of the hill in the shortest time you can,' Jack explained.

Jamie made a face. 'That doesn't sound very exciting.'

'It's not a straight track. They throw in a few hairpin bends just to test your mettle.' Olivier grinned. 'It's pretty hairy at top speed. And it can be down to a hundredth of a second.'

'In other words it's pretty lethal?'

'Well, yes, if you make a mistake, it could be,' admitted Olivier cheerfully.

'Whatever turns you on,' Jamie smiled, rolling her eyes in exasperation. All she could be grateful for was that Jack had retired gracefully from the enterprise, and was happy to compete vicariously through Olivier. She wondered for a moment who exactly was financing this foolhardiness; even she in her ignorance could see that it didn't come cheap and Olivier, by his own admission, didn't have a job. But then who was she to quibble? It had given her father something to think about. It was a small price to pay.

Not wanting to dampen their enthusiasm, she carried on nodding in what she thought were the right places, before pleading exhaustion just after ten and excusing herself.

She fell into bed, snuggling up under the rose-covered eiderdown she'd had since she was six. She could just hear the voices of Jack and Olivier two floors below, and the occasional boisterous laugh. Again she had that feeling of being an outsider, an interloper, then told herself to stop being oversensitive and paranoid. It was her house, her father. And there was no denying he'd been delighted to see her.

Her relationship with Jack had never been conventional. From a very young age, he'd treated Jamie like an adult, when she hadn't really wanted to be. In return, she had often treated him like a child, had been disapproving and reproachful of his behaviour. He wasn't to know how embarrassing she'd found him at times. He wasn't like anyone else's dad. He was too irresponsible, too carefree, too eager to break the rules. How she'd secretly longed for a father who was 'a' something: a doctor or a lawyer or a vet. Every time someone asked what he did, she died inwardly, because there was no answer. Import/export, he always told her to say, but that made it sound as if he was trafficking drugs. And in her more suspicious moments, Jamie thought perhaps he did – the Persian carpet business had definitely been a front for something. And it was always either feast or famine. Privately, Jamie preferred famine, because it meant everyone was at home and had to eat sensible meals round the table. Quite possibly the worst moment of her life had been when Jack had turned up to Speech Day in a helicopter, sending hats and the headmistress's speech flying, waving frantically to three hundred girls with upturned faces and open mouths.

And while Louisa wasn't a conventional mother, at least she was never overtly embarrassing. There was something very controlled and English about her, even if she wasn't cuddly and bustly like some of her friends' mothers. Jack was always a little too loud, a little too eager to push the boat out. He'd never really grown up.

Now she was more confident about herself, she could accept her father for what he was, and what he had done. He was over sixty now, so not only was he unlikely to change, but he was unlikely to get up to too much mischief. Her mother's death made her realize that Jack probably had little time left. And in a way, nor did she. She was the same age now as her mother had been when she'd had Jamie.

Looking at Jack this evening, all the resentment and bitterness she'd felt evaporated into pity. He looked so incredibly ... vulnerable. His once luxuriantly bright golden hair was dull and thin, scraped over his skull. His eyes, always so alive and full of mischief, seemed permanently bloodshot, as if he had been weeping – and perhaps he had. Even his voice now had a slight tremor in it that he didn't seem quite able to control. Jamie felt a sudden surge of fondness for him. She might not have approved of the way he lived his life, he may have done terrible things that she could never condone, but what was the point of holding it against him now?

She resolved to spend the next few months with her father; rebuild their relationship. And the house certainly needed some attention. She'd phone the agency tomorrow, tell them she was ready to go back on their books, but that she only wanted work locally. That way she could earn some money and concentrate on restoring Jack and Bucklebury at the same time. She was running through her plans in her mind, when there was a scrabbling and snuffling sound, and before she knew it her bedroom door was shoved open and Parsnip and Gumdrop bounded into the room and up on to her bed. She drifted off with the two little dogs asleep on her feet. They were like two lead weights and she didn't dare move for fear of disturbing them, but they made her feel wanted. They made her feel as if she belonged. As she fell into a delicious, much-needed sleep, she decided she'd definitely done the right thing by coming home.

8

There was a saying in Lower Faviell that the only good Deacon was a dead Deacon. And there was a line of tombstones in the churchyard that should have been reassuring. But every Sunday, without fail, the flowers on the graves were replaced with fresh blooms, indicating that there were bearers of that name still going strong.

The family were the bane of Lower Faviell. Any suggestion of badger-baiting, cock-fighting, poaching, missing livestock, stolen ponies or petty break-ins, and the finger of suspicion was always pointed Deaconwards. The men fought, they got drunk, they got girls pregnant. One or other of them was generally up before the magistrate; their names featured regularly in the local paper – driving without tax, driving while drunk, being drunk and disorderly, causing affray. And the distaff side weren't much better – hard as nails. You didn't mess with a Deacon girl, with their flashing dark eyes, their gypsy curls, their gold jewellery.

People often complained that something should be done – but what? And they could be useful, if you wanted a job done quickly for cash. They were all good with their hands, bricklaying and plastering and painting and decorating. And demolition – they were particularly good at that.

The biggest branch lived at Lower Faviell Farm, where they had been tenants for three generations, and were ruled over by John, the oldest of his brothers and a man of few words who had respect for no one but his wife, the redoubtable Nolly. Being the oldest son, he had inherited the tenancy when his father had died, and as his own family had grown, his brothers and sisters had gradually dispersed towards the town, each of them actually glad to be rid of the responsibility of trying to scratch a living from twenty acres.

John and Nolly's offspring were, on the whole, a good-looking bunch, built like the proverbial, fortuitously inheriting the best of their parents' features. There were eight of them altogether – five boys, three girls, tightly knit. Three of them had moved out to the council estate on the edge of Ludlow to join their aunts and uncles – even the warren-like rooms at Lower Faviell Farm couldn't hold all their partners and offspring. A couple of them were usually accommodated at Her Majesty's pleasure at any one time.

And already the next generation were well established. John and Nolly were the proud owners of nine grand-children, the eldest of whom were shipped into the village school at Lower Faviell by dint of their parents giving Lower Faviell Farm as their address. This was partly for convenience (so they could go from school straight to Nolly for their tea) and partly because the Deacons always stuck together and looked out for each other. The headmistress despaired, as she was desperately trying to improve the SATs results and get a decent Ofsted report. But of her sixty-four pupils, nearly ten per cent were Deacons. Not that some of them weren't sharp and cunning. If the little buggers could be made to apply themselves, they could do quite well. Rod Deacon was proof enough of that. It was generally agreed that, of all of them, Rod had done very well for himself and could, almost, be trusted.

Rod drove down his parents' pitted drive, not bothering to try and avoid the potholes, for it would have been impossible, but thanking God he was in the pick-up, and not his low-slung brand new sports car. He hadn't mentioned that to his family yet. He'd been hoping to keep it quiet for a while, although it was inevitable that he or Bella would be spotted in it sooner or later by one of the Deacon tribe. He'd be in for a right ribbing then. They thought the Mitsubishi Warrior was flashy enough, with its twin cabs, its chrome accessories, its dark green metallic paint. On the side, in discreet gold lettering, was inscribed 'Roderick Deacon, Handmade Bespoke Kitchens for the Discerning'.

'Who are they then?' his dad had asked. 'Is that a posh word for disabled or something?'

They'd wind him up about the Audi all right.

Rod had long accepted that his family were all hypocrites, with double standards, resenting anything that smacked of achievement. After all, it wasn't as if they didn't all spend their lives in pursuit of money. Any means, as long as it wasn't legitimate and preferably didn't involve hard work. They'd scorned him for setting up properly in business. Practically fell off their chairs laughing when they found out he refused to do cash deals. But Rod had learned the hard way not to trust anyone. If you did cash deals, it was only a matter of time before someone grassed you up to the Inland Revenue or the VAT man, and life was already complicated enough.

He swung the car into the yard in front of the house, avoiding the motley collection of bright plastic toys that had been reaped from car-boot sales over the years – two Cosy Coupes, a turtle sandbox, a Barbie bicycle, lethally abandoned rollerblades and a pair of quad bikes that had never worked since the day they'd been brought home. They had joined the queue of things waiting for repair: a battered old Land Rover, a washing machine with the drum removed. In the midst of this chaos stood a pristine set of iroko chairs and matching table shaded by a green parasol. Rod didn't like to think of its provenance. No one in his family would have dreamed of forking out the best part of a grand for garden furniture. Two fat white Alsatians lifted their heads in interest as he climbed out of the cab, then, satisfied that he wasn't an intruder, carried on their snoozing, their muddy tails thumping up and down to indicate they were pleased to see him but really couldn't be bothered to do anything about it.

From out of nowhere appeared three children: Stacey, in pink plastic mules and an Eminem T-shirt that came down to her knees, Casey in a nappy and Bob the Builder wellingtons, and Jordan in top-to-toe Diadora, trainers flashing wildly as he raced to be the first to embrace his uncle. Rod detested the way his various brothers and sisters used his mother ruthlessly as an unpaid child-minder for those of their offspring who were too young for school. Nolly insisted she didn't mind, that was what grandmothers were for, but Rod objected to the way his siblings never gave her a second thought, didn't consider that she might have a life of her own, and certainly never paid her for her time, or even gave her a box of chocolates or a bunch of flowers as a thank you. After all, Nolly was getting on now. He thought she deserved a rest, but she was far from likely to get one.

Rod disentangled himself gently from a tangle of arms and kisses. The smell of Bazooka bubblegum and poo overwhelmed him.

'Casey needs changing,' Stacey informed him in her twenty-a-day rasp, brushing her too-long fringe out of her eyes.

'Where's Nana?' asked Rod.

'On the net,' Jordan informed him solemnly. Rod rolled his eyes. His mother was no doubt trying to drum up publicity for his sister, Tanya, who had a Shania Twain tribute act called 36D. Nolly was her publicist, agent and manager rolled into one, which meant she spent most of her days emailing bigwigs and trying to get Tanya more prestigious slots than the third Monday of every month at the Drum and Monkey in Tidsworth. Tanya was the only sister who hadn't yet started whelping, and still lived with her parents. She worked her socks off as an instructor at a nearby riding school. Rod had a lot of time for her. She wasn't as lazy as the rest; she understood that life wasn't about finding the easiest way out all the time. Her lack of partner had led to rumours that she was a dyke, but Rod didn't believe them. Tanya didn't suffer fools gladly and she just hadn't yet found a man worthy of her respect.

He scooped up Casey and took her into the kitchen to change her. He wasn't squeamish, and he couldn't bear the thought of her trotting round dirty. He knew perfectly well her father wouldn't have ever changed her nappy. Dean was a sexist git through and through. All of his brothers were. It rankled Rod. If – no, when – he had kids, he'd be a hands-on father. He was quite happy to spend hours playing with his nieces and nephews; pushing them on the rope swing he'd put up, playing hide and seek, teaching them to ride bikes, holding their hands while they mastered roller skating.

It was ironic that his brothers and sisters had so many offspring between them and paid them so little attention. Instead of time, they lavished them with toys and games which were usually a five-minute wonder. Every few months or so one of his sisters or sisters-in-law would 'catch' for another one, and spend the next nine months moaning and groaning. Then, the minute it popped out, the baby became Nolly's responsibility most of the time, while its mother sat at home watching daytime telly, smoking and ordering things out of catalogues.

In the meantime, months had gone by since Bella and Rod had started trying, and there was still no sign ...

He didn't want to dwell on it. He'd got a lot of work to do. He shouted up to his mum that he was there, dished out Panda Pops for the three kids, plonked them in front of the forty-two-inch-screen television to watch *Rocky IV* on the DVD, and went out to the old shed he still used as his workshop.

As soon as he left school, where the only thing he had been good at was carpentry, Rod had started out fitting kitchens for one of the big DIY stores. The experience opened his eyes: he was appalled at how quickly he and the rest of the team slapped in a kitchen, how little care was taken both in the initial design and the installation, how corners were cut and things were botched. He was even more incensed by the differential between what the customer was charged and his pitiful hourly rate. But there was little he could do about it, so he kept his head down, and if he was more conscientious than his workmates, they were quite happy to let him get on with it. He ended up with the tricky jobs, because he could be bothered, and as a result there were fewer complaints. There was no sign of acknowledgement from the management, however, because the gaffer never gave him the credit. All Rod could gain was experience, hoping that he wouldn't be ground down and eventually become as cynical and slipshod as the rest of them because, as they pointed out, no one gave you any thanks for doing a good job so you might as well do a bad one and save yourself the trouble.

One day they'd gone to fit out a utility room in a beautiful Tudor manor, and Rod had been horrified by the appalling job they had done – not that anyone would know on the surface, but Rod knew that in six months' time all the shortcuts would reveal themselves; the drawers would jam, the work surface would split, the plumbing would come unravelled. All night it had eaten away at him, and the next morning he woke up determined.

The lady of the house had been just that – a Lady – and she had been utterly charmed by Rod's arrival on her doorstep. He'd explained his concerns, and told her it wouldn't take him more than a couple of hours to put it all right. She'd been flummoxed when it finally emerged he was doing it off his own bat, and wouldn't get paid; that he was giving up his own Saturday because he quite simply couldn't bear the thought of their shoddy workmanship in her beautiful house.

Lady Pamela tried her very best not to sound patronizing when she asked if he would like to see the main kitchen. She ushered him in and he was speechless; it was quite the most breathtaking room he had ever seen. He wandered round it in awe, stroking the smooth golden wood, pulling out the drawers that glided like silk, examining all the clever little cubbyholes, admiring the craftsmanship, the design, the thought that had gone into it. Pamela was fascinated by his enthusiasm. But then, he'd never seen a kitchen like this before. He didn't move in those circles; didn't buy those kinds of magazines. And now he'd seen what could be done, he knew that was what he wanted to do.

Two days later a huge parcel arrived at his house, containing a dozen brochures from top-notch kitchen companies and a note in Pamela's distinctive italics. They were, she said, doing up the gardener's cottage on the estate, and she wanted to give Rod first option on fitting the kitchen. He could have free rein with the design and she thought he might find inspiration in the enclosed.

He'd taken up the challenge eagerly. It took him three months to complete it, because he had to squeeze it in during his limited spare time, but Pamela had assured him there was no rush. The kitchen was only tiny, but he'd fitted it out using oak from the estate, and it was exquisite. He wasn't foolish enough to be over-ambitious on his first and clearly most important solo project, so he'd stuck with plain and simple and square.

Pamela was delighted with the result. Not only did she pay Rod handsomely for his work, but she nominated herself as his patron. She had an enormous circle of wealthy friends, to whom she trumpeted Rod's skills, until he found himself inundated with enquiries. As well as that, she made him an appointment with her own bank manager, who painstakingly talked Rod through the perils and pitfalls of being self-employed. And she insisted on bankrolling his first few freelance commissions, until he had enough of a profit to stand on his own two feet. He repaid her financially as soon as he could, but he knew that as long as he lived he couldn't repay her generosity of spirit. Lady Pamela, however, was sufficiently gratified by the fact that he was a resounding success, and that she had discovered him.

He had a lot to learn, of course. There was more to fitting a kitchen than making the cupboards match the wall space. And at this end of the market you had to cater for every whim. Financing it was terrifying. Initially he couldn't underwrite the enormously expensive appliances a lot of his customers wanted. He didn't know you could spend three thousand pounds on a fridge. So at first, the customers paid for their appliances direct, which meant of course that he made nothing on them.

But gradually the business grew, until he was able to meet the overheads properly. He learned how to pick and choose clients – spot the ones who were going to be more trouble than they were worth and change things for the sake of it, and go with ones who were as enthusiastic as he was about the end product, but who were happy to trust him and leave him to his own devices.

Now, ten years later, he was well established. He still worked from his parents' farm, in the shed his father had once used to bring on turkeys and fatten them up for Christmas, until the EEC rules and regulations had become so prohibitive as to make him lose interest. It wasn't a glamorous setting, and it was freezing in the winter, but he was able to lock the door and lose himself in his craft. He did about eight kitchens a year on average, working at his own pace. He could have taken on someone else, but he knew the trouble started when you bit off more than you could chew; when you were trying to run more than one job at a time. And he was a perfectionist. He would never be able to trust anyone to have his exacting standards. By doing it all himself, he could be sure both he and the customer were satisfied.

He was certainly reaping the rewards. He and his wife Bella had bought a tumbledown barn a couple of miles away, which they'd renovated and was now a luxurious home, Owl's Nest (Rod was conscious that the name was a little bit twee, but Bella collected owls – or at least things in the shape of owls, like biscuit barrels and hot-water-bottle covers). And in it, they enjoyed their creature comforts, which his family couldn't resist winding him up about. But, as he pointed out, the two of them both worked bloody hard for it.

This morning, he was putting the finishing touches to a free-standing larder unit, with tiny zinc-lined spice drawers, sea-grass vegetable baskets, a wine rack and even a shiny brass hook on which to hang strings of onions and garlic. He reminded himself to take a photo of it before it was finished. Now he had done one, the next would be easier, and he was charging a small fortune.

At eleven o'clock Nolly banged on the door with coffee and a bacon sandwich. To look at her now, you'd never realize that she had once been the belle of the county;

her hair was iron grey and straggly, and despite the fact that she ran round after her family all day, she was very overweight. Rod worried about her laboured breathing and the cough she'd developed, but no matter how he nagged she wouldn't give up her fags. The nicotine, she claimed, was holding her lungs together.

'How are things?'

Rod knew exactly what that meant. He just gave a thin-lipped smile.

'Oh, you know. Fingers crossed this month.'

She was the only person he'd spoken to about it. His brothers and sisters all thought he and Bella were enjoying their hedonistic existence too much to worry about children, that they would only cramp their style. They couldn't be more wrong.

'You should go and see someone. A specialist.'

'I know. If it's nothing doing this time ...'

Nolly pressed her lips together. 'You know what the problem is. She doesn't eat enough.'

'She eats, Mum. Honestly.'

She didn't, of course. Not properly. Bella was the only person he knew who had no interest in food whatsoever.

'Do you want me to do you some dinner? Lamb hotpot?'

Rod's mouth watered at the thought – big chump chops, the meat falling off the bone, chunks of potato, sweet melting leeks. But he had an assignation this lunchtime, with Bella. A vital assignation that couldn't be missed for all the hotpot in Shropshire.

Jamie awoke the next morning confused and disorientated. The dogs had long abandoned her, leaving a slightly hairy indentation on her bedcover. She pulled her curtains open, and smiled to see a jolly yellow sun hovering over the stable yard and the fields beyond – judging by its height it was almost midday. She padded down to the kitchen in her nightshirt. She was perturbed to see that, despite their assurances the night before as they'd urged her off to bed, neither Jack nor Olivier had done the washing-up from supper. The stout little brown teapot was still warm, so they'd managed to lever the kettle under the tap despite the dishes piled up in the sink.

She made a fresh pot of tea and sawed a chunk off the loaf she'd bought in the post office the day before. She spread it liberally with butter and jam, then stuck her feet into her hiking boots and went outside.

It was a glorious day, one which promised a gentle heat to soothe her aching bones and brought out the scent of roses by the back door. The old cockerel stood on the water butt, crowing defiantly for the benefit of anyone who would listen. She headed down towards the stables, walking in through the archway topped by the clock whose hands had stopped years ago. She felt a tinge of sadness to see all the loose boxes now empty; the concrete was cracking and grass was growing through. It had once been immaculate, not a speck of dust or stray strand of straw across the cobbles, the stable doors always freshly creosoted where now they had faded to a silvery grey, many of them hanging off their hinges. The flower baskets that Louisa had put up every year were dry and empty; some of them sprouted weeds in a ghostly imitation of what they had once been.

The far side of the yard had a five-bar gate leading to the top paddock and the fields beyond. Jamie was puzzled to see that a large part of this area had been marked out with stakes and orange plastic tape. She wondered if perhaps Jack was arranging to have it all re-concreted. Maybe he had plans to renovate it? She thought for a moment that perhaps they could open a livery yard. It would make quite a nice little cash business – DIY liveries almost ran themselves if you were well organized. She felt cheered by the idea. Bucklebury Farm needed horses.

She wandered over to the old barn that made up the fourth side of the courtyard. Inside, Jack and Olivier were bent over the Bugatti. Jack was in the driver's seat, foot on the throttle, thraping the engine, while Olivier peered with a frown under the bonnet, ear cocked to one side, not quite liking what he heard. Though how he could discern anything through such a deafening roar was a mystery.

When the revs finally died down, Jamie ventured a greeting. The two men looked up absently. Jamie felt rather as a woman might on entering a gentlemen's club, as waves of unspoken hostility told her she was stepping into forbidden territory. She received a somewhat cursory nod of acknowledgement from each of them. It was clearly a crucial moment. At a signal from Olivier, Jack turned off the engine. Olivier, hands black with oil, delved into the depths with a spanner and made a minor adjustment. Jack restarted the engine, and after listening carefully for a few moments the two men nodded at each other in satisfaction. Only then, and more out of politeness than because they wanted to, Jamie felt, did they turn their attention to her. She felt she had to justify her presence.

'I wondered if you fancied coffee?'

The enthusiasm with which they greeted her offer made Jamie realize her first mistake. If she didn't watch her step, she could easily become an unpaid skivvy. She'd do coffee this once, then things would have to change. She was about to turn and go when she remembered something.

'By the way, what are all the stakes in the yard for? And the orange tape?'

Olivier and Jack exchanged a glance. Jamie detected guilt. She frowned.

'What?'

Jack put down his spanner. 'I need to talk to you about that.'

Olivier looked awkward.

'I'll go and make the coffee, shall I?'

He headed for the door. Jack panicked.

'No. Stay. You can help me explain.'

'Explain what?' Somehow Jamie knew she'd hit upon the secret she felt had been kept from her ever since she'd arrived. The sense of exclusion, the paranoia she'd felt was not unfounded after all. So what was it all about? Was it police tape? Was there a body under the stable yard? Were teams of forensic officers about to start digging for bones?

Jack was looking uncharacteristically nervous.

'I'm not going to beat about the bush, Jamie. I'm broke. I haven't got a bean. I've got no income, no pensions, no capital ... Nothing to live on. And nothing to fall back on.' He paused awkwardly. 'Except Bucklebury. That is my only asset.'

'You're not selling the farm? You can't!'

'Not exactly. No.'

'What do you mean, not exactly? Either you are or you aren't.' Jamie hated it when her father prevaricated.

'It would kill me to leave Bucklebury. There's nowhere else I want to go. So I've come to a compromise.'

In Jamie's experience, compromise meant something that nobody liked. She looked at Jack suspiciously.

'What sort of compromise?'

She could see Jack was choosing his words carefully.

'I've done a deal with a developer. He's going to convert the stables and the barns into houses. I get to keep one of the barns, this workshop and the top paddock. And some cash – enough to see me out if I'm sensible with it.' Jack had the grace to look a little shamefaced at this. It would be the first time in his life he had been sensible with money. 'I can show you the plans. They're very sympathetic—'

But Jamie was shaking her head.

'You can't! You just can't! It would destroy the place.'

'I've racked my brains to think of a better solution. And there isn't one. If I stay here, the house is going to fall down around my ears.' He paused for dramatic effect. 'While I starve to death. At least this way I don't actually have to leave. And I've got something to live on.'

Jamie sat down on a dusty old bale of hay, staring dully into the middle distance while she took in the implications. Jack exchanged glances with Olivier, who gave him a wry, sympathetic smile of support. Encouraged, Jack went and put a reassuring hand on Jamie's shoulder.

'I know this must come as a shock. But everyone has to rationalize in their old age. Make changes they don't necessarily like.'

She stared up at him accusingly.

'Not people who've planned ahead. Not people who've put money aside all their life. Not people who save money when they make it, instead of blowing it on flash holidays and ridiculous get-rich-quick schemes that never bloody work—'

Jack put his hand up to stop the onslaught.

'Please, Jamie. Think it through.'

'I don't need to think it through. It's the most terrible idea I've ever heard.' She paused a moment as something else occurred to her. 'And who gets the house? The actual house?'

'The developer. He's keeping it for himself.'

Jamie looked grim.

'So who is this developer?'

Jack didn't answer immediately. He drew breath, ready to drop perhaps the biggest bombshell of them all.

'Rod Deacon.'

A swirling red mist came down. Jamie could barely speak.

'Rod Deacon? You're not seriously telling me you've done a deal with Rod Deacon—'

'He's as sound as a pound, Jamie.'

Jamie spluttered. 'I hope you counted your fingers after you shook his hand.'

Jack looked at his hand, as if he suddenly expected to see a digit missing.

'You misjudge Rod. He's not like the others—'

'You watch. They'll all be living here. They'll be swarming all over the place like bloody tinkers. Your washing won't be safe on the line.'

Jack stared at her bleakly. His voice became harsh; defensive.

'Unless you've got any better ideas, I've got no alternative.'

'I don't know how you dared go through with this without consulting me. This is my home too, you know.'

'You've been somewhat incommunicado. Or had you forgotten?'

'I won't allow it!'

'Jamie – it's a done deal. There's nothing you can do. It's in the hands of the solicitors.'

Jamie glared at her father. How could she have been lulled into a false sense of security? He was never going to change. He was going to go to his grave with a champagne lifestyle on a beer income, totally irresponsible, utterly selfish.

'You'll have to get rid of me first.'

She swept out of the barn, as dignified as she could be in a Snoopy nightshirt and hiking boots. Olivier shrank back into the corner as she went past, desperately wishing he was somewhere else. As soon as she'd gone, he looked at Jack, who looked like a dog that had been caught weeing on an expensive rug.

Jack smiled weakly.

'Let's take her for a spin, shall we?'

Olivier hesitated.

'I should go after her.'

Jack put up a warning hand.

'No. Give her a bit of time to think about it. Trust me. Jamie always goes off at the deep end – she'll calm down when she's had a chance to think about it.'

But Olivier felt the situation had been handled badly. He could see that Jamie was most upset by having a bombshell dropped upon her in front of a relative stranger, and he wanted to reassure her that he wasn't part of some evil plot. The look of distaste she had thrown him as she left the barn made it clear she thought he was colluding.

'I'm just going to make sure she's all right.'

He caught up with her by the back door.

'Jamie!'

'Fuck off.'

'You're bound to be upset.'

She snorted in derision. 'Upset?'

'I don't think your dad explained things very well—'

'Is it any of your business?'

'Of course not. I'm just trying to help.' Olivier was starting to realize he would have done better not to interfere. Jamie looked at him venomously.

'If you want to help,' she hissed at him, 'then do the washing-up. This place is a fucking pigsty.'

She stomped over the flagstones in her boots and up the stairs, wishing she hadn't said that. She wasn't the sort of person who bitched about dirty plates lying around. But anything was better than entering into a debate with Olivier about what she'd just heard.

9

Forty miles away, on the drive in front of a sprawling gentleman's residence in Edgbaston, Claudia Sedgeley sat astride the bonnet of *her* Bugatti, dressed in a white satin trouser suit and a matching fedora, her red-nailed feet bare and a huge Havana cigar clamped between her teeth. The photographer from the *Birmingham Post* snapped away in delight. The paper was running a series of features on local girls infiltrating worlds traditionally dominated by men, which certainly made a change from photographing the usual charity committees and be-chained dignitaries. Meanwhile, the stylist was sulking. The cigar had been Claudia's idea. And the bare feet. And it worked a treat.

From the grandeur of his portico, her father watched and smiled.

Anyone who called Ray Sedgeley a scrap-metal merchant was asking for trouble. He preferred steelbroker. Scrap metal was one up from being a rag-and-bone man. Though he couldn't deny he'd once ridden round Kidderminster on the back of his dad's flatbed truck, slinging in people's unwanted junk. He'd come a long way since then. Now there was a depot, offices, staff, a fleet of trucks. And a large house on the outskirts of Birmingham. Built in the thirties, Kingswood sat in grounds of nearly an acre in leafy Edgbaston, and had served Ray and his wife Barbara as a very comfortable family home for over twenty years.

Not that he ever tried to hide where he had come from. Ray was a rough diamond, and he didn't care who knew it. He made few attempts to soften his image or modulate his Black Country accent. With his brightly coloured silk shirts, close-cropped hair and Rolex the size of a dinner plate, he knew he looked like a gangster. In his opinion, that was a good thing. In his line of business, people had more respect for a hard nut than a suit with a posh accent.

Ray only had one weakness and that was his youngest daughter, Claudia. She was his Achilles heel, the one part of his life over which he had no control, but which really mattered to him. She was beautiful, untameable and mischievous and she was going to break his heart one day, when she finally got married and went off to make some other man's life hell.

She'd certainly led Ray a merry dance. Until she was twelve, she was merely lively. It was when the hormones kicked in at thirteen that the trouble started. She failed every single exam that she sat at the private school he paid through the nose for – he might not mind looking like a gangster, but he wanted his daughter to have polish. Her teachers despaired. Educational psychologists were brought in; discreet suggestions made of some attention deficit disorder or hyperactivity. But no one could make a conclusive diagnosis. They were all clear about one thing. Claudia was perfectly bright. If she applied herself she could do well.

But Claudia just wanted to play. And to be the centre

of attention. If she couldn't be the thinnest, richest and prettiest, she found some other way of outshining those around her. Ray tried very hard to think of her misdemeanours as youthful high spirits, but sometimes it made him shudder to think how close she came to danger.

He remembered when she was fourteen, and had ostensibly gone to a friend's house for the night. A chance phone call had ascertained that the mother of the friend thought *her* daughter was spending the night at Claudia's. A frantic search of all the bars and clubs on Broad Street had ensued. He'd finally found Claudia and Naomi at about one o'clock, being plied with champagne by unscrupulous-looking men in suits and black T-shirts.

A middle-aged man dragging a screaming, barely dressed pubescent girl out of a nightclub was bound to attract attention. Protestations that he was her father had received cynical glances, especially as Claudia volubly denied this, and declared him a pimp. The bouncers had turned nasty. The police had been called. Ray had to put in a call to a superintendent friend of his and only narrowly escaped being locked up. Claudia was unashamed, defiant. What did he expect, for spoiling her fun?

Grounding her had no effect. She just ignored it. Short of tying her up and locking her in her bedroom, there was nothing Ray could do. Stopping her allowance didn't help either. The one time he'd done that, she'd taken to shoplifting, coming home with bags of designer gear she'd brazenly pinched, totally unrepentant – even when she'd got caught. He'd had to spread some backhanders around that time. For years, he prayed that she would calm down, that someone or something would catch her eye and absorb her attention.

His wife Barbara eventually became battle-weary and withdrew from the fracas, writing Claudia off as a lost cause and concentrating her attention on Debbie and Andrea, Claudia's sensible and reliable older sisters. Left to deal with his daughter alone, Ray despaired time and again. He'd heard the phrase 'tough love'; he considered washing his hands of her entirely, throwing Claudia out on the streets to give her a short, sharp shock. But Ray Sedgeley, tough and uncompromising Ray Sedgeley, who'd been known to sack a man for a misdemeanour as minor as making private phone calls on his time, couldn't do it to his own flesh and blood.

For somehow, just when he'd reached the end of his tether, Claudia would always do an about-face and surprise him by playing the doting daughter, and she did it so well his heart would melt and he would forgive her for the hell she'd put him through. Overnight, she would become biddable and demure, loving, affectionate and thoughtful. He found it unsettling, because it usually heralded trouble. But he made sure he enjoyed it while it lasted.

Once she left school, Claudia's life had settled into a pattern. She would find something to occupy her, a new job or a new business project with a friend, and for a couple of months she would be totally absorbed and apparently fulfilled. Until the novelty wore off. Then there were usually disastrous financial consequences and a falling-out, followed by tears, tantrums and a credit card bending to make up for the fact that she, Claudia, had yet again been let down or betrayed or stitched up – because it was never her fault. And Ray was always there to pick up the pieces. What the hell else could he do?

He'd lost track of the ventures he'd subsidized. A sandwich delivery service. A tanning studio. And one involving counterfeit designer handbags that had resulted in a visit from the Customs and Excise people. Ray's name had been on all the paperwork and for a nasty moment he'd been convinced he was going to end up in jail. Claudia had drifted through the entire episode oblivious and unperturbed.

Thus Ray had accepted that things weren't going to change, until, miraculously, they did, one glorious Saturday in June. He'd been invited to a corporate day out by his stockbrokers; they were taking a hospitality tent at a vintage race meeting and had asked a select number of clients to come and watch the fun. Ray quite fancied going, as it sounded eccentric and English, but Barbara had promised to babysit for two of their grandchildren. He'd resigned himself to going on his own, when he found Claudia lounging in front of the telly at a loose end. Not thinking she'd take him up on it, he suggested she came with him. He was amazed when she agreed, even more amazed when she was standing by the car less than half an hour later, suitably dressed and seemingly looking forward to a day out with her dad.

They'd been well looked after, with a salmon and strawberry lunch. As for the racing, Ray thought at best it was a bunch of overgrown schoolboys tearing round a track, potentially bashing up cars that represented more money than most people would earn in a lifetime. Mildly amusing, but for him it didn't have the thrust of Formula One, the death-defying speed. He worried that Claudia was bored. There weren't any female retail opportunities; it wasn't something people dressed up for, so she couldn't look at the outfits.

To his amazement, she was utterly transfixed. The smell of oil, the roar of the engines, the dirt and smoke, the passion, the sweat, the concentration – she lapped it all up eagerly. As they watched the victor in his Bugatti circle the track in a lap of honour, a wreath of laurels round his neck, Claudia turned to her father, her eyes shining. 'That,' she declared, 'is what I want to do.'

To test his daughter's dedication, he sent her on several courses, so she could learn her skills and have the safety measures drummed into her. She passed her advanced motor-racing certificate almost effortlessly. He was satisfied she had proven herself. For her twenty-first birthday, he presented her with a Bugatti Type 35, parking it outside their front door with a huge pink ribbon tied around the long, black bonnet. He'd had it custom-built to his exacting specification, by a company that specialized in restoration. Of course, he could have bought a total replica, but by obtaining an old chassis, which entitled it to an authentically old registration, Ray had it fitted out with the best of everything. If people wanted to consider that cheating, let them. It didn't break any rules. It was eligible.

A combination of her 'too fast to live too young to die' attitude, her utter determination to be the best and an innate feel for the sport made Claudia deadly on the track. Of course, Ray was utterly terrified that she would kill herself in the process. But then, she'd always taken risks, and it was better for her to die in the pursuit of glory than to end up with a needle in her arm. She'd been to some dark places in the past, but at last Ray was able to see the fruits of Claudia's labours; the success she could achieve if she applied herself.

He found her a coach – a woman, because he felt sure a veteran female driver would recognize the forces driving Claudia and would be able to head off potential weaknesses and build on her strengths. Agnes Porter-Wright was an eccentric old bird from the Cotswolds who used to race Bentleys. She took absolutely no crap from Claudia, and Ray was once again amazed to see Claudia have respect for someone.

Repeatedly, he thanked God for saving Claudia from herself. And when she'd entered her first race the year before, even though she only clocked up twelfth place, he was bursting with pride. She'd run up to him in her overalls, eyes shining, and flung her arms round him in triumph, and for a moment he was taken back to her winning her first rosette at a gymkhana when she was nine. It was as if all the turbulent years in between had never happened.

Now, a year later, Ray was even more grateful that the novelty hadn't worn off. After each race he'd been terrified that she would become truculent and despondent. But it seemed to spur her on. Even over the long winter months, when there was no racing, she pored over old videos, spent hours in the garage, talked on the phone to Agnes.

Once, she'd taken Ray out on the road, and he'd been so terrified that he vowed never to repeat the experience. It wasn't that she was a reckless or dangerous driver. Far from it. It was the consummate skill with which she drove, the confidence with which she took corners, changed gear, judged distances, decelerating and accelerating as if it was second nature. Fast, furious, spine-tingling, exhilarating, a white-knuckle ride that Ray never wanted to relive.

There was no doubt she was a good driver, but he

knew it was his money that would guarantee her eventual success. He made sure she had the best. He did out the spare garage at Kingswood for her; had it air-conditioned and an inspection pit put in. Every tool, every spare she needed was neatly stored on an immaculate shelving system; catalogues were lined up; articles snipped out of magazines and filed neatly for future reference.

Now he was confident Claudia was gearing up for a good summer. She'd raced steadily so far, with no mishaps. And she was hotly tipped to win the Richard Corrigan Memorial Trophy in two weeks' time, a race for novice drivers who had been competing for less than two years. Claudia had set her heart on winning it. Ray was looking forward to seeing the trophy on the mantelpiece in the lounge.

But that race wasn't for another fortnight. There was the hill climb at Prescott to get through first, that coming weekend. Ray would be able to eye up the competition, see if there were any serious contenders for the Corrigan Trophy who might get in the way of Claudia's glory. For he was determined she was going to win it, and he had no compunction whatsoever about eliminating the opposition.

Claudia slipped into the silver lamé cat suit that was her final outfit of the shoot, then defiantly undid the zip down to her navel and climbed behind the wheel of her car, sitting with one stiletto heel up on the leather seat in a provocative pose that was pure porn with its clothes on. The photographer's eyes nearly popped out of his head in excitement, praying that the paper would allow these to be printed. The stylist came over to rearrange her hair and

Claudia gritted her teeth with annoyance. Patience had never been one of her virtues, and probably never would be, even though she'd changed quite considerably over the past twelve months.

When Claudia was twelve years old, her older sisters decided they were tired of her hogging the limelight and decided to bring her down a peg or two. They told her it was time she knew the truth, that she had been an accident, and that her parents had very nearly got rid of her. And that they had since been heard to wish that they had. Debbie and Andrea were no more spiteful than any other teenagers; jealousy and hormones made them cruel, and they had no idea of the long-lasting damage their fabrication had wrought on Claudia.

If Claudia had only had the common sense to go to her mother to corroborate the evidence, she could have saved them all a lot of heartache and had the pleasure of seeing Debbie and Andrea torn off a strip. But their spiteful slur had gone straight to her heart, where she nursed it and fed it until it grew and grew and tarnished her soul, which grew black with misery and anger and resentment. Each merry dance she led her parents had been a mixture of revenge and a cry for reassurance. She was a bewildered little girl whose self-esteem had plummeted so low that she took enormous risks. And she was so clever at hiding her insecurity: her stunning looks and her belligerent attitude belied her lack of confidence. Her inability to stick at anything was fear of failure. The moment anything she touched looked like becoming a success, she lost interest immediately. It was easier that way.

It was only now, at twenty-two, that she was finally becoming comfortable with herself and who she was, to her great relief. It was actually very exhausting being a wild child. It took perseverance and concentration and dedication to be such a spectacular failure at everything; to shock people continually and let them down at the moment of maximum impact.

But over the past year she had felt a sense of calm and a sense of self. She'd finally found an outlet for all that pent-up anger and energy. She was able to take her risks on the racetrack, and it was the greatest thrill of all, knowing that every decision she made could lead to either death or glory ... It was far more exhilarating than all those years of empty gestures and attention-seeking.

Not that she'd entirely sacrificed her exhibitionist streak. Not by any means. The race circuit was the perfect platform for showing off, the Bugatti the ultimate accessory: the status symbol that made every man's eyes glaze over with envy, the toy they all wanted. It turned her on every time, climbing defiantly behind the wheel of a car most of them could only dream of, then creaming the pants off the other competitors. And to rub their noses in it even further she played up her femininity, her sexuality, knowing that many of her audience would find it hard to choose between her Bugatti and her breasts ... She knew she'd been dubbed Penelope Pitstop behind her back, but she was secretly delighted. She didn't go quite as far as touching up her lipstick before a race, but she wasn't far off.

So Claudia was feeling a little more secure about herself. But old habits die hard. After all, you didn't turn from a snarling tiger into a pussycat overnight.

10

As she wriggled out of her nightshirt and pulled on her jeans, Jamie felt absolutely sick to her stomach as she went over and over what her father had told her. A housing development at Bucklebury Farm? She could just imagine it. Half-a-dozen units, divided up with plaster-board and fitted out with cheap light-fittings and plywood doors, each with a pocket handkerchief of garden which would end up with a rotary dryer and a swing set. The English countryside was dotted with similar projects, and she loathed them with a vengeance. Her mother would spin in her grave at the thought.

Jamie couldn't help thinking that her father had, as usual, fallen at the first fence, taken the easy option, hadn't bothered to do his homework and think things through. Thank God she'd got home when she had. Just in time, with any luck, to put an end to this madcap scheme and come up with another solution. It might be in the hands of the solicitors, but until the final 'i' was dotted and 't' was crossed, there would still be time to put a stop to it.

She laced up her boots, grabbed her car keys, and without even bothering to pull a comb through her hair flew out of the door.

At twenty-five past twelve, Rod put away his plane, locked up his workshop away from prying little fingers and drove home. The TT was in the drive, which meant Bella was home already. He opened the front door, quite literally girded his loins and made his way up to the bedroom.

Bella was crouched on the bed on all fours, in a stance similar to Kylie's wax effigy at Madame Tussaud's, rosy-cheeked bottom in the air. She'd obviously been at the Agent Provocateur catalogue again, as Rod hadn't seen this particular ensemble before. She tossed back her hair and smiled at him provocatively, inviting him to join her. Rod suddenly felt nervous. A year ago he'd have been right in there. But now, he didn't want a porn-star fantasy romping about on his bed. He didn't want sexual gymnastics; he just wanted to make love, pure and simple and natural. But with Bella, everything was rehearsed; everything was a slick performance, minutely choreographed, with not a hint of spontaneity allowed.

At first, he'd appreciated it. That was when it was new, before he'd got to know the routines. He remembered the first time he'd seen her. He was helping his brother Dean, who'd invested in a bouncy castle to hire out for kiddies' birthday parties. In a rare display of community spirit he'd brought it to the village fête, where he was charging fifty pence for ten minutes' bouncing to be split fifty-fifty with the fête committee – though of course the committee weren't to know how many coins actually passed through his hands, so he was hoping to do quite well out of it. Rod had gone along to help, because Dean had little patience where his own kids were concerned, let alone anyone else's, and would haul them out unceremoniously by the scruff of the neck when their time was up. So Rod supervised the children and Dean took the money.

Halfway through the afternoon, a distorted fanfare of music burst through the speakers, announcing a display by the Bella Robbins Dance Academy. Nineteen tiny moppets in pink leotards and tutus twisted and spun and pirouetted and jeté-d to a chorus of 'aaahs', then reappeared in red and black spangles for a tap demonstration (which didn't have quite the same effect on the drying grass of the vicarage as it would have had on a wooden stage), followed by a splendid pastiche of the River Dance, each of them concentrating hard to keep their upper bodies rigid as the legs twinkled in unison. Rod thought it a bit unfair that Bella went on to upstage them entirely, clad in a flame-red dress that was slashed to her buttocks and her navel front and back, with a medley of flamenco and tango and salsa that left every male dribbling into his Styrofoam cup of tea, and every woman determined to try and get to the gym three times a week.

'Fucking hell,' said Dean.

'Fucking heaven, more like,' said Rod.

Dean stuck out his hand, grinning. 'Duel,' he said. It was their ritual. Whenever they saw an attractive woman, they challenged each other to a duel, to see who could capture her attentions first. It had worked when they were young, before Dean had lost his hair and gained a belly courtesy of his five-pints-on-a-good-night habit. He knew he wouldn't have a hope in hell of attracting Bella – and besides, he was married with three kids and his wife Leanne might have something to say about it – but the ritual now meant that Rod had to honour the challenge.

Rod shook Dean's hand and took up the challenge happily. He gave his prettiest niece ballet lessons for her birthday, and when her mother moaned about the commitment he offered to take her every Saturday morning. It was no great hardship. Courtney had shown great promise, and Rod took the opportunity to discuss her progress earnestly and at length with Bella, who was charmed that he should take such an interest. By week four, he'd got her to agree to come out for a drink. By week six, it was dinner. By week seven, he was worshipping at the altar of her incredibly honed and pliable body, thinking himself in heaven.

Six months later they were married and now, three years on, he wasn't sure that it was so far from hell. Not that their situation was Bella's fault. They didn't, in fact, know whose fault it was, not as yet. But an added complication had arisen – so to speak – in that Rod was finding it increasingly difficult to perform to order.

He shut his eyes, willing himself to get hard. He felt Bella rubbing her breasts against his chest, her hand cupping his balls, coaxing him into life. He shuddered as one of her talons scratched along his scrotum. Relax, relax, he told himself, and gradually his faithful friend responded, nudging higher and higher into the air as blood poured into the stem. Bella was on her back by now, her pelvis tilted into the air – they'd read somewhere this was the best position in which to conceive. Rod knelt in front of her, careful to get his penis at the right height, and took aim.

Bingo! He slid in effortlessly, courtesy of some exotic lubricant she'd rubbed on to herself. He ground into her before his erection got any funny ideas about disappearing, hoping for enough friction to achieve the desired effect. It was ironic, really: in the olden days he would have had to think about something dull and prosaic in order to *stop* himself ejaculating.

He was just on the brink. Spillage was moments away, and he was praying that one – it only needed to be one – *one* of his little sperm would make the epic journey to Bella's egg and fuse into life. Mentally he visualized it, the power of positive thinking, as the familiar build-up to orgasm began until—

Brrrrring!

Bella shot out from underneath him like a scalded cat. His penis shrank back into nothingness. The doorbell rang again, even more insistently, if that were possible.

'Who is it?'

'I don't bloody know,' replied Rod irritably, grabbing his dressing gown. Great. His one chance for the Golden Shot had definitely vanished. He'd never be able to get it up again before it was time for Bella to go and do her Over Fifties' Flex 'n' Tone. And this was her optimum ovulation window. She'd be home too late tonight for either of them to feel up to much.

He hurried down the stairs as the bell went yet again, wondering if perhaps the house had caught fire without them knowing. He threw open the front door. For a moment he thought he was seeing things, then stepped aside hastily as a wild-eyed creature barged straight past him without waiting for an invitation.

'Jamie? What the hell are you doing here?'

'I want to talk to you.'

Her eyes were blazing, her hair flying out in a russet-coloured stream behind her. There were high spots of colour on her cheeks that Rod had seen twice before. Once when she was angry. And once—

'What the fuck do you think you're playing at?' Jamie demanded, her hands on her hips.

Rod blinked, feeling somewhat aggrieved. He might be engaging in a bit of lunchtime nookie, but it was in his own home, with his own wife. What right did she have to turn up here out of the blue questioning his actions?

'I'm sorry. What am I supposed to have done, exactly?'

She glared at him. Rod could see that in the ten months since he'd last seen her, at her mother's funeral, she'd changed considerably. Her face was thinner, and her body – the slenderness of her waist made her breasts look larger. Her hair had grown, and it looked tangled and wild. Her rage made her look wanton. And totally, utterly desirable. Rod swallowed. His penis was about to betray him again. While minutes ago it had been so reluctant to perform, now he could feel it straining behind the fabric of his underpants.

'Bloody well trying to con my father into selling Bucklebury Farm.'

'Con?'

'You should be locked up for it. Taking advantage of a grieving widower; preying on him like that—'

'Hold on a minute.'

Rod held up his hand to halt her stream of invective, then realized she was staring over his shoulder. He turned to see Bella gliding down the stairs, in pink velour hotpants and a matching hooded top, her long legs tanned and toned leading down to ankle socks and pristine white trainers. She stopped at the bottom of the stairs, her hand on the newel post, looking for all the world like a catwalk model striking a pose for the benefit of her audience.

'What's going on?' She looked Jamie up and down coolly. 'And who are you?'

'This is Jamie Wilding,' said Rod hastily. 'Her father owns Bucklebury Farm. We're just trying to clear up a bit of a misunderstanding.'

Jamie gave an indignant snort.

'There's no misunderstanding, I can assure you. I'm quite clear about what's happened. I just want to make sure *you* understand—'

Rod cut in icily. He really didn't want Bella witnessing this bawling match.

'Perhaps we could talk about this some other time? It's not convenient at the moment. My wife and I—'

Bella sailed past him waving a nonchalant hand in the air and picked up her Prada gym bag.

'Don't worry about me, darling. I've got to go. I've got a class to get to. You two carry on discussing your business.'

She smiled at Rod, and ran her finger down his chest. 'You can fill me in later.'

Her double entendre was quite clear. Bella left the house, her high ponytail swinging jauntily from side to side in perfect time with her taut buttocks. For a moment Rod felt rather proud. There weren't many wives who would leave with such blasé confidence, having found their husband in mid-row with a screaming harpy. And he was pleased to see that Jamie looked as if the wind had been taken out of her sails. He indicated the three-piece suite.

'Shall we sit down and talk about this sensibly?'

She ignored his invitation completely, and relaunched herself on the attack, this time her voice low with barely suppressed rage.

'How dare you! How dare you take advantage of my father like that? It's obvious he wasn't thinking straight – he's still in bits about my mother, for God's sake. But then that's typical of you, isn't it? Exploiting people. You always had the morals of a fucking snake.'

She paused for breath, to regain her composure, as if she'd realized she was ranting. Rod looked at her coolly.

'Am I going to be allowed to speak?'

She nodded.

'I found your dad falling off his bar stool in the Royal Oak. Blind drunk. Not for the first time either, according to Toby. We got chatting. He told me he was going to have to sell up. He was in total despair. He jokingly asked me if I wanted to buy it. It got me thinking...'

'Obviously.'

'You might call it exploiting him. But it seemed like the perfect answer to me. Your father's got no money, Jamie. You can't keep a place like Bucklebury Farm going with no capital. All I did was come up with a solution that I thought might help him. He was going to sell up completely, but I came up with a compromise.'

Jamie stamped her foot. 'If anyone else tells me it's a compromise... Well, there isn't going to be any compromise. It's out of the question. We'll find an alternative—'

Rod raised a quizzical eyebrow. 'The alternative is he sells the whole lot and buys some hideous bungalow somewhere. At least this way he keeps the view he's always loved, he's still on the same soil and he's got cash left over to live on—'

'And what do you get out of it? The big house? Won't you have done well for yourself?'

Her bitterness sliced through him like a knife. Rod sighed. She was obviously going to paint him black; no matter what he said he was going to be the villain of the piece. He gave a little shrug of resignation.

'Listen, if the deal falls through, I don't have a problem with it. It's not the end of the world for me. You've obviously got other ideas and I hope it works out for you.'

'It would be a travesty to split Bucklebury up. I'd rather sell it as a whole than see the stables converted.' Her tone was withering.

'Get real, Jamie. It's the way of the world. Why else do you think people do it? Because they couldn't afford to live in places like Bucklebury otherwise. Do you know what your dad was quoted for a new roof?'

He told her. He could see she was shocked, though she tried to not show it. Rod carried on.

'And I can tell you, if you ever did sell it as a whole, the surveyors would have a field day. The old part needs underpinning. Any purchaser would knock you down and knock you down on the price until you were practically paying them to take it off your hands. Twenty-seven acres in Shropshire is not an economically viable proposition. It's a white elephant.'

'Rubbish. Lots of people want to move to a big house in the country. People are relocating all the time.'

'Well, good luck.'

Jamie tilted her chin in the air defiantly, in a gesture he remembered so well.

'Anyway, we might not have to sell. I've got ... other ideas.'

Fighting his corner made him harsh.

'Good for you. If you've got a couple of hundred grand going for running repairs, and you can support your dad in his dotage, then I wish you all the luck in the world.'

He was horrified when she sank down into the nearest chair and put her head in her hands. He was expecting her to fight back. Fiery, feisty Jamie always did. But she suddenly seemed to deflate; her shoulders hunched forwards. Had he been too harsh? But then, why shouldn't he defend himself? She'd marched in here with all guns blazing, after all. And he didn't care what she thought, it had been a good plan. A fair plan. He'd had no intention of conning Jack Wilding. The idea was laughable in itself. Jack was as wily and cunning as a fox in his own way.

He waited a moment for her to respond, but there was nothing but silence.

'Jamie?'

She looked up, her face white, her eyes blazing with hatred. 'I suppose you're laughing your socks off. I suppose you think it's what we deserve. You with your bloody Robin Hood complex, robbing the rich. You've been waiting for this ...'

He came over and knelt in front of her. She was sobbing piteously. He tried to put a consoling arm round her but she shook him off.

'Leave me alone.'

'Jamie. Jamie ... Believe me, I only ever wanted to help.'

'Yeah – yourself.' Her tone was bitter. Vicious.

Rod sat patiently while she wept, knowing she couldn't go on indefinitely. And when her sobs began to subside, he took hold of her wrists and pulled them away from her face. She was calmer now, so he reached out and wiped a tear from her cheek, ever so gently. When she didn't protest he slid his hand round to the back of her head, stroking her hair.

'Listen – it's OK. I'll help you sort something out. And nothing in it for me, I promise.'

He carried on stroking, just as he'd watched his mother trying to calm a dog that had been badly treated. Time and patience, that's what it took. Gradually, he slid his other hand round her waist, until he was cradling her in his arms.

How could half an hour of sexual gymnastics with Bella leave him cold, while just touching Jamie's skin threw him into a blazing inferno? It was all he could do not to throw her on the floor: he had an incredible primal urge to do so, but his head told him that was not a good plan. Instead, he concentrated on calming her with gentle, soothing caresses. He could feel her relax; her sobs had subsided. Tentatively, he turned her face to his, and went to kiss her.

Jamie leaped up as if she'd been bitten by a snake.

'Forget it,' she snarled. 'If you think you're going to get Bucklebury Farm that way, you've got another thing coming.'

She strode across the room, turning just before the door.

'And in case you hadn't realized, the deal's off. You can find some other sucker to rip off.'

She flung open the front door and slammed it behind her. Rod winced, praying the glass wouldn't shatter.

'Shit. Shit shit shit,' he said.

Not a good day. He'd lost the chance to fertilize Bella, he'd lost the deal on Bucklebury Farm. And he'd lost his bloody heart. Again. He thought he'd got over her years ago.

II

The summer Jamie turned eighteen was a strange one for her. The very number was symbolic of growing up, and she really didn't want to. She knew she was going to have to start standing on her own two feet, decide what she wanted to do with her life, make her own way in the world. After all, she couldn't doss around at Bucklebury Farm for ever, riding horses and mucking about with her mates down at the pub.

The irony of it was her parents put no pressure on her at all to decide her future. Her friends were constantly being badgered by their mothers and fathers about what they were going to do; exam results were anxiously awaited, university applications agonized over. But Jack and Louisa seemed perfectly happy to go along with whatever Jamie wanted. She was always being told how lucky she was not to have her parents yapping on about career plans and further education and prospects. But actually, Jamie felt herself under more pressure because of her lack of parental input. She knew she was going to have to motivate herself, and that was very hard for an eighteen-year-old who didn't have much of an idea about the real world, having lived in such a fantasy environment all her life.

The summer she left school was a mad season of post-exam celebrations and hedonistic fun in the sun. She'd always had a very long rein, which meant she didn't really do all the things her friends were doing behind their parents' backs – smoking and getting paralytic and screwing each other senseless. She wasn't square or straight; put quite simply, smoking made her feel sick, she didn't like the way she behaved when she was drunk or the hideous hangover the next day, and she hadn't met anyone she wanted to screw. Besides, what was the point of trying to rebel when there was no one to rebel against? The advantage was that everyone came back to Bucklebury Farm to indulge in their nefarious activities, because there was no one to tut and spy and shout at them to turn the music down – Jack and Louisa didn't care how loud the music was, or how many bodies were scattered around the house next morning. But as each day passed, Jamie felt it was a day closer to the end of an era. Everyone was going to disappear off on their chosen paths, while she was left behind to drift, alone and directionless.

When her A-level results arrived, they were pretty average – a C in art and a couple of Ds – but her parents had congratulated her warmly nevertheless. This made Jamie feel deeply uncomfortable. Did they not care, or understand the importance? Or did they just not think she was capable of any better? Others of her friends had done much better but were still upbraided for not getting straight As, or not fulfilling the criteria for the university of their (or rather their parents') choice. Secretly, she longed for someone to sit her down and give her a stiff talking-to, then go through her options. Instead of which, she got an airy reassurance that they would go along with whatever she wanted to do. Which didn't bloody help at all.

She tried one morning to get them to talk seriously about it.

'Well,' said Louisa. 'What do you want to do?'

'That's just it,' said Jamie. 'I don't have a clue.'

'University of life,' said Jack. 'That was good enough for me.'

'I adored art college,' reflected Louisa dreamily. 'I'd have stayed there for ever if I could. Why don't you try that?'

'I don't really think I'm good enough at art,' said Jamie. 'Besides, that doesn't help with a career.'

'Do you really need a career?'

'I need to earn a living, yes!' Jamie was starting to get irritated. 'I thought about training to be a nanny.'

'A nanny?' Louisa looked far from impressed.

'What's wrong with that?'

Louisa shrugged. 'It sounds like hard work.'

'I'm not afraid of hard work.'

'No. But, darling – being at someone else's beck and call. It's drudgery.'

Jamie swallowed her frustration. 'Well, what do you suggest?'

Neither of them could suggest anything remotely realistic. Which wasn't that surprising. Jamie didn't think either of them had ever applied for a job in their lives, let alone had an interview. And they didn't quite seem to understand why Jamie needed to go down that route. It was the very nearest Jamie came to having a stand-up row with them, with the roles rather ironically reversed. But she wasn't used to confrontation, so instead she fled the kitchen before she burst into tears of total frustration which they wouldn't understand. All she'd wanted was some firm guidance, a flicker of an indication that they took her future seriously. She knew they loved her, but really – it was like talking to a pair of irresponsible teenagers.

She stormed out to the stable yard and tacked up Nutmeg. She had to get away for a couple of hours and clear her head. Maybe inspiration would strike her and she could come up with a plan. She jumped up into the saddle and dug her heels in, anxious to put as much distance between herself and Bucklebury Farm as quickly as possible.

She headed down through the top paddock, then through a gateway across another field until she reached a wide bridle path where she knew she could have a mind-clearing gallop. Nutmeg was totally wired, sensing Jamie's tension, and began prancing sideways until she was allowed her head.

Suddenly something scuttled across the path in front of them. A rabbit, a squirrel, Jamie couldn't be sure, but whatever it was Nutmeg panicked, veered madly to one side into the undergrowth, leaping and bucking in alarm. Jamie tried desperately to get the little horse under control, but there was so much adrenalin coursing through her veins, so much tension and stress, that she found it hard to stay calm. They were well off the path now, crashing through the trees. She had to keep her head down low to avoid the branches; she couldn't look up and find her way out. She saw a fence up ahead; they were bearing down on it relentlessly. The trees were too thick either side to avoid it. The only way was forwards and over the fence. She couldn't judge its height through her screwed-up eyes, so the only thing she could do was kick Nutmeg on and encourage her to make the leap. It was open field the other side; if Nutmeg wouldn't stop, she would have to run her round and round until she was exhausted.

As soon as they left the ground, Jamie knew she wasn't going to make it over in one piece. Nutmeg had taken off nearly two strides too soon, and she'd lost both her stirrups. In order to avoid falling under the horse, she bailed out halfway. Nutmeg just managed to get over without mishap, leaving Jamie to crash inelegantly on to the hedge and plop into a crumpled heap on to the grass.

Luckily, Nutmeg chose not to run off, just took a brief disinterested look round her and put her head down to graze. Jamie tried to scramble on to her feet, but a searing pain shot through her. She moaned and dropped back to the ground.

She realized where she was. Shit – she was on Deacon territory. She'd been so lost in her thoughts she'd strayed right off her usual patch. Her heart was hammering – the Deacons were the type to take pot-shots at anyone trespassing on their land. Which was pretty hypocritical, considering they were arch poachers.

All her life, she'd been warned off the Deacons. They were like evil characters in a fairy tale – some terrible fate would befall anyone who fell into their clutches. And they lay in wait, like the troll under the bridge, or the witch in her gingerbread prison. She knew all the myths and legends; all the wicked things they had ever done. She'd seen the evidence for most of it in the local paper.

The Deacons were absolutely the only people in the world her parents disapproved of.

With her heart in her mouth, Jamie realized she'd been seen. She had no idea which one it was, but one of them was watching her. He'd been mending the fence further up. Jamie wanted to scramble to her feet and run, but the pain in her ankle stopped her. And she wasn't going to leave Nutmeg. If the Deacons got their hands on her, she'd be in the next county before nightfall and they'd be drinking the profits between them.

To her amazement, however, he looked concerned.

'Bloody hell, you came a real cropper then. Are you OK?'

She was in too much agony to reply. He came over and squatted by her. He was about her age, she reckoned. He was stripped to the waist, and Jamie couldn't help noticing his build. His upper arms were as thick as her thigh, but pure muscle, his biceps sharply defined under his brown skin; his stomach was as flat as a washboard. His faded jeans, held up by a thick, silver-buckled belt, sat easily on his narrow hips. None of her male friends were built like that. They were all pretty puny. Despite herself, she was mesmerized.

What was even more fascinating was his gentleness. He picked up her leg to examine it, running his fingers deftly over the ankle bone to feel for swelling, then waggling her foot from side to side.

'Ow!' she squawked indignantly.

'I think it's just sprained. It would be agony if it was broken.'

'It is agony!'

Ignoring her protests, he stood up, then bent down and lifted her into his arms quite effortlessly.

'Put your arms around my neck,' he ordered.

'No way!'

She couldn't be carried across the fields by a Deacon, like a bride being carried over the threshold. She tried to wriggle out of his arms, but he tightened his grip, and she realized she was totally trapped. She looked up at him indignantly. He was obviously highly amused by her discomfort and the fact that she was powerless.

'Fucking well let go of me!' She was furious, and tried to kick at him with her good leg. To her fury, he just laughed, and dropped her unceremoniously back on to the grass.

'OK. Have it your own way. Maybe it wasn't such a good idea.'

He walked over to Nutmeg and grabbed her bridle. Jamie sat up in alarm. She wasn't going to let Nutmeg out of her sight. But there was nothing she could do about it.

'I'll take the horse back to our place; make sure she's safe. Then I'll come back for you.'

Jamie watched as he jumped into the saddle. He rode like a cowboy, with long legs and long reins, kicking the horse straight into a gallop from a standstill. Soon there was nothing left of them but a cloud of dust.

The wait was interminable. She felt sure he'd gone back to tell his family that he'd left her stranded and crippled, that they'd be loading Nutmeg on to a trailer any minute. Then she heard the distant sound of an engine. He came back on a quad bike.

'I thought this was the easiest way to get you back.'

Being left with little choice, she climbed on behind

him, sitting as far away from him as she could. Eventually, however, she had to relent and relax into his body to make the ride more comfortable. Every rut in the fields felt like fire shooting up her ankle, and by the time they got to Lower Faviell Farm she was nearly in tears. She reluctantly allowed him to take her arm as she hobbled into the farmhouse, where she was very relieved that the rest of the Deacons all seemed to be out. Despite the fact that her rescuer appeared to belie all the rumours, she would have been terrified to find herself in their midst.

He sat her down on an armchair while he made tea in quite the most chaotic kitchen she had ever seen. There was a basket of newborn kittens in one corner. Some-one had been cleaning tack on the kitchen table, leaving behind a tangled mass of reins and stirrup leathers. There were at least a dozen mugs lined up next to the sink, waiting to be washed. A huge bar built out of old cider barrels stood in one corner, with proper optics behind it for gin and whisky and rum, but as well as those the counter was smothered in bottles of every type of alcohol one could imagine. He picked up a bottle of brandy and poured a substantial slug into a mug of very hot, very sweet tea which he handed to her. She protested.

'I don't really drink.'

'It's medicinal. It'll do you good.'

She sipped at her mug obediently and soon felt the luxuriously numbing effects of the alcohol slide into her veins. Meanwhile, he applied some ointment to her ankle, evoking a curious mix of pain and pleasure: the sprain was agony, but his warm fingers on her skin were very soothing indeed.

'My sister uses this for bruising whenever she falls off. You probably know her. Tanya.'

Jamie certainly knew Tanya by sight, and repute. Tanya had a string of unlikely and rather moth-eaten ponies that she used to sweep up all the rosettes at local horse shows. She would strut around the showground with her shirt unbuttoned and knotted at the waist, a leopard-skin bra shamelessly visible underneath and a matching thong deliberately showing above the waistband of her skin-tight jodhpurs. Her hair varied in colour from peroxide white to magenta to blue-black. When the time came for her to go into the ring, she would button up her shirt, sling on her tie and show-jumping jacket, two sizes too small and with all the buttons missing, then, kicking the living daylights out of whatever dozing mount she'd chosen, nonchalantly pop every fence. Before she'd even left the ring she would have lit another cigarette, displaying no emotion at the reluctant round of applause that would follow her achievement. Jamie had been up against her in a clear round several times. She was terrified of Tanya. Everybody was. Not that she ever said anything to anyone; she just glowered, collected her rosettes ungraciously and left. The one time Jamie had scooped a rosette from under her nose, Tanya had given her a cool, appraising stare from between her spidery lashes, then looked away as she blew out a long stream of disparaging cigarette smoke, as if to say that the competition hadn't been worth the effort of winning.

As she sat curled up in the chair, taking in her surroundings, Jamie found herself drifting off. Perhaps it was the brandy, or the shock, or the rug that had been tucked round her, but she couldn't keep her eyes open. She awoke to find him brushing her hair gently away from her face, and realized she didn't even know his name.

'Which one are you, anyway?' she murmured sleepily.

He grinned, showing white even teeth.

'Rod. Second youngest. I was thinking ... maybe you'd like me to drop you home? The others will be back soon – it'll be chaos.'

She certainly didn't want to be an object of curiosity for the rest of the Deacons, like Goldilocks being peered at by the three bears, so she let him help her to a filthy old pick-up. He grinned ruefully, apologetic.

'Sorry – you need a tetanus jab to get in here.'

Inside, it was littered with old Coke cans, cigarette ends and Mars bar wrappers. But Jamie didn't mind. All she was worried about was the fact that, in a few minutes' time, she was going to have to say goodbye. And she absolutely didn't want to. And for the life of her she couldn't think of an excuse to see him again.

Luckily, Rod was two jumps ahead of her.

'I'll call you tomorrow, see how you are. Then we can make arrangements to bring your horse back. I'll get Tanya to ride her over.' He paused. 'Or I could ...'

He looked at her sideways and smiled.

Luckily for Jamie, her parents were both preoccupied that week. Louisa had gone to talk to a gallery owner in London about showing a new series of paintings, and Jack had gone with her to negotiate some deal. By the time the two of them got back, she had fallen head over heels in love.

To her amazement, she had found a kindred spirit in Rod. They both loved the outdoors and, while they enjoyed other people's company, were happiest when they were on their own. And they both shared the same frustrations: parents who were seemingly disinterested in their futures. Rod told her how he was fulfilling his dream to set up his own kitchen company, and how his father was pouring scorn upon it.

'He says a self-employed man is never his own man; he's always at someone else's beck and call. He reckons I should just stick to a wage and be done with it.'

Jamie told him her dilemma; how her parents seemed to think it perfectly reasonable for her to have no ambition whatsoever, and how frustrating she found that. And she was grateful for Rod's understanding. All her other friends just envied her not being pushed – they didn't get how it undermined her confidence.

She felt comfortable and safe with him, but at the same time tingly inside. When he wasn't looking, she feasted her eyes upon him, admiring his dark, gypsy curls, the eyes the colour of liquid amber that crinkled kindly at the corners when he laughed. His physique made her quite weak with longing, especially his hands with the long, brown fingers that were obviously so skilled at their craft. He wore faded jeans and Dr Martens, tight white T-shirts and soft cotton lumberjack shirts open over the top. Once, when he had left one of them in her car, she had taken it to bed with her. It smelled of his tangy, salty maleness, and it was almost as if he was with her. She wished fervently that he was, realizing that at long last she had met someone she felt sure was 'the one'. She felt alive with anticipation and expectation, wondering where it would all lead.

Added to this was the thrill of keeping Rod a secret.

She'd never done anything forbidden before, quite simply because nothing was forbidden to her. But something told her Jack and Louisa would not be happy about her liaising with a Deacon. Besides, if their relationship was out in the open, she'd be expected to bring him into the Wilding social life, and she had a feeling he wouldn't be comfortable with that. She couldn't bear the thought of him sitting at the table, a fish out of water trying to make polite conversation. Nor could she imagine him wafting about on the lawn sipping Pimm's, or standing with his back to a roaring log fire clutching a glass of mulled wine at Christmas. He wouldn't fit in to the Wildings' way of life. And she didn't want him to. She wanted him just as he was, and all to herself.

So, like a delicious square of chocolate surreptitiously enjoyed by a dieter, or a nip of whisky taken unobtrusively by the secret alcoholic, she revelled in the clandestine nature of her sin. She didn't even have to lie. Her parents trusted her so implicitly, would never have imagined in their wildest dreams what she was up to, that they rarely enquired as to her whereabouts.

They would never have believed what a gentleman Rod was. How he went to great lengths to find excursions to delight her, taking a boat out on the river, visiting a wildlife park, exploring the ruins of a castle. They went to the films in the middle of the afternoon, and sat holding hands with a box of popcorn between them.

Only once did something happen to shake her belief in Rod and remind her that there was no smoke without fire, that people hadn't branded the Deacons as gypsies, tramps and thieves for nothing. She'd gone to collect him from their secret meeting place, up a track that ran alongside one of their outlying fields. She didn't flatter herself that the Deacons knew about her any more than Jack and Louisa knew about him.

A horse was running up and down beside the fence, in the agitated way horses do when they arrive at a new location, before they have satisfied themselves of their surroundings. With its tail high and its ears pricked, it was snorting and whinnying through flared nostrils, muscles tightly bunched in preparation for flight should anything untoward appear. It was clearly highly strung and highly bred. Jamie looked at it with interest. It was stunning; not the Deacons' usual calibre at all.

'Wow!' she said, as Rod got into the front seat. 'What a fantastic horse.'

Rod gave it a cursory glance.

'It's Tanya's.'

'It must have cost a fortune.'

Rod shrugged. Jamie leaned out of the window to get a better look.

'Seriously.' She examined the immaculate conformation, its sleek, streamlined perfection. 'It looks like a racehorse.'

She looked at Rod, puzzled, not wanting to be so rude as to ask where they'd got the money.

'Let's go,' he said, turning on the radio. She frowned. He obviously didn't want to talk about it. Suddenly, a cold realization hit her.

'It's not stolen, is it?'

'Of course not.'

'Well, where did she get it?'

Again a disinterested shrug. 'Off some dealer.'

'You should check the paperwork very carefully. She

might have bought a stolen horse without knowing it. It must be worth thousands. Thousands and thousands.'

She knew she was right. This wasn't a gifted amateur's horse. It was quality, bred for speed and endurance. Surely they must realize? Jamie persisted.

'Maybe you should just check with the police. I mean, it would be awful if Tanya was found with it, and it turned out it had been stolen.'

Rod turned to look at her, his eyes hard.

'Jamie, the horse isn't stolen. OK?'

The tone in his voice told her she was supposed to shut up. But she wasn't going to give up that easily.

'How do you know?'

'It's ... on loan. Let's just leave it at that, OK?'

Jamie sat at the wheel, turning everything over in her mind. Why would anyone in their right mind want Tanya Deacon to be in charge of a valuable horse like that? And why was it being kept in the field that was furthest from the road, where no one was likely to clap eyes on it?

The penny dropped. She turned to look at Rod, who was staring ahead, frowning.

'It's an insurance job, isn't it? Someone's arranged to have it nicked, and you're looking after it.'

His lack of response was sufficient answer.

'That's terrible! That's absolutely terrible! You can't let them do that—'

'Look,' said Rod. 'I don't criticize your family. So don't criticize mine. OK?'

There was something in his tone that made her drop the subject immediately. But the incident had frightened her, unsettled her. Somebody somewhere had made a substantial claim on their insurance for a horse they'd declared stolen, knowing full well it was perfectly safe with the Deacons, who had no doubt received a generous payment for 'stealing' it. This made them out-and-out criminals. Rod, by doing nothing, clearly condoned this behaviour, even if he wasn't directly involved. She was quiet for the rest of the afternoon, unable to help wondering what else he was happy to accept. It was in his blood, after all.

In the end, she decided to keep quiet and not mention it again, though she couldn't help worrying if that made her as bad as they were. She'd toyed with the idea of phoning the police anonymously, but she was too frightened. She didn't want anything to come between her and Rod. And she was sure he hadn't had anything to do with it directly. He wasn't like the rest of them. And she didn't want to risk upsetting him, possibly losing him. Not when she'd finally found someone she wanted to spend time with; someone she thought about the minute she woke up, and fell asleep dreaming about. And who she was pretty sure felt the same way about her.

Thus they continued their sweet, rather old-fashioned courtship, enjoying innocent pastimes and days out that most people would have dismissed as dull, but they got their excitement from each other's company, discovering as much about each other as they could.

And then finally, one day, when they'd taken a picnic to a tranquil secluded spot by a river, they made love. It seemed entirely natural, not the terrifying, traumatic occasion Jamie had always imagined it to be. They were lying side by side on a rug under an oak tree, dozing after having devoured thick ham sandwiches and crisps and a cloudy bottle of local cider, when he leaned over and looked deep into her eyes.

He said just one word. Her name. And she knew in that single word was a question, a request for permission. And her reply was to reach her hand up behind his head and pull his lips to hers. She could taste the appley cider on him, rough yet sweet, just like his kisses, and she devoured the sensation eagerly. She was wearing a skimpy sundress, and as he pushed it up, caressing her thighs, she knew she had no intention of protesting, that she was going to let him go as far as he wanted, that she was totally happy to give herself up to whatever was to come. And as his firm, strong fingers began to explore her further, it was as if he'd unlocked a magic box. She pushed herself against his hand, which suddenly wasn't enough, urging him on with a frenetic desperation. He tried to calm her, a little frightened by what he had unleashed.

'I don't want to hurt you.'

'Please. Just do it. Please.'

He was incredibly tentative, and at first she felt nothing. Somehow, she'd expected pain, but there was none. Then gradually he began to move, and so did she, relaxing into his rhythm, shutting her eyes and letting herself go. Then a little tingle started right in the core of her belly, twisting round and round like a tiny tornado, elusive at first, seeming to tease her. As it grew stronger, and then stronger, she heard herself give a little whimper of pleasure, then felt Rod stop. She opened her eyes: he was looking at her in concern.

'Are you OK?' he whispered. She nodded, and as if to confirm it pulled him to her urgently, for fear the magical sensation would vanish. It didn't; on the contrary it spread, spilling through her insides like an upturned tin of golden syrup, seeping through her veins. Nothing else in the world mattered; she didn't care if the whole of Shropshire was lined up to see her.

All too soon, it was over. Rod lay on top of her, and she could feel their hearts hammering in unison, their breath gradually subsiding. For a moment she felt bereft; terrified that had been the first and last time. It couldn't possibly happen again. Not like that. It was ...

Heaven.

The next day Jamie was walking on air. She had hardly slept, just gone over and over what had happened that afternoon. It had been beyond her wildest dreams and expectations. She wondered if it was like that every time, and if it was like that for everyone. And if it had been as fantastic and momentous for him – though she didn't flatter herself that she'd been his first by any means. Not that she minded. She hugged his shirt to her, and every time she smelled him on it her insides turned over.

Eventually she dragged herself out of her bed and away from her daydreams, and went into Ludlow to run some errands. Rod was working, and they'd arranged to meet later that evening. She was in a frenzy of anticipation, longing to see him but somehow feeling shy as well. She didn't want to seem too cheap, too eager to have sex again, but the truth was she couldn't think about anything else. She let herself imagine the day when they could be together for ever, when they could fall asleep in each other's arms and wake up the same. She knew somehow that their relationship had changed, that it had gone up a gear, and that they were going to have to make some serious decisions. She would have to reveal the truth to her parents. How desperately she had wanted to tell Louisa what had happened, and ask her if it was like that for everyone. And had it been with anyone else, she would have done. Her mother was very open and frank. But Jamie had kept quiet. If she and Rod were going to come clean about their relationship, they would have to do it together. There was going to be uproar from both sides, she was sure of it, and they would have to demonstrate their conviction for each other in order to heal the rift between the two families.

Neither of them was too sure what dark history there was between the Deacons and the Wildings. Being such close neighbours, life would have been much easier if they had at least agreed to cooperate with each other. But for as long as both Rod and Jamie could remember, the Wilding name was anathema to the Deacons, and vice versa. Perhaps it was just the good old English feudal system, the haves and the have-nots. Or some petty disagreement years ago that had grown out of all proportion.

Maybe, thought Jamie, allowing her imagination to run away with her, maybe a wedding would heal the breach. Everyone loved a wedding, didn't they?

She was drifting past the market square, indulging in what she knew was a ridiculous fantasy, but which involved Nutmeg dressed up and pulling a little flower-decked cart and Jamie in a shepherdess frock, her hair in ringlets, and the church bells ringing all over Upper and Lower Faviell while the villagers turned out to witness—

'Hey – you've cost me good money, you have.'

A booted foot stretched out and blocked her path. It was Lee, the oldest and baddest of the Deacon brothers.

He was the one that had actually done time, several times. His black hair was slicked back, his skin was pitted from teenage acne, his fingers were bedecked with huge silver rings: a skull, a dragon's head, a serpent. His sideburns were pointed and reached nearly to the corners of his mouth. He was sitting at a table with his hand curled round a pint of rough cider that was, judging by his slurred words and glittering eyes, not his first.

'Fifty quid. Fifty quid I couldn't afford to lose.'

Jamie stopped short. 'What do you mean?'

Lee leered at her, eyes fixed on her camisole top. Jamie crossed her arms firmly across her chest.

'Rod. I bet him fifty quid he couldn't get into your knickers.'

'I beg your pardon?'

Jamie knew she sounded stuck-up as soon as she said it. She should have just laughed, tossed her hair and walked off. Lee was baiting her.

'Rod, I said to him, there's no way a top-drawer bit of skirt like you would let a bit of rough like him get his leg over. Seems I was wrong.'

Lee leered again. Jamie was tempted to pick up his glass and throw it all over him, but that was probably the sort of uptight reaction he expected. He was gazing at her crotch now, so she moved her handbag to cover it, wishing she hadn't cut her jeans off quite so short.

'He says you're a right little wildcat. Can't get enough of it. I'm going to have to pay him out now.'

Lee threw back his head and laughed long and loud.

Jamie tilted her chin in the air primly.

'I don't believe you. I don't believe he told you anything of the sort.'

'Pink panties.' Lee presented the proof matter-of-factly. 'Tiny little pink panties that wouldn't do you as a hankie, he said.'

Jamie felt sick. She had been wearing pink knickers; Marks & Spencers bikini briefs. Lee chortled at the expression on her face. He leaned forwards conspiratorially.

'Easiest fifty quid he's ever made. Just you make sure he buys you a drink out of it.'

Lee picked up his glass and took a long, satisfying pull as he watched the girl fly off in distress.

There hadn't been any such wager, of course. In fact, Rod hadn't told Lee anything about Jamie at all. It had been his somewhat furtive behaviour of late, his reluctance to join the rest of them down the pub as usual, combined with his sudden preoccupation with his appearance that had alerted Lee to the fact that his little brother was up to no good, and that it involved a woman.

He hadn't been spying on them as such. He just wanted to confirm his worst suspicions. Despite his brother's attempt at secrecy, Lee soon realized Rod was besotted with the Wilding girl. He'd followed him on a couple of occasions, just to make sure his hunch was correct, and his heart had sunk when he'd seen the two of them mooning over each other like love's young dream. And yesterday, he'd spied them by the river, using the powerful binoculars he had for keeping surveillance during a job. They'd given him a pretty clear view of his brother's seduction of Jamie, and her obvious enjoyment had struck fear into his heart. Things had gone too far.

So when he'd seen her like that, tripping across the market square without a care in the world, smiling the smile of the recently satisfied, he couldn't resist bursting her bubble. He was pretty confident that he'd put a spanner in the works. And even if he hadn't, it had been worth it for the look on Jamie's face. With any luck she'd send Rod packing with a flea in his ear. Lee wasn't worried about dropping his brother in it. It was for his own good.

He knew Rod had no real understanding of why it didn't do to get mixed up with people like Jamie Wilding. He'd always had a naive streak, had Rod. No doubt he fancied himself in love, and that the love was reciprocated. Lee knew better. You'd always be a toy, ready to be dropped as soon as the novelty wore off. Though they always made out you were the best thing since sliced bread at the time. Lee had been a bit of rough for enough middle-class women over the years to know all their tricks. They bloody loved it when you gave them a good seeing-to; the rougher the better usually. But if you started to get too close, started to ask anything of them, they became nervous. Nervous then cool. Then would come the excuses.

Lee didn't mind. He'd always got his revenge. Pleasuring these women in their own beds gave them a thrill, but also gave him a golden opportunity to case their houses. And when he did them over a few months later, they could never point the finger at him, not without incriminating themselves. Rough justice, maybe. But justice nevertheless.

Lee took another slug of cider. His brother might not realize it now, but he'd done him a favour in the long run. Cruel to be kind, thought Lee. Cruel to be kind.

Jamie hurried away as quickly as she could, Lee's derisive laughter still ringing in her ears, hot tears of humiliation stinging her eyelids.

Had she really just been a wager between the two Deacon brothers? She could imagine them in the pub laughing, Lee ruefully and reluctantly counting out fifty quid in used tenners, with Rod telling everyone who wanted to listen about her sexual performance, how pathetically grateful she'd been for his attentions, boasting about her prowess. It couldn't be true, surely. But then – how had Lee known she was wearing pink knickers? That couldn't have been a lucky guess.

What a total and utter bastard Rod had turned out to be. Well, she wasn't going to humiliate herself by confronting him and giving them all another chance to laugh at her. Jamie cursed her own stupidity. She should have known better: her own mother had always denounced the Deacons as black-hearted vagabonds that weren't to be trusted, and had warned Jamie away from them. How on earth had she managed to persuade herself Rod was any different from the rest? The stolen horse: surely that should have set off alarm bells? They were a feckless bunch of petty criminals, the whole lot of them. And she was a naive little fool.

She tried not to think about the moments of tenderness that had seemed so genuine. The way he traced his fingers gently over her face. The way he always seemed to know what she was thinking, what she wanted. How they agreed over so many things. And how utterly fantastic making love had been—

Only it wasn't making love. Not for him. It was a conquest, a challenge, a dare – a feat he'd probably be boasting about for weeks. And no doubt he was only good at it because he'd had so much practice.

She walked straight out from the market square into

the road, blinded by her tears. A mad tooting alerted her to the fact she'd stepped right in front of a car. The driver was leaning out of the window, about to berate her for her stupidity.

'Oh, fuck off!' she snarled, in no mood for recriminations.

'Jamie?' It was Kif, looking at her anxiously. 'Whatever's the matter?'

She couldn't deny there was something wrong. Kif leaped out of the car and put his arm round her, and she sobbed into his chest.

And from across the market place, Lee watched, his replenished glass in front of him, and smirked as Kif installed her gently into the front seat and drove her away. They always stuck together, the toffs. Well, so did the bloody Deacons. He'd take Rod out tonight, get him lashed, find him a girl who'd make him forget Jamie's ladylike ways, her lily-white thighs, her pretty pink panties. Foxy Marsden would do the trick.

Rod was puzzled when Jamie hadn't phoned him by half-six that night. She always phoned him, because no one in the Deacon house ever took any interest in phone calls that weren't for themselves. An hour later he was increasingly anxious, worrying that he'd upset her in some way.

At eight o'clock he broke their golden rule and telephoned Bucklebury Farm. He'd make up a name if either of her parents answered; try and put on a pseudo-posh, casual accent. But it was Jamie who picked up the phone.

'Jamie. Are you OK? What's the matter?'

Her icy tones cut through him like a bitter east wind.

'If you have to ask, then either you're more stupid than I thought, or you must think I'm stupid.'

'What?'

She sighed, wearily. 'Just fuck off. And don't bother phoning again.'

She hung up on him. Bewildered, Rod stared at the receiver his end. The temperature in the hallway seemed to drop, and he shivered fearfully. Something terrible had happened, but he didn't know what.

Yesterday had been so magical. They'd left each other with tender kisses and promises, each in agony at having to leave the other. What on earth had changed? He felt ill with foreboding. He hadn't forced her into having sex, he was sure of that. But he'd heard about girls who changed their minds, when they panicked after the event. Surely Jamie wouldn't do that? She wasn't the fickle, highly strung type who would blow the whistle on you just because they had doubts. And she'd had no doubts. There hadn't been a moment when he'd thought she didn't want to go through with it. There hadn't been a moment afterwards when he'd thought she regretted what they'd done.

Or had he misread the signs? Could he have coerced her in some way without realizing it? He couldn't bear to think that perhaps she was traumatized. He had to talk to her and find some way of discovering the truth. And if he had done wrong, he had to make amends ...

At Bucklebury Farm, Jamie picked up her duffel bag, which she filled with a couple of changes of clothing and her night things. Kif was on his way over. He'd promised to pick her up at eight. She'd left a note for her parents, telling them where she was going. Kif had invited her down to Bristol, where he was about to start his third year in English at the university. He was going back early to move into his own flat; she was going to go down and help him decorate. A total change of scene and a few days' hard work might help her forget the trauma of the past twenty-four hours.

At last she heard the sound of Kif's car outside. She slipped out of the kitchen door. Turning the key in its lock, she shoved it under the mat.

They passed Rod driving hell for leather up the drive.

'Don't stop. Just drive on,' commanded Jamie, and Kif obeyed her.

Bristol turned out to be the perfect tonic. Kif's flat was wonderful – on the second floor of a high-ceilinged, spacious house overlooking the Avon in Hotwells. They spent three days with buckets of white emulsion, eradicating the dubious tastes of the previous inhabitants, with Bob Marley and Sting and Dire Straits blaring out on Kif's sound system as the sun streamed in through the balcony windows.

Jamie loved Bristol. It had a buzz and an energy to it that she found totally seductive. She'd always thought she didn't like cities – she certainly hadn't particularly liked London, on the occasions her parents had taken her there with them – but Bristol was different. More intimate, less threatening. She was surprised to find she felt quite at home.

On the Saturday, to celebrate finishing and to say thank you, Kif took her out for dinner to Browns, where she met a crowd of his friends and they ate huge, fat juicy burgers and worked their way merrily down the cocktail list. Jamie for once allowed herself to get if not blind drunk then certainly very merry.

Later, they went on to a club, dark and sultry with unresolved sexual tension. Jamie lost herself in the throbbing music, totally uninhibited, relaxed by the alcohol and the atmosphere. She fell into a rhythm with Kif's flatmate, Alistair, and when he pulled her in closer as the dance floor got more crowded, she didn't protest, just melted against him. She felt dreamy, distant, languid and sensual; the air was thick with a strange sweet smell that she thought was probably dope. She felt cocooned from the real world, the world she had come from, the world she wanted to forget, where people shafted you and laughed behind your back, raised your hopes and then dashed them, and shattered your dreams.

Later, Alistair kissed her on the balcony of Kif's flat as the sun came up over the river. And if she only felt a pleasant trickle of warmth, not a raging torrent of desire, she tried not to be too disappointed and enjoyed the encounter for what it was. She went alone to bed at six o'clock, light-headed from too much alcohol and too little sleep and the realization that there was life beyond Bucklebury Farm.

In the next few days, she buried away what had happened earlier that summer, passing Rod off as an adolescent crush whom she'd imbued with magical qualities because he was forbidden fruit. She even managed to convince herself that she'd only slept with him out of curiosity and to divest herself of her virginity. Being away from Bucklebury Farm and getting a taste of a different life also helped make up her mind about her future. She definitely needed to broaden her horizons and get a taste of what was out there in the big wide world – then perhaps she wouldn't be gullible enough to be taken in by the likes of Rod Deacon again. She was going to go with her original idea to train to be a nanny, though she wasn't going to study at the local college as she'd first planned. She found a private college in Berkshire where she could study full time. She'd only need to come home in the holidays, when it wouldn't be too difficult to avoid Rod. They hardly moved in the same social circles, after all.

And so, that September, off she went to college.

And if sometimes, even years later, she woke from a dream that made her insides feel like melting chocolate, she knew she'd been dreaming of Rod, but she never admitted it to herself...

12

Jamie drove away from Owl's Nest that lunchtime filled with fury and despair, and unable to face going back to Bucklebury Farm. She didn't know what she would say to her father if she saw him. She needed to clear her mind a bit and get things into perspective, so instead of turning off for home, she headed straight along the main road back into Ludlow.

She felt drained; utterly humiliated that she'd broken down in front of Rod like that. But she'd suddenly been overwhelmed with despair. After the initial high of coming home the night before, thinking everything was all right, thinking that she was going to be able to cope and rebuild some sort of cosy idyllic life at Bucklebury Farm with Jack, she'd found that dream shattered. Jack the leopard was never going to change his spots, her mother was gone, the farm was going to be snatched away. Add to that the bitter irony of Rod Deacon being the one to benefit from the plan, and it was hardly surprising she'd lost it.

As she pulled into the market square, Jamie thought grimly that she'd certainly made a fool of herself. In front of Rod's perfect wife Bella as well – what must she have thought of the screaming fishwife in her living room? She remembered Bella's cool gaze upon her, the incredible composure, the dignified exit, while she ranted and raved like some harpy.

It occurred to her that today was the first time she had actually spoken to Rod face to face since that day by the river. She'd only clapped eyes on him a few times afterwards, which was incredible when you thought what a small community they lived in, and how close their boundaries were. The last time she'd seen him was in the congregation at her mother's funeral, when there had been too many emotions jostling for pole position for her to give his presence much thought. Thankfully, he hadn't come back to the house afterwards, so she hadn't had to face him, but there had been a note, brief but polite, on his headed paper, sending his condolences and signed 'with best wishes'. She hadn't written back, though she'd replied dutifully to every other letter of condolence. She didn't know what to say.

She'd seen the wedding photos in the local paper a few years earlier, Rod looking rakish in his morning suit, his eyes crinkling for the camera, and Bella looking utterly stunning in a low-cut white wedding dress. Jamie didn't even have the satisfaction of thinking she looked tarty; she didn't, just beautiful and radiant. The wedding had been in the church at Upper Faviell, with a reception afterwards at a country house hotel, which must have cost a fortune – even before you took into account the amount of drink the Deacons were likely to consume between them. But then, Rod's kitchen business was doing very well. A Rod Deacon kitchen had become something of a status symbol locally. She'd seen a feature on him in *Shropshire Life* when she'd been to the dentist a year or so ago. It had been a three-page colour spread, with photographs of him in his workshop and examples of his handiwork, which she'd had to admit were exquisite. And a photograph of him and Bella in their kitchen at Owl's Nest, the epitome of domestic bliss, hands curled round mugs of coffee, beaming for the camera, the perfect couple, successful and content. Jamie's ensuing root canal treatment had been less painful than seeing those photos.

She knew of Bella. She'd been to classes at her mother's dance academy with Kate and Emma, when she was about seven, before pony mania overtook the desire to be a ballet dancer. Bella had been a precocious tot even then, immaculate in her tutu with her black hair scraped back into a bun, always used by her mother to demonstrate the correct moves, which she did with an air of smug satisfaction as if to say 'You will never be as good as me as long as you live.' Jamie was sure Bella and Rod were happy together. They obviously couldn't keep their hands off each other, nipping home for lunchtime sex . . .

As she pulled into a parking space, Jamie tried not to dwell on the image of the two of them in bed together, and focused instead on the spending spree she'd promised herself. She desperately needed a good splurge in the chemist to make up for neglecting herself over the past few months. And, she noticed, with her mother gone, the house had lost some of its softness. Jamie resolved to give it the feminine touch it was sorely lacking.

The town was thriving, and she smiled to see it. Like a lot of country towns dependent on agriculture and tourism, it had suffered badly a few years ago from the foot-and-mouth crisis, and a lot of businesses had gone under as a result. But Ludlow was now happily resplendent again. It lifted her mood. She spent the next hour exploring, investigating the changes and indulging in her old favourite haunts. As well as the predictable antique shops, there were many unusual emporiums selling things that were hardly essential to life, but were totally irresistible nevertheless. She bought a dozen beeswax candles, and some muslin lavender bags, several bunches of flowers, fresh coffee and loose leaf tea, then deposited her purchases back in the car before setting out on her own transformation.

Her woes were temporarily forgotten as she indulged herself in some serious retail therapy – she couldn't remember the last time she'd really splashed out on herself. First she bought rehydrating face packs and hair masks in the hope of replenishing the moisture the relentless South American sun had dried out. Then she bought deliciously scented bath oil and body lotion. This was the ultimate luxury: she hadn't bought anything heavily perfumed for years. She didn't use it in her job, in case the babies had an allergy, but also to keep rampant fathers at bay. It was amazing how many of them had strange ideas about what a maternity nurse's duties might include. Though to be fair many of them had been deprived of sexual activity for months already, with no glimmer of light at the end of the tunnel. Finally, she bought some lipstick and nail polish, blusher and a new mascara, promising herself a therapeutic spa evening and a total makeover.

As she carried her booty back to her car, she realized she was parked only a stone's throw from Drace's estate agents. She decided she'd go and call in on Kif, surprise him. Jack had told her about Hamilton. And about Christopher and Zoe moving back to Lydbrook. She felt guilty that she hadn't been in touch during her absence, but she had explained things to Christopher on the phone before she left, and he'd understood. He didn't expect anything from her. Nor she him. They had the perfect friendship. And she'd remembered Sebastian's birthday; she was his godmother, and a good one. She sent him zany postcards from the crazy places she'd been to, with funny messages.

Kif was just the person she needed to see, to lift her spirits and also put her feet back on the ground. He'd give her an objective opinion about what had happened with her father. He was level-headed and pragmatic, but would also understand her misgivings. He'd soon tell her if she'd overreacted – but without making her feel like a fool.

Drace's was at the top of a small side street just off the market place. It had an old-fashioned frontage with two huge bay windows that were perfect for displaying house details. Inside it was very traditional. An inviting chesterfield sofa with a low coffee table in front, scattered with copies of *Country Life* and the *Daily Telegraph*, sat in one of the bay windows for potential purchasers to browse through details in comfort. The atmosphere very cleverly evoked the sort of lifestyle you were buying into by purchasing a house through them. There was no doubt Drace's pitched themselves at the upper end of the property market. Jamie peered in through the window. There he was, at a large, leather-topped desk, with his reddish-blond fringe flopping down into his eyes, pushing it back every few seconds with his freckled hand. Jamie felt a sudden burst of fondness.

She pushed open the door eagerly. Christopher got to his feet automatically. He afforded every customer this courtesy. It was free, and it made them feel valued. His polite Drace's smile broke into a huge grin as soon as he realized who his customer was.

'Jamie! My God! What the hell are you doing here? How fantastic!'

He crossed the floor to her in three easy strides, and pulled her to him.

'I'm so sorry about your dad. I'm so sorry.' Jamie thought she was in danger of crying into his scratchy tweedy chest. His arms round her were so comforting yet unthreatening.

'I know,' he said, hugging her to him for comfort in his turn, because if there was anyone in the world who would understand what he was going through it was Jamie.

Tiona was completely unamused to find Christopher with a stunning redhead in his arms when she came out of her office. Well, OK, maybe not stunning. Her hair was dreadful and her clothes were diabolical – old jeans, a polo shirt and hiking boots. But she was incredibly pretty in a totally unmade-up way – big, dark, Bambi eyes and a cute, freckle-spattered nose. And a to-die-for tan, being one of those unusual redheads who went brown rather than pink. And she was tall-and-thin-with-tits, which Tiona knew spelled trouble. She herself was small-and-round-with-tits, which was great once you actually got men into bed because that was what they really wanted, something to get hold of. But thin-with-tits was what they always thought they wanted.

Christopher introduced Jamie as his oldest and dearest friend. Tiona was charmingly and prettily polite as she mentally cast a hex on Jamie. If she was going to break up Christopher's marriage, she certainly didn't want his oldest and dearest friend around giving him advice.

'Are you staying in Ludlow long?' she ventured.

Jamie looked momentarily troubled.

'I don't know what I'm doing. Everything's in a bit of a mess. In fact, I need to talk to you, Kif. I'm badly in need of some advice.'

Kif? thought Tiona, disgusted. What sort of a name was that? And to make matters worse, Christopher was looking at his watch.

'I was going to go over to the printers. But I could do with a cup of tea. Let's go over to de Grays. I'll buy you a cream cake.' He prodded her playfully in the ribs. 'You look as if you could do with feeding up.'

Tiona watched, eyes narrowed, as Christopher escorted Jamie out of the door.

Going into de Gray's was like going back thirty, or even fifty years. As you went in, you were confronted by glass cabinets full of toothsome treats – old-fashioned cakes and buns and biscuits displayed in white paper cases, some oozing cream and jam, others encrusted with raisins and nuts, others topped with succulent sugary icing or chocolate. The smell was quite dizzying, topped off with the scent of roasting coffee. Through the back was a huge traditional tearoom. Jamie was ravenous. She hadn't had any lunch. To Kif's amusement she ordered a cream tea, rather like a tourist.

Christopher poured them both Earl Grey when it arrived, listening sympathetically while Jamie spilled the beans about the deal her father had done with Rod

Deacon. Her heart sank when he nodded sagely, and said he wasn't in the least bit surprised.

'I know because of Lydbrook. These old houses are absolute millstones, to be honest. They gobble up cash, especially if they haven't been modernized.'

'So do you think ... Dad should go through with the deal?'

Christopher surveyed her anxious brown eyes.

'I'd feel the same way as you, Jamie. Lydbrook would go over my dead body. I'd hate to see it turned into a nursing home, or apartments. It needs a family in it.' He smiled self-deprecatingly. 'I know it's terrible for an estate agent to be sentimental about houses. I'm always telling my clients not to get emotionally involved, as it only leads to heartache. But when a house has been in your family for generations; when it's almost in your blood—'

Jamie nodded in passionate agreement.

'Exactly. That's how I feel about Bucklebury. It would be like selling a relative. I don't know how Dad can even give it a second thought.'

'It wasn't in his family, though, was it? It was your mother's. He hasn't got the same attachment.'

'But I would have thought – there's so much of my mother in it. I don't know how he can bear to let it go.'

'Maybe that's the only way he can forget,' Christopher suggested very gently. 'And he isn't letting go completely, is he? Maybe he sees this as a—'

Jamie put her hand up to stop him.

'Please. Don't say the word compromise.' She managed to laugh, though she felt like crying. 'Kif – are you saying ... do you think it's a good idea?'

Christopher considered his answer carefully.

'I think it's a very practical, economically viable proposition—'

Jamie's shoulders slumped in despair.

'—but it's not the only solution. Not now you're in the equation, and happy to shoulder some of the responsibility.'

'I am. Definitely. I'm happy to do whatever it takes.'

The waitress arrived with two huge floury scones and two glass bowls, one filled with ruby-bright raspberry jam, the other a sinful mound of deep-yellow clotted cream.

'Come on,' said Christopher. 'Eat up.'

He watched as Jamie performed the ritual, splitting open the scone. She was a cream first, jam on top person, he noted. As she bit into her handiwork, he dragged his mind back to the problem in hand.

'You're not going to make any money out of Bucklebury by farming – at least, not for years, by which time you'd be up to your neck in debt. We all know there's no real money to be made out of horses – just backbreaking hard work and blisters for little thanks. And as this area is only really kept afloat by tourism, I'd say your obvious answer was to jump on the bandwagon.'

Jamie's mind was racing to keep up. She thought she knew where Kif was leading.

'You mean ... open a hotel?'

'Not a hotel. Not straight away, anyway. The standards are too high these days. You'd have to have a proper restaurant, all sorts of facilities. No, I was thinking more like ... farmhouse B&B. Bucklebury would be ideal. It's only three miles out of Ludlow. And it's a gorgeous setting.'

Jamie nodded, turning the idea over in her mind as Christopher elaborated.

'You'd have to be totally professional and businesslike. It's a competitive market. And you'd have to think of some way of making it a little bit different. A gimmick to make it stand out from the rest. The area's hardly short of accommodation, after all.'

'I think it's a wonderful idea.'

'Hold your horses. It's not just a question of buying some new duvet covers and a set of matching mugs, Jamie. It's bloody hard work. Ask anyone who does it. You need to do your research. And think about how you're going to finance it.'

Jamie groaned. 'Oh God. Here we go. Money again.'

'Yeah, well, that's what it's all about, isn't it? Everything's down to money at the end of the day.'

He took his wallet out of his pocket, rifled through it and pulled out a card.

'Go and see the business manager at my bank. He's a good bloke. He helped me out of seven sorts of shit when I was trying to sort out the agency. He can see the big picture – he won't just crunch numbers into his computer and give you a "No". He's got a bit of vision. I think you'll find him helpful.'

Jamie licked the last of the cream from her fingers and took the card. As she looked at it, she felt her heart beating fast. All of a sudden she found herself rather frightened by the prospect; this was all terribly grown-up and serious. But it was down to her – if she sat back and did nothing, the worst would happen.

She could see Bella Deacon in the kitchen at Bucklebury, nibbling daintily on a slice of melon. She could imagine how she would rip the heart out of it, filling it with whimsical china teapots and cookie jars, with ruffled blinds at the windows and sprigged tablecloths with matching serviettes, tea towels and oven gloves ... A sterile and rather twee environment that would miss the whole point entirely.

She decided to use this image as her motivation. Every time she faltered in her task she would visualize Bella and Rod smiling for the camera in their next magazine article, and the caption underneath: 'Rod and Bella Deacon in their idyllic farmhouse kitchen ...'

'Thanks, Kif.' She put her hand over his, knowing he understood, knowing she didn't have to reiterate her appreciation too often. 'And I'm sorry. Here I am babbling on about my problems, when you must be having a nightmare as well. How are things?'

Christopher thought about cheerily telling her everything was fine. It was what he kept telling himself, after all. But he was walking a continual tightrope. Sooner or later there was going to be a catastrophe. He needed a sounding board, and could think of no one better than Jamie.

'Fucking bloody awful,' he admitted.

'Your poor father. I must go and see him.'

'I wouldn't bother. He won't even know you're there.'

'And how's your mum?'

'Pretty dreadful. But she never complains. You know Mum ...' Christopher trailed off, stirring his tea absentmindedly with his spoon, even though he didn't have sugar. 'Actually, it's not either of them that's the real problem. It's Zoe. She's absolutely miserable and I don't know what to do about it.'

He looked so totally stricken, Jamie was alarmed. She'd never seen Kif rattled. He was always so calm, so capable, and always had an answer.

'Is there anything I can do?'

Christopher chucked the spoon on the table in a gesture of defeat, shrugging.

'Why don't you come for supper tomorrow night? See what you think. Maybe you can find a way of snapping her out of it.'

Fired with enthusiasm, Jamie left Christopher with promises to see him the next night and went straight into the tourist office. There she spent a good hour picking up as many leaflets as she could, comparing prices and what existing establishments had on offer. They varied wildly, from what sounded fairly spartan shared bathroom facilities to unashamed luxury. Like anyone with a new idea, she veered from unburstable optimism to black gloom.

It was feasible.

It was impossible.

It was the answer to her prayers.

She couldn't pull it off in a million years.

One freeze-frame of Bella dipping her spoon into a low-fat yogurt spurred her on. She came out into the bright light of the market square. It was late afternoon and the stallholders were packing up. The last of the tourists were wending their way back to the car park. She imagined some of them making their way to Bucklebury for tea and shortbread on the lawn before going up the stairs for a nap, followed by a hot bath.

She nipped into the bank just before it closed. A combination of charm and luck secured her an appointment with Edward Lincoln the next morning. She felt slightly sick – what on earth was she going to say to him? She needed to get a vague set of figures sorted out before their meeting or he'd think she was an idiot. She went into WHSmith and bought an efficient-looking notebook and a rollerball pen. She should probably go in armed with spreadsheets and projections, but there was no computer at Bucklebury and never likely to be. Well, if Edward Lincoln laughed her out of the bank tomorrow, she was ready for it. But she had to at least try.

When Jamie got home, she realized she had one more thing to do before she sat down and worked out her figures. She had to go and talk to Jack. She thought perhaps she owed him an apology. She'd gone off at the deep end, without looking at things from his perspective. What else was he supposed to do, widowed, broke, his daughter sulking on the other side of the world, subject to the wiles of a cunning, silver-tongued gypsy? If his situation was anyone's fault, it was hers. If she'd been there to support him from the start...

At six o'clock, she made two proper hefty gin and tonics, in heavy tumblers, with plenty of ice and thick wedges of lemon and Indian tonic water. She found Jack in the barn, not actually doing anything, just sitting on the bale of hay she'd collapsed on earlier, staring at the car. She was suddenly struck by how old and tired and sad he looked, and she felt riddled with guilt.

She handed him a glass and he took it, smiling his thanks. She cleared her throat awkwardly.

'I'm sorry I was so beastly about your plan earlier. It was a shock, that's all. I didn't expect it.'

'I didn't expect you to like it. And I can't say that I'm that taken with it either. But at least now you can see I was faced with little choice.'

'Not at the time, no.'

Jack looked at her sharply. He knew his daughter well enough to realize there was something else coming. He raised a quizzical eyebrow. Jamie couldn't help smiling, a little abashed.

'Um – I've had a sort of idea. About how we could make the farm work for us, without having to sell any of it off.'

She looked at him hesitantly.

'Well, go on then. Tell me.'

After her trip to the tourist office, Jamie had a clearer idea of what she had in mind, and she began to outline it. She saw Bucklebury Farm as an upmarket farmhouse bed and breakfast for stressed-out urban couples with young children who wanted a real break, not just a change of scene where life was even more difficult. As well as accommodation, her background meant she could provide qualified childcare during the day. And that didn't just mean sticking kids in front of a video, but involving them in proper countryside activities: pony rides and picnics and pond-dipping and treasure hunts – all the things Jamie had enjoyed when she was little and that were so sadly lacking from today's childhood. The parents could please themselves, either relaxing at the farm or going out for the day to explore Ludlow. And in the evenings, after giving the children a traditional high tea, the parents could potter back into Ludlow and enjoy one of the restaurants safe in the knowledge that their children were being looked after by a qualified nanny who would also be there to nurse their little darlings next morning while they nursed their hangovers. Marketing would be a challenge, but it was the sort of enterprise that would take off through word of mouth.

'We'd only need to lure one celebrity couple here, or get a feature in one of the Sunday papers, and we'd be made,' Jamie finished, her eyes shining with her enthusiasm for the project.

'It sounds fantastic,' Jack agreed. 'There's just one thing. The sort of set-up you're talking about – surely it would cost a fortune? Stressed-out urban couples don't take kindly to stressed-out rural plumbing, for a start.'

'I've worked out we'd need at least a hundred thousand. For Phase One. Repairs, renovations and bringing it up to tourist-board standards.' Jamie said it briskly. It didn't sound so much that way. It was, in fact, a round figure she'd just plucked out of the air. Jack looked at her blankly.

'But we haven't got a hundred thousand.'

'No. But we could raise it.'

'How?'

This was the moment when she had to tread very carefully.

'If you handed the farm over to me – put it in my name – I could use it as collateral. For a loan. Or a mortgage.'

'It sounds like a lot of hard work.'

'I'm not afraid of hard work.'

Jamie tried not to sound tart, or imply that Jack was. But he persisted.

'It sounds like one of those ideas that are fantastic on

paper, but it could turn into a living nightmare. People are very hard to please, you know.'

'Can we at least think about it? Kif's put me in touch with someone who can give me some financial advice and work out the figures. I'm going to see him tomorrow.' She put her hand beseechingly on Jack's arm. 'I don't want to lose the farm, Dad. I really don't. And if this is the only way ...'

Jack smiled. 'Of course we can think about it, darling. Dreaming never hurt anybody. You go and sort the figures out and we'll have a look.'

Jamie couldn't help feeling that he was just playing along with her, and that he was being a tiny bit patronizing. But at least he hadn't said no. She shoved the fact that she'd already been to see Rod and told him the deal was off to the back of her mind. With any luck they wouldn't be in contact over the next few days, by which time she would have her business plan intact and a loan in place, and Jack wouldn't be able to argue.

And as she lay in bed that night, she fell asleep dreaming of her plans. She saw Bucklebury Farm restored to its former glory. She wanted to retain the arty, bohemian atmosphere that had been instilled by her mother, but was realistic enough to know that to satisfy today's customer one couldn't just rely on quirkiness, that a few mod cons would have to be installed to bring it from merely comfortable up to luxurious. Even impractical Jack had spotted that. They'd need central heating that worked, for a start. And big baths with huge taps that gushed scalding-hot water, deep carpets in the bedrooms, squashy chairs and sofas for guests to lounge in reading the novels that they'd been meaning to read for months. She'd cook them gargantuan breakfasts – thick bacon with proper fat that sizzled and didn't turn to water, freshly laid eggs and freshly picked mushrooms, fat sausages that burst their skins. Black pudding, spicy, groaty black pudding that would make men groan with pleasure and their wives frown disapprovingly. Home-made marmalade dark with bitter-sweet slices of Seville orange spread on to bread just out of the oven.

And for the children, a pair of fat Shetland ponies, chickens whose eggs they could help collect, perhaps a dear little goat. She could have a tree house built, and a Wendy house with proper curtains. As she finally drifted off, she smiled to realize that she'd already gone wildly over budget, but firmly convinced that Bucklebury Farm was going to be a huge success...

That evening, Bella didn't take the news about the deal on Bucklebury Farm being off very well at all. In fact, she became almost hysterical. Rod didn't quite understand her reaction.

'I thought you were happy at Owl's Nest? I thought you loved it here?'

'I do. But we've been here long enough. It's been two years since it was finished. We always said we'd move on. Onwards and upwards, that's what you said. Don't let the grass grow under your feet, you said. Move one rung up the property ladder every two years, you said.'

This was true. Rod could hear himself saying it as she spoke. When they'd converted Owl's Nest, they'd always agreed they would turn it round as soon as possible. It was perfect for a professional couple. The bedroom was in the gallery, with a spacious en suite. Downstairs was a kitchen-cum-living area – large and airy, admittedly, with room for a dining table and a three-piece suite. But apart from a laundry room and another small room where Rod kept the computer to do the books and Bella's leaflets and publicity for the dance school, there was no spare space. Any addition to the family would definitely necessitate a move.

'Something else will come up,' he murmured soothingly.

'Not something like Bucklebury Farm. You said it was a once in a lifetime opportunity. The only way we'd be able to afford a proper big family home without waiting another ten years.'

This was true as well. Rod sometimes wished he could keep his big mouth shut. But he'd been so excited by the plan. And if you couldn't share your plans with your own wife ... But by painting too rosy a picture, he'd also painted himself into a corner. It was going to be very difficult to sell any alternative to Bella. Once she'd set her mind on something ...

It was a bloody nuisance. The only silver lining in the cloud that Rod could see was that Bella's mother would be out of the equation. Pauline still helped at the dance school she'd founded, even though she'd handed it over to Bella and it no longer bore her name. She still taught the ballroom-dancing classes for the older generation, as she kept things at a more sedate pace and didn't cause a stir by exposing her midriff. Just after they were married, Bella and Rod had raised the money to allow Pauline to buy her council house – she'd got it for less than a hundred thousand, and it was worth nearer two at today's prices. The plan now was for her to sell the house and move into

Bucklebury Farm with them – they couldn't have pulled the deal off without her input. Rod had been wary of the idea, for although he was fond of Pauline she could be extremely bossy and opinionated. But as Bella pointed out, she would be a very useful asset if and when a baby came along – a built-in babysitter and childminder.

Bella was weeping bitterly.

'What are we going to do, Rod? What are we going to do?'

Rod knew that this was more than just about disappointment. This was about frustration, of hopes cruelly dashed, of trying and failing and not pointing the finger of blame. These bouts of uncontrolled sobbing were becoming a regular feature of their life; monthly, to be precise, every time Mother Nature taunted Bella with evidence that once again she wasn't pregnant. He did his best to console her, but it was very hard – not least because his own hopes had been cruelly dashed. She wasn't to know quite how desperate he was to become a father. He didn't want to put undue pressure on her, so he had to pretend to be resilient and optimistic. And each month he tried to make it up to her and take her mind off the ordeal; each month the consolation prize got more elaborate. He'd started with a voucher for a massage at a local beauty salon; last month's offering had been the Audi, even though he couldn't really afford it. The novelty had taken her mind off things for a while.

He looked round at everything they'd done; everything they'd achieved. They were both incredibly successful; they had a beautiful home. They had everything they wanted. Except what they really wanted.

Bella looked up. He felt relieved; she was wiping away

her tears and seemed to have pulled herself together. She took in a shuddering breath.

'Well, it makes one thing clear.'

'What's that?'

'We'll have to stop trying for a baby until everything's sorted out. I'm so completely stressed. I can't cope with this and trying to ... trying to—'

She dissolved into tears again. Rod was at her side in two bounds.

'No, sweetheart. Nothing's going to get in the way of that. I want you to stop worrying right now. Things will sort themselves out, I promise you. This is just a glitch.'

He pulled her to him as she nuzzled into his chest for comfort. She was so incredibly fragile. It was his duty to protect her. With a supreme effort of will, he managed to erase from his mind the fact that he'd thought of nothing but Jamie Wilding all afternoon. He buried his face in Bella's soft, silky hair, murmuring reassurance.

'We'll get Bucklebury Farm, I promise you.'

13

Strictly speaking, Zoe couldn't be described as beauti-ful. Her face was too round, her mouth was too wide and her eyes were too small. But she had a wonderful personality that brought all these imperfect features to life: a glow within her that lit up her smile and made her eyes sparkle, so although she wasn't technically beautiful, people often thought she was.

Most of the time, that is. Today, the light had definitely gone out; the fuse had blown, the bulb had gone. As she looked in the mirror, she thought with a heavy heart that she looked closer to forty than thirty. Her face was puffy and her eyes bloodshot. Her skin was sludgy and grey.

But that's what you got for falling asleep half-pissed in the afternoon.

When Christopher had told her at breakfast that Jamie was coming round for supper, Zoe had resolved to make a real effort for once and cook something nice. She really had. In fact, she'd phoned Natalie at eleven o'clock, to ask her what she should cook. Natalie was great at recipes that even Zoe could manage. She gave her instructions for something relatively uncomplicated involving chicken breasts and chestnut mushrooms and tinfoil that just got bunged in the oven and forgotten about.

'You'll be able to get all the ingredients in Tesco. Serve it with some buttery noodles and a green salad. Then go and pick some of that soft fruit you've been moaning about. Slosh a tub of crème fraîche over the top and a load of brown sugar and stick it under the grill for five minutes. It'll be scrummy, I promise.'

They'd gone on to talk about Natalie's birthday the day before yesterday. The girls had all missed Zoe like mad, apparently. Nat filled her in on all the gossip – one of their friends was plucking up the courage to go for a tummy tuck, and they debated the relative merits and dangers of plastic surgery. While they chatted, Zoe gravitated towards the fridge, the phone tucked between her shoulder and her ear. If she couldn't actually go for a girlie lunch, a chat on the phone and a glass of wine were second best. There was nothing wrong with that, surely? By the time she came off the phone, she felt depressed, so she topped herself up again, and sat down to watch telly just for ten minutes.

And now here she was, at ten past four, looking like shit with her head throbbing slightly from the three big glasses of wine she'd drunk. She only had twenty minutes to get to Twelvetrees to collect Hugo and Sebastian. And she hadn't been to Tesco. She couldn't go now; the boys absolutely loathed going round the supermarket and she didn't think it was fair to inflict it on them after a day at school. They needed to run round and let off a bit of steam.

She had a quick look in the cupboard for inspiration. Pasta and salad. Even she couldn't screw that up. And she'd get the boys to go and pick some of those sodding raspberries from the garden for pudding. She could get cream and some fresh Parmesan from the post office. Surely that would do for what was only a casual supper? She didn't know why she was putting herself under pressure.

She was trying to prove herself, that's why, a little voice told her. The truth was, Zoe had always felt a bit ... well, threatened by Jamie. It wasn't that she didn't like her. She did, very much. It was just that she felt that Jamie was everything Christopher secretly wanted *her* to be. And they shared so much of their past. They were comfy with each other; each fitted the other like a pair of old slippers. They had no need to pretend. Zoe felt as if Christopher was his true self when Jamie was around.

And Jamie made Zoe feel shallow and superficial. She was the sort of girl who wasn't all that bothered about clothes and make-up. Zoe couldn't imagine her hyperventilating in LK Bennett or Whistles, or going for a quick fix in Space.NK. No, she was the sort of girl who would nonchalantly pull on whatever was at the front of her wardrobe and look irritatingly fantastic in it.

Zoe remembered her coming to Christopher's birthday barbecue at Elmdon Road a couple of years ago. Jamie had worn jeans, flip-flops – not designer ones, but the kind your mum bought you from Woolworths when you were a kid – and a little white vest top that made it screamingly obvious she had no bra on underneath. Every man in the room had been dribbling, while every other woman spat tacks – they'd all gone to vast expense to make themselves look understated and casual. Sixty quid Zoe had paid for *her* flip-flops, and the bloody flower that had made them that price had fallen off after she'd worn them twice. But the men had flocked round Jamie like bees round a honeypot.

Yes, Jamie definitely had a way of making her realize what a silly, superficial cow she was. Not that she meant to, Zoe was sure of that. In fact, she always admired what Zoe was wearing and was utterly genuine, bemoaning the fact that she was unadventurous when it came to clothes, never had the time to go shopping and didn't really have anywhere to wear nice things even if she bought them. Which just made Zoe feel even more like a spoilt lazy bitch.

Zoe imagined Jamie in her position. She would cherish Lydbrook as it was; she wouldn't wander round longing for a lilac Aga – she'd be happy with the nasty blue one. She would no doubt be incredibly supportive of Christopher, instead of moaning at him as soon as he walked in through the door of an evening. She wouldn't be impatient with Rosemary – she'd probably go for long walks with her and her horrible, dribbly dogs. She would have picked all the runner beans by now, sliced them up and blanched them and put them in the freezer. She'd take homemade cakes to Hamilton and go and read to him three times a week. Zoe had been very fond of Hamilton, but she couldn't bring herself to go and visit him. The home depressed her. The other inmates terrified her. The nurses intimidated her. A couple of times she'd lied to Christopher and said she'd been – after all, Hamilton was hardly likely to contradict her. Anyway, Zoe reasoned, Christopher felt less guilty if he thought someone had been in to see his father. He didn't get the chance to go as often as he felt he should, and his sisters, Kate and

Emma, lived too far away to visit regularly. So a little white lie on her part made everyone feel better.

Zoe picked up her car keys with a heavy heart. She was a lousy, rotten wife. Why couldn't she just snap out of it and enjoy what she'd got? Why did that big, black cloud of negativity follow her round, making her hate everyone and everything – not least herself? And why was Christopher so incredibly patient with her, when clearly what she needed was a good slap?

Sometimes, she longed for her friends from London to come up, just so they could sympathize with her plight. She remembered when she'd left, how they'd all promised to come for the weekend as soon as she was settled. But none of them had. Nobody wanted to pile into the car on a Friday evening and battle with the London traffic, then have a four-hour journey with the kids screaming in the back, only to repeat the exercise in reverse after lunch on Sunday. In some ways, Zoe was grateful that they hadn't fulfilled their promises. She hadn't been able to admit to any of them quite how awful it was; she went along with their impression that she was living in some *Homes & Gardens* heaven. She didn't want to disillusion them. She couldn't bear the thought of them all sitting round in the Bluebird Café the following week, saying 'Poor, poor Zoe…'

Jamie bounded in through the front door of Lydbrook at seven o'clock that evening, just as she always had as a child, and then stopped short in the hallway. Perhaps she shouldn't be so familiar now? Things had changed. She knew Kif wouldn't mind her barging in like this, but Zoe might have other ideas, and she was the mistress of the house now. It probably wasn't the done thing in London, to wander into someone's house without knocking. Not that you'd be able to – Jamie remembered the armoury of Yale locks and bolts and chains on Kif's house in Shepherd's Bush. She was about to backtrack and knock on the door when she realized she'd been spotted. There was a figure at the bottom of the stairs. A ghostly, pale figure that it took Jamie several seconds to recognize.

'Rosemary?'

Rosemary was standing rooted to the spot, clutching a plate. On it was a rather grey slice of dried meat and a spoonful of coleslaw.

'Jamie.' She gave a weary smile. 'I heard you were coming. I was just going upstairs for my supper ...'

'Aren't you going to join us?' Jamie stepped closer. Was it her imagination or did Rosemary seem to recoil?

'No. No, no. I'll let you young ones have fun. I'm not very good company these days, I'm afraid.'

Rosemary was already halfway up the stairs.

'Wait!'

Rosemary halted, without turning round.

'I'm so sorry about Hamilton,' said Jamie. 'I really am. It must be awful for you.'

Rosemary said nothing for a moment, just stared down at her unappetizing plate of food.

'Yes, it is.'

And before Jamie could commiserate any further, she'd disappeared up the stairs.

Jamie stood in the hallway, rather puzzled and unsure what to do. That was a very strange reception indeed. Why on earth had Rosemary bolted like that? She'd seemed almost eager to get away from her. Perhaps, because it was inevitable that the conversation would turn to Hamilton, Rosemary found it too painful and wanted to avoid sympathy and platitudes. Jamie knew from experience how sometimes you desperately wanted people to talk about anything but your own problems. Perhaps she should have gone bowling cheerfully up to her and told her how lovely the garden was looking, or asked her for a recipe for tomato chutney? She remembered only too well seeing people after Louisa had died, steeling herself for the inevitable commiseration, wishing that someone would come up and say something completely frivolous, so she could have a normal conversation instead of being reminded of the hideous truth …

And Rosemary had always been rather reticent. She'd never been a social animal like Hamilton; she'd always kept herself to herself. Jamie remembered her as a kindly, shadowy figure hovering in the background. Louisa had once rather cruelly referred to her as a bit of a drip, and said she didn't know why on earth Hamilton had married her. But then Jamie had no doubt that Rosemary was just the sort of wife an energetic, robust and sociable creature like Hamilton needed. Someone to run the house, look after the children and clean his hunting boots. That didn't make him a chauvinist; he was an English country gent and he'd been brought up to expect that sort of treatment. And Rosemary had always seemed quite happy with her role. She wasn't downtrodden by any means. She in turn was an English country gentlewoman, with her dogs and her garden to keep her amused, her faded prettiness, her pink cheeks from spending so much time outside, her Liberty lawn blouses and needlecord skirts and sensible shoes.

When Kif's sisters, Kate and Emma, came over to play at Bucklebury, they always wanted to sneak into Louisa's dressing room. This was a tiny little boxroom opposite the master bedroom – an enormous mahogany wardrobe took up most of it, and it was stuffed with Louisa's clothes: racks of silk and lace and chiffon. The floor of the wardrobe was covered in shoes, the top of it in hats and handbags. Everything was carelessly flung back after whatever social occasion it had been aired at – a gallery opening, Ladies Day at the races, a hunt ball. To a trio of teenage girls it was dressing-up heaven. They burrowed in her make-up and perfume, draped themselves in her jewellery, tried on the dizzyingly high heels and paraded around in outfits that came in every colour of the rainbow.

'Mum's only got powder and one lipstick that she wears to church. And I know she didn't buy that. Someone left it behind in the bathroom once when they came to stay.' Emma sounded rather disgusted as she sat at Louisa's dressing table underneath the window, slapping on her Elizabeth Arden blusher. They were deeply envious that Jamie could borrow whatever she wanted.

'God, imagine wanting to borrow any of Mum's clothes.' Kate snorted with laughter at the thought. 'Only if you wanted to dress up as Worzel Gummidge.'

'That's unkind,' Jamie had protested.

'The trouble with Mum is she just doesn't care what she looks like. All she cares about is the dogs,' pronounced Emma.

'And you. She cares about you.' Jamie was stout in her defence of Rosemary. Kate and Emma obviously didn't appreciate her one bit.

Thinking about it now, Jamie wondered if Rosemary

had been as happy with her lot as they'd all assumed. Sometimes, when there'd been a huge crowd round the dinner table at Bucklebury, all roaring with laughter and knocking back the booze as if it was a competition, she'd glimpsed Rosemary looking rather pained. She didn't really drink, and no doubt it was hard to find the conversation as uproariously funny as everyone else, as it deteriorated into the sort of smut and double entendre only the inebriated found amusing.

One particular night, when Jamie was about thirteen, she remembered Louisa sneaking into her bedroom, thinking she was asleep, and taking one of her games from on top of the wardrobe. Mystified, Jamie had crept down the stairs after her.

Louisa was standing triumphantly in the dining-room doorway.

'Right, everybody. Let's play Strip Twister,' Louisa had said, her eyes sparkling with mischief. Rosemary had panicked, and stood up sharply, making her excuses, trying to persuade Hamilton to come with her. He had refused, and Jamie remembered Rosemary scuttling off into the night, clearly terrified, as Hamilton gamely seized the dice. Jamie had shot back up to her bedroom before she was discovered.

'Jamie, hi!' Zoe came bounding down the stairs looking flustered, a tea towel over one shoulder. 'I've just been putting the boys to bed so we can have supper in peace and quiet.'

The two girls embraced in the hallway.

'I just walked in – sorry, I should have knocked.' Jamie thought she should apologize.

'Don't be silly.' Come and have a glass of wine. Christopher phoned five minutes ago. He's on his way.'

'Actually, I wondered if I could go and see the boys? I won't get them overexcited, I promise.' Jamie held up a Woolworths bag. 'I got them something hideous and plastic each – I hope you don't mind.'

'No – they'll love it. I don't have a problem with hideous and plastic.' Zoe grinned. 'Their room's upstairs; first on the—'

'Kif's old room. Don't worry – I know.' Jamie ran lightly up the stairs.

Zoe watched her. And couldn't help wondering what exactly they'd got up to in Kif's old room, all those years ago.

Half an hour later, Christopher had arrived home, and they all went out on to the terrace to enjoy the last of the evening sun. Christopher had mowed the lawn the evening before: the soft green velvet stripes led down to the white metal railings of the fence that separated the garden from the banks of the river, which could just be heard burbling in the distance. Beyond that lay undulating farmland punctuated by huge oaks.

'I'd forgotten how lovely it was here,' said Jamie. 'It must be heaven after London.'

'Apart from the fact that it takes three bloody hours to mow the lawn,' agreed Christopher. Zoe said nothing; just helped herself to a Pringle from the bowl she'd put on the wrought-iron table. She remembered she'd been going to buy olives and dips. Maybe it was easier not to make resolutions. That way you couldn't break them. It was like going on a diet. The minute you decided you were on one, you started bingeing. Oh well, at least she'd put them in a bowl – she usually scoffed them straight from the cardboard tube.

Christopher picked up the bottle of Oyster Bay that was sitting in its chiller pouch.

'Top-up, anyone?'

Jamie shook her head; she'd barely touched hers. Zoe poked her empty glass across the table towards Christopher. She thought she detected the tiniest flicker of disapproval before he poured her a miserly third of a glass, then filled his own three-quarters full.

'So – how did it go with Edward?' he asked Jamie.

'He was fantastic. Incredibly helpful,' she replied.

'I told you he was a good bloke.'

'He couldn't have done more for me. I was in there nearly two hours.'

'And?'

'It doesn't look too promising.' Jamie made a face. 'I'd worked out some rough figures the night before, but being a complete novice I'd left out all sorts of things. Like the interest on the repayments. And public liability insurance. Which made me look a bit of a fool.'

'You've got to start somewhere. Edward would know that. He's done enough start-ups to know not everyone's John Harvey-Jones.'

'Oh yes – he was very sweet about it. Not at all patronizing. Anyway, he helped me work out some more realistic sums. Then came the crunch. How much capital we were going to need. And whether they'd give it to us.'

Jamie took a gulp of wine.

'The problem is, neither Dad nor I have any liquid assets. I've got a couple of grand left from my savings.

Dad's got bugger all, as far as I know. Yes, in theory, we can borrow against Bucklebury, but we need to prove we've got the means to pay it back. The figures Edward and I worked out don't show a healthy return for at least five years, and that's presuming the business is a success. Which makes any loan a huge risk, because not only do we not have any cash, we don't have any experience, or track record, to give them confidence in our ability to run a successful business.'

'Oh dear.'

'Very oh dear,' agreed Jamie. 'And I've been dossing about for nearly a year, not earning any money, which doesn't look good. And the business isn't related to what I was doing before that, even though I was earning a good salary. So I'm not a good risk. And as we know, Dad's business ventures ... well, like they say, let's not even go there. In fact, I left him out of the picture altogether. I didn't want anyone digging about in his past.'

'So what was the bottom line?'

'The bottom line is I bought two lottery tickets on the way over here. I think I've got more chance of hitting the jackpot than getting the money we need out of the bank.'

'Jamie, I'm sorry. I feel guilty about coming up with the idea in the first place.'

'Don't be daft. You've got to have a go, haven't you?'

'So what *are* you going to do?'

'Edward did suggest another of his clients might be interested in investing. Though I don't really want anyone else involved – I think that's dangerous.'

'I agree. Keep it clean and on your terms.'

'Meanwhile, I'm going to rack my brains. And keep my fingers crossed for the bonus ball ...'

Zoe had finished her miserly top-up. She didn't want to attract attention by asking for more. She stood up, the legs of her chair scraping along the stone terrace and setting her teeth on edge.

'I'm going to go and check on supper.'

'Lovely,' said Christopher, smiling at her.

I doubt it, thought Zoe, going straight into the kitchen and pouring herself a glass of the Merlot Christopher had opened and left to warm on the Aga. At least she didn't have Rosemary hovering around trying to be helpful, offering to go and snip fresh parsley out of the garden. She had taken a plate up to her room earlier, said she had one of her heads. Zoe poked at the swirling pan full of fusilli with a fork, managed to extricate one, and put it in her mouth to see if it was done.

'Fuck!' It was boiling hot. She spat it back on to the worktop, but too late – she'd scalded her mouth. She felt hot tears prick the backs of her eyes as she took two jars of tomato and basil sauce out of the cupboard. Thank God for Loyd Grossman.

She humped the saucepan over to the sink and drained its contents into the colander. It was definitely done, if not overdone. She'd meant to try and keep it al dente, like you were supposed to, but she'd lost concentration for a minute. Now it was soggy and flabby and the fusilli were starting to unravel. She slopped it back into the pan and took it back over to the Aga, not noticing through the clouds of steam that Soot and Honey had parked themselves in the middle of the kitchen floor.

Zoe went flying. As did the pan of pasta, much to the delight of Soot and Honey. A minute later, Jamie and Christopher came in from the garden to find her on her hands and knees, desperately trying to scoop the remains of the fusilli back into the saucepan, hoping no one would notice the grit and the dog hairs, while the dogs gobbled frantically.

'It's OK, it's under control,' said Zoe desperately. 'Fuck off, Soot.'

Christopher looked alarmed. 'We can't eat that!'

Why did they have to have come in? They'd never have noticed.

'There's nothing else!'

'There must be.'

'Well, there isn't.'

Christopher tried to remain robust and cheerful. He didn't want to come across as some chauvinistic, tight-lipped husband who tut-tutted at his wife's inadequacies. He peered into the fridge optimistically. A lamb bone, two roast potatoes and three tubs of Munch Bunch fromage frais.

'I was going to do a big shop tomorrow,' Zoe fibbed.

'Eggs. You must have eggs. Or baked beans? I'm not fussy,' Jamie suggested helpfully.

There was a stony silence. Christopher smiled.

'We'll get a take-away. I'll drive back into Ludlow.'

'They'll be hours. It'll take hours!'

'No, it won't. Not if we phone ahead.'

Zoe plonked herself down at the kitchen table. 'I'm useless. I'm so fucking useless.'

'No, you're not. It was an accident,' said Jamie soothingly. 'Look – why don't I nip home? I know we've got eggs. We can do omelettes.'

Jamie came back ten minutes later with big, fat, free-range eggs, a lump of Gruyère and a fistful of fresh herbs she'd picked from the garden. Zoe sat slurping miserably at her Merlot, watching her produce three fluffy omelettes that were just the right side of gooey.

Christopher managed to temper his appreciation so that Zoe wouldn't feel too bad – it was the kiss of death to wax lyrical about another woman's cooking, especially when it was performed in your own kitchen.

But when he saw Jamie out later, he thanked her profusely. She waved away his thanks.

'She's not very happy, is she?'

'No. But I don't know what to do. She absolutely loathes it here.'

'She's not the Zoe I remember.'

'She's like a fish out of water.'

Jamie screwed up her face in puzzlement.

'I don't understand,' she said. 'Most people would give their eye teeth to live somewhere like Lydbrook. It's idyllic.'

'Well, apparently not.'

Jamie was surprised to hear the normally good-natured Christopher apparently running out of patience. He looked at her with something that bordered on despair.

'I don't know what to do. I mean, you can't help some-one who won't help themselves, can you?'

'Maybe she's depressed?'

'What the hell has she got to be depressed about? I mean, look at you. You've got serious problems, but you manage not to collapse on the floor in a snivelling, drunken heap.'

'I'm not as brave as you might think.' Jamie remembered the state she had got herself into at Owl's Nest the day before. 'You just need to be patient.'

Patient, thought Christopher glumly. Frankly, he thought he'd been patient long enough.

That night, Rod and Bella tried to make love again, just in case there was still a fertile egg lurking in her tubes. But this time Rod found himself totally incapable – his penis was as soft and squashy as a marshmallow, stubbornly refusing to respond, no matter how Bella coaxed and cajoled. They went to sleep without discussing it, disconcerted by this latest spanner in the works.

Later, Rod woke to find Bella lying on her back, gazing at the ceiling, and he tried to apologize.

'I'm sorry. I don't know what's the matter with me. It's probably stress; worrying over Bucklebury Farm.'

Bella turned to face him. He could see her cleavage, the dark of her nipples peeping over the top of her nightdress. But still nothing doing... She was talking to him, her tone comforting.

'Don't worry, baby. Maybe it's for the best. Maybe we should just forget everything for a couple of months. Enjoy what's left of the summer. Have some fun. I mean, it's all become a bit of a chore, hasn't it?'

She hugged him reassuringly and Rod smiled at her gratefully. Ten minutes later she was asleep, leaving him gazing at the ceiling, wide awake, wondering why his prick of a prick had decided to betray him, when it had been so perky and receptive all of his life. But then it seemed as if everything was going pear-shaped at the moment. Bucklebury Farm, for a start. It was all very well Bella telling him not to worry, but she obviously didn't realize quite how much the project meant to him.

Ever since he'd struck the deal with Jack Wilding, he'd

spent days and nights fantasizing about what he was going to do there. Starting with the kitchen, of course, as that could double as a showroom – a living, breathing example of his work that he could show to prospective customers, instead of them flipping through his album of Polaroids. He wanted to do something incredibly modern in contrast to the beams and flagstones; but not one of the clinical, abattoir-like designs that seemed to be in fashion. Something with curves, rounded edges and perhaps warm, pink marble work surfaces; something with impact yet at the same time warm and welcoming, as every heart of the home should be. Then he would move on to the bedrooms at the very top of the house. He planned to do them out like a ship's cabin – high bunk beds with lots of cunning drawers and cupboards underneath where children could store all their treasures. Then in the garden, a wooden pirate ship where they could sail away on their own private adventures... The drawing table in his workshop was covered in doodles and daydreams. He was, he knew, obsessed with creating the perfect family home, an environment where life was idyllic, the stuff of storybooks, a Sunday supplement fantasy. For all Rod wanted, all he'd ever really wanted, was a family of his own...

He'd got it all worked out. Three children was the perfect number. He'd like more, but that was unrealistic. Rod knew from experience that in very large families you had to stand on your own two feet, not expect any mollycoddling. He wanted to be able to give his own kids equal attention. No one had ever sat down and explained the mysteries of where the extra ten actually came from in subtraction, or tested him on his spellings, or stuck his paintings up on the kitchen wall. He didn't blame his parents: they had a tough life, his father eking out a living from the land, Nolly holding down two or three jobs for extra cash to feed all the mouths. They simply didn't have time to harbour aspirations for their children, or to put in the effort that would enable them to better themselves. So Rod had determined to give his own children everything he had missed, but also everything he had gained from being in a warm, noisy family who stuck together and looked out for each other.

He'd always known he'd married Bella on the rebound. After Jamie had vanished, Rod had become a recluse for about six months. It had coincided with the time Lady Pamela had commissioned him to build her kitchen, so he had gratefully buried himself in his work. Eventually, when it became clear that Jamie wasn't going to make a miraculous reappearance, or even contact him to explain, his brothers had coaxed him out and his social life had revived. He'd spent a few years having casual flings, never giving any woman the full benefit of his charms, expecting nothing from them and giving little in return. It was a chauvinistic, hedonistic lifestyle that went against the grain because, underneath it all, Rod was monogamous through and through. All the while, he was keeping his eyes peeled for Miss Right, the one he could marry and fulfil his dreams with.

When he'd met Bella, she had seemed like the one. He admired her for her work; she was incredibly dedicated to the dance school. But then, he was married to his work too. He could lose hours in his workshop, absorbed in crafting the perfect join. But because of their dedication to their individual careers, they understood each other perfectly – she didn't moan when he was so absorbed in a project that he didn't get home till gone midnight; he didn't complain when she was wrapped up in ballet exams or a show that meant constant rehearsal. Plus she was beautiful and sexy. Rod wouldn't have been human if he hadn't enjoyed the envious glances other men gave him when they were out together. Bella had the body of a goddess, and dressed it to suit, without ever looking tarty or tacky. And the sex had always been pretty amazing – until recent events and pressures had taken over, that is.

So Rod had gone to the altar quite happy that he had made the right choice. But he sometimes felt that there was something missing. It was almost as if they were both operating on automatic pilot, mannequins living out an idyllic existence, perfect specimens in a perfect house with perfect careers. They had all the material ticks in all the boxes. But Rod knew he was deceiving himself, because although he loved Bella, worshipped at the temple that was her body, enjoyed her company, respected her opinion – all the things that were necessary in a successful marriage – he knew she didn't set his heart alight. He had hoped that perhaps children would bring that spark, that when they held a tiny being they'd created together, they too would bond, but now that hope was becoming more and more elusive, and their desperate efforts to procreate were gradually driving them apart. And deep down, he suspected that the spark he was yearning for couldn't be manufactured. It was something that came naturally and spontaneously; an ethereal tingle whose ingredients couldn't be pinned down. But when they were there, you knew about it.

He knew that, because he'd had it with Jamie. That

wonderful, floating feeling that was comfort and security and togetherness, together with a special glow that made you feel warm inside whenever you thought about the other person. He'd felt so sure it was reciprocated. But to this day, he didn't understand why Jamie had fled without a word. Surely it didn't get better than what they'd had? What was there to run away from?

When he'd seen Jamie sobbing the day before, all the feelings he'd been repressing for so long had come flooding back. When Bella had cried over the loss of Bucklebury Farm, he'd comforted her, but her angst hadn't hit him in the core of his belly. He hadn't had an overwhelming urge to make things right for her. He'd reassured her out of duty, not passion. But Jamie: he'd go to the ends of the earth to make things right for her, even now. He'd wanted to scoop her up, make it better, make her smile – never mind that she'd come barging into his home with all guns blazing.

As he lay there reliving their confrontation, he wondered if the real reason he'd tried to buy Bucklebury Farm was because he knew, eventually, Jamie would find out what he was trying to do, and would do everything in her power to stop him. Was it his twisted way of bringing her back into his life? Because if so, he'd succeeded.

Dawn came, and Rod eventually fell into a troubled sleep. There were so many problems turning over in his mind that he didn't know which to address, especially as he knew there was bugger all he could do about any of them.

Zoe woke at four in the morning with a pounding head and a raging thirst, the memory of last night's disaster needling at her conscience. If they'd been in London, if they'd been in Shepherd's Bush, they could have phoned Zaffran's and within twenty minutes the little waiter would have been at the door with steaming foil cartons full of tandoori chicken masala and still-warm poppadoms.

But they weren't. And she'd shown herself up in front of Jamie, who'd been so nice and sympathetic about the whole thing that she couldn't hate her. And Christopher had been upset. He hadn't said anything, because he was so spectacularly non-confrontational, but she could see it in his face, and the way he lay in bed that night. She felt ashamed, like a badly behaved little girl who'd let her parents down in front of a special visitor. She hated herself. Why on earth couldn't she have kept it together?

The whole time Jamie had been there, Zoe had felt like a gooseberry. She and Christopher had chattered on about their houses as though they were people, until Zoe almost expected Lydbrook and Bucklebury to take on human form and join them for supper. She found it all slightly nauseating and sentimental. But then, she'd been brought up in a modern four-bedroomed detached on the outskirts of Guildford – perfectly pleasant, but not something to get attached to. Perhaps if she'd had the legacy of a country pile, she'd feel the same way.

And the way Jamie called Christopher 'Kif' – it was so intimate, so excluding, somehow. It made Zoe feel as if she didn't know her own husband. It smacked of childhood secrets and adventures, teenage escapades that she hadn't been a part of. Even though it was she who was married to Christopher, she who shared his bed and had borne his children, she felt as if Jamie was more privy to the real him.

And she began to wonder about Christopher's feelings for Jamie. When she'd waltzed back in with that clutch of farm-fresh eggs and done her domestic goddess bit, Zoe hadn't missed the admiration in his eyes. She could almost hear him thinking, 'Why couldn't Zoe do that?'

Feeling thoroughly sorry for herself, Zoe rolled out of bed, padded down to the kitchen and poured herself a glass of water from the tap. Another day, another hangover. Hey-ho. At least it was Saturday. She could lie in bed all morning and sleep it off. Christopher could get up and give the boys breakfast before he went to work.

14

Jamie woke up the next morning determined to forget all her troubles for the rest of the weekend. After all, sometimes inspiration struck when you weren't thinking. And there was certainly no point in trying to have a sensible conversation with Jack today. He and Olivier were as excited as two small boys about today's hill climb. They'd spent the evening before in the garage, fine-tuning – they were still in there fettling when Jamie had got home from Lydbrook. And to her surprise, they were both up by half past six. By the time she came down to the kitchen at seven, they were in the yard loading the Bugatti on to a rusty old trailer that looked as if it defied every safety regulation in the book. They'd daubed the licence number of the Land Rover on to a bit of old cardboard and tied it on with some baler twine.

'You'll get stopped by the police,' warned Jamie, but they seemed unperturbed.

'We'd better be off,' said Jack, looking anxiously at his watch and calculating the day's timetable backwards. 'Scrutineering starts at ten.'

'Are you coming with us?' Olivier asked Jamie.

'I think I'll follow in my car. Have a leisurely breakfast

and not take my life into my hands,' said Jamie, looking dubiously at the towbar.

A familiar fanfare heralded Lettice's arrival. The Bentley bounced into the stable yard and out she popped, clearly as excited at the prospect of the day ahead as Jack and Olivier.

'I've done us a picnic,' she yodelled. 'Man's food – game pie, cold sausages and piccalilli. Plenty of protein to help you concentrate.' She squeezed Olivier's upper arm, then turned to Jamie. 'You can come with me, darling. We'll travel in style – not in that old bone-shaker.'

Jamie was about to protest. The last thing she wanted was to drive to Prescott with Lettice wittering in her ear. She wanted some time alone, to think. But she knew there was no point in refusing. Lettice wasn't one to take no for an answer. And half an hour later, she was glad she had capitulated. The Bentley was incredibly comfortable, gliding smoothly through the Shropshire lanes and over the hills towards Hereford, then down towards Gloucestershire. As the day's sun became gently warmer, Jamie found her eyes closing and consciousness gradually slipping away. She hadn't slept well the night before – spreadsheets and business plans and proposals had been whirling round in her head, and she was determined to put them to the back of her mind. And in a strange way she was looking forward to today – the others' excitement had been infectious, and she thought it would be churlish not to join in the fun.

Rod woke up with a heavy heart when the alarm went off, convinced he had only just dropped off to sleep. Bella bounced out of bed, seemingly refreshed and no longer under the cloud of last night's fruitless encounter. Dressed in a baby-blue towelling tracksuit, smelling of zingy shower gel, she brought Rod a cup of tea and a toasted muffin in bed and was out of the house by half past eight – Saturday was her busiest day, with her first ballet class starting at nine.

Rod sipped his tea gloomily and decided to go into the workshop. It would take his mind off things, and he had some designs to finish off for a prospective client. He took the Audi, not caring if it elicited ridicule from his siblings. It was a beautiful day, and he whizzed through the lanes with the top down, trying hard to feel cheered by his surroundings.

By nine-thirty, he could barely see or breathe. Something blossomed at this time of year that made Rod's nose stream and his eyes run incessantly. It made his life a misery; made work almost impossible. There was nothing for it but serious antihistamines: he phoned up the doctor to get a repeat prescription. They would make him dopey and drowsy, but at least he'd be able to see.

He drove to the surgery, this time with the roof up to shield himself from the pollen that was becoming more intense as the day became warmer. Inside, he joined the queue and was gratified to see that there were two other sufferers sniffing and dabbing their noses with their handkerchiefs. He wasn't the only one debilitated by the time of year. The receptionist riffled through the box and plucked out his prescription. Her coral-tipped nails hovered over the one behind his.

'There's one here for your wife as well. You might as well take it.'

She handed it over to him with a smile, not realizing that she was passing him an unexploded bomb.

He didn't bother to look at Bella's prescription until he joined the queue in the chemist. He was about to sign on the line, to say he was the patient's representative, when he read '6 x Ovranette'. For a moment he didn't register. He thought perhaps it was some exotic prenatal concoction containing vitamins and folic acid. Then the penny dropped. He knew the name rang a bell. He'd seen the pink boxes on her bedside table when they'd first got together.

The contraceptive pill. Six months' worth of anti-baby tablets.

The hill climb at Prescott, in its glorious Cotswold setting, was renowned as a testing course for even the most experienced drivers, and today's historic meeting was an annual event that drew enthusiasts from far and wide. The sky was a dazzling Wedgwood blue with only the occasional fluffy cloud providing respite from the glorious sunshine. The track itself was only visible to the initiated, cutting a swathe through the verdant greenery on the hillside, a tortuous corkscrew of tarmac that from a distance seemed benign, but was undeniably demanding.

Spectators and entrants alike gathered in an orchard at the foot of the hill. The competitors' cars were lined up in neat rows, each with their own numbered space where they prepared their vehicles, refuelled and waited for their class to begin. The atmosphere, thought Jamie, was garden party meets *Wacky Races*. It was definitely a social occasion – most people seemed to know each other – but there was a buzz of excitement in the air that only the promise of competition can bring.

The cars, even to a girl whose only interest in vehicles was that they got her from A to B, were incredible – stylish, glamorous, sleek objects of beauty. And, Jamie had to admit, a lot of the drivers were worth admiring as well. A young woman in search of a husband could do worse than hang out here, she mused to herself. It undoubtedly wasn't a poor man's sport, though nobody was here to show off their wealth. It just went without saying. There was a good broad section of people: some inherited wealth, obviously, drivers whose cars had been handed down to them through the family. And a generous sprinkling of new money: it was an ideal sport for the entrepreneur looking for a novel way to spend his hard-earned cash and get his thrills. Then there were the enthusiasts, those who were simply mad about the sport, who probably worked hard in order to play hard, spent all their spare cash on their hobby and no doubt went without holidays and other luxuries in order to pursue it.

She wasn't quite sure which category Jack and Olivier fell into. Just plain obsessed, she thought. They were checking over the car meticulously now, making sure it hadn't sustained any damage during the journey. Olivier was striding around masterfully in a pair of Jack's faded and patched old overalls, oblivious to the admiring glances he was getting from the other drivers' wives and girlfriends, rebuffing Lettice's offers of refreshment, totally focused on his task. Jamie smiled to herself, thinking that whoever ended up marrying Olivier would have to be an absolute paragon.

She decided to go off and explore her surroundings.

The atmosphere was intoxicating, even for someone who wasn't an enthusiast. The noise and the smell; the heat and the sense of expectation; the rivalry mixed with camaraderie – for this was a sport fuelled by passion, a passion which was often passed down through generations. She wandered through the paddock, admiring the different marques of car whose names conjured up another era: Bentley and Lagonda, Frazer Nash, Morgan, Riley. Each marque had its own following, with the owners believing their chosen vehicle had superiority over the rest, but it was a healthy competitiveness. Even the colours of the cars seemed exotic and enticing: British racing green, French blue, Bordeaux red, Royal ivory. And then there were the specials: the zany little cars that were designed specifically to conquer the hill, as light and as powerful as possible, some of them looking straight out of *Mad Max*, with nicknames like The Hornet and The Wasp.

Another Bugatti, similar to Jack and Olivier's, was parked up at the end of the paddock, and Jamie was interested to see a girl considerably younger than herself leaning against the bonnet. She was wearing regulation overalls, which highlighted the fact that her legs were enviably long. Her hair was tied up in a high ponytail, and her eyes were hidden behind a pair of Ray-Ban aviator sunglasses. She looked like a model on a fashion shoot. But then she undid the leather strap on the bonnet of the car she was posing next to, lifting the flap to expose the engine underneath, and began to inspect the interior with something resembling expertise. Jamie watched, fascinated, as she actually got her hands dirty adjusting something, then wiped them on an oily bit of rag before closing up the engine again in apparent satisfaction. She really looked as if she knew what she was doing. A man – her father? – brought over a cup of coffee for her, and they had an animated conversation. Jamie was intrigued, and wondered what had attracted the girl to the sport. No doubt it was the perverse thrill of being female in what was undoubtedly a fairly male preserve. She ran her eye down the list of competitors in the programme, and decided by process of elimination that she must be Claudia Sedgeley.

Claudia was feeling most peculiar. She'd had the feeling before, when she'd raced at Donington Park in April. Then again at the vintage meeting at Silverstone. And it wasn't the imminent hill climb that was making her feel like this.

She remembered seeing Madonna interviewed once. She'd been asked how she'd felt when she'd first seen Guy Ritchie, and she said he made her insides feel squishy. At the time, Claudia hadn't a clue what she meant. But the first time she saw Olivier Templeton standing by his car in the paddock, chatting to the scrutineer and running his hand absent-mindedly through his hair, Claudia's insides had dissolved and at that moment she knew, absolutely, what Madonna had meant.

Until then, Claudia's opinion of men had been that, on the whole, they weren't worth bothering about. They were always trying to control her, clearly threatened by her independent spirit. It was so easy to wind them up and make them insecure, and the moment she sensed their anxiety she lost all respect. Didn't they realize that to tame her they had to loosen the leash, not tighten it? The only person in the world who seemed to understand how she worked was her dad. And she certainly wasn't looking for a replacement father figure. She didn't need another Ray. She needed someone who excited her, intrigued her, and presented her with a challenge. Someone unpredictable. Perhaps a little bit dangerous.

Most of the men she'd been out with were older than she was, because she had expensive tastes. And she liked to learn from their experience. A lot of them were successful entrepreneurs and businessmen who'd made their money on the back of Britain's booming second city. They were men to whom appearance was everything. They dressed in tailored suits, teamed with slightly quirky shirts or ties or shoes to show their individuality. Claudia knew that she was just another accessory to most of them – a good-looking bird to go with the prestige motor and the penthouse. They took her out to the myriad restaurants that had opened up in Birmingham: once known only for its balti houses, it was now brimming with chic, modernist eateries where people went to see and be seen – Zinc, Denial, The Living Room, Mal Maison. While Claudia toyed with a Thai fish cake or monkfish tail, her suitors loved talking about themselves and what they'd done, and Claudia paid very close attention to the details, not remotely bored. It was, after all, far better to learn from other people's mistakes than your own. Besides, young men of her own age bored her. They talked about football, then got drunk and wanted sex, at which they were usually pretty abysmal. The older men were a little bit wiser, and didn't forget that they were more likely to get a repeat performance if they satisfied her as well as themselves. But so far, Claudia hadn't met anyone that made her pulse race or her heart beat faster. They were all carbon copies of each other, with the same aspirations and the same insecurities. They might all walk and talk tough but, underneath, their egos were pathetically fragile. It amused her to undermine them, to string them along then drop them like hot potatoes for no apparent reason.

But as soon as she'd clapped eyes on Olivier Templeton, she knew he was the one. The one she didn't know how to handle. The one whose rulebook she couldn't follow. She'd always known that the man for her would be a wild card, a renegade, a maverick, and Olivier was certainly that. She couldn't pigeonhole him for the life of her. When she'd watched him from afar at the first meeting of the season, driving his Bugatti into the paddock, one hand on the wheel, his streaky blond locks tousled by the April breeze, she could easily have dismissed him as just another trust-fund poseur trashing expensive cars for thrills. But something about his lack of self-consciousness told her that here was something different.

Olivier intrigued her. He kept himself to himself, but he wasn't aloof – he treated everyone, including her, with the same measured friendliness. She hadn't yet been able to find a way of breaking down the barrier. Over the past few meetings, they had become natural rivals. Each new to the game, with the same make and model of car, it was inevitable that they would attract attention; that people would be watching with interest to see who would come out on top. Olivier had Jack Wilding's technical expertise to back him up; Claudia had her father's chequebook. They were each fearless drivers, and what they lacked in experience they made up for in determination. And they were both hungry for glory. Claudia knew that specula- tion over who was going to claim the imminent Corrigan

Trophy was rife, and had been in no doubt whatsoever that it should be her, no matter what it took. But all of a sudden, Claudia's desire to win was being overridden by another, far more powerful urge.

From the moment she'd seen him arrive today, she hadn't been able to concentrate. She was watching him now, from behind her reflective shades. He was bent over the bonnet of his car, occasionally brushing back the long fringe that fell into his eyes, stripped to the waist in the warmth of the midsummer sun. From her vantage point, she admired his physique, the sinuous muscle under his golden skin hard and toned. He was like a wild animal, naturally fit, his metabolism perfectly balanced – not so lean as to become scrawny, but certainly not carrying any excess. Just like herself, in fact. Claudia amused herself for a moment imagining what they would look like in bed together. A classical sculpture, the perfect contrast of hard and soft, sinew and muscle versus flesh and curves. She wondered for a moment where she might find a mirrored ceiling, then checked herself. She was going a bit too fast.

Taking her sunglasses off and tucking them into her cleavage, she strode over. She didn't need to check her appearance first – she knew it was perfect. The woman at the MAC counter at the new Harvey Nichols in Birmingham had worked her out a routine that made her look as natural and fresh as a daisy. It might take half an hour to apply first thing in the morning, but it lasted all day and only needed the occasional touch-up with a barely there lipstick.

'Hi.' She managed to encompass antagonism and a provocative flirtatiousness into her greeting. Olivier looked up with disinterest, and managed a smile.

'Hello,' he offered in return, before turning back to what he was doing.

'It's hot, isn't it?' she heard herself saying.

He raised an eyebrow at the crass obviousness of her statement.

'Certainly is,' he replied, and closed his bonnet.

She racked her brain for something more interesting to say.

'All ready for this afternoon?' she ventured, cringing inwardly.

He gave her a bemused little smile.

'Just about. And you?' His tone was playful; only just short of sarcastic. Claudia realized he was teasing her.

'I think so.'

'Good.' He put a hand on her elbow to usher her out of the way. 'Excuse me,' he said politely, as he swung one long leg over the side of the car, slid into the driver's seat and started up the engine, the conversation clearly over.

Claudia turned on her heel and stalked off, wondering how she could have made such an idiot of herself. She, who was never at a loss for words, had stood there and talked about the weather! She had imagined enticing him into some sort of flirtatious banter, with her getting the last word in, sauntering off and leaving him panting with longing. Instead, she felt a total fool. She crushed her cup and tossed it into a nearby bin. The rebuff had merely fuelled her libido. She was going to break Olivier Templeton, get under his skin and torment him – make him come crawling to her. She was going to start that very afternoon, by snatching the victory from under his nose.

*

From the corner of his eye, Olivier watched Claudia flounce off and smiled to himself. As soon as he'd seen her at that very first race meeting in April, he'd smelled trouble. Spoilt, capricious and used to getting her way, he correctly surmised. He'd met enough Claudias on the slopes and on the tennis courts during his career, and had learned how to deal with them by keeping them firmly at arm's length. Though he had to admit that as princesses went, Claudia had a little more backbone than most. He admired her driving skills and her determination. But he wasn't going to let her know that *just* yet, because the most fun to be had with a princess was to make it seem you weren't remotely interested. It drove them insane, as they were so used to men falling at their feet. So he treated her as he might a check-out girl: polite, certainly not rude, but with total disinterest. Not a flicker. It amused him highly, almost as much as it frustrated her.

What gave a further edge to their antagonism was that each knew the other was their greatest threat. Olivier knew if he had to beat anyone this afternoon, it was Claudia. Not that he had anything to prove. Just for the hell of it, and to wind her up.

The scrutineer arrived, ready to run the rigorous safety checks that ensured the car was fit to race – not too much play in the steering, no oil leaking over the engine. As the scrutineer began ticking off points on his clipboard, Olivier put Claudia to the back of his mind, totally focused on the challenge ahead.

Jamie and Lettice had finally come to the conclusion that they weren't going to get either a civil or a sensible word out of Jack and Olivier until the day was over, and so, carrying the picnic basket between them, they'd crossed over the wooden bridge that led from the competitors' paddock to the public parking area, and climbed the hill with the rest of the spectators to find a suitable vantage point from which to view the afternoon's sport. It was impossible to see the whole of the course in one go, so they chose a spot halfway up which gave them a clear view of the most demanding section: the notorious hairpin known as Ettore's Bend (after Ettore Bugatti, the car's designer), followed by the run up to the Esses, a section of deceptively challenging S-bends. Strategically placed commentators would keep them informed of each car's progress elsewhere. They settled themselves safely behind the fence and spread out the rug.

Lettice unscrewed the lid of a mammoth tartan flask and poured them each a coffee.

'You know, it's marvellous that your father's found an interest. I honestly believe that car has been his saving grace.'

'Really?'

'He took your mother's death very hard, you know.'

'Yes, I do,' said Jamie, in a tone of voice that made it clear she didn't really want to carry on the conversation. However, Lettice wasn't the type to take subtle hints.

'I was very worried about him at one point. He was drinking very heavily. Some days he didn't even get dressed. I used to come and check up on him, chivvy him along. Make sure he had something to eat.' She smiled ruefully at the memory. 'One day I actually frogmarched him upstairs and made him have a bath and a shave.'

Jamie wondered if she was supposed to be grateful.

'That's very kind of you.'

'Not really. After all, I'd been through it myself,' said Lettice. 'I knew exactly how he was feeling. When my husband died I was bereft for a long time. Everyone had given up on me. I was a lost cause. I looked like a bag lady. I had to have whisky in my morning tea to help me get through the day.' Lettice's face clouded over at the memory. She paused for a moment. 'I was an absolute pain in the arse. I realize that now. But at the time all I could think about was myself – poor old me – and I expected everyone's sympathy, expected them to make allowances.'

'So – what made you pull yourself together?' Despite herself, Jamie was curious. Lettice's description of her former self certainly didn't match the ebullient, flamboyant figure sitting next to her.

'I reached rock bottom. It was Christmas time and some friends dragged me out to Midnight Mass. Christmas is always the worst time if you've been bereaved. Well, I knew I'd never get through it without sustenance. I stuck a hip flask in my coat pocket to top myself up throughout the service. By the time we got to the third lesson I was completely legless. I could barely stand up, swaying in the pew. I could see all the youngsters laughing at me. I could just imagine what they were thinking: drunken old bag. Then I ...' Lettice swallowed; it was difficult to get the next few words out. 'I wet myself, during "Hark the Herald Angels". Stood there with piddle trickling down my legs trying to sing along with everyone else ...'

She trailed off, her face screwed up with pain at the memory. The image was so comical, Jamie was tempted to laugh out loud. But she found she didn't want to. It had obviously cost Lettice a lot to tell her this story, and she told it with such dignity.

'So what happened?' she asked gently.

'My friends took me home, got me cleaned up and put me to bed. Which was more than I deserved. A few days later they made me call my GP. I think they thought it was time to pass the buck, and they didn't want to spend the rest of their lives checking up on an incontinent old bag. Anyway, this girl came out to see me. She'd just joined the local practice. She was so young – I couldn't believe she was even qualified. But she gave it to me straight between the eyes. She didn't pull any punches. She told me if I carried on the way I was, I'd be joining Larry before I knew it. From then on, she came out to see me every morning on her way into the surgery – made sure I was up and dressed and had a plan for the day. It was a very slow process. I still had my black days. Well, I still do. But gradually they got further and further apart.'

Jamie saw that there were tears shimmering in Lettice's eyes that she hastily blinked back. She pressed her lips together and looked away for a moment while she gathered herself, then turned back to Jamie, smiling.

'So, you see, I knew what Jack was going through, and where he was heading. I was determined to help him like Sarah had helped me. It was an uphill struggle, I can tell you. I couldn't get him interested in anything. I tried all sorts. Golf. Bridge. He went along with it but I could tell he was just humouring me. Then Olivier turned up, and all of a sudden he came to life. It's miraculous, really.'

Jamie felt humbled, and ashamed that she could have thought such horrid things about Lettice, when she'd obviously done so much to help Jack. Lettice was letting

Olivier take the credit, but Jamie felt sure that if she hadn't put in the time and the effort, Jack wouldn't have been so receptive.

She thanked her, hesitantly.

'I'm … very grateful to you, Lettice. I know I shouldn't have … I should have …' Jamie was finding it hard to go on as an uninvited lump came into her throat.

'Listen, darling – don't you go blaming yourself. It must have been very hard for you too. Everyone seems to have forgotten that.'

Lettice reached out and squeezed her hand. Jamie could feel the edges of the old girl's diamond rings digging into her flesh, and was grateful for the pain.

Just before the start of his class, Olivier was pale, tight-lipped and silent. Watching the first two classes had done nothing to settle his nerves, and he'd had to take himself off for a quiet walk, even though he could still hear the roar of the engines and the excited babble of the commentators. He always felt jittery in that half-hour build-up before competing. It was a necessary part of psyching himself up: part fear, part anticipation, part a hideously all-consuming desire to win that was bordering on the unsportsmanlike – he had to muster up hatred for his fellow competitors, even though deep down he knew he had the utmost respect for all of them.

In the paddock, the cars were starting to line up ready to take their places at the start. He was fifth to go. He manoeuvred himself into place behind a Frazer Nash whose driver looked as cool as a cucumber.

The commentator was talking the crowds through each entrant, the loudspeaker desperately competing with the sound of engines revving up and turning over. He heard his own name mentioned.

'... Olivier Templeton, in the Type 35B once competed in by his father Eric, who veterans amongst you might remember winning here on occasion back in the eighties. This is Olivier's first time out at Prescott, though he put in a good time at Shelsley Walsh a few weeks ago. It's also first time here for Claudia Sedgeley in *her* Type 35. It'll be interesting to see how these two newcomers fare: the conditions are good for them today; but there's no doubt experience counts for a lot at Prescott ...'

If Olivier had felt edgy before, this public announce-ment of his need to perform turned his insides to liquid. Not only had he been compared to his father, but the gauntlet had been thrown down and it was now a matter of pride for him to beat Claudia. He looked over his shoulder to see where she was.

Three places behind him in the queue. She was pulling on a balaclava, tucking in her long hair, prior to slipping on her safety helmet over the top. The bile in his stomach turned to adrenalin and supercharged his veins. Taking a couple of deep breaths to quell the last of the butterflies in his stomach, he edged forwards to take his place on the starting line. He could see the tail end of the competitor in front flying under the bridge, then disappear around the first corner. It was his turn next.

Claudia sat at the wheel, every muscle in her body tensed, every nerve end buzzing, making the hairs on the back of her neck stand up. She shivered with the sensation, ran her eyes over the dials on the dashboard and drummed her kid-clad fingers lightly on the steering wheel, wanting to prolong the moment yet desperate for her turn.

For the final impetus, she looked at Olivier in front of her as he took his place on the start line. She imagined his aquiline features under his helmet, his eyes coolly surveying the track ahead. She was going to beat him. She had to. She felt an adrenalin rush as she moved forwards a place in the queue. Then, as the light turned to green and Olivier roared up the hill, Claudia felt a sudden and unexpected pang for his safety ...

Jamie could hardly bear to watch. She knew the modern cars that went up this hill, the Lotuses, the Caterhams, the Westfields, could go from bottom to top in less than forty seconds. For a vintage vehicle, anything less than a minute was pretty impressive going: the record for a Bugatti was just over fifty-two seconds. So in comparison, Olivier was travelling at a pretty insignificant speed. But her heart was still in her mouth. The whine of the engine as he ran through the gearbox gave the impression of death-defying acceleration. And he was certainly going fast enough to do himself serious damage if they made a wrong move. Lettice, who was as blind as a bat, surveyed the proceedings with a pair of field glasses, alternately swearing and cheering at Olivier's progress.

Jack was deathly silent, his jaw clenched. This was his moment as much as Olivier's. He'd put in the preparation, he'd given him the game plan and the benefit of his experience. He made a mental note of every single move Olivier made, ready to debrief him afterwards. He mopped at his brow with a handkerchief. For a moment, he felt as if he'd gone back twenty years, as if it was Eric he was watching on the ascent. He couldn't begin to count the afternoons they'd spent on this very track, and nothing much had changed. It was almost as if it had been frozen in time.

They'd been carefree days. All his problems had been ahead of him then; he'd been blissfully unaware of what was round the corner. Although for the moment he was living in a little cameo, focusing his attention on Olivier's performance, after the excitement had worn off there would still be the memories to face, decisions to make, mistakes to regret.

If he could have gone back in time, what would he have changed? Everything, he thought. If only he hadn't been so weak ... But then, wouldn't everyone change things, given the benefit of hindsight? Wishing he'd done it all differently wasn't going to help him now – it was too bloody late. He just felt desperately sad that it was Jamie who was paying for the past. Sad, guilty, helpless, useless, his only legacy to her was a litany of failures and disappointments. And it wasn't as if he could justify his position by telling her the truth. That would be the coward's way out, and Jack knew that the very last vestiges of his self-respect, already meagre, would vanish into thin air if he took that route ...

The first two hundred yards were torture: in his eagerness to get off to a flying start, Olivier had to decelerate hard to negotiate the lethal hairpin of Ettore's Bend. But afterwards, after he'd regained his composure and his heart rate had slowed down a little, the rest of the course unfolded in front of him like a movie he had seen a hundred times. For these few glorious moments the world was his, as if he was invincible. There was a split second, when he approached the Esses and put his foot on the brake a little too late, when he thought the car wasn't going to stop, that she was going to go flying over the edge and glide through the air over the miles and miles of countryside he could see below him. But with a finely judged twitch of the steering wheel, he took the corner just in time, just as he knew he should, just as he had practised. He flew smoothly round the final semicircle, then, with a sense of relief and achievement, put his foot down hard for the final stretch.

A thousand yards below him, Claudia listened with her heart in her mouth as the commentator announced Olivier had arrived safely at the finish. She didn't have time to listen to what time he'd done. As she took her place on the start line, Olivier's existence went entirely out of her head. She pressed her foot down on the throttle, felt the engine respond enthusiastically as if to reassure her they were in tune, then dropped her foot off the clutch as soon as she saw the light go green. Her whoop of excitement couldn't be heard above the roar of the engines as she accelerated away.

It was all going so smoothly. She felt totally in control. And so she should be: she'd prepared thoroughly enough for today. She'd been to the driving school at Prescott twice where she'd been put through her paces by the instructors; she'd watched the reruns of the videos they'd taken of her performances; she'd walked the course with her father to refresh her memory. She should have been able to get to the top without mishap.

But as she came out of the second hairpin and

accelerated up the hill, she was momentarily blinded by the sun. She lost the line she was taking, overcompensated, totally misjudged the camber and, to her horror, felt herself leaving the road. There were a few moments of sheer terror as she wondered if she was going to slew into the metal girders that protected the spectators from the track. She braced herself, trying to keep calm as she dropped down the gearbox to slow down. Her heart was thudding wildly; she felt for a moment as if she was going to pass out, as if her system couldn't cope with the sky-high surge of adrenalin. Then suddenly the panic was over and she felt mere frustration as she hurtled over the gravel that edged the track where the car ground to a halt, stalling inelegantly.

Swearing profusely, she restarted the engine. It stalled again, refusing to cooperate, as if traumatized by its treatment. She took a deep breath and tried once more. Thankfully, it purred into life. She slammed the car into first, desperately trying to get it back on track as quickly as possible. Precious seconds were ticking by. The wheels spun round in vain, buried deep in the gravel, churning it up. She eased off the throttle, trying to gain traction, and the car eventually lurched forwards.

She rejoined the track, cheeks burning with humiliation, wanting the ground to open and swallow her up, imagining the knowing smirks of the audience, how they were telling each other that a silly little girl like her couldn't possibly begin to handle such a powerful car.

Olivier came seventh, with a very respectable time of seventy-two seconds. Jamie found herself jumping up and down in delight. The man next to her smiled. His small son was perched on his shoulders, sporting a pair of ear defenders to protect him from the noise and a dangerous-looking ice-cream cornet that was about to drip on to his father's neck.

'Nice sport if you can afford it,' the man remarked conversationally. 'It's all right for some, of course. Most of these cars are worth more than my bloody house is.'

'Seriously?' said Jamie, somewhat startled by this announcement.

'Well, yes – when it comes to a toss-up between a Bugatti and a family home, normal people like me don't have the luxury of being able to make the choice. Not when you've got the school fees to think about.' He threw his eyes up to his son in a gesture of mock exasperation. 'I just get my kicks out of watching. Most of these guys can afford both, of course.'

'So – how much is one worth? On average?' Jamie tried to sound casual.

The man shrugged. 'A Bugatti? You wouldn't get much change out of quarter of a million, for a decent model in reasonable nick. More, if it's got a good history.'

Jamie tried not to look shocked. She had no idea that was what they were worth. If pressed, she'd have guessed between twenty and thirty thousand, which to her was a lot of money for what was essentially a toy. But a quarter of a million? That was a ridiculous amount of money. Immoral. Irresponsible. Outrageous.

It was also life-changing. Potentially.

She had to tell Jack. It was absolutely typical of him, to be naively harbouring something that was the answer to all their problems. Her mind raced through the implications – even if his car was worth bottom book, with his half share there'd be enough to do up Bucklebury and have change.

She couldn't tell him now. Besides, she didn't want to bring the matter up in front of Olivier and Lettice. She'd wait till they were alone later that evening. Then they could crack open the champagne.

Claudia hadn't even been placed. She was going to have the ignominy of FAIL next to her name when the results came out. As she drove back down the return road she cringed inwardly, trying to make herself unnoticeable, thinking that if anyone commiserated with her she'd burst into tears. Back in the paddock she parked hastily, took off her helmet and scurried off towards the bar with her head down. She needed a gin and tonic – her father had promised to drive the trailer home, so she could drown her sorrows with impunity.

The bar was full to bursting. She'd just joined the queue, hoping no one would notice her, when she felt a hand on her shoulder. She turned to see Olivier smiling at her.

'Hey,' he said. 'I'm sorry to hear you wiped out.'

Wiped out? What did he mean, wiped out? They weren't fucking surfing. Claudia glared at him.

'Sorry? Why would you be sorry?' she demanded belligerently.

He looked a little bewildered, then shrugged. 'Well, you know. It happens to the best of us.'

'Oh, I see. So you're the best, are you?' Claudia retorted.

'It's just an expression.' Olivier recoiled from her riposte, looking at her with something bordering on distaste. 'You know, you shouldn't take part if you can't cope with losing,' he told her.

Claudia realized at once that she'd been too defensive, that she was guilty of being a bad sport, which was infinitely worse than being a bad driver. And to her horror, tears of humiliation sprang into her eyes at his reproach. She blinked them back, wishing she'd remembered her shades, praying Olivier wouldn't notice. But before she could turn away, he peered at her.

'Listen, I'm sorry—' he began to apologize, but she jerked away from him.

'Get off.'

For a moment they glared at each other.

'Fine,' he said, shrugging. 'See you at Sapersley, then. For the Corrigan Trophy. May the best man win.'

Claudia didn't miss the hint of mockery in his tone. She wanted to say sorry, beg him to come and have a drink, prove to him that she wasn't a bad loser, but the words stuck in her throat. And before she could swallow her pride, he had turned away from her and was pushing his way out of the bar. She watched him walking off towards the orchard. As he disappeared amongst the throng, she felt filled with desolation, wondering why she always had to spoil everything.

As he made his way back to the paddock, Olivier wondered if perhaps he'd been a little too sharp with Claudia, even if she was behaving like a spoilt brat. She was only young, and it took a lot of bottle to get up that hill; he knew as well as anyone that the stress could play havoc with your nerves. He shouldn't have goaded her like that. It would have been far more sportsmanlike of him to have taken the time to placate rather than chastise her; he should have bought her a drink, not torn her off a strip. Besides, he'd have quite liked a chat with her, to see what made her tick and find out why a girl that looked as if she belonged on the catwalk was happier on the racetrack. He resolved to make a real effort to befriend her at Sapersley: if they were going to be rivals, they might as well be friends.

On the way home, Claudia's thunderous mood enveloped the cab of the Winnebago, hanging ominously in the air. Ray tried trickling out a few platitudes, like 'You win some, you lose some.' He had been rewarded with a particularly venomous scowl. He thought it best not to follow it up with 'It's not the winning, it's the taking part.'

She put her feet up on the dashboard defiantly. The stroppy, troublesome teenager of years gone by had re-appeared.

'Fuck it. I might as well not bother any more.' She thumped her fist on her leg in frustration. 'I drove like a bloody girl.'

'Cherub, look upon it as experience. You won't make the same mistake again.'

'No. I won't. Because I'm not bloody driving again.'

Ray's heart lurched and ended up somewhere near his lunch. This was the moment he'd been dreading. The moment when Claudia became bored and lost interest. He'd had a year's grace; a year when he'd been able to stop worrying about her and what she was going to do with her life.

'You can't give up. It's the Corrigan Trophy the week

after next. This is what you've been working up to for weeks.' He tried desperately to think of something that might persuade her it was worthwhile. 'Think of Agnes. Think of all the hard work she's put in. She'd be so disappointed.'

She glared at him, bolshy and defiant.

'Well, if I don't win that, that's it. Forget it.'

Ray negotiated his entry on to the M5 extra carefully. His heart was beating so fast he couldn't concentrate. He was going to have to get his thinking cap on. Claudia was going to win the Corrigan Trophy no matter what it cost him.

15

Jamie waited until they were alone before tackling her father about the Bugatti's worth. She wanted his undivided attention. And she certainly didn't want to discuss money in front of Lettice and Olivier. They'd all come back to Bucklebury for a celebration supper: only cold chicken and potato salad, but it was a merry meal, with Jack and Olivier dissecting everyone's performance. Eventually Lettice declared herself exhausted.

'Even more exhausting and exhilarating to watch than horse racing. I thought I was going to have a heart attack when that little girl came off the track. I was sure she was a goner.'

'Don't worry. Claudia knows exactly what she's doing.' Olivier's tone was dry.

'She's certainly got a lot of gumption.' Lettice prodded Jamie. 'You should have a go. Looks as if they need more girls in the sport. Glam it up a bit.'

'No fear,' said Jamie.

'You're a daredevil on a horse,' said Jack.

'That's different. A horse has got a brain.'

'It's exactly the same theory. Spurs and reins; throttles and brakes.'

Jamie smiled, shaking her head, not wanting to pursue

the subject any further in the light of what she was going to say. Lettice finally drove off home happily, and she breathed a sigh of relief.

Olivier was piling the washing-up into the sink, squirting Fairy liberally all over the plates. Ever since her jibe the other morning, he had been anxious to pull his weight. But Jamie wanted to be alone with her dad.

'Listen, I'll do it. You've had a long day. Go and have a hot bath. I bought some fantastic bubbly stuff the other day – if you're very good I'll let you steal a bit.'

Olivier smiled gratefully.

'I must admit I'm knackered. My neck's killing me. What I really need's a good massage.'

He rolled his shoulders and twisted his head to try and relieve the tension. Jamie poked him with the washing-up brush.

'Go on. Go and get a good night's sleep.'

He finally went, as Jack brought in the wine glasses from the garden. There was just enough for a glass each left in the bottom of the bottle.

'Finish it off with me?' he asked. Normally, Jamie would refuse, but tonight she accepted.

'Let's go and sit down. I need to talk to you.'

'Sounds ominous.'

'No. Not at all. In fact, I think it's good news.'

They curled up in the living room. Jamie lit the half-dozen candles on the wrought-iron candelabra by the fireplace, and the room glowed. The windows were still open. Outside, it had begun to rain gently, and the scent of damp earth that had been warmed by the summer sun wafted in from the garden.

Jack stretched his legs out luxuriously in front of him.

'So – what's the big secret?'

'Dad. The Bugatti. You do know how much it's worth?'

Jack looked at her warily.

'Well, not exactly, no. It's not an exact science, valuing a car like that. It depends on all sorts of things. Model, condition, specification, demand ...'

'But roughly?' Jamie persisted.

Jack shrugged. He had that look in his eye that suggested he'd been caught doing something he shouldn't.

In a split second she realized that of course he knew. If anyone had their finger on the pulse of what things were worth, it was her father. The implications took her breath away. Surely he wasn't prepared to sacrifice Bucklebury Farm for a bloody car? Then she remembered her father embracing Olivier after the hill climb, clapping him on the back, and the look of total, utter delight on both of their faces. Of course he would. Of course he bloody would.

'I was told,' she said slowly, 'that a car like that would be worth somewhere in the region of a quarter of a million.'

Jack didn't answer at first.

'Give or take ten grand,' he agreed reluctantly. 'But you'd have to wait for the right buyer ...'

'But if you did sell. You do realize what this could mean?' Jamie was becoming impatient. 'Dad – if you got your half share out of the car, we could restore Bucklebury. We'd be talking about at least a hundred thousand pounds.'

'It's not as simple as that.'

Jamie narrowed her eyes. 'Why not?'

'I can't do it to Olivier. He can't afford to buy me out.'

'But the other half's his, isn't it? Well, his father's, anyway. And surely Eric would buy you out? Then he could flog the lot if he wanted to.'

'I don't want to bring Eric into it.'

'Why not?'

'He's shown no interest in the car over the past fifteen years. I'd rather keep it that way.'

'But surely he knows Olivier's been racing it?'

Jack looked shifty. 'No.'

'What?' Jamie's jaw dropped in disbelief. 'You can't be serious. That's ... criminally irresponsible.'

'No, it isn't. The car's half mine. He's obviously not interested—'

'Have you asked him?'

'No.'

'Why not?'

'I ... don't really want to get in contact. You know the expression. Let sleeping dogs lie.'

Fury made Jamie vicious.

'Well, maybe you should have thought twice about fucking his wife all those years ago.'

Jack recoiled as if he had been slapped. 'What?'

'Don't be naive. I might only have been fifteen at the time, but I could put two and two together.'

It was a wild accusation, one she would never normally have made even if she had suspected it. But Jack's pained expression told her that her suppositions were only too correct. Jamie ploughed on.

'You are so unbelievably irresponsible. Though I don't know why I'm surprised! All my life you've let us down. You can't ever take life seriously, can you? Or do things straight? We've got a golden opportunity to save

Bucklebury, but because of your disgusting behaviour, your sordid past ...'

'That's enough!'

Jack's voice was low, but something about his tone stopped Jamie in mid-diatribe. For a moment she was frightened. He was very pale. And trembling slightly. Whether from fear or anger she couldn't be sure. Eventually he spoke, in a very quiet voice that had no fight in it at all.

'I'm sorry I've been such a disappointment to you, Jamie. I really am.'

To her horror, she saw his mouth working up and down as if he was trying hard not to cry. But before she could say or do anything, backtrack or apologize or defend her position, he put down his glass and hurried out of the room.

Jamie slumped back in her chair with a despairing sigh. What a mess! She hadn't meant to be so harsh, but her father was infuriating. She thought it was probably the first time anyone had given it to him straight between the eyes.

The door opened, and a tentative Olivier put his head round, sleek from his bath.

'Are you OK?'

'Yes. No. Who cares?'

He came into the room.

'I thought I heard shouting.'

Jamie fixed him with a hostile glare.

'Yes, you did. But you needn't worry. No one's going to spoil your fun.'

Olivier looked wounded, not sure what he'd done to deserve such a response.

'Do you want to tell me what's going on?'

'I've just found out that fucking car you've been messing about in all afternoon is worth enough to save this farm. But everyone else in this house seems to be operating on a different set of priorities to me. Evidently whizzing up a hill in pursuit of a battered old trophy is more important than saving our family home—'

'Hold on a minute!' Olivier felt he had the right to be indignant. 'I don't think you've got the full picture.'

'Which bit am I missing, exactly?' Jamie's tone was scornful.

Olivier sighed.

'The registration documents are in Dad's name. He and your father may have had a gentleman's agreement to share it, but there's no evidence on paper to prove it. And I know Dad. He'd flog it and keep the lot for himself.'

'No doubt he'd think it was a suitable revenge.'

Olivier frowned. 'What do you mean?'

'You know. My dad and your mother. That summer in Cap Ferrat.'

Olivier went very quiet and thoughtful. He walked over to the drinks cupboard and poured himself a brandy. Then he looked over at Jamie and poured her one as well.

'You can't hold people's pasts against them for ever.' He handed her the glass. Jamie hesitated for a moment. She wasn't a spirit drinker, but perhaps this conversation required a bit of Dutch courage.

'Can't I?' She took a hefty slug, and swallowed hard. 'My father has never given a moment's thought to anyone else in his entire life. Except when it suited him. He's always done exactly as he pleases. He's never made a contingency plan. He lives for the moment, and if that doesn't fit in with everyone else – tough luck. Which is why we're in the situation we are now. And it just ... frustrates me to think that the answer is sitting there in that garage. It's just typical that because of his total self-indulgence, we can't do anything about it.'

'I think you're being rather harsh.'

'That's because you haven't had to live with it. My mother put up with it all her life. Never knowing when or if the next penny was coming in. Never being sure where he was. Never knowing if he was going to spring dinner for twelve on you, or whisk you off somewhere.'

'Sounds rather exciting. At least life was never dull,' said Olivier lightly.

'I used to pray for it to be dull, I can tell you. There is such a thing as a happy medium. The Christmas we ran out of oil and nearly froze to death wasn't much fun. Nearly having to be sent home from school because Dad hadn't paid the fees for two terms wasn't fun. Having to sell my pony to some fat-bottomed, rich little brat from Shrewsbury wasn't fun. It was a bloody rollercoaster ride, I can tell you.'

Jamie felt hot tears rising, of anger and frustration. She clenched her teeth in an effort to stop the flow, feeling foolish that she'd broken down in front of Olivier. She seemed to be making a speciality of losing control lately. She tried to smile an apology.

'Sorry. It's just so frustrating. I can't bear the thought of losing Bucklebury.'

'Maybe what you need to do is find yourself a rich husband. And fast.'

She looked at him, appalled.

'I suppose you wouldn't take it seriously. It's not your home, is it?'

Olivier knew he sounded flippant, but Jamie was looking for answers he couldn't give her. His tone softened. 'You know, Jamie, change isn't always a bad thing. The fear of it is sometimes worse than the reality.'

'I can't bear the thought of someone else's stuff in here!' she protested. 'I can just imagine what Bella Deacon would do to it. It'll be wall-to-wall cream carpet and bowls of pot-pourri and nasty twee prints in gold frames and a huge blow-up photograph of her and Rod made to look like a painting hanging over the fireplace—'

Olivier looked around the room and had to admit the prospect was grim. Tattered, shabby, comfy and cosy, it was years of accumulated possessions. Candle wax had dripped on to the hearth. Gumdrop and Parsnip were snoozing by the fire. The prospect of anyone wanting to change a thing was almost unimaginable.

Olivier had never felt sentimental about where he lived. Whenever his parents upgraded to a new house, he had no regrets about leaving the old one. As long as he had his sound system, a comfy bed and a wardrobe to stuff everything into, he was happy. There was a nomadic streak in him. Wherever he laid his hat…

He wasn't going to admit it to Jamie, but Bucklebury Farm was the first place he'd ever felt at home. The only place he had never wanted to leave. Telling her that would only add fuel to her argument.

'Life's not about places, Jamie. It's about people. They're the only things that really matter. The worst thing would be if you fell out with your father over this. Believe me, I envy your relationship with him more than anything.

What wouldn't I give for a father who thinks the world of me?'

There was a certain bitterness in his tone as he spoke, and Jamie felt a sudden twinge of guilt. Perhaps she was being a brat? Infuriating though Jack was, he would never in a million years undermine her or deride her, like Eric had Olivier.

'I know you love Bucklebury, but at the end of the day, it's just bricks and mortar. Nothing more. It's the people in it that make it really special.'

Olivier wasn't used to waxing so lyrical. Even more surprising was the fact that he meant it. Jack and Jamie *were* special.

Quite how special, he was only just starting to realize …

When Bella got back to Owl's Nest after a gruelling day teaching aspiring Darcys and Britneys, she found the table laid, the lights dimmed, soft candlelight flickering and David Gray gently tickling the ivories in the background. At each place was a plate of oak-smoked salmon, on a bed of watercress and rocket, with triangles of granary bread. Zinc in the fish. And plenty of iron in the garnish. Rod was an expert on what the conceiving couple should be eating and often presented her with carefully prepared meals.

Bella sat down as he handed her a glass of wine. She smiled brightly.

'So, what's all this in aid of?'

'I've been thinking,' answered Rod carefully. 'I think it's about time we saw someone. I've made an appointment for us with the doctor, so we can be referred.'

Bella started to protest.

'But it often takes—'

'It's been nearly a year, Bella. And neither of us are spring chickens any more. We need to sort it sooner rather than later.'

Bella took a careful sip from her glass without answering. Rod looked at her.

'I know neither of us wants to be told there's something wrong. But it could be something very simple; something that could be put right straight away.'

Bella nodded and smiled.

'Maybe you're right. I suppose we can just ... have a chat. It can't do any harm.'

Rod walked over to the dresser, opened a drawer and pulled out a package.

'This is for you, I thought it might help.'

Bella reached out eagerly. She adored presents, and Rod was so good at them; so thoughtful. She wondered what on earth it could be. The package was beautifully wrapped in white tissue paper with silver ribbons, but with no label, no indication as to which shop it had come from. She looked to Rod for permission to open it, and he smiled indulgently. Bella was like a little girl when it came to presents. She picked it up and shook it tentatively, looking for a clue. It was very light, but rattled slightly. It was too large for a ring, but then she wouldn't put it past Rod to be deceptive in his wrapping; to enjoy keeping her guessing. She tried to brace herself for the worst-case scenario – a bottle of perfume or body lotion – but then reassured herself: Rod wouldn't have gone to all this trouble for something insignificant. She pulled at the strings of the ribbon, picked impatiently at the knots with her nails, then ripped apart the paper.

Inside were six boxes. Six very familiar pink oblong boxes. Her face fell. Her heart pounded. She looked up again at Rod. His gaze was no longer indulgent. His eyes were hard.

Bella was a quick thinker. She did her best to extricate herself from the situation.

'I ... I don't understand,' she floundered. 'Why do you want me to go back on the pill?'

'Nice try, Bella, but it won't work.' He held up a piece of paper. 'You ordered this by phone yesterday. Repeat prescription.'

She frowned, shaking her head.

'No. I didn't. There must have been some mistake. You know what they're like at that surgery. Totally inefficient. Always getting things wrong ...'

She trailed off. Rod's face was impassive, disbelieving. Her face crumpled and she dissolved into noisy sobs. 'You don't understand.'

'No. I don't.' His voice was careful, and she wasn't to know it was because he was trying very hard not to cry himself. 'I don't understand at all. For nearly a year, you've strung me along. Every month I've been through torture, wondering if this would be the month. My heart's bled for you. Watching you, whenever you realized you weren't pregnant – it tore me apart. I did everything in my power to make it up to you.'

He thought about how desperately he'd tried to compensate. The trips away, the five-star hotels, the jewellery. The bloody Audi! How she must have crowed inwardly when he presented her with the keys only a month ago, after the last time he'd found her sobbing in their en suite. Time and again he'd showered her with material goods because he'd been so afraid that it was his fault, when all along he'd been duped.

'How could you do it to me, Bella? What did I do?' He shook his head in bewilderment. 'You must really hate me.'

'No! Of course I don't. I love you—'

'Really?' He looked at her, his face twisted into a cynical smile. 'So what do you do for an encore?'

Bella swallowed. Rod walked over to the window.

'I thought we were in this together. I thought you wanted the same as I did. I thought you wanted kids—'

'I do!'

He looked over at the incriminating pile of pill boxes.

'Yeah, right,' he scoffed. 'Didn't your mother tell you about the birds and the bees? Or did she just teach you how to find a sucker; take him for a ride ...'

'It's not like that.' Bella's voice was a desperate whimper.

'Then what is it? What am I supposed to think?' He gestured at the boxes. 'That's just annihilated everything I thought we were about. For God's sake, did I force you into it? You could have said, if you'd wanted to wait. Or if you didn't want children at all. Instead of putting us through all that agony ...'

He trailed off, his voice cracking with the emotion. Bella was sobbing bitterly.

'Please, Rod ... You don't understand.'

'No. No, I don't,' he said, his fists clenching and unclenching.

Bella took a deep, shuddering breath inwards, her eyes as wide as saucers as she twisted her hands with distress.

'It's just ... I was so afraid. I wasn't ready. I didn't know if I could cope with ...' She trailed off in despair. 'I'm sorry. I'm so, so sorry.'

'So am I,' Rod said bleakly. 'I had no idea we'd got it so wrong.'

'We can ... try again,' she ventured.

Rod shook his head. 'I don't think so,' he said. 'How could I trust you? When I think of all those times I felt guilty, wishing I could take your pain away ...'

He turned away sharply, not wanting her to see him struggling to fight back tears. Bella looked at the floor, shamefaced.

'Do you want me to go?' she asked, in a small voice.

'There doesn't seem much point in us carrying on. Does there?'

There was a challenge in his voice. Bella looked up, and for one moment it seemed as if she was on the point of saying something, was prepared to fight for her marriage. Then she turned, picked up the phone with shaking hands, looked at the taxi number on the card pinned on to the board and punched out the number.

'I'd like a cab, please.' Her voice was almost a whisper. 'Owl's Nest, Sandstone Lane, Upper Faviell. Thanks.'

She put the phone down and ran upstairs to pack.

Ten minutes later the doorbell rang and Bella came down the stairs slowly with her bag. Rod had opened the door and the taxi driver was hovering uncomfortably on the doormat, sensing tension.

'Where to, love?'

'Manor Close.'

The driver raised an eyebrow. She was going down in

the world all right. He held out a hand to take her bag nevertheless. Bella turned in the doorway to say goodbye to Rod, to appeal to him one last time, but he'd turned his back on her, his body language firmly indicating that there was nothing more to be discussed.

Bella followed the taxi driver to the car, as if following her executioner to the gallows.

As soon as the door closed behind him, Rod found tears sliding down his face. He couldn't remember the last time he'd cried. They were tears of anger: anger at Bella for deceiving him, and at himself for letting himself be deceived. Tears of bitterness for the total sham that had been his marriage. He thought of all the times he'd held her, focusing on her grief rather than his, because somehow it was accepted that the disappointment was worse for a woman, that it called into question her *raison d'être*. There had been no such support for him. Nolly, of course, had tried, but Rod had kept her sympathy at arm's length, bottling everything up, because the minute he expressed his fears would be the minute they were realized.

Mixed in amongst them, however, were tears of relief. Relief that he probably wasn't sterile or impotent, as he had been starting to fear over the past few months. He might have lost his mate, but now he knew the truth: he had as much chance as the next bloke of becoming a father.

As the taxi drove through the lanes back towards Ludlow, Bella opened the window in the back and took in big gulps of fresh air to suppress her hysteria. She didn't want to break down and make a scene in front of the driver. He was curious enough already. It was obvious she'd been turfed out of Owl's Nest, and he kept glancing in the rear-view mirror to assess her state of mind.

Instead, she chewed frantically on her perfect finger-nails as she contemplated her bad luck. She'd been so careful. She'd hidden the packets at the dance studio, deep in a filing cabinet, and each month she popped each of the twenty-one pills out of its foil wrap and decanted them into an empty folic acid bottle, which she took home. She then took one each day in front of Rod. It had been a foolproof deception.

Until today. What were the chances of Rod picking up her prescription like that? She'd only ordered them yesterday; she'd been going to pick them up on Monday and squirrel them away as usual. Now the cat was well and truly out of the bag.

She hadn't been given a chance to explain, but then how could she? How could she make him understand that the thought of getting pregnant and carrying a child not only terrified but repulsed her? She couldn't bear the thought of not being in control of her body, of all that weight distorting her beyond recognition. She'd seen pregnant women in the high street, with their huge distended lumps. They barely looked human. And she'd seen the after-effects in her toning classes often enough – the hideous silvery stretch marks, the wrinkles, the deflated bellies that would never regain their elasticity, the pendulous breasts with the blue veins. And she'd heard talk of disfigurements that were not visible – the stitches, the scars, the incontinence.

And that was before you took the pain of shitting a Ford Fiesta into account.

Every month she gave herself a pep talk. Every month

she promised herself that she would stop taking the pill; that she'd give it a go. But every time she bottled out, finding some spurious reason. She hated herself for it. Once she'd managed three whole days without it before panicking and rushing to the packet with shaking hands and taking the pills she'd missed all at once, then still going for the morning-after pill when she and Rod had sex that month, just in case.

And when she used to cry when she came on, she wasn't faking it. They weren't crocodile tears. They were tears of shame that she wasn't able to give Rod what he wanted, no matter how hard she tried to do battle with her head. She wept because she felt she wasn't normal – all normal women wanted babies, didn't they? Once you were happily married, which she certainly was, it was a natural progression. But nothing she did could conquer her fear. She peered into prams, examining newborns, hoping they would emanate some sort of magic scent that would make her broody. Once, she was charmed by a particularly winsome specimen giving her a heart-melting grin from beneath a white velour beanie hat. Bella felt a tiny little flicker of something inside her, and wondered if at long last her maternal instincts were kicking in. But one look at the mother changed her mind. She'd once attended Bella's aerobic classes, and had been lean and toned. Now, with her drooping breasts and thickened waistline, combined with dark rings under her eyes from lack of sleep, she was barely recognizable. Bella recoiled in horror, all inclinations to procreate vanishing into thin air.

The taxi turned into the road that led to her mother's house. Bella's heart sank. As council houses went, it was perfectly pleasant. All the old windows had been replaced with smart UPVC leaded windows; the garden was tidy. But not all their neighbours were as conscientious with their upkeep. The estate was notorious as a dumping ground for the villains of the area. Not least several of Rod's brothers, who ruled the estate with a rod of iron. Cars destined for the scrap heap, some of them without wheels, littered the roadside. Broken fences, peeling paint, front lawns worn bare by relentless football practice – it was a predominantly depressing neighbourhood, despite the efforts of some.

Bella sighed. She'd worked so bloody hard to get herself out of here. She thought of the long days and nights she and Rod had spent doing up Owl's Nest. Her nails had been ruined, but she hadn't minded. She'd worked tirelessly, sanding and stripping and scraping, then painting and staining and polishing. Now here she was, back to square one. She felt her heart slither down to her boots, just like Snakes and Ladders, when the counter slid back down the snake after landing on an unlucky square.

She'd landed on an unlucky square all right. But it had been of her own making.

Pauline answered the door, and looked questioningly at Bella's suitcase.

'We've had,' said Bella, very carefully so she didn't cry, 'a bit of an argument. I don't want to talk about it at the moment. But can I come and stay?'

As Jamie tossed and turned in her bed that night, trying to get to sleep, she went over and over what Olivier had said to her, and realized he was right.

It was a sobering thought, but Jack was now her only living relative – the only one that meant anything, that is, though there was the odd aunt and a few cousins floating around. Until she got a husband of her own, and had children, which seemed a long way off if not totally unlikely, he was all she had in the world. She had to do everything in her power to preserve her relationship with him. And she didn't want to be filled with regret. She knew now that you could never be sure what was round the corner. Her mother's death had taught her that.

Maybe it was part of growing up to accept that you couldn't make everything right, to learn to live with things as they are. Hundreds of clichés spun round her head – make the best of a bad job, like it or lump it, every cloud has a silver lining. She couldn't change the past or wave a magic wand and save Bucklebury. Jack had been right to salvage what he could from the wreckage. By coming along and throwing her hands up in horror, Jamie realized she'd shown herself up as naive, unrealistic, reactionary.

Maybe things wouldn't be so bad. And this way was less of a risk. Jamie saw now that her head had been in the clouds. What did she know about running a country hotel, or any sort of business for that matter? Her expertise was childcare, getting newborn babies to sleep through the night, not pandering to the whims of demanding, querulous house guests. She should stick to what she was good at. She could have ended up making a very expensive mistake, putting a lot of time and effort into a project that ultimately lost them everything.

With Jack's plan, at least they still had a toehold. He could still wake up and enjoy the same view he'd had for forty years; breathe the same air. And presumably they would have a certain amount of control over how the development looked – she'd get Kif's advice; make sure that there were certain stipulations built into the contract. No hideous UPVC conservatories; no ghastly fast-growing conifers. From what little she'd seen of Owl's Nest, Rod was a sympathetic renovator, using authentic materials that blended in with the surroundings. And anyway, if he was going to be living in the farmhouse, he wouldn't want to look out on anything unattractive; no doubt he'd take as much care over the conversion of the stables as he would the renovation of the house.

By the time Jamie fell asleep, she felt happier. She'd resigned herself to the fact that buildings didn't matter, that the most important thing to preserve was her relationship with Jack, and she wasn't going to fall out with the one person she had left in the world over a pile of old bricks.

16

Having made her resolution, the very last thing Jamie wanted to do was go and apologize to Rod Deacon. But she had to, before it was too late. She prayed to God that he hadn't de-instructed his solicitors on the back of what she'd told him, but as they'd heard nothing to indicate that, she presumed he was just biding his time. Meanwhile, she was going to have to bite the bullet. Eat humble pie. Swallow her pride. She cursed herself for her impulsiveness. If only she hadn't flown off the handle the week before, she wouldn't have to humiliate herself now.

On Monday morning, she dressed carefully for the confrontation, wanting to look calm and collected and to dispel the image of last week's ranting harpy. She put on the linen skirt she'd worn to the bank and tied back her hair neatly. Happy that she looked businesslike, and trying to ignore the dread that was churning in her stomach, she ran out to the car before she could change her mind and bottle out.

To her annoyance, both cars were parked outside Owl's Nest. She didn't really want Bella as an audience while she grovelled, but she had little choice. She rapped on the door and waited. And waited. After what seemed like an age, but was probably only a minute, she rapped again.

She had to admit she felt a certain relief when there was still no reply. She needn't have the conversation she'd been dreading after all. She was scrabbling in her bag to find a pen and paper, in order to write a note and explain the situation, when Rod answered the door.

He looked absolutely terrible. He was wearing a white T-shirt and boxer shorts, still not dressed even though it was lunchtime. He hadn't shaved either, and his eyes were bloodshot. His hair stuck out at all angles. There was a definite smell of last night's beer.

Jamie recoiled slightly, but was grateful. If he'd come to the door looking crisp and fresh and irresistible, she would have found the task even harder.

She coughed to clear her throat.

'I've come to apologize,' she began carefully. 'And to say – just ignore what I said the other day. I overreacted. I was exhausted. And a bit ... emotional. I've got everything a bit more in perspective now.' She smiled. 'The deal's still on. Pretend I never said anything. As soon as the solicitors have done their thing, we can sign.'

He stared at her dully. When he spoke his voice was gruff.

'There's not a lot of point now.'

Jamie frowned. This wasn't quite what she'd been steeling herself for. 'What do you mean?'

'Bella and I have split up. So there's no need for the comfortable family home any more.' His tone dripped acid bitterness. 'Added to which, I won't be able to afford it. Not with an ex-wife to support.'

Jamie tried to take in what he was saying, genuinely shocked. Rod and Bella had seemed so together the other day. For heaven's sake, they'd both come home in their lunch hour for a romp. What on earth could have happened?

'I'm sorry,' Jamie faltered, really not sure what to say.

'Don't be.'

There was an uncomfortable silence.

'Do you want to ... talk about it?'

He looked at her without really seeing her.

'No. I don't think I do.'

But he made no move to shut the door. Jamie hovered awkwardly, not sure what she was supposed to do. She hated to leave him in this state. He looked utterly distraught, and her initial instinct was to comfort him. He looked bereft, distressed, inconsolable, like a small boy who'd lost his mummy while out shopping. The urge to take him in her arms was almost instinctive.

But then she remembered how she herself had suffered at his hands. Perhaps Bella had undergone a similar indignity; flown the coop because of some callous, unfeeling action on Rod's part. She remembered how desperate she had been to get away from him, all those years ago. She felt all her pity evaporate at the memory, and her heart harden.

'Well, no doubt you did something to deserve it,' she said, unable to stop the words coming out. He looked as if he'd been slapped.

'What?' His expression was pained.

'Come on, Rod. We both know what you're capable of. You don't appreciate what you've got, and then you go and dump on them from a great height. Basically because you can only think about yourself.'

'What are you talking about?'

243

'Are you telling me you can't remember? Did it all mean so little to you?'

Shit, thought Jamie. She was losing control again. This was exactly what she hadn't meant to do, open old wounds and show her feelings. Why couldn't she keep her trap shut? She should have phoned. Or written a letter. Or contacted him through his solicitor.

But then, why shouldn't she say her piece? Did he honestly think he could sail through life treating women so badly? At the time, of course, she hadn't had the strength to confront him. She had felt so hurt, she'd just wanted to hide, pretend it had never happened.

He was gaping at her, uncomprehending.

'Jamie. Please explain. I never did understand what went wrong. Why did you disappear like that? That day by the river. I thought ... I mean ... it was special, wasn't it?'

He was almost pleading with her for reassurance. Jamie gave a cynical laugh.

'Yeah. So special that you went and told your brother. You told your brother, Rod, and made me a laughing stock. You might as well have taken an advert out in the *Ludlow Herald* ...'

Even now, Jamie could feel the bitter humiliation and anger burning up inside her, just as it had when Lee had laughed at her in the market place.

'What?' Rod was looking at her in bewilderment.

'Surely you didn't expect Lee to keep his mouth shut? I suppose you couldn't resist boasting, could you? That's what blokes do, isn't it? I suppose it was my fault for thinking you were different. But you couldn't resist crowing about getting your leg over. Because that's all it was to you, wasn't it? A quick how's your father down by the river, then back to the pub to tell your mates. Stupid me, for thinking it was something special. But no, it was just a bet. A fifty-quid bonk. How do you think that made me feel?'

Feeling sure she'd said enough, Jamie backed hastily towards her car, snatching for the handle. She had to get away. All the fury she'd felt was as all-consuming as it had been that day, and she wanted to pour out her feelings, make him realize what he'd done to her. Tell him that she'd never been able to trust anyone since. She was opening the door to get in when Rod grabbed her by the arm.

'Jamie,' he said. 'I've got no idea what you're talking about. But I promise you I didn't breathe a word. Not to anyone.'

She stared at him, wanting to believe. But the wounds were still raw, even after all these years.

'You would say that, wouldn't you? I mean, you couldn't admit to it, could you? It was a despicable, cowardly—' she groped around for the final insult '—ungentlemanly thing to do.'

She looked down at his hand on her arm, as if his very touch repulsed her.

'Excuse me.'

He released her immediately, backing off. She slid into the seat and turned the ignition with shaking hands. As she drove away, she wiped away the tears from her eyes as she realized that not only had she behaved like a complete idiot yet again, but Bucklebury Farm was well and truly fucked and she'd only got herself to blame.

*

Rod stared disbelievingly after Jamie's car, finding it hard to comprehend what he had just heard, and trying to ascertain in his head just what it was he'd been accused of. He walked back into his house in a daze, got dressed, picked up his car keys and walked out again, as if sleep-walking. The few facts she'd given him were churning round, gradually connecting, until everything finally fell into place. He headed determinedly for the town, roaring up through the sweeping streets, causing heads to turn and pedestrians to jump out of the way, unused as the inhabitants of Ludlow were to aggressive driving.

He abandoned his car recklessly in the market place, not caring if he got a parking ticket, and strode along the pavement, eyes fixed straight ahead, jaw clenched. Shoppers and tourists scurried out of his way, realizing that this was a man on a mission. He reached the pub where he knew he'd find his brother. He pushed open the door, ignoring the surprised greeting of people he'd known for years, trying to accustom his eyes to the smoky gloom. The thud and boom of a fruit machine drowned out a tinny tape of sixties hits that had been played so many times it was stretched beyond recognition.

Lee was sitting at the bar as usual, holding court amongst his minions, a packet of John Player Special topped by a huge gold lighter resting next to his fresh pint.

'Hey, bro – to what do we owe the pleasure? Another pint for my little brother, please, barman.'

Rod's expression didn't falter as he jabbed towards the door with his thumb.

'Outside.'

'What?'

'I said outside. I want a word.'

Lee made a mystified face to his fellow drinkers, shrugged and followed Rod out into the market place.

'What's this all about?'

Rod replied with a well-aimed blow to Lee's jaw.

'Jesus!' Lee reeled back in shock, clutching his face, indignant. 'What the bloody hell was that for?'

'What did you say to her?'

'Who?'

'Jamie Wilding. What the fuck did you say to her, you bastard?'

'Jamie Wilding?' Lee looked every inch the aggrieved innocent. 'I haven't seen her for years.'

'Exactly. Neither have I. Because of something you told her.'

A dim light of recollection came on in Lee's eyes.

'Ah ...'

A little knowing smirk appeared on his lips at the long-buried memory. Enraged, Rod rewarded his brother with another punch. Then another. By the time he'd reached the fourth, Lee realized that if he didn't start defending himself he'd be dead meat. He aimed a blow at Rod in retaliation, who stepped neatly out of the way and tripped him up. Lee lay sprawled in the gutter. He was about to scrabble to his feet when he found Rod's trainer resting on his neck. He grabbed his ankle, desperately trying to pull him off.

'You're choking me! Get off.'

Rod had put just enough weight on his throat to stop him moving. Lee shut his eyes, thinking that if he could feign unconsciousness Rod might remove his foot. But his brother remained steadfast.

'Not until you tell me what you said to her.'

By now, punters were pouring out of the pub to watch the fun, cheering the brothers on. It certainly livened up a dull Monday lunchtime. Behind them, the landlord was jumping up and down in agitation.

'Leave it out, lads. I don't want trouble here. You'll have the coppers round any minute.'

Rod leaned forwards, increasing the pressure slightly. Lee gave a strangled gargle.

'OK, OK! I told her you'd shagged her for a bet.'

'Right. Thank you.' Rod took his foot away and Lee sprang to his feet. The two brothers faced each other in a standoff, Lee on the defensive, fists clenched, and Rod fixing him with a cold, hard, steely glare.

'Do you want to tell me why?'

'She wasn't good enough for you, Rod. She'd have chewed you up and spat you out. Her sort don't give a toss for the likes of us.'

'You never gave me the chance to find out for myself, did you?'

Lee jabbed Rod in the chest, cocky now he was back on his own two feet.

'She was toying with you, mate. You were her little bit of rough; a cheap thrill. I did you a favour. Trust me.'

The next moment, Lee found himself hurtling backwards through the air as Rod aimed a vicious blow at his stomach. He gave a roar of rage and came back at him, fists flailing indiscriminately. As the brawl became more vicious, a couple of the regulars waded in to pull the brothers apart. By the end of it, Lee was in the gutter again, groaning. He was more used to fighting than Rod, but he wasn't fuelled by blind fury, and the beer had slowed him up. He spat a tooth out into the road, prodding the bloody gap gingerly with his tongue.

''Kin' 'ell,' he lamented, looking after his brother's retreating back. 'Didn't know he had it in him.'

Moments later the police arrived, and questioned Lee, who made an aggrieved statement saying he'd been set upon by someone but he had no idea who or what for. The police hadn't believed a word but as no one else seemed able to give evidence either, they left Lee with a dark warning. Then he cadged a lift to the hospital to get himself stitched up; see if his nose was actually broken. He was going to have to lie low for a couple of days. He certainly didn't want his mother asking questions. If he thought Rod had given him a hard time, it was nothing to what Nolly would do to him if she knew the truth.

Rod drove to his workshop, gripping the wheel to stop his hands from trembling. He wasn't a violent person, but his discovery had unearthed a terrible rage, and he'd needed to vent it straight away. He'd never be able to make Lee understand what he'd done. There wasn't a romantic bone in his body. He wouldn't appreciate what he'd destroyed. Getting his face smashed in was the only language Lee understood. And Rod was horrified to realize that he'd enjoyed the splat of his knuckles against Lee's lips. Beating him to a pulp wasn't going to change anything, least of all the past, but it had made him feel better.

He reached the sanctuary of his workshop and took several deep breaths to calm himself down. He stared blankly at the work in progress, wondering how on earth it could stay so resolutely the same when his life was in such turmoil.

Bella had left. Bella had betrayed him. And Jamie had come back into his life, but seemed further out of reach than ever.

He made a half-hearted effort to finish a job, but he couldn't possibly concentrate. What crazy set of rules was he supposed to be playing by? What was he supposed to do next? He thought he'd done his best to make the most of his life after Jamie had gone. He'd built up a business, got married, built a home for his wife, been – he thought – a pretty good husband and was hoping to become a father. Now the whole fucking lot had come crashing down around him, and his past had come back to have a bloody good belly laugh at it all. Where the hell had he gone wrong? By obeying the rules and being a naive fool. He might as well have just lain down and asked everyone to walk over him.

He went over to a cabinet he kept locked in the corner of the workshop. With trembling hands he undid the padlock. Inside was an exquisite, hand-carved, hand-painted Noah's Ark, about two feet long and a foot high. There was a roof that came off to reveal the animals inside, and a ramp that slid out for them all to walk on board. With it came Noah and Mrs Noah and their sons and, at the last count, about thirty pairs of animals: all the usual, and some more unusual – gnus and warthogs and armadillos, all accurate down to the last whisker.

He'd started it just after they'd begun trying for a baby, wanting his firstborn to have an heirloom that showed his love. He realized now it had been presumptuous. The ark was a jinx. He should never have started it. He remembered all the old wives' tales, like not bringing a pram into the house before the baby was born. If that was bad luck, then pouring your heart and soul and love and hope into something was definitely portentous.

He opened the door to his wood-burning stove and, before he could stop and think about it, thrust all the animals inside. He tossed in an old rag covered in turps, then threw on a match. Then he snapped the ark over his knee until it resembled pieces of kindling, throwing the splintered remains on to the flames that were beginning to take hold. Hours and hours of painstaking work were demolished in seconds.

OK. That was it. No more Mr Nice Guy. He wasn't going to sit around mooning, dreaming silly romantic dreams about a perfect future any more. He was going to behave like a normal person. Be immoral, selfish, self-centred – just like his brothers, who all seemed to live the life of Riley. He was going to go out on the piss, shag women, treat them like dirt. That way, he couldn't get hurt …

Jamie was sitting on the gate in the top paddock at Bucklebury, gazing over the rolling fields of pasture. In the very far distance, you could just see the line of oak trees that followed the tributary of the Teme running along the border of Lydbrook House. Jamie remembered how on a summer's day like this, she would run out with a halter and catch her pony, leap on to it bareback and canter down over the fields till she reached the river. There was one shallow spot where it was safe to cross, where the water burbled unthreateningly over the pebbles. Then she would circumnavigate the lawn and call for Emma and Kate to tack up their ponies. They could happily spend the whole day roaming the countryside, armed with a

Tupperware box of hard-boiled eggs and a plastic bottle of squash.

She felt a hand on her shoulder and turned. It was Olivier, in cut-off jeans and covered in oil. He'd been tinkering with the car in the stable yard and was on his way inside for a beer when he'd spied Jamie. Something about the set of her shoulders told him something was badly wrong.

'Are you OK?' He looked concerned.

'I have, as they say, fucked up big time.' She looked bleakly over the fields, too despondent even for tears. When she finally spoke again, her tone was flat. 'We're going to have to sell the whole lot.'

There was a mixture of concern and jubilation later in the kitchen at Lower Faviell Farm when Rod spilled the beans about Bella's betrayal to a select audience of Deacons. He had to tell his mother. She'd been his pillar of strength over the past few months, and besides, he'd always told Nolly everything. Except ... well, there was one thing he'd kept to himself all these years. And he told Tanya. He told Tanya because he wanted reassurance that he was to be pitied. And he knew he could rely on his outspoken sister to say all the things he was thinking in his head.

'Well, I can't say I'm surprised. She's always been a selfish bitch. Lucky escape, Rod. Lucky escape!' She jabbed the air with her cigarette to emphasize how strongly she felt. 'Just think, if she had got pregnant – you'd have ended up with some devil child, chained to her for ever.'

Nolly nursed her cup of tea, deeply upset. She would never admit it to anyone, but of all her children, Rod was her favourite. And she'd been looking forward to the day he gave her a grandchild, because it would have held a special place in her heart – even though she had nine others which she already loved dearly. And no mother likes to see their child hurt, even when he's nearly thirty and big enough and ugly enough to look after himself. She was finding it very hard to know what to say. The last thing she wanted to encourage was a reconciliation with Bella. What a wicked, wicked thing to do.

Tanya hurled herself into a chair and stuck her feet up on the kitchen table. She was in jodhpurs, purple chaps and a crop top bearing the slogan 'Beat Me, Bite Me, Whip Me, Fuck Me'. Rod wondered what on earth the parents who brought their little darlings for riding lessons with her thought. But then, Tanya was Tanya. You either liked it or lumped it. She lit another cigarette with the end of her old one, and tossed the nub end into the sink where it landed in the washing-up water with a spiteful hiss.

'Well,' she said in a tone of finality. 'At least we can look forward to getting the old Rod back.'

Rod looked startled. 'What do you mean?'

'You've always thought you were a bit special, ever since you were with Bella. To be honest, you were becoming a real knob. Poncey clothes, poncey cars, poncey holidays. Too good to come for Sunday lunch with the rest of us.'

Rod looked pained. He'd always wanted to come to Sunday lunch, but Bella had refused, arguing that Sunday was the only day they had off together. Why should they go and spend it with his family?

'And Christmas?' Tanya went on. 'Fucking off skiing. What a poseur.'

That had been the only solution. Bella had refused to go to Lower Faviell Farm for Christmas lunch as well.

'I'm not having your drunken brothers touching me up,' she'd said. 'And those kids smearing chocolate all over me.'

That should have rung alarm bells, surely? He knew some of his nieces and nephews were badly behaved when they got overexcited, but it was Christmas – she could have made allowances. But she'd stood fast. And the only way to avoid deeply offending his mother was to say they were going away. They could hardly sit at Owl's Nest with the rest of them only half a mile up the road.

Tanya was glaring at him accusingly.

'Yeah. Fucking off skiing and leaving behind flashy presents for everyone that none of us could afford. All wrapped in shiny gold wrapping paper with ribbons and bows. Which made us all look like cheapskates.'

Rod was mortified. OK, so he'd bought his mum a bread-maker. But only because he thought she'd like it; she'd seen it on the telly and admired it. Not because he wanted to show off, but because he wanted her to know he'd thought about her.

'Tanya, that's enough,' interjected Nolly, feeling that once again her outspoken daughter was going too far.

'I'm telling him for his own good.' Tanya jumped up to give Rod a hug. 'I love you, you know that. We all love you. And you're better off without her.'

Rod found himself smothered in Tanya's CKOne-drenched cleavage and wild black mane. He pushed her away, laughing.

'All right, all right. I get the message.'

'Come to the gig tonight, then. You haven't been for over a year.'

Rod was surprised to hear genuine reproach in her voice. He didn't think Tanya had noticed, or cared, that he hadn't been to see her perform for so long.

'It wasn't really Bella's scene, to be honest.'

'No, because she was jealous.' Tanya was brazenly matter-of-fact. 'Anyway, were the Ice-Skating Championships she dragged you to your scene? Was going to see Enrique Iglesias your scene? Surely marriage is about give and take?' she finished, with an uncharacteristic insight into relationships. Tanya had never managed to stay with anyone more than two weeks. They quite simply couldn't cope.

As the sun began to slip down behind the trees like a golden penny, Olivier and Jamie wandered along the river. Olivier did his best to reassure her that the deal falling through wasn't her fault.

'His wife would still have left him, so the deal would have fallen through anyway. It was nothing to do with you. So stop blaming yourself.'

Jamie looked doubtful.

'Anyway, maybe selling up will give you a chance for a new start, a clean slate for you and your dad.'

'But I don't want a clean slate,' protested Jamie. 'I was happy with the way things were.'

'What about in six months' time, when the central heating's packed in? It's on the blink, I can tell you. And when the next council tax bill comes in. And the drive needs tarmacking, the downstairs windows all need replacing—'

Jamie smiled, despite the doom and gloom.

'I'm starting to get the picture.'

'Honestly, it would be a constant worry. You're too young to take on the responsibility of a place like that. And Jack's too old.'

He lit a cigarette, gesturing with it to emphasize his points.

'Flog it. Take the money and run. I would.'

'Would you?' Jamie sounded far from convinced.

'I can totally see why you love Bucklebury. But I think the price is too high. You'd never get on top of it. You'd never enjoy it. There'd be too much to worry about.'

Jamie surveyed him thoughtfully. 'So what will you do? If we do sell?'

'You know me. I'm long overdue a change. I never stay in one place too long.'

Jamie sighed. 'You're right. It's time to move on. I just couldn't help hoping ...'

Olivier put an arm round her and gave her an affectionate squeeze. For a moment she nestled into him, put her head on his shoulder. He felt his heart quicken at the contact. Alarmed by his response, he moved away as if he'd been scalded. They were just coming back up the hill to the gate where he'd found her.

'I better go and put the car away,' he said hastily and, leaping over the gate, walked swiftly across the yard to where the Bugatti was parked.

He didn't like to admit it, but he was totally unconvinced by his own arguments. He felt like a total hypocrite. For the first time in his life he was dreading the prospect of moving on. Having thought all his life that he was immune to sentiment, he would have done anything in his power to help the Wildings protect their legacy and save the farm. But what could he do? He was a no-good ski-bum with no prospects, no cash, no power, no influence.

Olivier drove the car carefully in through the barn doors and sat in the driving seat for a few moments. All he could hear was the clicking of the engine as it cooled down, and the old rooster giving a defiant crow. The mustiness of years of hay and straw combined with the last of the exhaust fumes filled his nostrils. In the early evening warmth he could feel his eyes closing, his mind drifting away.

For one wild moment, he wondered about going to ask his father for the money to save the farm. He could dress it up as some sort of watertight investment opportunity that would guarantee a great return. But no – that was far too dangerous. Eric wasn't the sort of man who gallantly helped people out of financial difficulty. He was the type to take advantage of others' misfortunes. And given the history between Eric and Jack...

Anyway, Olivier had to prove himself to Eric before he could go back to him. And the only way he could do that was by walking back into the showroom with the Corrigan Trophy under his arm. For a moment he let his mind wander to the one other person who was standing in his way. Of all the other possible entrants, it was only Claudia Sedgeley who was going to put up any serious competition. How important was the trophy to her? Did she have something to prove like he did? Just how hungry was she for the glory?

He wondered why he felt so threatened by her, when she was just a girl. Surely he didn't have any scruples about trouncing her? Then he remembered that moment in the tent, when she'd looked so vulnerable, so crestfallen, and his heart had gone out to her, just before she'd turned on him again.

He put Claudia firmly to the back of his mind. He was going to have to treat her just like any other competitor. She was just a number. If you started making allowances, that was when you lost your edge.

17

By nine o'clock that evening, the Drum and Monkey at Tidsworth was stifling, rammed with hot bodies and smelling of spilled beer and fags and sweat. To Rod, it felt like heaven. He hadn't been anywhere like this for years; this would have been absolute anathema to Bella, who liked designer purity, clinical minimalism, wipe-clean chic. Not earthy, raw, peasant fun. There were no poseurs in here, just people who knew how to let their hair down and didn't mind making fools of themselves.

As a Shania Twain tribute, Tanya had her own serious following; die-hard fans who turned out dutifully to every gig. As well as that, line-dancing clubs often had coach trips to see her. She was bloody good; she could belt out the tunes in a faithful reproduction of her tribute, she had a rapport with her audience, it was obvious she revelled in being on stage and showing off. And she looked great; she worked hard to keep in shape for her figure-hugging stage costumes. Tonight she was in a black lace body stocking, lace-up stiletto boots and a huge belt with an eagle's head for a buckle, her hair in wild, snaky ringlets that had taken Nolly hours with a pair of curling tongs. She looked sensational; she'd have put Shania herself to shame.

To Rod, coming to the Drum and Monkey was a bit

like coming home. Nothing had changed since he was last here, not even the bar staff. He nodded to people he knew, and was gratified that many of them slapped him on the back in genuine pleasure at seeing him there. He felt guilty that he hadn't turned out to support his sister more often. He felt someone tickle him just above his waistband and turned to find Foxy Marsden peering up at him through her peroxide fringe.

Foxy's eyes were small and black, but so alive – they snapped and crackled with vivacity and mischief. Her mouth was permanently twisted into a naughty little grin. She never seemed to take anything seriously; life was one long party. She was wearing hot-pink bondage trousers and a tight white leather biker jacket with her name emblazoned in rhinestones on the back. She was drinking Dirty Diesel – Guinness with a Vimto top – and it clearly wasn't her first. It was hard to believe that by day she worked in a local solicitor's office, dressed demurely in a navy-blue skirt and white blouse, dealing with people's queries politely and efficiently.

'Rodders! Long time no see! Tanya said you were going to be here, but I didn't believe her.' Foxy was genuinely delighted to see him. She checked him out with a mischievous grin. 'You're looking gorgeous.'

Rod ruffled her hair.

'So are you.'

Pre-Bella, Tanya, Foxy and Rod had been a bit of a threesome, going out on the town, driving to clubs in Shrewsbury and Worcester and Hereford where they'd danced the night away. Rod had been their minder, and made sure Tanya and Foxy didn't get out of control, always forcing them back into the car at the end of the evening no matter how much they protested. It was often like trying to control a box of frogs, as they were as highly spirited as each other. But it had been fun, and the three of them had been close.

But when he got married, everything changed. And now he felt guilty that he'd cut the likes of Foxy out of his life so ruthlessly. He hadn't even invited her to the wedding. God, what a prick. Did she, like Tanya, think he'd got ideas above himself, that he'd turned into a supercilious git once he'd married Bella? Not that it was Bella's fault that he'd cut himself off from people who mattered. He'd done it subconsciously, knowing that there was no point in trying to mix his two worlds. Which made him a prize wanker. But Foxy didn't seem to hold it against him. She was more generous of spirit than that. It was almost as if they'd slipped straight back into the old times.

They stood together in a sea of heaving, dancing bodies as Tanya belted out her repertoire, the appreciative audience singing along with her: 'Man, I Feel Like a Woman', 'I'm Gonna Get You Good', 'That Don't Impress Me Much'. Rod found that scarcely a moment went by without a bottle of beer being thrust into his hand. He'd forgotten how hospitable and generous the old crowd were: when you went to the bar, you made sure everyone was all right for a drink. He made sure he reciprocated, passing out bottles of Beck's to faces he knew, getting a nod of thanks in return. It wasn't long before he realized he was well and truly plastered, but he didn't care. So was everyone else, and he was up for a laugh. He hadn't had a session for months. All the advice he'd read on conception had advised going easy on alcohol. Well, tonight he was making up for lost time.

*

Jamie had a heart-to-heart with Jack that evening. They sat out on the camomile lawn, and she broke the news that Rod had decided to back out of the deal. They both agreed there was nothing for it but to sell up lock, stock and barrel.

'I'll get Kif to come out and value it. I don't know if now is the best time to put it on the market, with people going off on holiday. And we need to tidy the place up a bit. I think we'll probably be looking at September.' As she said it, she couldn't believe she sounded so matter-of-fact. 'And I'll get him to send us some details of other places on the market. You'll need to start looking for somewhere else.'

For a few minutes they discussed where he might look. It was rare for anything to come on the market in Upper Faviell, and when it did it was usually madly overpriced, but there were a couple of villages on the way into Ludlow that they thought might be suitable.

'What about you?' asked Jack. 'What are you going to do? I mean, obviously wherever I go there'll be room for you.'

'Phone the agency. Tell them I'm back on the books. They'll be delighted.'

But Jamie wasn't sure she was looking forward to going back to her old lifestyle. It had always been her return to Bucklebury in between jobs that had sustained her; knowing she could chill out at home and recover, catch up with her friends, enjoy the countryside. She wasn't sure that checking into the spare room of whatever house Jack ended up in was going to be quite the same tonic. Obviously, what she needed was a place of her own. She was old enough. She earned enough. Perhaps she'd ask Kif to look out for a place in Ludlow for her. A little terraced house that wouldn't need much looking after if she wasn't there. Maybe she could rent it out as a holiday let while she was working... For a moment, she felt quite excited by the prospect. She'd never had somewhere to call hers, and maybe that's what she needed to compensate for the desolation she felt at leaving Bucklebury. A focus.

It was funny, she thought. Olivier had been right: now she'd come to terms with the idea of selling up, the future was full of possibilities. She mused on how she'd written him off as a bit of a layabout, too obsessed with playing to have any grip on reality. But he was obviously quite sussed underneath it all. And she was grateful for his support; he'd been sweet—

'You know what we ought to do?' said Jack, breaking into her reverie. 'Have a bloody great party.'

Jamie looked at him in amazement.

'A party? What on earth is there to celebrate?'

'It's my birthday next weekend.'

Jamie clapped her hand to her mouth.

'Of course it is. I'd forgotten. Well, I hadn't forgotten, but I hadn't really thought about it. I'm so sorry, Dad.'

She felt stricken with guilt. Jack's birthday, falling as it did in the middle of July, had always been an excuse for the Wildings to have a huge party. It hadn't seemed appropriate this year, with Louisa gone.

'Don't be. I wasn't going to bother. But in the circumstances, I think we should go out with a bang.'

Jamie thought about it. Maybe Jack was right. A final bash at Bucklebury would do no harm. They'd make sure that whoever took over the farm from them could never live up to their reputation for party-giving. She grinned, suddenly excited by the idea.

'Why not?'

'I'll organize the booze,' said Jack, 'if you do the food.'

Jamie looked indignant.

'And I'll sort out the garden,' added Jack hastily, realizing that the division of labour wasn't quite fair. 'I know I've let it run away. But I haven't really had a reason to tackle it up until now.'

As the end of her set approached, Tanya launched into a slow, romantic ballad, and the audience needed no second telling to couple up and indulge in a good smooch. Alcohol and the heat had made them all amorous. Heads nuzzled into shoulders; wandering hands strayed over bare, warm flesh; lips and tongues introduced themselves to each other and made their probing acquaintances.

Foxy pulled Rod towards her, putting her hands round his waist as they danced – or tried to – amidst the crush. Foxy took the opportunity to grind her groin against his, grinning lasciviously. She'd taken her jacket off, and underneath all she wore was what looked like a bandanna tied on with string round her neck, her breasts underneath like playful puppies. He felt a sudden rush of fondness for her. A rush of fondness that ran straight down to his groin. Rod was astonished to feel himself grow as hard as iron. Astonished and delighted. He'd convinced himself that he was never going to get a decent erection again, yet the evidence in his trousers couldn't be argued with. And it hadn't gone unnoticed by Foxy either. As the song came to an end to rapturous applause, and Tanya took her bow, smiling and blowing kisses to her admirers, Foxy led

Rod by the hand through the throng and into the men's. Against his better judgement, overruled by pure animal instinct, he followed her.

Rod pressed her up against the wall, finding himself driven wild by her passionate response, her warm hands exploring his body, tugging up his T-shirt, scrabbling at his flies. He wanted to lose himself in the experience; indulge in sheer, unadulterated lust; a damn good fuck that didn't involve a military-style planning campaign and an agonizing wait to see if it had had the desired effect.

But even in his inebriated state, a little warning bell went off. He might be desperate for a shag, but he needed to be careful. As he kissed her, his left hand was struggling for loose change in his jeans. He found a pound coin and, without taking his mouth off hers, inserted it into the condom machine. He grappled for the small packet, then led her into the nearest empty cubicle for some privacy, shutting the door and sliding the lock into place.

But as he looked at the graffiti-splattered wall, the extreme tackiness of the situation struck him. What the hell was he doing, having it off with Foxy Marsden in a public toilet? He'd never, even in his most dissolute days, done anything like it. Was he totally desperate? Yes, probably, on reflection. Even in his drink-addled state, he tried to put things into perspective. He was going to regret this in the morning. Not that Foxy would make any demands on him, or read anything into it. But, actually, she deserved better. He liked Foxy. More than that, he respected her. He didn't want to use her, like some backstreet whore he could just throw away.

He leaned back against the door, putting his hands up.

His head was spinning slightly, from the booze and the heat and the intensity of their passion.

'I'm sorry. I don't think I can do this.'

She protested and grumbled, then cajoled.

'Come on, Rod. You're the last one on the list. I never thought I was going to be able to get you. I'd have a full house – the only girl in Shropshire to have had all the Deacon brothers.'

If Rod had thought it was a bad idea before, this really brought it home. He'd always been the enigmatic one. He wasn't going to blot his copybook now.

'Listen, Foxy – if I'm going to screw you, I want to do it properly. Dinner, candlelight, champagne – the full works.'

Foxy rolled her eyes. 'Where did that romantic bollocks ever get you?'

She put a hand on his zip and felt underneath. He was still rock hard. She shook her head regretfully.

'What a waste.'

Later, Rod staggered out to the car park to call a cab on his mobile, impressed with his self-control. And even more impressed with his hard-on. He might have had a narrow escape with Foxy, but at least he knew he still had lead in his pencil. He'd been afraid that all that high-pressure copulation with Bella had taken its toll, but it obviously hadn't. When he fell into bed that night, managing to remove his shoes but nothing else, he congratulated himself on a fantastic night. He'd had a good few drinks, a few laughs with his old mates and brought himself back down to earth. Perhaps the future wasn't so bleak after all.

*

266

Pauline Robbins was beside herself with anxiety, anxiety that was bordering on distress. Since Bella had turned up on the doorstep on Saturday evening, distraught but tight-lipped, she hadn't emerged from her bedroom. And no matter how hard Pauline coaxed her, she wouldn't reveal what was the matter.

In the meantime, Pauline didn't know how on earth she was going to hold things together at the dance school. It was obvious Bella wasn't in a fit state to teach. Pauline could manage most classes, but Street Funk for six- to nine-year-olds was beyond even her choreographic skills. At fifty-six, she would look ridiculous wiggling and thrusting in imitation of J-Lo and Christina Aguilera. In between classes she was rushing back to see if there was any improvement in her daughter. After just one day, she was exhausted and in despair.

She knew she was guilty of living her life through Bella. Ever since her feckless husband had taken off when Bella was eleven, they had been incredibly close. And Pauline was gratified that Bella had followed in her footsteps by taking over the dance school. She'd started it in the local village hall twenty-six years ago, when Bella was three, racking her brains as to how to earn a bit of extra cash that she could keep from her bully of a husband in order to clothe the kids and give them a few treats. It had taken off at once, and probably been instrumental in Len's departure – he was insanely jealous of her success, and tried all sorts of tricks to stop her teaching, even ... well, Pauline didn't want to remember the effects of his fists, just thanked God that he had taken the easy option and buggered off with Carole-Ann Rogers like that.

Even now she and Bella were very close. Pauline tried

hard not to let their relationship impinge on Bella's marriage, but the truth was she didn't have much else in her life. She was a very attractive woman still at fifty-six, she took good care of herself, but she really couldn't be bothered with men. She'd tried a couple of times – it was all champagne and roses to start with, elaborate promises. Then the real bloke emerged, farting, whinging, snoring, demanding kinky sex – the bloody Internet had a lot to answer for, in Pauline's view. She was quite happy to be independent. She loved the dance school – she dreaded the day when her joints would become too stiff to teach. All in all, she felt, life was good. She was in control.

Bella appearing like that had been rather a bolt from the blue. Pauline had been convinced she and Rod had a strong marriage. And she was very fond of her son-in-law. Despite her generally low opinion of men, she wouldn't have thought he was the type to have an affair, which was the only reason she could think of for her daughter's distress.

She knocked gently and walked into Bella's room. Bella was curled up under the duvet, wide awake, staring dully into space. The curtains were half-drawn, the windows closed. The room was incredibly stuffy. There was a glass and a half-empty bottle of mineral water, but no sign that Bella had eaten anything.

Pauline decided she had to be firm. She sat on the bed.

'Right,' she said. 'I can't help you if I don't know what's going on. I want some answers. And if you don't give them to me, I'm going to go and ask Rod what it's all about.'

Bella's reaction was most alarming. She clung to her mother, sobbing hysterically, begging her not to contact

Rod. She would only be making things worse. Pauline was horrified by what she'd unleashed and backtracked immediately, assuring Bella she wouldn't say a word, desperately trying to soothe her. Bella slumped back on to her pillows, exhausted, and Pauline stroked her daughter's brow, noticing her hair was lank with grease and sweat. She didn't think she'd ever seen her look this awful.

Eventually Bella's eyes closed, and she fell asleep. Pauline sat and watched her till she was sure she wasn't going to stir again, desperately wondering what was troubling her. All sorts of scenarios ran through Pauline's mind. What evil had the bastard been inflicting on her precious daughter? She might be fond of Rod, but not being a great fan of the male species she had a low opinion of what any of them were capable of. Had he been beating her? She hadn't seen any sign of bruising, but then Pauline knew only too well how clever wife-beaters were at concealing the fruits of their labour. God, if he had ... Her own fists clenched at the very thought.

With the loyalty of a mother, it never once occurred to her that in fact it was Bella who was in the wrong.

18

There was, thought Jamie, nothing like planning a party for taking your mind off things. And she was going to make this a good one. If this was going to be their last celebration at Bucklebury, she wanted it to go down in local history.

She and Jack compiled a guest list then split it between them and phoned round. Happily, most people seemed able to come, even though it was short notice. They were obviously delighted that the institution had been re-established: Jack's birthday had always been an import-ant date on the local calendar. You knew whether or not you'd made it socially by whether or not you received an invitation.

By the time they'd finished, the final number was seventy, and Jamie knew from experience that what with gatecrashers and last-minute invitations and people bringing their long-lost cousins who had turned up at the eleventh hour, it was likely to be closer to eighty. They would just have to pray that the weather stayed fine.

It had always been the tradition for Jack's birthday party to have some sort of theme. There had been the Pink Party, the Come As Your Alter Ego party, the S and M party, when everyone came dressed as something beginning with S or M: there were soldiers and spacemen and morris dancers and mandarins, and they'd eaten sausages and mash followed by strawberries and meringues. Jamie remembered that her mother had been a mermaid, a glittering, shimmering siren outshone by nobody, while drab little Rosemary Drace had come dressed as a mouse. Louisa had laughingly told her how clever she was to come as herself...

For some reason the memory made Jamie feel uncomfortable. She decided it was too late to expect people to come in fancy dress, but nevertheless she wanted to create a magical atmosphere, a backdrop, something to tie the event together and make it a talking point rather than just a mundane garden party.

She rummaged through the house and outbuildings in search of inspiration. Bucklebury had long been a treasure trove, as Jack and Louisa were both great hoarders, magpies who found a use for items most people were glad to see the back of: Jack because he was always convinced he could make a profit out of the most trivial piece of rubbish; Louisa because her artistic nature meant she could turn the most unwanted item into an object of beauty. Inevitably, they did nothing with their salvage, but it made Jamie's search an interesting one, and brought memories flooding back. Halfway through, she wondered what on earth they were going to do with all of it when they moved out. It was two lifetimes of accumulated junk that no one else would give houseroom.

Eventually, she hit gold when she discovered the remnants of one of Jack's business ventures stuffed into a stable — flood-damaged stock from an emporium that sold ethnic goods, that he'd been planning to sell on and never got round to. There were embroidered bedspreads and cushions, lanterns, incense sticks, huge wooden bowls and chalices. They were all a bit mouldy and damp, but that didn't matter. Thus she decided on a Middle Eastern theme – very loosely interpreted and not authentically correct, but colourful and exotic.

She had her props, and now she had to decide on the food. For that amount of people, it would have to be a buffet. Jamie spent an afternoon in the sunshine with her mother's old cookery books, copying out recipes and making lists of ingredients, until she'd compiled a menu that she thought she could manage – food that could be cooked in advance and wouldn't spoil. Spicy lamb kebabs threaded with peppers and tomatoes that she would bung on the barbecue. An enormous chicken tagine, with almonds and apricots. Huge earthenware bowls filled with hummus, slick with olive oil and pungent with garlic, and sesame-seed-encrusted pitta breads to dip in or stuff with salad. Couscous mixed with pine kernels and sultanas and fresh coriander. Deep, rich red plum tomatoes and chunks of cucumber tossed with shiny, wrinkly black olives and squares of crumbling feta cheese. A yogurt dip fortified with handfuls of freshly chopped mint.

And for pudding, she'd make baklava – little diamonds of layered filo pastry filled with a delicious honey-drenched mixture of pistachio nuts and almonds. And cubes of rose-scented Turkish delight dusted with icing sugar. And figs, roasted on the barbecue, then slashed open to reveal their gloriously decadent purple interiors into which even more gloriously decadent mascarpone cheese could be dolloped.

As she scribbled out lists and more lists, she could hear

the metallic snip of Jack's hedge clippers as he coaxed the box hedge into shape. Even he seemed happier, and at one with himself. It appeared that once you'd made a decision, even if it was the hardest one you'd ever made in your life, things then got easier.

Zoe and Christopher had their very first serious row over Jamie's party invitation. Zoe had already made arrangements with Natalie earlier in the week to go and spend the weekend with her, and couldn't even admit to herself how ridiculously excited she was about the prospect. Christopher couldn't for the life of him see why she couldn't postpone it.

'It's a chance for you to meet some more people. Jack's birthday party is a legend in its own lifetime. And it'll be a fun crowd.' Zoe just raised an eyebrow, which incensed him. 'Frankly, if you're not even going to make the effort—'

'You'll have much more fun without me. You'll be able to catch up with all your old friends. You won't have to worry about whether I'm enjoying myself. I don't want to inhibit you.'

'Zoe – you wouldn't inhibit me. You're my wife, for God's sake. I want you to be there.'

Zoe looked stubborn. 'I've already told Nat I'm coming. And I've got an appointment for my hair.'

Christopher wondered if he should put his foot down for the first time in his life. But it wasn't his style. And he wasn't sure what sort of reaction he'd get. So, in the end, he didn't. He just sighed.

'Fine. If you think that's more important.'

'It wouldn't be a problem if there was a decent hair-dresser in this godforsaken neck of the woods.'

Christopher looked at her witheringly.

'Not that you've actually tried any of them. You've just made assumptions. Just as you have about Jamie's party guests. And all of the mothers you've met at Twelvetrees. It's not like you to be so judgemental, Zoe. I don't know what's come over you. I really don't.'

He stalked out of the room. Zoe bit her lip. She knew that every accusation he'd levelled at her was a fair one. Whenever she heard her own voice, she hated herself. But she didn't know how to drag herself out of the rut.

Then she told herself she'd been perfectly reasonable. It wasn't as if Jamie's invitation was a longstanding one. On the contrary, it was very last minute. And very presumptuous of the Wildings to assume everyone would be available at such short notice. But then, Zoe reminded herself, most people round here probably didn't have anything better to do.

Early on Thursday morning, Jamie was in the post office buying ingredients for the party. Hilly was caught up in the excitement.

'It's about time somebody had a decent party round here. It's one of the things I miss most about your mum. She was so spontaneous – always popping in here and buying the place out because she'd got twelve for dinner. And you never knew who you'd be sat next to. A trapeze artist or a celebrity gynaecologist or a pig farmer. She had such a knack of mixing up guests. Never worried about whether they'd get on – it was up to them. She was a wonderful hostess.'

274

That was one of the things Jamie loved about Hilly. She wasn't coy about mentioning Louisa. And if anyone would understand her other reasons for the party, Hilly would. She decided to mention it to her; see if she thought she was being fanciful.

'I know this sounds bonkers, but this party's sort of my memorial to her. It's the last party we'll probably have at Bucklebury, And I feel ready to celebrate her life now. I didn't at the funeral.'

'Well, no. Who does? It's all such a blur; you're still in shock from them dying, aren't you? And you're so hidebound by tradition. Roger's funeral was hideous; it wasn't the send-off he deserved at all.' She leaned in confidentially. 'I took a few close friends to Claridge's a couple of months after. We stuffed ourselves silly on oysters and champagne and told funny stories about him. We had a riot, and Roger would have loved it. It was so therapeutic. It helped me enormously.'

At that moment the door opened, and Rod walked in. Jamie immediately felt a flush run up over her cheeks. He walked over to the fridge to collect a pint of milk before he noticed her.

'Hi.' He put the milk down on the counter and burrowed in his pocket for change. He looked a hell of a lot better than the last time she'd seen him, Jamie thought. Somehow she managed to find her voice.

'Hello,' she said coolly, hoping that he would pay and leave as quickly as possible. But he didn't.

'Can we talk?'

'Um ...' Jamie shrugged. 'I suppose so.'

She waited for him to carry on. He stood there awkwardly. Hilly gestured vaguely at all Jamie's purchases.

'A box. You're going to need a box. I think I've got some in the stockroom.'

She disappeared tactfully. Rod picked up a Mars bar, placing it carefully next to his pint of milk.

'I spoke to Lee. He told me what he'd told you. About it being a bet.'

Jamie nodded. Just keep your mouth shut, she told herself. Keep your dignity this time.

'I know you might not want to believe me,' Rod carried on. 'But there was no bet. And I didn't say a word to Lee. I promise you. That day ... meant more to me than any other day, before or since. I never knew why you went off: it haunted me for years. But I understand now. And I wanted to say, even though I didn't do what you thought I'd done, that I'm sorry.'

They stood there in silence. Twelve years, thought Jamie. Twelve years because Rod's sick, twisted brother went and put a spanner in the works. Neither of them had any idea what to say. They couldn't just go back and wipe the slate clean, not after all this time. Jamie decided that it was in both of their interests to make light of it, not embarrass each other by wallowing about in something that had happened half a lifetime ago. She kept her tone light and casual.

'Oh well. Never mind. There's been a lot of water under the bridge since then. We were only kids ...'

'I guess so,' agreed Rod hastily, not wanting to make more of it than necessary.

Jamie ploughed on hastily.

'By the way, I'm having a party this Saturday. A sort of ... farewell to Bucklebury.'

'You're putting it on the market, then?'

'We've got no choice.'

There was a pause. Rod looked awkward, knowing he was partly to blame for the situation.

'I'm sorry. It's a very special house.'

He held out a pound to Jamie. 'Give this to Hilly, would you? I'm in a bit of a rush. Tell her to put the change in the blind box.'

He was about to go. He scooped up his Mars bar and put it in the top pocket of his denim jacket.

'Rod—'

He turned in the doorway.

'I'd love you to come. If you could. If you're not doing anything.'

Their eyes met. There was an awful lot more she wanted to say, but the middle of the post office wasn't the place to do it.

Rod looked awkward. 'I'm not sure what I'm up to. Can I leave it open?'

'Sure. It's only casual. Eightish. Buffet supper. Outside hopefully, if the weather's kind. Loads of booze. Dancing. You know the sort of thing. Bring a bottle.'

Jamie knew she was babbling, but it was the only way to stop herself saying what she really felt, and she'd sworn to herself not to lose control again. Rod smiled at her from the safety of the doorway.

'Maybe see you then.'

He was gone. Moments later, Hilly reappeared with a box.

'I knew I had some somewhere,' she said triumphantly, then looked at Jamie shrewdly. 'Is he coming?'

'I don't know,' said Jamie slowly.

'He's a lovely lad,' said Hilly. 'He gave me a kitchen,

you know. For the flat upstairs. He was fitting a new one down the road and had to take the old one out. It would have been far easier for him to skip it, but he brought it up here on the back of his truck. And he only charged me a hundred quid to put it in.'

Jamie was impressed at Rod's thoughtfulness. He obviously knew that, even though on the surface the post office always seemed busy, it was a struggle for Hilly financially, that the profits on stamps and newspapers and pints of milk, which were the bulk of her trade, were not substantial.

Hilly leaned forwards confidentially. 'I'm not usually indiscreet. People use this place like a confessional. They trust me, and I don't like to gossip. But the word is his wife's left him.'

'Yes, she has,' said Jamie. 'But there's a lot of baggage.'

'Bugger the baggage!' snorted Hilly. 'People just use that as an excuse not to move on. He should forget about her.'

Jamie didn't like to say she didn't mean the baggage between Rod and Bella, but between Rod and herself. Twelve years of baggage that still hung thick in the air between them whenever they met. Why on earth had she gone and asked him to the party? She wasn't going to be able to think about anything else between now and Saturday.

Because she couldn't deny it, his revelation had turned her upside down. Their relationship – the only relationship she had ever found meaningful – had been destroyed on a misunderstanding. And now they had come full circle, were both free and available, to all intents and purposes. Jamie found her heart was beating ten to the dozen with the realization. For even after all these years, she found him as attractive as ever. Their conversation had set her pulse racing, his proximity had made her feel faint with longing. There had been one moment when she'd almost thrown herself into his arms, but caution had won. She wasn't going to lay herself open again. She wasn't going to make a fool of herself by pursuing him.

Gathering up her box of goodies, Jamie decided she'd done her bit. She'd asked him to the party. If he was interested, he'd turn up. And if not ...

As she left the shop, Hilly watched after her thoughtfully. In her opinion, Jamie and Rod would make a perfect match. Hilly didn't suffer fools gladly, but she had a lot of time for Rod. And she'd never really warmed to Bella. She was perfectly pleasant and polite, but she never seemed quite real. Like a Barbie doll – plastic perfection but nothing underneath. She wondered what on earth Rod had ever seen in her, apart from her obvious attributes. But then, men were funny creatures. A pair of perky breasts often went a long way.

For the next two days, the kitchen at Bucklebury became a fug of browning spices and bubbling, scented syrup as Jamie cooked like a mad thing. Outside was a hive of activity as Olivier and Jack set to in the garden with enthusiasm if not expertise, transforming the overgrown wilderness. They had strict instructions from Jamie not to make it look too manicured, but there wasn't much danger of that happening: it was going to be all they could do to get the grass cut, the hedges trimmed and the beds weeded in time for Saturday.

Surprisingly, Lettice turned out to be a godsend. Totally

unfazed by cooking for large numbers, she insisted on helping. The two of them had a hoot, with the windows thrown open, Louis Jordan blaring out on the sound system, singing and chopping and dancing and stirring and swearing profusely whenever a finger was burned or a plate was dropped. Every now and then the four of them would stop for a break, sitting out on the lawn with a pitcher of ginger beer, Jack and Olivier and Lettice smoking as if their lives depended on it; Jamie lying back in the hopes of topping up her South American tan which had faded disconcertingly quickly.

In the midst of it all, something happened to unsettle Jamie. An envelope was pushed through the front door at midday on Friday. It contained a stiff little note from Rosemary, politely declining their invitation. Jamie felt a little hurt that she hadn't felt able to talk to her in person: she perfectly understood that Rosemary probably wasn't in the mood for mad socializing, given Hamilton's condition.

This led her to realize she hadn't been to visit Ham yet, and she felt riddled with guilt. Even though everyone insisted that he wouldn't know if she'd been or not, Jamie didn't think that was quite the point. She resolved to go and see him as soon as she had time; once the party was over and they'd got over the trauma of putting Bucklebury on the market. It was the least she could do, after all. Kif had been so sweet about helping, even though that plan had come to nothing. And perhaps it was about time she thought about someone other than herself for a change.

And throughout all the preparations, with a supreme effort of will, she put her invitation to Rod to the back of her mind. Of course he wouldn't come. He was obviously still raw from his sudden split, and Jamie hadn't exactly behaved decorously at their reunion the other day. The last thing he'd want to do was fall out of the frying pan into the fire.

19

Friday morning did not start well for Christopher. Zoe was overexcited about her trip, and was too preoccupied with getting ready to care that there were only enough Frosties left in the packet for one bowl. Christopher patiently divided them between Hugo and Sebastian and sliced the last banana on top to bulk them out. There was none of his favourite marmalade left either – the thick-cut, dark stuff. He didn't complain. There was no point in starting a row about something as trivial as marmalade.

His mother was taking the boys to school so he could drop Zoe at the station en route to work. They didn't really speak much on the way. Christopher pulled up outside the ticket office. She got out of the car and leaned in through the driver's window to give him a kiss.

'Have a lovely party tomorrow.'

Christopher gave a resigned smile, resisting the urge to snipe at her once more.

'Have a good time. Send my love to Nat and Edwin.'

He watched her scamper off clutching her weekend bag, only just remembering to turn back and give him a wave. She obviously couldn't get out of there fast enough. Christopher sighed as he started up the engine. What was the saying? You can't keep all of the people happy all of the time…

He'd only been at the office ten minutes before his spirits were restored. They were having an office meeting, to assess their progress over the past two months, and see where they could make further improvements. There was a pot of fresh coffee on the table and a plate of almond pastries. Christopher sank gratefully into his chair at the head of the table, poured himself a cup of coffee and decided he really was turning into an old fogey because he was pleased to see the milk in a proper jug.

The meeting got off to a flying start. Tiona was delighted to report that the number of houses they'd sold since May was equal to the amount they'd sold since Hamilton had taken ill, so things were really taking off again. Samples of updated artwork – a revamped brochure and proposed new layout of their property details – had come in from the PR company, and they all agreed the new image was fresh and exciting yet still put them across as traditional and upmarket. Luke, the new boy that Tiona had taken on as her assistant, was congratulated on his hard work and dedication, and it was agreed that he should be allowed to do viewings on his own and should start studying for his estate agency exams.

It was only when Tiona put in a plea for another new member of staff that Christopher smelled trouble on the horizon. He'd already noticed that whenever Norma tried to contribute, Tiona cut her off in irritation. Often the point that Norma made was perfectly valid, but she wasn't being allowed her twopence-worth. She had, after all, been at the office longer than any of them. She'd worked for Hamilton for as long as Christopher could remember, she was Ludlow born and bred and a stalwart of the local scene, so her opinion was important.

Tiona gave a brief profile of exactly what they needed.

'We need someone who can update the computer – there's no point in having one unless the information is totally up to the minute – as well as the website – ditto. And someone who can lay out the weekly photographs for the newspaper. That will leave Luke and me free for viewings and valuations. And leave Norma free to answer the phone and send out details, as well as providing your administrative support.'

Tiona flashed Christopher a brilliant smile that assured him he was far too important to be expected to type out his own letters, even though he was perfectly computer literate and capable of typing out a letter faster than he could dictate it. At the same time she had managed to diminish Norma's role, making her sound like a glorified dogsbody. Of course, Norma wasn't capable of carrying out the job Tiona was describing – at nearly sixty she didn't have the technological skills and was unlikely to acquire them – but there was no need to undermine the very good job she did do.

Christopher tackled Tiona about it in private later on, when Norma had nipped out for her vegetable puff from the bakery down the road. Tiona stood firm.

'I know I get irritated by her, and I'm sorry, but I find it very frustrating that she tries to stand in the way of every innovation I try and bring in—'

'I don't think she's trying to stand in the way as such—' objected Christopher mildly.

'Believe me, she is. When you're not here, she

undermines me at every opportunity. And if you ask me, it's extremely dangerous. We need a spirit of cooperation here, not a struggle for supremacy. We're all equally important. It's not a competition. But Norma seems desperate to stamp her authority. She's under the impression that she knows best. But how can she? She hasn't done her estate agency exams. She's just answered the phone here for two hundred years.'

'Are you saying we should get rid of her?'

'I'm saying we should make it clear what her place is. Which is answering the phone and sending out details. Not getting involved in making offers and chasing up solicitors. She's nearly made two deals go down this week by passing on incorrect information at the wrong time.'

Christopher sighed. This was one part of the job he wasn't overly good at, man management. He could appreciate Tiona's dilemma, but Norma was practically part of the furniture. And she was a fantastic source of local gossip – she knew when people were moving almost before they knew themselves. Anyway, he was pretty sure they couldn't get rid of her for no reason, whatever Tiona said.

'Luke's doing brilliantly,' Tiona persisted. 'I can have him out valuing by the end of the month. We're getting so busy, we'll both be out of the office seventy per cent of the time. We need somebody else at that front desk; someone bright and young who can be trained up as well. Not a grumpy old Rottweiler.'

Through the bull's-eye window, Christopher could see Norma coming back from her lunch break.

'Look, why don't we chat about this ... over dinner?'

Tiona looked faintly startled.

'I've been meaning to treat you to say thanks for

everything you've done. Zoe's buggered off to London for the weekend. I don't want to sit with an omelette in front of *Midsomer Murders*. Why don't we thrash these problems out after work? If you're not doing anything, that is,' he added hastily, realizing he'd been a bit presumptuous.

Tiona laughed. 'It was going to be pizza in front of *Midsomer Murders*.'

Christopher paused for a moment, wondering if he was being rash, then told himself it was perfectly acceptable to reward a conscientious member of staff with dinner out.

'I'll have to nip home and give the boys their supper. I'm sure Mum won't mind babysitting. What about if I book us a table for eightish?'

'Perfect.' Tiona flashed him a smile.

Christopher walked back to his desk and sat down as Norma came in through the door, trying to ignore the fizz of excitement he felt in the bottom of his belly.

Zoe sat on the train, willing the wheels to turn faster and bring her closer to London. She'd bought *Elle* at the station and had devoured it carefully from cover to cover, making several notes in her Filofax for things she wanted to buy – a new light-deflecting foundation, some cork-heeled wedges and a bra that promised miracles. She couldn't believe how ridiculously excited she was, and how she must have once taken everything so much for granted. She had an appointment to have her hair done at two, something she once did automatically every six weeks without a second thought. She'd found a picture of a supermodel with a fluffy, urchin cut shot through with streaks of paprika and cinnamon. She knew it would suit her. And that Christopher wouldn't like it much. He was always trying to get her to grow her hair; he said it made her look more feminine. Frumpy, more like. She supposed he wanted her to look like Jamie, with her long, unkempt mop that always made her look as if she'd been dragged through a hedge backwards – and not in a designer way.

Eventually the fields became fewer and the houses began to build up. Just as some people yearned for grass and trees and blue sky, so Zoe yearned for bricks and concrete, and as they hurtled past industrial estates and warehouses and tower blocks she began to relax. Open space made her nervous. It was the city where she belonged. Why did nobody seem able to understand that humans suffered outside their natural habitat just as much as animals?

By the time she arrived at Paddington, the Friday afternoon rush had already begun. The roar of the crowds, the boom of the announcements, the distant hooting of trains, the chaos, the impatience, the rushing, the rudeness, the smell of Costa coffee all felt like paradise. She bought Natalie a huge bunch of overpriced flowers from a stall and nearly broke her neck rushing down the stairs to the Circle Line. She was going to be late for her hair appointment but she didn't care. She was back where she belonged.

That evening, Christopher dutifully made Hugo and Sebastian macaroni cheese and practised a few wickets with them in the garden. Then he chucked them into the bath while he got changed. Once they were in their pyjamas and happily ensconced with his mother in front of the telly, he went out to the cab he had called earlier.

He got the taxi to drop him off at the top of Corve

Street. The evening sun provided a rosy glow to the pinky-red brick of the Georgian facades that stood to attention either side of the wide, sweeping street, crowned by the black-and-white beamed Feathers Hotel. The sound of live jazz and laughter spilled out from the courtyard of a nearby pub. The shop windows were stuffed with all kinds of fascinating treasures: antiques and bric-a-brac, unusual gifts, paintings – nothing at all that you actually needed, just things designed to bring pleasure. By the time Christopher reached Hibiscus, a discreet, square-fronted building painted a deep cream, he'd mentally bought a French wirework jardinière for the terrace, a painting of a square-bottomed Herefordshire cow and a stained-glass window that he thought might look nice over the front door at Lydbrook.

He was really looking forward to going to Hibiscus, which had a Michelin star and, more importantly, a laid-back, relaxed atmosphere. He'd read so many rave reviews, heard so many people heap praise upon the talents of the young French chef, Claude Bosi, but Zoe had never shown any inclination to go. And there wasn't much point in pushing her if she wasn't going to appreciate it. Tiona had been utterly delighted when he'd phoned her earlier to tell her where to meet, and had been amazed he'd been able to get a table. As had he. God was obviously smiling on him tonight.

He arrived five minutes early, just long enough to peruse the wine list and decide on what to start with. Not champagne. That was over the top and a bit presumptuous. Christopher felt champagne was overused these days. People seemed to pop a bottle at the drop of a hat. It had lost its mystique and its sense of occasion. Instead he chose a good white burgundy. By the time the bottle had appeared at his table, so had Tiona.

She looked ravishingly pretty, in a lilac dress that at first glance seemed very demure and girlish, but on closer inspection was tantalizingly low-cut, and made of a soft, silky fabric that clung to her curves. They exchanged polite kisses on each cheek, and he ushered her into her seat and poured her a drink.

For a few moments they had fun people-watching: a table of eight celebrating a milestone birthday, people from out of town who were spending the weekend on a gastronomic tour of Ludlow, locals who made a habit of frequenting the outstanding restaurants on their doorstep. Christopher felt slightly relieved that there was no one in there he knew. Not that he had a guilty conscience, for he had a perfectly above-board reason for being there, and had Zoe bothered to phone him from London he would have told her where he was going and why. But people did have a tendency to jump to conclusions.

They lingered over the menu, agonizing over what to choose, and finally settled on the *menu gastronomique* – seven surprise courses carefully chosen and executed by the chef, demonstrating his repertoire and exploring a vista of ingredients. It took the responsibility of making a decision out of their hands and, thought Christopher, would prolong the evening pleasantly – you could hardly gallop through seven different dishes.

As they worked their way down the first bottle of wine, Christopher found he was unburdening himself to Tiona about Zoe, and how unhappy she seemed. She was so sympathetic and concerned, and it was nice to share the problem with someone. He hadn't until now. He'd hinted to Jamie, but she had her own problems. By the time the first course arrived, he'd almost talked himself into some sort of separation.

'It's obvious she's desperate to go back to London,' he explained. 'But how can I go back, with the business? And I don't want the boys going back.'

It was true. Hugo and Sebastian had thoroughly blossomed in their six months in Shropshire. They were bonny, active boys, not pale, insipid Londoners permanently plugged into their PlayStations. They loved the country life; they adored Twelvetrees and all its outdoor activities – archery, golf, even cross-country running. It would be a crime to force them back into the filth and dirt and grime of the city.

'I suppose we'd have to have some hideous split life. Zoe could go back to London – she'd have to get a job, though. We couldn't afford it otherwise. And we'd have to take it in turns – me going to London one weekend, her coming up here the next. Or something.' Christopher frowned. It sounded incredibly complicated. 'And who would the boys live with? I'd keep them here with me if I could, but I can't if I'm working. Not with the hours I do.'

'Why don't the boys board at Twelvetrees? They do weekly boarding. Tons of people do it. And the kids have a whale of a time. Half of them don't want to come home at the weekends, apparently.'

'How on earth do you know that?' Christopher was curious.

'It's part of my job to know everything, isn't it? It's the first thing people ask about when they're thinking of relocating – what are the schools like? I'm telling you,

Twelvetrees has clinched more sales round here than the fact that the restaurants are to die for.'

Christopher looked down at his tiny white cup of melon cappuccino. Perhaps Tiona had a point. Then he stopped himself. He was being ridiculous. He and Zoe weren't going to split up, for heaven's sake.

He looked over at Tiona, who was sipping her soup reverently.

'This is divine. I can't tell you what a treat this is. I've been dying to come here ever since it opened, but for some reason they haven't been queueing up to take me.'

'It's a pleasure,' said Christopher, and it was. He sloshed another few inches of wine into their glasses.

'Now,' he said. 'What about Norma?'

Tiona wrinkled her nose. 'Let's not spoil a lovely evening by talking about Norma.'

She put her elbow on the table, cupping her chin in her hand and looking into his eyes. He was transfixed by a string of river pearls dangling between her breasts.

'OK then,' he said carefully. 'Tell me ... where you see yourself in a year's time.'

Tiona tilted her head to one side, considering the question, a dreamy little smile on her lips. Then she leaned forwards.

'Opening another branch of Drace's,' she said. 'In Shrewsbury. Or Hereford. Or preferably both.'

Christopher was knocked sideways by her dedication. As the pan-fried foie gras arrived, he marvelled at what a treasure she was, and how lucky he was to have her on his side. And her loyalty wasn't her only attribute. Christopher had always been a chest man. Zoe's were like a couple of fried eggs ...

Later, he walked Tiona home through the streets. There were still plenty of people around. Even though the night was warm, Tiona seemed chilly in her dress and he lent her his jumper. She looked adorable, vulnerable – the sleeves hanging over her fingertips.

At the front door of her little terraced house, she put the key in the lock, turned to him and smiled.

'Coffee? Brandy?'

Christopher shook his head.

'I'd better get home. I think I'll walk back to the market place and get a cab. Clear my head.'

'Sure you don't want to come inside and wait?'

Of course he did. It was what he wanted more than anything – to step over her threshold, enter her world. He hesitated. But it was too late.

'Actually, you're probably right,' Tiona was saying. 'We'd better call it a night. We've got a hectic day at the office tomorrow, after all. Last thing you want is another brandy sloshing about on top of all that lovely food.'

Her tone was brisk, almost businesslike. Any hint of invitation Christopher thought he'd heard in her voice a moment ago had vanished. Thank God he hadn't gone and made a fool of himself. He turned to go.

'Wait!'

She went to take off his jumper. As she pulled it up over her head, he couldn't take his eyes off her breasts underneath the lilac fabric. She folded the jumper neatly, handing it back to him.

'Thank you so much for a lovely evening.'

Her voice was soft, delicious, like a caress. She leaned in to give him a kiss goodnight. Her lips brushed his lightly, so lightly he couldn't be sure if they had in fact made contact. And as he drew back, she put a finger on his cheek, giving it the gentlest stroke, before disappearing inside and shutting the door. It was such a fleeting gesture that he couldn't be sure of its meaning. But all the way home in the taxi, he relived the moment. Had it been affection? Appreciation? Or an invitation? He really couldn't be sure. He lifted up his sweater and held it to his nose. Her scent still clung to it, making his stomach clench with desire and giving him a sudden schoolboy urge ...

20

By five o'clock on Saturday afternoon, Jamie thought that everything that needed to be done had been done. The garden looked stunning – the box hedges had been clipped and the honeysuckle and clematis and roses were cooperating by showing off their best blooms. All the food had been prepared and was lying under tea towels on the cold slab in the larder or in the fridge. Using the rose-covered pergola on the back lawn as a base, and two gazebos she'd begged off the village fête committee, she'd used the flood-damaged bedspreads to construct a sort of Bedouin tent effect. Inside, she covered trestle tables with white tablecloths and scattered them with rose petals on which to lay out the food when the time came. She'd strung dozens of tiny tin lanterns with tea lights on a washing line. Hay bales covered in yet more bedspreads and Ali Baba cushions and gaily striped durries provided seating. She sent Jack down to the gate at the end of the drive to tie on a bunch of gold balloons, for the few guests who hadn't been to Bucklebury before.

Olivier had mowed the lawns, and the air was heavy with the delicious scent of freshly cut grass. The sound system had been placed by the French windows, with the speakers perched on the patio, and Jamie had gone through their entire record, tape and CD collection compiling a suitable selection of music: cool atmospheric jazz to kick off the proceedings, then something more up tempo and up to date for dancing.

As she wandered barefoot back into the kitchen, she felt satisfied with her preparations. There was nothing she'd forgotten – she'd even got up early to listen to *Farming Today* and get the forecast. Tonight was going to be warm and dry; there was no threat of rain.

She was amused to find Olivier in the kitchen doing battle with the ironing board, running the ancient old iron that rarely saw the light of day over a pale blue linen shirt.

'I'm impressed.' She grinned.

'My mother trained us all rigorously in the art of ironing. You know what the French are like when it comes to looking well turned out.'

'I don't think I've ever seen you in anything but jeans.'

'I can do understated chic.' He indicated a pair of cream chinos that had already undergone his attentions. A pair of conker-brown loafers was on the floor, polished and gleaming.

'You haven't forgotten you're in charge of the barbecue.' Jamie didn't like the thought of his pristine outfit covered in marinade.

Olivier held up a white chef's apron. 'I borrowed this from Toby at the Royal Oak.'

Jamie was touched. Olivier had made so much effort. He'd been running round doing all the last-minute errands for her; nothing was too much trouble. He'd borrowed extra chairs from the village hall, gone into Ludlow for mineral water and mixers, and brought back an enormous bunch of orange lilies mixed with exotic greenery as a centrepiece for the drinks table.

She realized she'd kept him somewhat at arm's length during his stay, but looking back at it now he'd been incredibly supportive. She supposed she'd been suspicious of his motives at first, wondering why he was so keen to hang around Jack. Was he just a freeloader, taking advantage of her father's generosity in order to pursue his own quest for glory? She knew now that wasn't the case, that Olivier and Jack were a partnership, that Olivier more than pulled his weight in his own way. He was a good friend, and she hadn't really acknowledged it, with all that had happened.

'Anything you want ironing, while I'm at it?'

Olivier was looking at her questioningly, holding the iron aloft. He cut a comical figure, the picture of masculinity behind an ironing board, a domestic god whose sexuality couldn't be questioned, even for a second. The perfect husband for someone, mused Jamie. Surely that was what every girl wanted...

'Well?'

His question brought her back to the matter in hand with a jolt of alarm, as she realized she hadn't given a thought to tonight's outfit. The first visitors were going to start arriving in less than two hours and she hadn't even had a bath.

'Shit! I'd better go and sort out what I'm going to wear. I haven't had a chance to think about it...'

She fled the kitchen in a panic. She'd meant to go out and buy something new, but what with all the preparations, she hadn't had time. She knew she didn't have anything suitable in her own wardrobe. She wanted something slightly glamorous but not too dressy. Something feminine, sexy and colourful, but practical if she was going to be rushing round hostessing. She thought about ringing Zoe and asking if she could borrow something, but then remembered that Kif had phoned to tell her Zoe had a prior engagement in London and wouldn't be coming.

There was nothing for it but to raid her mother's wardrobe.

Christopher had had a bitch of a day. Some days estate agency could be very satisfying: putting the perfect deal in place, helping people realize their dreams. But often it was a nightmare, especially when people's dreams were jeopardized, when a chain broke, or a smug solicitor discovered some hideous glitch on the deeds and pushed the panic button. Or when people pulled out at the very last minute without a word of apology or explanation. That's when the estate agent, as the middle man, got it in the neck, and had to call on every last drop of diplomacy to soothe ruffled feathers. Three deals had gone sour today, and Christopher had felt as if he was treading water as he desperately tried to salvage them and calm hysterical vendors who saw the house of their dreams slipping through their fingers. And of course, being the weekend, there was a lot he couldn't do, as solicitors weren't working and banks didn't answer the telephone. At the same time, the world and his wife wanted to view: nosing round other people's properties when you had no intention whatsoever of putting in an offer seemed to be a national pastime.

Tiona had been a trouper, as ever, pouring oil on troubled waters, her gentle voice calming the most irate of clients. Norma got very stressed and ratty if asked to do more than one thing at once. Christopher wondered if Tiona was right, and perhaps it was time she went. Then he chastised himself for being intolerant. He hadn't had a hangover as such, but the rich food and wine of the night before, followed by a rather sleepless night, made him feel as if he was wading through treacle. The backs of his eyelids felt like sandpaper, the bottom of his mouth like the proverbial parrot cage, and he was slightly light-headed.

He hadn't had a moment to swap notes with Tiona about the evening, which was probably a good thing, as he wouldn't have had a clue what to say. But just as she was leaving, she stopped by his desk to thank him for a lovely dinner.

'It was great, wasn't it?' replied Christopher, a trifle non-committally.

'Yes. It's spoilt me rather. My pizza will seem dreadfully dull after all that wonderful food.'

Christopher wasn't sure if she was dropping a hint or not.

'I'm going to a party, I'm afraid. Otherwise I'd say pop round for supper with me and the boys.' There. That sounded friendly and open but not too incriminating.

'That's very sweet. But I could probably do with an early night.'

Christopher wondered, for one wild moment, if Jamie would mind if he brought Tiona to the party. It wouldn't be that extraordinary a request. And he knew the Wildings. The more the merrier. Then he realized it was a crazy, dangerous idea, because he knew his reasons for it were less than innocent.

Tiona leaned down to pick up her handbag. She obviously had no idea, Christopher thought, that from a certain angle you could see right down her front in that cardigan. The river pearls were there again, slithering back into their place between her cleavage as she stood up. He gulped. Tiona waved her fingers in farewell.

'Have a lovely party. Think of me curled up on the sofa in my jimjams.'

And off she went. Christopher groaned inwardly. The image of Tiona in her jimjams was going to haunt him all bloody evening.

No one had ever cleared out Louisa's dressing room. It wasn't that it was a shrine. Jamie simply hadn't had time before she had flown off on her travels to address the problem, and Jack had found it too painful to face. Everything was still hanging there. Rows and rows of couture frocks and jackets and coats and trouser suits. It was only now that Jamie really appreciated how exquisite they all were. Balenciaga, St Laurent, Dior – feminine and unfussy. And on the floor of the cupboard, boxes and boxes of shoes, many with matching handbags.

Louisa had never come across as a label freak – not like Olivier's mother – and ninety per cent of the time she'd been in jeans or jodhpurs. But there was no denying that when she did dress up, she had a presence and an elegance that was inimitable – the class and style of Jackie O, Audrey Hepburn and Grace Kelly rolled into one, with a little bit of Bloomsbury bohemian thrown in. It was her tiny frame, her flawless complexion and her colouring that stopped men in their tracks and made women grind their teeth with envy. Most infuriating of all was the impression she gave that she hadn't really tried. Jamie sighed. Something would have to be done with it all. It was almost worthy of a museum.

She searched through the wardrobe, trying on and discarding, wanting to find the perfect fit. She was taller than her mother, and her breasts were slightly larger, but she had inherited her tiny waist and her slim, boyish hips. Eventually she settled on a simple sleeveless shift dress made of Shanghai silk. The material was sensational – deep, hot pink shot with threads of gold. It fitted her perfectly; any tighter and it would have been tarty, but instead its simplicity made it classy. On Louisa, Jamie remembered, it had come to just below the knee, but on Jamie it was just above, which made it look more modern. She backcombed her hair to give it height around her face, then tied the rest in a loose plait which she wore over one shoulder. On her feet she wore a pair of wedge-heeled espadrilles with canvas ribbons that tied round her ankles like ballet shoes.

Looking at herself in the mirror for approval, she wondered if she'd done the right thing. Was it tasteless to wear a dress belonging to her mother? She soon reassured herself. People wore jewellery belonging to the deceased, hung their pictures on the wall, utilized their furniture. Why not wear their clothes?

On impulse, she finished off with a squirt of the perfume bottle that was still sitting on the dressing table. For a moment her mother was there in the room with her. When Jamie was a little girl, she would always go into Louisa's dressing room just before a party, just before she went down to greet her guests. They had a little ritual: Louisa would do a twirl for Jamie's benefit, and Jamie would survey the final effect before giving a nod of approval. Louisa would finish by spraying a cloud of perfume into the air, then walking into it. Then she would squirt a tiny cloud for Jamie, who would go to bed smelling of Schiaparelli's Shocking, and listening to the sounds of merriment downstairs.

Now, smelling it again, she was surprised she didn't feel sad. Instead, she felt quite ready to go downstairs, greet her guests and host the party of a lifetime.

By half-six when Christopher got home, he very nearly bottled out of the party altogether. All he wanted was a light supper and, frankly, bed. To make matters worse, Zoe phoned to talk to the boys. She fizzed and bubbled down the telephone, sounding just like the old Zoe, the girl he'd married. Not the harbinger of doom he came home to every evening. He felt thoroughly depressed. What was the point? Life was one long juggling act – despite his hard work and best intentions today he'd ended up making no one happy. And his wife was only herself when she was two hundred miles away in the bosom of someone else's family, not her own.

He snapped himself out of it. He couldn't not go to the party. Jamie was his best mate, for heaven's sake. And he might feel better when he got there. It was a given, that the less you looked forward to something the more you enjoyed it, and vice versa. By that token, tonight should be a bloody riot, he thought, as he pulled on a fresh pair of jeans and a navy-blue shirt.

He went to kiss the boys goodnight. They were roaring with laughter in front of some Saturday evening game show and weren't in the least perturbed by his departure.

Rosemary was in the kitchen washing up by hand. Even though they'd brought the dishwasher up from Elmdon Road and plumbed it in, she still insisted on doing things the hard way.

'Thanks for holding the fort again, Mum.' He put an arm round her shoulder and gave her an affectionate squeeze.

'I'll probably stay over if I have too much to drink, if that's OK,' he added, ever so casually, and Rosemary smiled her consent.

Jack was in the kitchen mixing huge pitchers of deadly fruit punch with an alchemist's precision when Jamie came in. Olivier was washing up the last of the glasses they'd unearthed from the larder. He stared at Jamie in open admiration.

'You do scrub up well,' he said. She realized he hadn't seen her in anything but scruffy jeans. Suddenly she felt a bit self-conscious. There was time to change into something less dressy. Then she thought no – this was an occasion. She was the hostess – she should look as if she'd made an effort. And she was actually enjoying the effect she was having.

'You don't look so bad yourself,' she replied, and it was true. Gone was the jeans-wearing, slightly scruffy ski-bum. In his place was an elegantly casual young man, looking like the perfect host as he buffed up the glasses with a linen cloth and lined them up on a tray.

Jack, dapper as usual in a pale pink shirt, cavalry twills and spotted cravat, had long prided himself on his cocktail-making capabilities. Tonight, he'd mixed together puréed raspberries, lime juice, gin, grenadine and ginger ale which, combined with copious amounts of ice, was deliciously refreshing, and tasted of summer, but packed a kick that would put the most reserved of guests into a party mood.

When he saw Jamie, his heart leaped into his mouth. For a moment, again, he'd thought it was Louisa coming into the kitchen. How many times had they been through this ritual, preparing for a party? He'd loved the sense of anticipation almost more than the event itself. He would always bring Louisa a glass of his latest concoction to taste in the bath, to get her approval.

He took a huge slurp himself instead to steady his nerves, not trusting himself to speak. Luckily, at that moment Lettice arrived, resplendent in turquoise silk and adorned with strings of amber necklaces.

'Happy birthday, darling,' she boomed, throwing her arms round Jack, thrusting a huge box of Havana cigars at him by way of a gift and demanding to taste the punch. Her arrival broke the moment, dragged him out of his reverie and extinguished the ghost in an instant, for which he was very grateful.

Ensconced in her old stamping ground in Shepherd's Bush, Zoe now knew that she wasn't going mad. She didn't care that she'd got chewing gum stuck to the bottom of her shoe on the way back from getting some fags from the shop. That she nearly got run over crossing the road. That she had to wash her hair because it was clogged with dirt and smog, whereas in Shropshire it lasted three days. She was happy again. She was in her natural habitat and, like an animal returned to the wild after some time in captivity, she began to thrive.

Tonight, Natalie's husband Edwin was babysitting for their two little girls, Daisy and Millie, and Natalie and Zoe were going out on the town, together with Natalie's au pair Marcella. Zoe couldn't believe how excited she was about something she'd once taken for granted. It had been a heavenly couple of days. She'd had some serious retail therapy the day before, after her hairdresser had followed her instructions to the letter and created a new look. Today she'd got up late, scoffed brioches and coffee with Natalie on the decking, wandered into Barkers of Kensington to top up her make-up bag, had her nails done at a nail bar and bought quite the most outrageous dress she'd seen in the window of Morgan – she suspected she was the wrong side of thirty for Morgan, but she didn't care. Made of a silver, chain-mail-effect fabric, it had a halter neck and not a lot else. It plunged at the back right down to her bum. She'd obviously never be able to wear it in deepest, darkest Shropshire, so she was going to make the most of it by christening it that very evening. She wore it with bare legs, which she'd carefully St Tropezed right up to her bikini line, and a pair of black R.Soles cowboy boots so she didn't look too tarty. Just funky, out for a laugh.

Natalie, relatively understated in jeans, a black lace shirt and killer ankle boots, looked at her askance as she came into the living room.

'Bloody hell, Zo.'

'Why not? I don't go out very often. Ever, in fact. I'm going to make the most of it.'

'I suppose I haven't got the nerve. Or the legs.'

Marcella came in and her eyes widened when she saw Zoe. She was a dumpy creature, with a tendency towards seventies hair and make-up, her fringe carefully tonged and her eyebrows over-plucked into startled arches. Her tight top and hipster trousers did nothing to disguise the pot-belly that came from spending most of her money on English sweets.

The three of them all paraded for Daisy and Millie, who clapped their approval. Edwin came in and grinned.

'Terrifying. Absolutely terrifying. Have fun.'

Claudia's bedroom looked like the first day of Rackhams summer sale. There were designer clothes strewn everywhere, falling off hangers, slung on to the bed, lying in crumpled heaps where they had been discarded.

Jack Wilding had phoned earlier in the week to invite them to a garden party. Unbeknownst to her, Ray and Jack had got chatting in the paddock at Prescott, both discussing the merits of their protégés. And from the moment her father had told her about the Wildings' invitation, she had been in a frenzy of indecision.

What the hell did you wear to a garden party? It meant hat and heels at Buck House, but it could mean jeans and T-shirt. She had no way of knowing, and she certainly wasn't going to phone and ask. Olivier might answer the phone and she'd die on the spot.

Her mother knocked gently and opened the door. Claudia let out a wail.

'Help me, Mum. What the hell am I going to wear?'

Barbara blinked in surprise. She didn't think Claudia had ever asked her advice on clothes. Barbara was committed to Jacques Vert for smart, Marks & Sparks for casual; her signature colours were emerald green and navy. Her dress sense was a million miles away from her daughter's. What was going on?

Barbara had begun to notice that Claudia had mellowed over the past few months. She'd been particularly quiet and thoughtful over the past week. They'd had a couple of chats that almost verged on heart-to-hearts, something Barbara had shared with Debbie and Andrea but never Claudia. But Claudia had asked her some searching questions. Had Barbara known when she'd met Ray that he was The One? And did Barbara think it was time she moved out – she was twenty-two; wasn't she too old to be living with her mum and dad? Barbara had found herself reassuring Claudia that she could live with them as long as she liked. Afterwards, she was amazed. For as long as she could remember she'd longed for Claudia to move out. But she was starting to like the softer, more vulnerable creature that was emerging, the creature that wasn't quite so sure of herself. Barbara had found the last ten years emotionally exhausting: Claudia's behaviour had often put a strain on her marriage to Ray. It was with an enormous sense of relief that she wondered whether at last they were to have some respite.

Swiftly, she helped Claudia restore some sort of order to her wardrobe, putting away the outfits that were unsuitable so they weren't distracting and gradually narrowing the possibilities down until they hit on the perfect ensemble.

'Are you sure I look OK?' Claudia asked anxiously. Claudia, who always strode through the house and out of the front door confident that no one came close to looking as good as she did.

'You look beautiful,' Barbara reassured her.

She was more than a little disconcerted when Claudia gave her a hug of thanks. Disconcerted, but very gratified. And very curious as to who had wrought such a change in her daughter. But she didn't pry. Not yet. She just crossed her fingers and prayed for her difficult, prickly, feisty little daughter's happiness. Rather selfishly, perhaps, because what Barbara was looking forward to more than anything was enjoying Ray's retirement, just three years away, and they could only do that if Claudia was settled and off their hands.

Rod had no intention whatsoever of going to the Wildings' party. No way. It would be emotional bloody suicide, being in such close proximity to Jamie. And he was deeply into self-preservation at the moment. He'd had some time alone over the past few days, and had come to the conclusion that the only time he didn't get hurt was when he behaved like a complete and utter bastard. He'd lost his heart to Jamie all those years ago and been damaged beyond repair. He'd managed to scrape himself back off the floor after some years and had found a certain happiness with Bella, only to be kicked in the teeth again when all he'd ever done was to try and make her happy. So the only answer was to behave like a caveman. Like most of his brothers, in fact. They behaved as they liked, with no regard to law, employers or wedlock, and as a result were perfectly contented. Whether anybody that lived with them was didn't really come into it. The Deacon motto was 'Me, Myself, I', and Rod thought that it was about time he lived by it.

Foxy had texted him earlier asking him to come out, with a complicated itinerary involving two counties, three pubs and a nightclub. He'd take the Warrior, give a few people a lift, have a laugh, catch up with some old mates. It meant he couldn't have a drink, but that didn't matter so much.

It was only when he opened the wardrobe to get out his suede jacket and saw Bella's clothes hanging there that he wondered what she was doing. She hadn't phoned or tried to contact him, which he considered to be an admission of guilt and evidence of her shame. What a complete and utter fool he'd been …

He slammed the wardrobe door shut, put on his jacket and texted Foxy to say he was on his way.

Ray Sedgeley's Jag bumped over the rutted track that a bunch of gold balloons had indicated led to Bucklebury Farm. He'd been delighted when Jack Wilding had phoned and asked them to the party. He and Jack had, by dint of sponsoring the two great white hopes of the summer, chatted at various race meetings and had struck up if not a friendship then an easy acquaintance. Barbara had been invited, of course, but was babysitting yet again for Andrea. Ray thought privately that his other two daughters took advantage of their mum's good nature, but he didn't say anything.

Claudia sat next to him, uncharacteristically quiet. She kept flipping through the CD-changer, which drove him demented, but he didn't risk a mouthful by telling her to stop. He was immensely relieved that, after sulking for three days, Claudia had got over her disastrous wipe-out at Prescott the previous week and seemed to be back on track. She'd been out with Agnes Porter-Wright, who'd given her a thorough chewing for being a bad sport when Claudia had moaned about her debacle.

'You only learn by your mistakes, my girl. It's like riding a horse. Every good rider has to fall off. I'd be very worried if you had a perfect track record. It would mean that you weren't taking risks. Only those who dare, win.'

Claudia didn't retaliate rudely, as Ray would have expected, for she had a healthy respect for the old girl. She'd seen jerky black-and-white film footage of her tearing round Brooklands in her Bentley, in the days when the racing was for real, when the track was a platform for showing off a car's capabilities as it came off the production line, when the split-second timing could make or break a car's commercial success. She'd been a glamorous figure in her time, had Agnes, a blonde bombshell with balls and attitude in the days when most women were still chained to the kitchen sink. Claudia admired her maverick, pioneering spirit, and as a result listened to her advice.

Later, Ray had caught Claudia clearing a space on the mantelpiece for the Corrigan Trophy.

'It's visualization,' she explained. 'If I imagine it there, I'll make it happen.'

Ray was very doubtful. His own plan was far more likely to be effective. He hadn't made a bomb out of scrap metal by indulging in flaky American New Age bollocks. It was just a question of waiting for the right moment. And Ray was good at that. In life, as in business, timing was everything.

In the passenger seat, Claudia's tummy was churning, worse than ever it had before a race. She was nervous about meeting Olivier on neutral territory; wondered if perhaps he wouldn't seem as alluring away from the thrust and glamour of the racetrack, though she knew that was unlikely. His attraction was in his elusiveness; those brilliant eyes that could laugh one minute and look straight through her the next, his casual indifference, his total willingness to accept her as a fellow competitor and not be fazed; to be man enough not to crow when he beat her. Most men wouldn't be able to resist keeping her in her place by flaunting their victory. But Olivier treated her as an equal, as if he was studiously ignoring the very obvious differences between them, and Claudia realized that wasn't what she wanted at all.

Maybe off the track their relationship would alter: maybe away from the pressures of competition they could relax and he could treat her like the woman she so obviously was. She prayed the outfit she and her mum had settled on would strike the right note: cropped satin cargo trousers with 'God's Gift' embroidered on the bum, a white fishnet jumper that showed off her tanned midriff, and low-heeled Grecian sandals that laced up her calves. He'd have to be made of stone to ignore her, surely?

Ray parked the car in the top paddock and wandered through the stable yard up to the house, where people were already milling about on the terrace outside the French windows. It was the perfect summer's evening for a party, with the sun still beaming down but not too stiflingly hot. The garden looked like a slightly surreal film set – Moroccan souk meets Vita Sackville-West – the flower beds rampant with soft, tangled blooms, Bedouin tents and hammocks and embroidered cushions slung about the lawns, huge terracotta pots stuffed with hot-pink pelargoniums, and the smell of incense mixing with the scent of recently cut grass.

Ray and Claudia greeted Jack and Jamie, presenting Jack with a magnum of champagne for his birthday. They were immediately introduced to more people than they could remember and plied with glasses of Jack's wicked punch, which he'd nicknamed Bucklebury Folly. The guests were an eclectic mix of arty, county, bohemian, sophisticated and down to earth, ranging in age from early twenties to late sixties.

Claudia realized at once that she was wearing totally the wrong thing. The clothes that had felt so right in her bedroom in Birmingham suddenly made her feel like a bit of a footballer's wife: satin and fishnet might be smart casual in the city, but here it looked flashy, trashy and cheap, despite the hefty price tag. She was left with the feeling that she'd tried a bit too hard; that there was too much of her body on show, even though the flesh underneath was faultless. Quite a few of the women were stunningly attractive, but obviously didn't feel the need to draw attention to themselves by their clothing – or lack of it. It was all very relaxed and understated: linen trousers and sloppy cotton sweaters or jeans with floaty tops; jewellery that was arty rather than expensive. In fact, the dressiest person there was Jamie, who, to Claudia's annoyance, looked stunning in a pink Suzie Wong frock. And it didn't take Claudia long to clock that Olivier, who was in charge of the barbecue, couldn't take his eyes off her.

Her heart missed a beat when she saw him, dressed in a blue linen shirt and cream trousers, wielding a pair of tongs as he supervised a row of kebabs. The week's sunshine had deepened his tan and lightened his hair, and his eyes seemed an even more startling aquamarine by contrast. *David Ginola*, thought Claudia. That's who he reminded her of. She'd seen Ginola out on the town in Birmingham a few times, when he'd been playing for

Aston Villa. Olivier had the same Gallic good looks, the same ability to wear his hair slightly too long without looking either effeminate or dated, the same mesmerizing eyes...

She had to go over and say hello. But Claudia felt tongue-tied. She couldn't for the life of her think of an opening gambit. She cringed when she remembered the drivel she had come out with the Saturday before. And all she could think of now were inane questions. She could hardly go and ask how his kebabs were doing. She took a big gulp of Bucklebury Folly, wishing fervently for inspiration and realizing that this was how normal people felt when faced with the object of their desires: awkward, bashful, terrified. But then, she supposed, it had never mattered to her before what anyone thought of her. She'd always been in control. She was the intimidating one, the unapproachable siren, the one who called the shots.

Before she could decide on a plan of action, Jamie descended on her and took her by the arm.

'Come and meet the Preston brothers,' she said, and led her firmly away. Next moment, Claudia found herself being introduced to three mischievous-looking young Hoorays, who were thoroughly appreciative of her trousers and her midriff and raised her spirits a little – though she couldn't help wondering if Jamie had distracted her on purpose.

Jamie was thrilled that the party was going so well. She had been a bit nervous, never having hosted something on this scale by herself before. But she realized now there was no need to be nervous when you were amongst friends. There was Clemency, her mother's old art teacher from London. Cyd and Nancy, the highly strung American princesses who ran a town-house bed and breakfast in Ludlow, who'd always had Louisa's paintings in their dining room and been responsible for most of her sales. Leo the cheesemonger, who'd brought her a huge basket of his wares – Stinking Bishop and Berkswell and Shropshire Blue. Hilly, of course. Kif, looking a bit lost, she thought. Pip and Rose Preston, local landed gentry and their three heartbreaking sons who she'd just introduced to Claudia Sedgeley – she grinned to herself as she contemplated the possible outcome of their encounter.

Time and again she found herself hugged and kissed and admired by people who had been part of her life for as long as she could remember, bringing home the bitter-sweet reality that this was the last time they would all come together like this. And many of them exclaimed how like her mother she looked when she was young. Jamie felt proud. Louisa had, in a way, been her role model. She knew that by throwing this party she had been trying to live up to the standards she'd set, trying to emulate everything she had admired about her mother. And she thought she'd succeeded, because so many people told her it was almost as if Louisa was going to turn up any moment, that she'd captured the magical atmosphere and the chemistry of those infamous parties of the past.

High on the congratulations, and the pleasure of seeing all the people she loved enjoying themselves, she didn't have time to wonder whether Rod was going to turn up. Anyway, she knew he wouldn't, not in a million years.

At nine o'clock, the kebabs were pronounced ready and everyone was commanded to dig in. By dint of their seniority, Lettice and Jack were sitting at one of the tables Jamie had set up on the terrace. Other people were sprawled on the lawn, or perched on the stone retaining walls of the flower beds.

'I wanted to have a word with you,' said Lettice, digging her fork into a mound of golden couscous. 'I'm not sure if this is the right time. But then again, I don't know if there is a right time.'

Jack made a face. 'Sounds ominous.'

'I'm thinking of moving to South Africa,' she explained carefully. 'Actually, not thinking. I am. I've put an offer in on a house in Cape Town.'

Jack started in surprise. Lettice looked a little shamefaced at dropping such a bombshell.

'I'm fed up with the winters here,' she went on to explain. 'They thoroughly depress me. There's nothing for an old woman my age to do except huddle up in her thermal knickers. I can't hunt any more. That bloody house of mine costs a fortune to heat and I only use two rooms. It's crazy.' She paused. 'I can get a beautiful bungalow in Cape Town, with a swimming pool and a guest cottage, for a fraction of what I'd get for my place. And I thought I'd just get somewhere small here for when I want to come back. Something that won't crumble to a ruin the minute I turn my back.'

'That sounds like a very good idea,' said Jack equably, trying not to look too crestfallen. He suddenly realized how dependent he'd become on Lettice of late, and how he looked forward to seeing her. The thought of not having her around any more was a depressing one.

'I've thought about it long and hard,' she went on. 'And I have to admit that the only thing really holding me back is the thought of having to leave you behind.'

Jack felt immensely flattered. Lettice leaned forwards and lowered her voice, which in itself was unusual.

'We both know that we're not the love of each other's lives. Because we've both had the loves of our lives. And lost them. But I don't mind telling you I've become very fond of you, Jack. I wanted to ask if you'd come with me.' She paused. 'Actually, not ask. Invite. I think that's a better word, and doesn't put you under any pressure. It's taken me a long time to realize that perhaps a clean slate is the only answer. I still get reminded of Larry ten, fifteen, thirty times a day. Not that I want to forget him, of course. It might be the answer for you too, Jack. I know it hasn't been as long. But you're still haunted.'

Jack looked away, pained.

'Yes,' he said. 'Especially at times like this. Jamie ... reminds me so much of Louisa. Yet in some ways, not at all.'

Lettice folded her freckled hand over his.

'It's an open invitation. I don't expect an answer straight away. The offer will always be there, Jack. And purely selfishly, I'd just like you to know I'd love you to be there with me.'

Jack just about managed a smile, slightly choked by her generosity of spirit.

'Can I think about it? It certainly sounds tempting. But there's a lot to sort out here. More than anything, I need to make sure Jamie's settled before I make any decisions.'

Olivier was sitting on the stone wall by the barbecue, guarding the last of the figs which were slowly softening in the warmth of the glowing embers, when Ray Sedgeley approached, sitting next to him and offering him a cigar.

Olivier shook his head, taking out one of his own Disque Bleu in preference. Ray made a great ritual of snipping the end off his cigar, before finally clearing his throat.

'I wanted to have a word.'

'Sure.'

Olivier flicked his lighter and Ray bent his head to light his cigar. He blew out a thick stream of smoke before enlightening him.

'I'm not going to beat about the bush. I want you to throw the race for the Corrigan Trophy.' Ray brushed the glowing end of the cigar against the wall casually, shaving off the ash, before looking up and meeting Olivier's eye to prove he meant what he was saying. 'I'd make it worth your while.'

Olivier looked at him, astounded. This was like something out of a film. He half expected Vinnie Jones to walk round the corner, or Guy Ritchie to shout 'Cut!'

'What do you mean?'

'I mean ... a hundred grand?'

Ray's gaze was steady. Olivier laughed. He was obviously winding him up. He had a strange sense of humour.

'You've got to be joking.'

'I've never been more serious. I need Claudia to win that race.'

Olivier raised an eyebrow.

'I don't think bribing other people to throw the race quite counts as winning.'

Ray knew he was being patronized, but in his experience even the most principled people caved in at the right price. He waved away Olivier's objection.

'As long as she thinks she has. That's all that matters.'

'What about all the other entrants? Are you going to pay them off too?'

Ray gave a curt shake of his head.

'We all know it's a two-horse race. There isn't another car entered that's powerful enough to touch you or Claudia. And I'll be honest, I think you've got the edge. You're the better driver, though she'd kill me for saying it.'

'So – you're going to deprive her of the opportunity to prove you wrong? By buying me off?'

Olivier's tone was polite, not sneering, but there was no denying his underlying disgust.

Ray flicked his unfinished cigar on to the grass and ground it out with his heel. It had obviously been a prop, an excuse to sit down and feign companionship.

'Let me explain something to you. This time three years ago, I was spending four hundred pounds a day on a private clinic for Claudia. Rehab, I believe the popular term is. Beloved of celebrities and superstars and, apparently, highly strung little girls whose wealthy fathers don't give them enough attention. I've made it my mission to rectify that ever since she came out.'

He paused for a moment. Olivier wondered if perhaps he was finding this confession difficult, but decided no – Ray was pausing merely for effect, a master of rhetoric, letting his words sink in before he continued.

'A hundred grand to keep her on the straight and narrow is nothing to me. If she wins that trophy, that buys me another season, another year, maybe more. If she loses, she'll lose interest, and then it will only be a matter of time before she falls back into her old ways.'

'I'm sorry,' said Olivier. 'I can appreciate your dilemma.

I'm sure as a father you feel you're doing the right thing. But I'm afraid I'm old-fashioned.'

'Don't tell me – it's not cricket.' Ray gave a short, cynical bark. 'Well, if today's cricketers are anything to go by, you'd be a fool not to take the money and run.'

'Then I'm a fool,' said Olivier politely. 'But a fool that can sleep at night.'

He held out his hand.

'We didn't have this conversation.' He looked Ray in the eye. 'If the racing authorities got wind of it …'

Ray shook his hand with a bluff, genial smile whose warmth didn't reach his eyes.

'They'd have to prove it first,' he said equably. 'And if you make any allegations, I'll sue you for libel.'

Which parting shot left Olivier in little doubt about the sort of man he was dealing with.

Rod was sitting with Foxy and a bunch of mates in the same pub he'd dragged his brother out of a few days before. He'd drunk up to his limit and now he was bored: the conversation was the usual bawdy innuendo that was hilarious to the inebriated. One of the blokes with them was talking about going to score some Es, and Rod felt uncomfortable with it. He wasn't a prude, but drugs weren't his scene. Added to his discomfort was the knowledge that, if he'd had the courage, he could be at Bucklebury Farm now. He'd gone over and over Jamie's invitation in his head, common sense telling him that if she hadn't wanted him to come, she wouldn't have asked him. But then insecurity kicked in: she was just being polite, she wouldn't give a stuff whether he turned up or not, probably wouldn't even notice …

It was Saturday night and the lottery results were coming out on the TV behind the bar. As the balls rolled out, Rod remembered the slogan. *You've got to be in it to win it.*

If he didn't take Jamie up on her invitation, if he didn't put his head on the chopping block, he'd never know how she felt about him. There'd been a moment in the post office when he'd felt a connection between them, before she'd closed down and backed off; dismissed their affair as a teenage dalliance.

What was the worst that could happen if he went? Jamie greeting him politely and then having to stand around at the party like a spare part? He'd feel a fool, but, after everything that had happened to him recently, it would be no great hardship.

Foxy poked him in the ribs with a sharp finger.

'Hey – wake up. You're not exactly the life and soul. What's up?'

Rod ran his hand through his hair. What was he going to do? Risk his dignity? Or get totally hammered and end up with a sympathy shag from Foxy, because the worst thing would be to lie in bed alone, knowing that he hadn't had the courage of his convictions and had bottled out of pursuing the one thing he really wanted? Visions of an empty life stretched out in front of him, a life littered with too much beer and too many one-night stands to try and patch over the hole in his heart ...

'Listen, Foxy – I'm feeling a bit rough. I think I'm going to go home; get some kip. Will you be all right for a lift?'

'Lightweight.' Her twinkling black eyes mocked him for a moment, then she softened. 'Don't worry. I can tell you don't want to be here. Go and sleep it off.'

She kissed him on the cheek, and he slid out of the pub before the others could protest. He didn't feel too guilty about leaving her. Foxy never found herself short of company.

At ten, when everyone had eaten their fill and more, the guests were distracted from their gossiping and flirting by Jamie emerging from the kitchen with an enormous birthday cake spiked with long white tapered candles. As she walked towards Jack, grinning, a rousing chorus of 'Happy Birthday' struck up.

Everyone gathered round as Jack blew out the candles.

'Make a wish!' shouted someone.

He knew it was pointless, but as he slid the knife through the sugary white icing and into the sponge, he wished that somehow he could save Bucklebury. Not for himself, but for Jamie, for posterity, for the grandchildren he felt sure he would one day have ...

'Speech,' shouted someone else, and Jack put up his hand in protest. Usually voluble when called upon to speak, he felt too emotionally vulnerable at that moment. Touched by Lettice's generosity and Jamie's gesture with the birthday cake, and filled with sentimentality that this was the very last birthday party he would celebrate here, he didn't know what he could say or refer to without making a fool of himself or, quite frankly, bursting into tears.

To his surprise, Jamie stepped forwards instead.

'There's just a few things I wanted to say. Firstly, of course, happy birthday to Dad. I've no idea how old he actually is, so there's no point in counting the candles. But many happy returns of the day, Dad.'

Everyone raised their glass to toast him, and Jack bowed his head modestly, thinking that really he couldn't take much more of this.

Jamie went on.

'Secondly, for those of you who don't know, Dad and I have decided that very sadly we're going to have to sell Bucklebury Farm. It's no longer practical, we can't do the place justice. So this is our last bash here and we want you to enjoy yourselves.' There was a murmur of consternation from those who hadn't realized. Jamie gave a wry smile. 'Anyone who fancies making an offer should go and see Christopher Drace – we're going to be instructing him to put it on the market next week.'

Christopher, who was sitting on a nearby hay bale, looked a bit embarrassed, feeling as if he was somehow profiting from the Wildings' misfortune.

Jamie continued.

'Finally, the last time I saw most of you was at Mum's funeral. And I don't think anyone was in a fit state to pay her tribute at the time, or look back on her life in the manner which she deserved. So for me this party has been as much in her honour as Dad's. I'm sure she's up there now, wishing she was here with all of us. So please, everyone, raise your glasses ... to Louisa!'

'To Louisa!' chorused everyone obediently.

It was Lettice who noticed Jack scurry back inside, on the pretext of changing a CD, and found him wiping away a tear in the drinks cupboard.

As the sun finally set and the night-scented stocks began to throw out their delicate perfume, Jamie lit the tea lights while her guests sat around gossiping, drinking and laughing. Others lolled on cushions in the Bedouin tent, gorging themselves on the syrup-drenched pastries that proved too much of a temptation even for the most abstemious. Some danced, entwined dreamily in each other's arms as music trickled out over the lawn.

Jamie stretched out her hand to Olivier, who had finally doused the barbecue coals.

'Olivier, come and dance with me.'

The music floated on the night breeze, the notes drifting across the valley as far as Lydbrook.

'Lucky we haven't got neighbours,' joked Jamie drily.

Olivier couldn't remember the last time he'd actually held a girl in his arms to dance with her. The ski resorts he worked in favoured boisterous, noisy discos, with everyone drinking to excess to kill the aches and pains of the day's sport. Jamie snuggled comfortably into him. He put one hand in the small of her back and linked the fingers of his other hand in hers. It could hardly be called dancing; they were just moving slowly in time to the music. But for Olivier, it was as if everyone else had disappeared, as if the music was playing just for them. He wanted, so badly, to kiss her hair. He could smell the baby shampoo she used. And her scent. A very faint trace of a perfume that seemed familiar somehow, though he was sure he hadn't smelled it on Jamie. He racked his brain, trying to remember, when suddenly it came to him, and he realized it was the perfume her mother had always worn. His stomach lurched with the memory. The thought distracted him so much, it was a moment before he became aware that Jamie was talking to him.

'I wanted to say thank you. For so many things. For sorting Dad out for a start. And for being so supportive;

helping me see things more clearly.' She gave a grin. 'And for mowing the lawns.'

'That's OK. It's the least I could do.'

'You're a real mate.'

Olivier didn't answer. He didn't want to be a mate. That was such a sexless word. Holding Jamie in his arms like this was sheer torture; it was like a physical taunt. But at the same time, he didn't want this moment to end.

From inside the makeshift gazebo, Claudia lay sprawled on a cushion, watching Olivier and Jamie with narrowed eyes. She hadn't had a chance to get near Olivier all evening, except for a polite and perfunctory kiss just after they'd arrived – he'd touched her on the elbow, smiled and said he'd catch her later. While Jack and Jamie were the official hosts of the evening, Olivier had obviously taken it on himself to provide them with back-up so they could spend time talking to their guests rather than looking after them. He'd spent the entire evening topping up glasses and supervising the barbecue, leaving Claudia with no window of opportunity to bestow her charms upon him.

She'd let the Preston brothers provide her entertainment instead. She had to admit they were good value: they alternately teased and admired her, showering her with compliments and sexual innuendoes that were endearing rather than insulting. As a result Claudia was feeling surprisingly relaxed, further helped by the spliff they were sharing, made from some grass one of the lads had grown on his father's estate.

'Bloody excellent cash crop,' he explained to Claudia. 'I've told Dad it's a rare French lettuce leaf that all the posh restaurants in Ludlow are after. He's putting aside another field so we can grow some more.'

The four of them rolled around on the cushions, help-less with laughter, but Claudia didn't take her eyes off Olivier for a second.

Olivier's heart was thudding. Just do it, he told himself. Just kiss her. For God's sake, of all the women he had kissed in his life, not many had objected. She was definitely relaxed; they were snuggled up quite cosily together. He'd only need to drop his head, brush his lips against her in a gesture that could be seen as affection or invitation – it would be up to her to decide. She could respond if she wanted to.

But every time he convinced himself it was the right moment, he bottled out. The record was nearly coming to an end: he'd lose the opportunity if he wasn't careful. She looked up at him and smiled. Encouraged, he mustered up the last of his courage and bent his head.

Olivier felt Jamie tense. Hastily he backed away, then realized she wasn't resisting his imminent kiss. She'd seen something over his shoulder. She dropped his hand like a hot potato and pulled away.

'Excuse me. Late arrival. I'd … better go and say hello.'

She hurried off, and Olivier peered into the darkness to see who it was. A dark bloke, about his own age, gypsy good looks … The penny dropped. Rod Deacon. He remembered Jack pointing him out in the Royal Oak. What the hell was he doing here? He'd bummed out on the deal on Bucklebury. Olivier couldn't imagine for a moment why he'd think he was welcome.

But from the way Jamie was scurrying over to him, she didn't seem to bear him any grudges whatsoever.

*

Jamie walked across the grass towards Rod, her heart banging against her ribs like a songbird trapped in a cage. He was looking round self-consciously. As he saw her approach, his face broke into a tentative smile.

What was he doing here? she wondered. Was he just bored – had he turned up to cadge a few free drinks and see what talent was available? Or did he want to see her? He'd seemed very cautious when she'd invited him; he hadn't exactly responded with enthusiasm.

'Hi.'

She was two feet away from him. He stuck his hands in his pockets awkwardly, and grinned.

'Hi. Sorry – you did say. I thought ... well, I wasn't doing anything. So ...'

'No, that's great. It's great to see you. Do you want a drink? There's wine, beer ...'

'I'm fine for the moment.'

There was an awkward silence.

'Looks like it's been a good party.'

Jamie nodded. She couldn't find her voice; couldn't bring herself to say what she really wanted. She didn't want to make herself look a fool, by saying that it was the best party in the world now that he'd turned up. He was looking at her, and she felt herself blush. She must be a bit of a mess by now – her hair was all over the place, her make-up had worn off and she'd taken off her shoes.

'You look gorgeous.' His voice was low and soft.

'Thank you ...'

There was another moment's silence that seemed to last a hundred years, before the opening chords of the next track floated over the lawn towards them. 'Summer

326

Breeze', by the Isley Brothers. Jamie used to have it on a compilation tape she'd painstakingly made up on her parents' sound system. She remembered playing it on the cassette in Rod's car that summer; they'd rewound it and rewound it till the tape had finally worn thin and snapped. She wondered if he remembered it too.

She looked into his eyes, and the smile in them told her that he did. He held out his arms. Wordlessly, she moved into his grasp, sliding her arms around his waist under the suede of his jacket. She felt herself melting into his warmth – there was no trepidation, no fear, no question. She pressed herself against his chest and felt his heart beating in unison with hers. As he squeezed her tight, she felt as if she was waking from her recurring dream – only this time it was for real. The stranger that held the key to her happiness, that had taken her to the height of bliss and ecstasy in her sleep so many times, only to slip through her fingers when she woke, was here at last in her arms.

22

For the whole time since she'd been at her mother's, no food had passed Bella's lips. She'd lain in her bed, gazing at the faded patches on the wallpaper, ghostly reminders of the posters she'd hung there during her teenage years. Her head was throbbing with dehydration. She felt as weak as a kitten. She put her hands up to her face: she could feel her cheekbones, reassuringly razor sharp. She circled her wrist with her thumb and middle finger, admiring how easily they met as she contemplated her plight.

It was only a matter of time before her mum found out the truth. As soon as she came into contact with Rod, he'd put her straight. And Bella knew she couldn't keep them apart for ever. Her mum was already baying for Rod's blood. And once Pauline knew, that would be it. She wouldn't support Bella after that. She'd be horrified by what she had done. Because it was evil. Bella knew that. It was downright wicked and evil and she didn't deserve anyone's forgiveness, not her mum's, not Rod's, not anyone's.

She'd had a whole week to think about it, and had decided what she had to do. She'd had to wait for Pauline to go out for her ritual girls' night with the women she taught Latin American ballroom dancing. Her mother hadn't wanted to leave her, but Bella had insisted she would be fine, and promised to call her mobile if anything was wrong. Pauline had left, reluctantly, at eight, promising to be back before midnight.

It had taken Bella until now to gather the strength for what she had to do. She swung her legs out of bed and got experimentally to her feet. She had to put a hand on the wall to steady herself. Her head was swimming, her legs weak. Slowly, carefully, she made her way to the bathroom. She stared at herself in the mirror over the sink for a moment. Her face was as white as a sheet, her eyes sunken and surrounded by purplish rings. Her black hair hung round her face, stringy and greasy. She felt a sudden urge to smash the mirror, pick up the shattered shards and hack at her reflection. Hate. That was the only emotion she could muster up now. Not self-pity, not regret, not desolation. Just hideous, ugly, black hatred for the monster that was staring back at her.

She opened up the medicine cabinet. From it, she extracted a bottle of paracetamol, a bottle of cough mixture, some prescription painkillers her mother used when her back was giving her trouble and a bottle of sleeping tablets. She carried her stash downstairs and placed it carefully on the dining table. Then she went over to the sideboard and opened the door that contained her mother's drink supply. Pauline wasn't a great boozer, but she liked to have a bottle of most things to hand for when people called. Bella carefully selected a bottle of Baileys. Then she opened her mother's chocolate drawer. Pauline didn't have much of a sweet tooth either, but her pupils often gave her boxes of chocolates on her birthday or at Christmas or to say thank you, and she stored them away ready for an opportune occasion to share them or pass them on to someone else.

Now Bella found it difficult to choose. There was Terry's All Gold, Black Magic, Ferrero Rocher, After Eights, chocolate brazils. Her mouth watered in anticipation. She scooped them all up greedily and plonked them on the table next to the bottles of medicine. She could have what she liked this time. She didn't have to worry about what effect they might have on her waistline or her bottom. She didn't have to run up to the scales afterwards and survey the needle anxiously, or stick her fingers down her throat. She could gorge herself on the whole lot without so much as a pang of guilt.

She might as well go out enjoying herself.

At the Electric Bar and Grill on the Portobello Road, Zoe, Natalie and Marcella had trashed four bottles of white wine and two packets of cigarettes between them. At half past ten, Natalie decided she was ready to go home. Zoe looked at her aghast.

'You can't be! It's not even eleven yet! This is my big night out.'

'Zo – I'm tired. Daisy and Millie are going to be up at the crack of dawn tomorrow. And frankly, I'm bored. It's not as if you can even have a conversation in here.'

This was true. They were bellowing at each other over the noise. Zoe turned pleadingly to Marcella.

'You'll stay, won't you, Marcella? You're not going to be a party pooper?'

'Sure. I'll stay.' The Czechoslovakian smiled obligingly. Natalie picked up her bag and stood up. She kissed Zoe apologetically.

'I'm really sorry, Zo. I know I'm boring but I just can't do late nights any more. The price is too high. Have fun, OK?'

Natalie the traitor disappeared off into the night.

'Right,' said Zoe with relish to Marcella. 'Where next?'

Bella had lined up a selection of chocolates on the chenille tablecloth, and carefully inserted a tablet into each. Then she poured herself a glass of Baileys. Ceremoniously she began her feast, slowly at first, running her tongue luxuriously through the cocoa-encrusted globules of fat, probing for the underlying flavour – tangy orange, buttery caramel, vibrant mint – revelling in the luxury of not having to torture herself again, of not having to deprive herself and not having to punish herself if she gave in.

Rod had never known how much she had struggled with her disorder. By the time they were married, she was very practised at hiding it. When he came down to breakfast, her plate would already be in the sink, a few crumbs carefully scattered over it, together with a knife which she had scraped through the butter and dunked in the jam. They rarely ate together at lunchtime, but she would regale him with descriptions of the baguettes, jacket potatoes and slices of pizza she had consumed. She left chocolate wrappers and crisp packets that she found on the floor of the dance school in the car. And if she was forced to eat too much, a surreptitious vomit or a dose of laxatives soon redressed the balance. Rod genuinely believed that Bella was merely disinterested in food. How was he to know that every bacon sandwich he'd devoured in front of her had haunted her for the rest of the day?

How she'd imagined its crispy saltiness, the fat-soaked bread.

Her only reward was admiring her concave stomach, the tiny childlike buttocks. She joked about her high metabolism. And, of course, the exercise helped. She made sure that for every leg raise her pupils did, she would do three. And they were only doing one class. She was doing at least five a day.

Well, she wouldn't have to go through that punishing regime any more. She didn't have to feel her limbs scream for mercy.

After every few chocolates, she cleansed her palate with a mouthful of Baileys, rinsing away the residue with the unctuous liquid, allowing the cool, smooth nectar to slither down her throat. She barely noticed the pills, just stuffing in another sweet if a trace of medicinal bitterness crept through.

After fifteen minutes of gorging and swilling, she slumped back in her chair, needing a rest. She looked down and saw her chest was smeared in crumbs of chocolate. She brushed them away, and a thought occurred to her. If she was going to die, she didn't want to be found in this grotty old T-shirt and tracksuit bottoms. They might bury her in it. God, that would be awful – lying in your coffin for all eternity in a nylon tracksuit. She lurched back up the stairs to her room, feeling faintly queasy. She rummaged about until she found her favourite nightdress. It was long black satin, piped with cream, with criss-cross straps across the back.

Bella gave a little burp, and a trickle of liquid spurted up into her mouth. It tasted of Baileys and After Eights and cough mixture. Shuddering, she swallowed it back down as she struggled to get the nightdress over her head. She couldn't get her arms in the right place; the straps were everywhere they shouldn't be, tying her up into a satin straitjacket – it had always been difficult to get on at the best of times.

Happy that at least it was on, she staggered out of the room and back down the stairs, clutching the handrail for support. She could see two dining tables swooping in and out, sometimes merging into one, then drawing apart again. She reached out for the bottle of Baileys but it moved at the last minute and she came crashing down on to the table, knocking over the rest of the cough medicine. She stared at it intently, then slowly, deliberately, reached her hand out.

'Got you.' The bottle felt cool in her hand. She lifted it to her lips; she couldn't face trying to capture her glass. She started to drink it down. The lights were dancing round the room. Just like Tinkerbell in *Peter Pan*, she thought hazily ...

By eleven o'clock, Zoe and Marcella were in a crowded bar up the road. They were drinking BMWs – Baileys, Malibu and whisky – a deadly concoction with a kick like a donkey. By midnight, Zoe was flying. Natalie was boring. Christopher was boring. Bloody Shropshire was boring, boring, boring. Marcella was her new best friend.

A group of three young men bought them the next round. Zoe couldn't keep her eyes off the ringleader – a pretty boy with wicked eyes and an incredibly kissable mouth. He introduced himself to her as Zak.

'Zak and Zoe. That's cool,' she mused, liking the poetry.

'How old are you, then?'

'How old do you think?' Zoe twinkled flirtatiously, knowing this was a dangerous question, but she was feeling confident. She knew she looked good. Zak looked her up and down appraisingly, letting his eyes rove over her body. He gave her a cheeky grin.

'Twenty-eight?'

Zoe gave him a kiss on the cheek. 'Thank you, darling.'

He leaned into her.

'Your friend's a bit of a dog. Can't you get rid of her and we'll go on somewhere else?'

'I can't. She's my friend's au pair. Anyway, she's Czechoslovakian.'

Zak looked puzzled, not entirely sure what this explained. He picked up Zoe's hand and ran a finger lightly up the inside of her arm.

'I've got some serious shit back at my place. Come and have a smoke.'

Zoe shook her head.

'I don't smoke. Not "shit", anyway.' She held out her empty glass to him. 'I'll have another drink, though.'

The boy handed her a crumpled twenty-pound note.

'You go to the bar. You'll get served much quicker than me.'

Zoe staggered her way through the crowds and bought another trio of BMWs. When she got back, Marcella had vanished.

'She said she felt ill,' Zak said. 'No stamina, these foreigners. Not like you, baby – eh?'

He tousled Zoe's hair roughly. She raised her glass to him with a smile, and knocked back her drink. Things were definitely looking up now she'd dumped Natalie and Marcella.

Christopher left the party at half-eleven. It was obviously going to go on for hours yet, but he was sober, unlike the majority of the guests. And he'd chatted to everyone he wanted to. Why the bloody hell couldn't Zoe have come with him? She'd have enjoyed herself, surely? Nobody had been standoffish or snooty or countrified; they'd all been up for a good time.

He slipped away without saying goodbye to Jack or Jamie, because he knew they would protest that he was going and he didn't have the strength to argue. Besides, Jamie was engrossed. She was sitting on a rug, her arms round her knees, talking earnestly to Rod Deacon, who for some mysterious reason had turned up. Christopher wondered if he'd changed his mind about the Bucklebury development deal. He hoped so. He was dreading drawing up the details of the house that had been so much part of his childhood. It also reminded him how precarious his own position was. There was absolutely no doubt his life would be easier if they sold Lydbrook and downsized. It was a huge financial drain. But if Zoe wasn't happy in a big house in Shropshire, she sure as hell wouldn't be in a small one.

He drove his car carefully out of the paddock, down the drive, then stopped at the end before turning right on to the road that led to Lydbrook. He'd go home, have a big glass of brandy, then get a good night's sleep. He could have a lie-in tomorrow. His mum had mentioned something about taking the boys to church. They'd probably moan, but he'd have a couple of hours' total peace and quiet, to think life over.

Then he thought ... no. It was only half-eleven. She'd probably still be up ...

Knowing deep down that was what he had intended to do all along, he turned left instead of right.

It was closing time, and all the bars were being emptied unceremoniously out on to the street. Zoe realized that at this time of the night, with all these crowds, there was no hope whatsoever of getting a taxi. She wondered how long it would take her to walk back to Shepherd's Bush. Bloody hours. And her feet were killing her already.

Zak was trying to persuade her to come back to his place. His mate was waiting down the road in his car. Through the effects of all the drink she'd had, Zoe tried to weigh up the pros and cons sensibly.

'Come on, baby. Come on.' He brushed his beautiful lips along her collarbone, then looked at her with his teasing, soulful eyes. She could feel herself dissolve into acquiescence, despite thinking that his mate was probably blind drunk, and she didn't have a clue where he lived. Or who he was. And that he was probably closer in age to Hugo than to her.

Zak pulled her to him and started to kiss her passion-ately. In full view of all the departing punters, she kissed him back. She felt his hands run up the insides of her thighs, and heard a resounding cheer go up as he pushed her up against the wall. She grinned, despite herself. She felt sexy, abandoned, excited – alive! She'd never been an exhibitionist before, but the attention was thrilling: people were egging them on. Her dress was riding higher and higher; Zak was biting her neck. She hooked one leg round him to pull him closer, not minding that everyone could probably now see her knickers.

Suddenly the cheers were turning to boos. Zoe opened her eyes and saw two policemen approaching.

'Come on, you two. Cut it out. This is a public place.'

Zoe flashed him her most charming, seductive smile.

'Just a bit of fun, officer. Sure you don't want to join us?'

'I don't think so, love.'

There was a look on his face that made her feel somewhat aggrieved. She looked stunning, didn't she? She was certainly the best offer he was going to get, with his rubbery lips and eyebrows that met in the middle. Unwinding herself from her paramour, she laced her fingers in his and strode off into the night, swaying her hips, to a round of ragged applause from the onlookers.

23

Tiona Tutton-Price made it her mission in life to surround herself with pretty, feminine things. She had nothing, absolutely nothing, ugly or utilitarian in her little house. Firstly, she was a great believer in white: towels, bedding, china, tea towels, loo paper and under-wear – they all had to be pristine, snowy white. And she was also a great believer in butter dishes and sugar bowls and jam spoons – there was nothing guaranteed to turn her stomach more than the sight of someone hoicking marmalade out of a jar with their knife. If that made her old-fashioned, so what?

Her living room was light and airy, with stripped pine floorboards and duck-egg blue walls. There were two large sofas covered in cream calico. A neat row of gilt-framed botanical prints hung along one wall; the limestone fireplace held a huge glass vase of parrot tulips, their ragged edges tinged with a vibrant pink. On the mantelpiece were two cut-glass candlesticks with vanilla-scented candles, and her collection of Beswick Alice in Wonderland figurines.

In the corner of her living room, where most people would have placed a television, was the most magnificent doll's house, a replica of a Georgian town house. It was the only relic she had from her childhood: it had been given to her by the kindly owner of the first home where her mother had been housekeeper. It had gone everywhere with Tiona since.

It had always just been Tiona and her mother. She had no idea who her father was; didn't even know if her mother knew. He was never mentioned. From the age of three to fourteen, Tiona had lived in an assortment of grand houses, always relegated to the servants' quarters by dint of her mother being housekeeper.

Susan Tutton was excellent at her job. She ruled the rest of the staff with a rod of iron. Everything was on time, in its place, as it should be. Crisp linen, gleaming cutlery. Fresh blooms cut from the gardens every day, colour-coded to match the individual decor of each room. She was the mistress of delegation and a stickler for detail. Thus Tiona had it drummed into her from an early age how a grand country house should be run. She learned how to gut trout, pluck pheasants, lay a table for a dinner party, make a proper bed, polish silver, at what temperature to serve wine, how to answer the door and the telephone, how to address servants and tradespeople. Although it was rather a peculiar existence for a little girl, Tiona had never minded. It was like living inside a film. She would sit in the kitchens and watch with wide eyes as magnificent banquets were prepared. She would peer through her bedroom window as stunningly elegant ladies and immaculate gentlemen rolled up to balls and dances and dinners, dreaming that one day it would be her descending from a stately motor car in her finery.

It was only when she was thrust into the reality of the outside world that she found life difficult. She was usually dispatched to the nearest village school, where she suffered from being not properly posh, yet being one up from the rest of the children as she lived at the Big House. As a result, she found herself misunderstood and excluded. She never had anyone back to play, as it wouldn't have been considered the done thing, and was never asked back anywhere in return. And her mother was always too busy to worry. It was a twenty-four-hour-a-day job, running a country house.

When Tiona was eleven, they moved to Overswood Manor in the Oxfordshire countryside, and Tiona went in by bus to Oxford every day to school. Two years passed, during which time Tiona became utterly infatuated with Lord and Lady Overswood's eldest son, Richard, who needless to say paid her no attention whatsoever when he blew in casually on exeat from Marlborough College. Why would he look at her? She was dumpy, mousy, poor and not even very clever.

At Richard's eighteenth, there was a massive marquee on the lawn and her mother was more keyed up than ever, determined that everything should run like clockwork. Banished to her bedroom on pain of death, the hapless thirteen-year-old Tiona watched longingly from her attic window as carefree, laughing, confident creatures in strapless taffeta tossed their shining manes over their shoulders and drank copious quantities of champagne that they couldn't handle. By the end of the evening they didn't look so glamorous as they charged around having piggybacks from Richard and his friends, also now dishevelled and missing their ties. Tiona crawled miserably into bed. It was torture, being on the fringes of such a decadent and hedonistic lifestyle when she had no hope whatsoever of joining in the fun. Sometimes she wished she had a normal, ordinary family who lived in a normal, ordinary house. Then she wouldn't have any idea of what she was missing. As she fell asleep, she swore to herself that one day she would have a life like this, that she would be mistress of a country house, with a handsome, aristocratic husband and heaps and heaps of posh, beautiful friends and non-stop parties and endless champagne ...

One day, when she was fourteen, Tiona walked back from the bus stop in the village and arrived home to find two police cars in the driveway. Lady Overswood spotted her and escorted her firmly into the library, where she was instructed not to move. Bewildered, she waited for someone to shed light on the situation. Eventually she was rewarded with the sight of her mother being led out to one of the police cars and driven away. Then Lady Overswood and one of the other police officers came in with matching grave expressions to tell her what had happened.

It seemed that Susan Tutton had been embezzling her employers by clever manipulation of the household accounts. Lord and Lady Overswood had no qualms about pressing charges, and the resulting enquiry revealed that Susan had done the same at all her previous places of employment, accruing quite an impressive little nest egg. The judge was entirely unsympathetic to her pleas of being a struggling single mother trying to do her best for her daughter. She had, he said, abused a position of trust. In fact, several.

For the two years that her mother was in jail, Tiona was taken into care. There was no one else to take her under their wing. Her mother had no relatives or friends to whom she could entrust her daughter, and none of their previous employers were going to touch her with a bargepole. She'd ended up in Liversmead House, an unprepossessing sixties building on the outskirts of Oxford that was home for thirty or so girls who were in unfortunate circumstances like herself.

The inmates of Liversmead House were a tough lot whose backgrounds and stories were harrowing and heartbreaking. They were wild and volatile. Cat fights often broke out. Yet for some strange reason, they were intrigued by Tiona, and didn't exclude her. Due to her accent and manners, they dubbed her 'Lady Di', and set about educating her in their ways.

Thus Tiona learned about credit-card fraud, fiddling the DSS – sick benefit, housing benefit – how to tell good drugs from bad, how to turn tricks for men, how to shoplift then take back the goods for a refund, how to pick a lock, hotwire a car. Not that she was planning on using most of the information. But it certainly gave her the tools for survival, because she was going to have to learn to stand on her own two feet.

She left the care home the day she was sixteen. By then, she had lost her puppy fat and become curvaceous rather than dumpy. Her hair had lost its greasy, lank appearance and was thick, soft and bouncy. She didn't care about her mother, where she was or whether she was coping. Tiona was just looking out for number one.

By using a combination of what she'd learned at Overswood and Liversmead, Tiona carved out quite a little lifestyle for herself. Her Sloaney exterior belied the criminal tendencies underneath. No one ever suspected her of theft or fraud. Her upper-class accent and perfect manners, combined with her feminine dress sense and china-doll prettiness, put her beyond suspicion. Tacking Price on to Tutton to give herself a double-barrelled surname added to the smokescreen. She glided from job to job, carrying out her duties impeccably but always finding a devious way to line her own pocket, moving on well before the alarm was raised, taking with her glowing references. If she'd learned one thing from her mother it was not to be complacent: looking back on it, Susan Tutton had got too comfortable at Overswood Manor, and had become greedy.

She moved around the countryside in search of the ideal town in which to settle. So far she had eschewed Bath, Guildford, York, Cheltenham and Windsor. When she arrived in Ludlow, she knew she'd found her resting place. A country town with a hint of sophistication, that wasn't either too bumpkinish or pretentious, where she could blend into the background. And it was far enough from London for the inhabitants to have a certain lack of cynicism, so she would be able to operate without rousing suspicion.

She secured herself a position at Drace's, and soon became Hamilton's right-hand woman, taking over all the valuations. It wasn't long before she met the unscrupulous and sexually magnetic Simon Lomax. He wasn't her ideal man – he was too flash, too rough round the edges, while she wanted someone refined and educated – but they recognized a bit of themselves in each other, a mutual willingness to take risks, and it sparked a chemistry between them. They indulged in several boozy lunches and some filthy sex before hitting upon their mutually profitable scam. Before long Tiona had accrued enough cash out of it for a substantial deposit on a house.

What she never quite realized was that she was the one being compromised by the deal, that she was being manipulated, that she was the only one with anything to lose. For if she had few scruples, Simon Lomax had none, and he was happy to use his hold over her to get what he wanted. For the time being she was hooked on the two needs he could supply: sex and money.

Her one remaining ambition was to recreate for herself the lifestyle she had grown up on the edge of. She still wanted to be lady of the house, though her aspirations weren't as high as they once had been. She didn't want anything as grand as Overswood; she knew now that the responsibility of a house like that was bloody hard work. One was forever having to let the paying public crawl all over the place or serve teas or open a safari park, which wasn't the idea at all. Tiona wanted an easy life.

The day she met Christopher Drace, she knew he was the one to give her what she wanted. He might not be titled or extraordinarily wealthy, but she knew she would be able to catch him in her snare. She'd seen Lydbrook House, as Hamilton had often invited her for supper over the past couple of years. To Tiona, it was perfection. She imagined presiding over dinner parties in the dining room, her own little pair of gun dogs sprawled in the hallway, buying a pretty little chestnut mare to put in the long-disused stable block, joining the hunt …

She didn't worry that Christopher was already married with children. In fact, that almost made it easier. And it took the pressure off her to produce an heir. English men were obsessed with procreation, and Christopher already had two fine, healthy sons who, if her calculations were correct, would be off to boarding school before two years were out – she congratulated herself on planting that seed the evening before.

This evening, as the hands of her pretty carriage clock moved towards midnight, Tiona knelt in front of her doll's house and opened the doors. They swung open to reveal three elegant floors, all meticulously fitted out in period detail and where she spent long hours living out her fantasies. There was the little Tiona figure – a blonde doll with an array of swishy, elegant clothes. At the moment she was naked, in the rolltop bath, wallowing in her scented suds before getting ready to go out for the evening. Tucked up in the nursery on the next floor were four beautiful blonde children, fast asleep. In the room next door was nanny, thick-ankled and hairy-lipped, as nannies should always be.

And in his dressing room, putting in his dress studs in front of a cheval mirror, was a tall, elegant man with sandy hair. Christopher.

Tiona smiled as she picked him up and walked him into the bathroom.

'Darling, we're going to be late for the hunt ball.'

The Tiona doll stepped elegantly out of the bath. The Christopher doll picked up a towel from the rail and came over to dry her. He found her damp, deliciously scented body so irresistible that it wasn't long before he was pleasuring her on the bathroom floor.

'You're gorgeous. Delicious. I just want to eat you all up,' groaned the Christopher doll, as he brought the Tiona doll to the brink of an earth-shattering climax.

Just then, in real life, there was a gentle rat-a-tat-tat on the door. Tiona's lips curled into the sweetest of smiles. OK, it had taken him twenty-four hours – twenty-four hours that in her opinion could have been better spent – but she had been confident. If he'd needed time to think about it then so much the better – it meant he'd made up his mind in the cold light of day that it was the right thing to do. Gently, she popped the Tiona doll back in the bath, sent Christopher back to his dressing room, closed the front of the house and went to open her own front door.

He stood leaning against the door jamb, swinging a bottle of champagne between his fingers. Tiona thought he looked divine. He wasn't classically handsome, but with those long rangy limbs, that boyish smile, that reticence combined with confidence, he was the archetypal Merchant Ivory hero.

'I wondered if you fancied a nightcap?'

Tiona stood back to let him in.

24

As soon as she'd spotted Jamie leave Olivier's side and greet the new arrival, Claudia had given an inward cheer and planned her next move. Olivier's face had fallen like the guillotine, and he'd stalked into the house through the French windows. This was the chance she'd been waiting for. Three glasses of Bucklebury Folly and the Preston brothers' herbal offerings had numbed her anxiety. The boys had spent all evening telling her she was the most gorgeous female at the party, giving her the confidence boost she needed. She felt quite her old self.

She rose gracefully to her feet, ignoring the protests from the Preston brothers. They were supine on the rug beside her, too stoned to get up. They tugged at her trouser legs, begging her not to go. She kicked them off good-naturedly.

'For heaven's sake, I'm only going to the loo.'

Satisfied with her explanation, and urging her not to be long, they fell back on to the rug.

Olivier was sitting cross-legged in front of the fireplace, lighting matches from a box of Swan Vesta and tossing them on to the unlit logs. Claudia flopped into a nearby battered leather chair.

'Penny for them,' she said softly.

Olivier looked up.

'Only a penny?' he said drily. He wondered if she had any idea of the offer her father had made him earlier in the evening. Judging by her reaction, he decided not, as she looked at him rather oddly.

'It's a fantastic house, isn't it?' she said, looking round the room.

It was a million miles from Kingswood, with its heavily gilded Italian furniture bought from a swanky showroom in Birmingham, the elaborately swagged curtains – or drapes, as the interior designer called them – hanging off poles as thick as a man's arm, the plush Axminster carpet that ran through the entire ground floor of the house like Astroturf. Everything was perfectly coordinated – right down to the jardinières stuffed with artificial flowers and twizzly bits of stick sprayed gold.

But in this room, absolutely nothing matched. Faded chintz chair covers were peppered with tapestry cushions trimmed with velvet, billowing striped silk curtains puddled on to the dark oak floorboards, a tartan rug was thrown over the back of a fraying chair. And the walls could barely be seen, as they were totally smothered in works of art in mismatched frames.

'Amazing pictures,' said Claudia, somewhat in awe. The artwork at Kingswood consisted of reproduction Russell Flints and garish still lifes of fruit run up by nimble-fingered Taiwanese.

'Paintings,' Olivier corrected her. 'Jamie's mother did most of them.'

'It's really sad,' said Claudia wistfully. 'Did you know her? Jamie's mother?'

'Yep,' said Olivier shortly.

'What was she like?'

348

Olivier shrugged.

'She was a vain, self-centred, hypocritical, neurotic bitch.'

Claudia looked at him in horror.

'You're kidding?'

Olivier didn't answer for a second.

'In my opinion. Most people thought she was a fucking goddess.'

Claudia raised an eyebrow at his bitterness.

'So is Jamie like her?' she asked casually. She thought it was better to bring the opposition into the equation, just to gauge his reaction.

'No,' said Olivier, very definitely. 'Jamie's absolutely nothing like her at all.'

There was silence for a moment. Olivier stared moodily into the fireplace, as if there was some sort of answer lurking in there, and carried on lighting matches. Claudia reached into one of the pockets of her cargo trousers and pulled out an immaculately rolled joint that the baby Preston had given her for a rainy day.

'Do you want to light this, before you run out of matches?'

Olivier took it from her wordlessly. He looked at it for a moment, remembering what Ray had said about Claudia being in rehab, wondering if this was going to send her hurtling back down some slippery slope. Then he decided he didn't care. She wasn't his responsibility, after all.

Rod was sitting back on a pile of cushions, an empty plate beside him and a full glass in his hand, thanking God for giving him the courage.

His dance with Jamie had been interrupted by an insensitive guest about to make his departure who hadn't recognized the invisible bubble they were in, the enchanted circle that set them apart from everyone else. But it didn't matter, because in that precious few moments the twelve years they had spent apart had been reduced to as many seconds. And Rod recognized that the spark he had always felt was missing in his marriage was not totally elusive. It was just a question of finding it with the right person.

He shuddered to think what he would have missed if he'd lost his bottle in the pub and sought solace with Foxy instead. He would probably never have been given the chance again. The slender, silken thread of magic that joined his soul to Jamie's would never have been reconnected; it would have remained floating unhappily in the air, like a snapped spider's web, searching in vain for something to latch on to.

Now the two of them were willing the party to end, biding their time, waiting for the moment when they could be alone to rediscover each other. Every now and then Jamie flitted off to say goodbye to one of her guests, who – now it was gone midnight – were starting to drift off, albeit reluctantly. And Rod found himself circulating. He knew quite a few of the people there. He'd done the Prestons' kitchen, and some of their friends'. Hilly, of course, was thrilled to see him there, and had to bite her tongue to stop herself from saying something indiscreet. She was a romantic old soul, and wise. She knew when two people belonged together.

Half an hour later, Olivier's mood had lifted. He'd been irritated at first when Claudia had invaded his space, but she was proving quite a welcome distraction. She'd kicked off her shoes and was sprawled over her chair, her legs hooked over one arm, her long, tousled hair hanging over the other.

'I've only been skiing twice,' she was telling him. 'Once with school and once with some mates. We had a chalet in Val d'Isère. It was fantastic.'

Olivier nodded. 'There's nothing like it.' He sucked the very last of the sweet smoke from the joint and tossed it into the fireplace. 'Although racing comes close. You get the same sense of speed, that feeling that you're not quite in control.'

'Yes,' agreed Claudia softly. 'Kind of like the very best sex.'

Olivier looked up and grinned in acquiescence. He'd used that very metaphor the other day.

'Dangerous sex,' Claudia carried on boldly. 'Sex with someone you shouldn't be having sex with.'

'I don't know about that,' said Olivier lightly.

'Ah, well,' said Claudia. 'Then you don't know what you're missing.'

She yawned and stretched out her arms, arching her back as she did so, and Olivier couldn't help but notice her top riding up, exposing a toned and tanned midriff that he would have to have been a monk not to appreciate. He was fairly certain that this was an act, that she was deliberately tempting him. He decided to call her bluff. He reached out a hand and tugged down her top so she was covered back up.

'You'll catch your death,' he warned teasingly, and she met his gaze boldly. There was no mistaking the invitation in her eyes. Olivier debated luring her upstairs. Then he decided that it would be unfair to use her like that. She might be a little minx, blatantly asking for it, but actually he respected her, in a funny sort of way. She wasn't your average bit of eye candy. There was definitely more to her than he'd first thought.

To his relief, Ray poked his head round the door, breaking the moment.

'Claudia, love, I think it's time we went.'

'But, Dad—'

'It's nearly one o'clock. And it's going to take at least an hour to drive home.'

Claudia looked mutinous. Ray looked meaningfully at Olivier, who looked at his watch, anxious to avoid a scene. He stood up hastily.

'I ought to give a hand clearing up, anyway.'

Ray nodded his approval. 'I'll go and fetch the car.'

He disappeared. Claudia and Olivier stood awkwardly by the fire for a moment, until she leaned forwards to give Olivier a peck goodbye, her silky hair brushing his cheek.

'I'll see you next weekend.'

He smiled. 'Certainly will.'

Her face was on a level with his. She looked into his eyes, her own dancing mischievously.

'I'm going to cream your ass.'

His left eyebrow raised a millimetre.

'Like you did last week, you mean?'

Claudia recoiled as he looked at her mockingly.

'Anyway, I'm sure Daddy's sorted it all out for you. Made sure you've got the very best,' he went on. 'That's what it's all about, isn't it? Buying your way in?'

As soon as he said it, Olivier regretted being so sharp. But he'd suddenly felt the need to put some distance between them. He was fairly sure that Ray Sedgeley, given his behaviour earlier, and the look on his face when he'd seen them together, would hardly take kindly to Olivier taking advantage of his daughter.

At Olivier's jibe, Claudia felt as if a bucket of icy water had been thrown over her. Suddenly she was twelve years old again, at the local gymkhana, lining up on her pony to receive the rosette for first place in the showjumping. And as she trotted off proudly, she heard – for she was meant to – the spiteful tones of Penny Lockwood, the girl who had come second.

'Of course, she only won 'cos her dad can afford to buy her the best pony. She's a crap rider. It was Marmalade that took her round. She wouldn't have a hope on Silvester. She'd have to know what she was doing ...'

Claudia heard the other little girls murmuring in agreement. And their words had cut her to the quick. What was the point in winning if everyone scorned your success? And it wasn't true. She wasn't a crap rider. She'd spent hours and hours going over practice jumps, learning how to set the pony straight, when to urge him on and when to rein him in so as to get the perfect stride.

It was the last time she competed on Marmalade. He sat in his stable in the livery yard for weeks while Ray cajoled her to get back on. But Claudia wasn't going to put herself through the humiliation again. Six months later Barbara put her foot down and put an ad in the paper. Penny Lockwood's father bought Marmalade for Penny's thirteenth birthday, and Barbara put the proceeds in the Halifax building society on Claudia's behalf.

And now history was repeating itself. Olivier was mocking her capabilities, implying that her father was buying her success. Claudia took in a deep breath to keep her fury at bay and gave him a little smile.

'We'll see, shall we?'

Then she walked off, giving him the full benefit of her rear view, swearing to herself that the arrogant little shit wouldn't get the chance to crow over her again.

Pauline slid her key into the lock and opened the front door gently. If Bella was sleeping, she didn't want to wake her. She'd had a good evening; she and the girls had arranged to go on holiday that autumn, on a tour of Andalusia. She realized Bella was still awake, and it looked as if she had ventured downstairs. The lights were all on, and the stereo was blaring out. Pauline smiled – perhaps she was on the mend.

She pushed open the door to the dining room, her face covered in a smile of greeting. The dining table was smothered in opened boxes of chocolates, multicoloured foil wrappers scattered with gay abandon. A bottle of cough medicine had spewed its lurid contents across the tablecloth. Pauline automatically stretched out her hand to set it upright, then her stomach contracted in fear as she spotted the empty tablet bottles.

Then she saw her daughter, spreadeagled on the floor in the lounge, face down, her satin nightdress rucked up round her thighs.

'Bella!' Pauline flew to her side, lifted up her head and recoiled at the sight of the pool of vomit on the floor. The ends of Bella's hair were trailing in it and the sour stench leaped up at her, mingled with a sickly undertone of chocolate and alcohol. Pauline ran for the phone, desperately punching out 999, wondering if she was wasting her time, if she was too late. Thinking clearly despite the horror of the situation, she gathered up as many medicine bottles as she could find, in order to give the paramedics a full description of what Bella might have taken, and prepared herself to receive their instructions, steeling herself for the unpleasant prospect of having to give her daughter mouth-to-mouth resuscitation.

An hour and a half later, all the guests had finally gone or, if they were beyond driving, crashed out in one of the spare bedrooms. Lettice and Hilly, bless them, had surreptitiously organized a small posse of helpers to clear up, for which Jamie was hugely grateful – instead of the usual debris littered everywhere, which would have taken three days to get through, there were ranks of gleaming glasses drying on the side, stacks of clean plates and cutlery, and boxes full of the empty beer and wine bottles that had been found scattered round the garden. Jack had disappeared off to bed and so, presumably, had Olivier, as he was nowhere to be seen.

Rod and Jamie found themselves alone at last. Jamie suddenly felt herself ridiculously shy and self-conscious. This was the moment of truth. What if she'd imagined that her feelings had been reciprocated; if to him their reunion had just been that of two old friends, not a momentous realization, the fulfilment of years of unrequited dreams?

She pulled a bottle of cold champagne out of the fridge. She'd hardly had a drink all evening. She picked at the foil top in frustration, finding her fingers were all thumbs in the confusion of the moment.

'Let me.'

Rod took the bottle out of her hand and peeled off the foil. As he untwisted the wire and eased the cork out, she picked two glasses off the draining board, searching for something to say.

'I thought they'd never all go.'

'Neither did I,' said Rod.

She held out the glasses for him to pour, then passed him one. He raised it in a toast.

'What shall we drink to?'

'To ... old friends?' she suggested brightly.

'More than that, I hope,' he answered. He chinked his glass gently against the side of hers. 'To us ...'

Jamie smiled and took a hasty sip. She felt incredibly nervous. Maybe he was hoping to get his leg over as a matter of pride, a macho thing, revenge for being dumped all those years ago. Another dare from his brother? Her imagination was running riot – could she have imagined the incredible feeling that had sprung up between them as they'd danced earlier?

'What made you come in the end?' she asked lightly.

He ran his finger round and round the rim of his glass before answering.

'Jamie – I had to know. Whether you felt the same.' He spoke earnestly. 'It haunted me for bloody years, wondering what had happened that day. I thought ... I thought maybe your parents had found out about us. I thought they'd threatened you – or even paid you not to come near me again.'

Jamie looked at him in horror.

'Of course not! They wouldn't do that!'

Rod shrugged.

'It was better than thinking I'd been a disappointment to you. That I'd been a letdown ...'

Jamie shook her head vigorously.

'No way. Not at all. In fact ...'

She trailed off, embarrassed.

'What?'

She swallowed before speaking.

'It's never been the same since. No one else has ever made me feel like you did.'

He was silent for a moment, and she cringed inwardly. She'd never revealed herself like that to anybody. Oh God, how humiliating. Was he going to laugh? Had she given him more fodder to boast to his brothers about? She forced herself to look him in the eye. He was looking at her strangely.

'Nor me,' he said.

'What?' Jamie wasn't sure whether to try and laugh it off. But he put down his glass and came over to her. Then took her glass out of her hand and cupped her face in his hands.

'I've spent all my life since that day hoping I'd feel like that about someone again. But I never have. Sometimes I'd torture myself hoping you might come back into my life, but I stopped doing that in the end because it hurt too much.'

For a moment, Jamie panicked. It wasn't every day your dreams came true. Surely it wasn't that easy? Maybe they were just cruising for a fall. They'd each harboured a secret desire for each other for so long, maybe the person they each remembered was a total fabrication, a moulding of fantasy and selective memories.

'It's been twelve years. Maybe we're different people.'

Rod shook his head. 'You're the same. I can feel it.'

'What about ... Bella?' she stammered. This was all very well, but at the end of the day Rod was still married. What if he and Bella had just had a silly tiff; if this evening was a little flirtation to make him feel better about himself before he went back to his wife?

But Rod's face contorted with pain, almost grief, at the mention of Bella's name.

'We're over. Trust me,' he said shortly, then realized to convince Jamie he had to substantiate this claim. 'We were trying for a baby. We were desperate. At least, I was. She was on the pill all the time.'

Jamie looked horrified.

'That's awful!'

'I know.' It had cost Rod a lot to admit the truth. He still felt humiliated. 'But thank God. What if she had got pregnant? I'd never have found you again.'

Jamie's heart flooded with joy as it dawned on her that there were no more obstacles. And as his lips finally touched hers, she felt herself melting inside, as if for all these years she'd been preserved in ice, her heart frozen. As they kissed, her fears and doubts melted away too. This was real, this was passion, this was the heaven of knowing that at last you'd found the key to happiness. Her memory hadn't failed her – he smelled the same, tasted the same, felt the same, as she explored his bare skin like electric velvet under her fingertips.

As the two of them climbed the stairs hand in hand to her little attic bedroom, they each felt their hearts pounding, wondering if this was yet another dream they were going to wake from, disheartened and disappointed. But the reality was ten times better than anything either of them had ever imagined, and for both of them it was like drowning in honey.

And later, as the very first cheepings of the dawn chorus insinuated their way in through the bedroom window, they slipped into the sleep of the blissfully happy and contented, wrapped in each other's arms.

25

Zoe awoke, or more accurately regained consciousness, at quarter to ten on Sunday morning, and could barely lift her head. In the semi-gloom she ascertained that she was one of several bodies sprawled over what, judging by its size, must be someone's living room, though there was no furniture to confirm this – only an enormous PA system, a plant pot and two greasy denim bean bags. In the midst of the bodies were empty bottles and saucers containing fag ends and roaches. The air was still thick with the rank residue of marijuana. Zoe tried not to breathe it in as she felt sick, sick, sick. Struggling to sit up, she felt a volcanic rush to her head as a tide of nausea overcame her; a tide she knew she couldn't ignore. She scrambled to her feet as quickly as she could, found the door, then in the corridor outside tried to estimate where a downstairs cloakroom might be. There was no time. There was already hot vomit in her mouth. Instead, she opened the front door and just managed to avoid the front step, spewing over what in normal circumstances might have been a flower bed but in this case was bare earth punctuated with litter.

The heavenly relief of emptying her guts of every-thing she had imbibed the night before was marred by the feeling that someone had taken an axe to her head. Sweating, she looked up, wiping the last trickles of sour saliva from her mouth, to see a wide-eyed child gaze at her in disgust then hurry on.

She realized she didn't even know what she was wearing. She looked down: still the dress from the night before, but it had a split in the side seam that reached the top of her thigh. She hurried back inside, found her bag and made her escape. She hadn't a clue where she was. She asked a woman for directions to the nearest tube, feeling too ill to be embarrassed by her dishevelled appearance.

She had to get off the tube twice to be sick. She didn't think she could possibly have anything left inside her, but she still managed putrid yellow bile. At one point she was tempted to lie down on a bench and hope for a speedy death, for she didn't think she could go on living. She didn't know which was worst: the nausea, the headache, the giddiness or the memories of the night before that were slowly coming back to her frame by frame.

At the second to last station she was reduced to dry retching, then managed to buy a Coke in an attempt to rehydrate, hoping that its syrupy sweetness would settle her stomach. She ran a tongue over her cracked lips, wondering how on earth a grown woman could voluntarily do herself so much damage in the name of fun. Eventually the ghastly journey came to an end and she struggled to the surface of Shepherd's Bush station.

The day outside was irritatingly bright and cheerful. Zoe shrank back into the shadows and tried to summon up the strength for the two-hundred-yard walk back to Natalie's. Feeling horribly self-conscious, she began her journey, praying she wouldn't see someone she knew.

Her prayers weren't answered. Heading straight for her was her old next-door-but-one neighbour, on his way, no doubt, for the Sunday papers, one child in each hand. She steeled herself for his greeting, but none came. Instead, he averted his gaze and firmly steered the children around her, hurrying on as quickly as he could. Zoe didn't blame him for ignoring her, then realized he wasn't – he hadn't even recognized her. He'd obviously mistaken her for some raddled old tart on her way home from working the streets.

Eventually she got to Natalie's house and rang the bell. Natalie opened the door and looked as if she'd seen a particularly terrifying apparition.

'Zoe! My God – where have you been? I was going to give you another hour, then I was going to call the police.'

She stepped back as Zoe stumbled in over the doorstep. Behind Natalie appeared Marcella, looking bandbox fresh and as if butter wouldn't melt.

'Marcella said you went off with some real lowlifes. She said she couldn't get you to come home.' She lowered her voice and spoke in a vicious whisper. 'For God's sake, Zoe. You could have been raped. Or gang-banged. Or anything. There're some real weirdos about.'

Zoe realized with a sickening lurch that for all she knew she could have been. She couldn't remember a bloody thing. She certainly felt as if an entire rugby team had had its wicked way with her. And she would have deserved it. She had a dim memory of dancing to 'Lady Marmalade', holding her arms above her head and thrusting her hips and her chest suggestively at anyone who would bother to look. She'd been asking for it all right.

Natalie was looking at her with distaste.

'For God's sake go and have a shower.'

'Thanks,' Zoe managed to croak, and stumbled past the two of them, not missing Marcella exchange a look of disdainful disapproval with Natalie. Hypocrite.

When she looked in the bathroom mirror, she recoiled in horror. Her eyes had almost vanished; they were puffy slits with huge bags slung underneath. Her skin was deathly pale and waxy; her lips cracked and blackened. Slowly, she took off her clothes. Her muscles ached unbearably, presumably from dancing all night. At least she hoped that was the case.

She thought about what Natalie had said. Had she had sex with Zak? Or one of his mates? Or worse, both? Willingly or unwillingly? Knowingly or unknowingly? Should she go to a police station – get herself checked out, have a forensic examination? Though she didn't know if she wanted to know. And she didn't know how she'd be received. And if she had – what then? What would she do about it? She could hardly expect any sympathy.

She had the shakes now. She sat down on the loo, trying to assess her predicament and failing. She tried desperately to work out how long it would be before she would feel human again. If she'd stopped being sick, she might be able to manage first some tea, and then some toast.

She poured a liberal amount of Natalie's bubble bath under the tap, then sank into the cleansing bubbles. She washed her hair and scrubbed her body, then when the last of the bath water had drained away she stood under the shower for ten minutes, wishing fervently that the memories – or rather lack of them – from the night before would disappear down the plughole as well.

She put her dress and her G-string into a spare carrier bag and tied a knot in it, then thrust it into the bin on the landing. She put on reassuringly clean underwear, her jeans and a T-shirt. She looked in the mirror again. She was still deathly pale, but her eyes had opened a fraction, now revealing bloodshot eyeballs underneath. She smothered her lips in Lypsyl and attempted repair with some Beauty Flash Balm.

She looked and felt like hell.

She edged herself gingerly down the stairs, sneaking past the playroom where Daisy and Millie were watching television. She was too ashamed to let them see what a state she was in; a hideous contrast to the sparkling party girl they'd applauded last night.

When she finally made it into the kitchen, Natalie gave her a look that would turn milk sour.

'I don't suppose you can face breakfast. Not that it's breakfast time any longer.'

Her voice was dripping acid. Zoe quailed.

'Tea? Hot sweet tea? And have you got any Frosties?' she asked meekly.

Natalie dumped a box of Frosties on the table and flicked the kettle on. Zoe sat down at the breakfast bar, feeling as if her legs were about to give way. She wasn't sure if she'd reached the stage when she'd be able to eat, but all the hangover cures she'd ever read had urged some sort of carbohydrate intake to speed up the healing process.

Natalie crossed her arms, waiting for the kettle to boil, and glared at her balefully.

'So, madam – what have you got to say for yourself?'

Zoe swallowed. She felt like a naughty little girl.

'For God's sake, Zoe. You're thirty-four. Not nineteen. I still can't believe the way you behaved last night.'

'It was our girls' night out. A bit of fun.'

'Fun? You call dressing up like a slag, getting paralytically drunk, then going off and screwing half of West London—'

'I didn't!' retorted Zoe, but rather lamely because she couldn't be sure even now what she had and hadn't done. Natalie went about making the tea, slamming cupboard doors.

'I don't know what's got into you, but I think you need to sort yourself out. You phone me up five times a week, pissed, usually, moaning about your terrible life. Then you come here and abuse my hospitality—'

Zoe looked up, shocked at this latest accusation.

'Yes. You weren't interested in my company last night. You weren't interested in anything I had to say. You had your own bloody agenda. You made me feel as if I was cramping your style. Then you don't come home, don't ring to tell me where you are, leave me worried sick and about to phone the police—'

'I'm sorry,' mumbled Zoe. 'I'm just having a bit of a shit time at the moment.'

'So you keep telling me. But you know what I think? You're the one making it shit. You're not making an effort. You're determined to hate your new life.'

Zoe wanted to clamp her hands over her ears to try and block out what Natalie was saying.

'All of us here would give our eye teeth to have a lovely house in the countryside. You're living our dream for us, Zoe, and you're ruining it. And not just for you, but for

Christopher. If you want the honest truth, it's him I feel sorry for.'

She slammed a cup of tea down in front of her. Zoe jumped.

'Sorry, Zo, but you can always rely on me to tell it like it is. I was going to have a word with you anyway this weekend, tell you to buck your ideas up. But I'd no idea you'd completely fucking lost it.'

Zoe was outraged. How dare Natalie lecture her as if she was her mother? Natalie, who'd been a notorious party animal herself not so long ago. She was a bloody hypocrite. A sanctimonious hypocrite who had absolutely no idea what she was going through. She opened her mouth to protest. But then, all of a sudden, a wave of desolation came over her and she wanted to weep.

'I think Christopher's in love with someone else,' she wailed.

'What?'

'You met her. Jamie Wilding. She went to his birthday barbecue.'

'The one that looks like a Barbour advert?'

'Yes. Little Miss Windswept, sparkly-eyed, don't need make-up, butter wouldn't melt …' Zoe trailed off, unable to think of any more adjectives. 'He thinks the world of her. I can tell. When he talks to her, it's as if I don't exist. He asks her advice. Not mine! And of course, she can cook. And she loves dogs. Those horrible stinking fucking dogs of his mother's.'

Zoe went on to describe the disastrous evening when Jamie had come over for supper, and how threatened she had felt by the whole thing. Then she laid her head down in her arms and began to sob. Natalie waited until she'd cried herself out before giving her a thorough talking-to.

'Zoe – you're paranoid. You need to get things into perspective here. Number one: Christopher married you. He's known Jamie since year dot – if he loved her that much, surely he'd have married her years ago, but he didn't. They're just mates. And number two: Jamie's doing all the things that you should be doing. Providing him with a sympathetic ear. Supporting him. For heaven's sake, see things from Christopher's point of view. He's under serious pressure, and you're not helping one bit. How do you think he feels, uprooted, his dad seriously ill, trying to keep the business together? And all he's got is you bitching because they don't sell Eve Lom in the local chemist.'

Natalie paused to draw breath. Zoe looked utterly shell-shocked, even though Natalie was saying things she already knew.

'I've known you and Christopher long enough. He loves you, because you're scatty, fun, lively, bright, sexy, sociable … You've given him two gorgeous boys. But for God's sake, snap out of it, or you will lose him. And at the end of the day, it's not as if you've been sent to bloody Siberia. If you could be arsed to make the effort, you'd make friends. Don't be such a snotty, uptight cow, judging people by their appearances. It's so superficial, and you're not. Otherwise, you wouldn't be *my* friend.'

Natalie paused, thinking she'd probably said enough for the time being. Zoe just looked frozen with misery.

'I'd better go and pack,' A tear rolled down her cheek and plopped into her Frosties. 'Do you think Edwin would give me a lift to the station?'

Natalie softened, and came and gave her a hug.

'I didn't mean to be harsh. But I'm only telling you for your own good. You're very lucky, Zoe. If only you could see that.'

As her friend rocked her in her arms, Zoe realized that everything Natalie said was right. And she knew exactly where she wanted to be right now. Sitting on the terrace at Lydbrook House with Christopher, reading the Sunday papers with a pot of coffee, while the boys swatted in vain at a shuttlecock on the lawn. Any minute now, she would go inside and start preparing Sunday lunch. Rosemary would come in with some freshly dug potatoes and she would thank her warmly, then pop out to the herb garden for mint to go with the lamb. She would happily scrape carrots and shell peas, then peel some of last autumn's apples for a crumble.

How stupid she'd been, hankering after the bright lights and nightlife and cheap thrills, when everything that was truly important was right under her nose. If she didn't die from alcohol poisoning – and judging by the way she was still feeling this was an acute possibility – she'd make it up to them as soon as she got back. She'd be the perfect country wife and mother. She'd make jam and learn to ride and do pony club with the boys. She'd pluck pheasants and gut trout unflinchingly.

She just hoped that she hadn't left it too late.

Christopher woke up on Sunday morning and thought, perhaps, that he might be in heaven. He was in the softest, sweetest-smelling bed. It was like resting on a cloud. White sheets embroidered with tiny rosebuds and their scent as well; the soft crackle of goose down. Somewhere a church bell was ringing.

Tiona appeared in the doorway in a white lace-trimmed camisole and French knickers, her curls loose and falling on to her shoulders. Her gentle blue eyes shone with affection when she saw he was awake.

'Breakfast,' she murmured, and he breathed in her smell. Toothpaste and roses. She poured them each a glass of champagne and handed one to him. Without taking her eyes off his she undid the tiny buttons on her camisole, revealing her deliciously round breasts, white and perky as meringues. He dipped his finger into his glass and traced a ring of champagne around her nipple, watching it harden under his touch. He bent his head to lick it off and she gave a little whimper of contentment, tipping back her head, arching her back in delight. When he stopped, she took a mouthful of champagne, pulled his head to hers and kissed him. Their tongues danced amongst the bubbles, the liquid spilling from their mouths as they licked every last drop from each other. She put down her glass and pulled him to her, falling back on to the bed. Just as their tongues had entwined now so did their limbs.

It was like fucking a fairy princess. He was spellbound. Enchanted. Bewitched. There was nothing he could do now.

Jamie woke, momentarily perplexed by the huge bubble of happiness inside her that started at her toes and ran all the way to her fingertips. It was a long-forgotten feeling. Most mornings over the past couple of weeks she had woken with a lump of anxiety that she had battled to dispel. But this – this was utter bliss. It took her a few moments to locate the reason, and when she did, the bubble threatened to grow even larger, until she thought she would burst with joy.

Rod's arm was hooked around her waist. He was holding her tightly, as if he would never let her go. She snuggled deeper into him, revelling in the cosiness, and in his sleep he hugged her even tighter as if he feared she was trying to escape. Jamie half closed her eyes and drifted away on a cocktail of contentment and anticipation. Half of her wanted to wake him and make love again, but this time in the light of day, so she could be sure it was real. But the other half wanted to lie there and revel in the memory of the night before. The curtains were slightly open and the morning light streamed in. Motes of dust swirled in a sunbeam. Jamie remembered how she always used to pretend they were tiny fairies, dancing in the air. She imagined herself one of them now, arms outstretched, spinning in a triumphant pirouette of happiness.

Beside her, Rod stirred. She wriggled out from under his grasp and turned to face him just as his eyes opened. She could see by his expression that he was undergoing the same blissful slide into realization that she'd just felt. They lay and looked at each other, unable to stop smiling. And they made love again. This time it was slow, the movements imperceptible, culminating in the intimate, all-consuming ecstasy that can only be evoked by love, not lust.

At last, one of them broke the silence.

'So – what do we do now?' asked Jamie.

'We're meant to be, aren't we?' answered Rod simply.

'We've wasted all those years; waited all that time. I don't know about you, but I haven't got any doubts.'

Jamie's heart hammered. She knew if she analysed it logically and dispassionately, she might hear warning bells. Childhood sweethearts meeting up after twelve years, falling into bed and declaring undying love for each other? It wasn't a firm foundation on which to build a future. At best, it was romanticizing.

But her heart told her she wasn't going to let this chance slip away. The feeling she'd thought she'd never have again in her life had resurrected itself. She wasn't going to sacrifice that by being practical and sensible. She wanted to spend every moment with him. They lay in each other's arms a little longer, not wanting to break the spell. Then Jamie turned to Rod with a grin.

'Do you know what?'

'What?'

'I'm absolutely starving.'

When Olivier heard two sets of footsteps coming down the stairs, and Jamie talking and laughing excitedly, he didn't need telling who the other pair belonged to. He'd seen the way she'd looked at Rod the night before, watched them slip away hand in hand. The last thing he wanted to do was give them a cheery greeting and offer them coffee. He didn't want to see her sparkling eyes, her besotted aura. With a heavy heart, he slipped quietly out of the back door just as they came into the room.

They sat out in the garden with a pot of tea, eating toast and blackberry jam. There was no sign of anyone else: the remaining guests had either gone or were still sleeping off their hangovers. It was almost impossible to believe that the garden had been heaving with nearly a hundred revellers the night before. Jamie made a mental note to buy Lettice a big bunch of flowers to thank her for her hard work – she had a heart of gold, once you got through the rather overpowering facade. Lettice and Jack had gone off somewhere – she'd heard the purr of the Bentley earlier this morning – for which she was rather grateful. Jack was very open-minded; he wouldn't necessarily be shocked to find her sharing breakfast with Rod, but Jamie felt the need to let things breathe a little before the two of them declared their love to the world.

'So,' she said, flapping a wasp away from the jam with her hand. 'Where do we take it from here?'

Rod considered his reply carefully.

'What's happening to this place? Are you still going to sell?'

Jamie sighed, feeling her bubble deflate slightly. At the end of the day, you might have found your true love, but there were still practicalities to consider.

'It's going on the market next week. There's no way we can afford to keep it going. Well, you know that – you know Dad's financial situation. I had all sorts of grand ideas about opening a country hotel, but the figures were terrifying. We didn't have a hope.' She looked rueful.

Rod munched on his toast thoughtfully.

'What about,' he ventured, 'if you and I bought Bucklebury Farm off your dad?'

Jamie stared at him. He carried on, feeling a flutter of excitement in his stomach as he warmed to his idea.

'We can go back to my original plan. With a few minor adjustments. We can convert the stables and give your father one of them to live in. But instead of selling the rest off, we could turn them into holiday cottages. It gives us an income, your father realizes his capital, and we've got the farmhouse.'

He didn't add the bit about filling it with fat, happy babies. Not just yet.

Jamie stared at him, her heart pounding.

'Do you think that's possible?'

'I don't see why not.'

Jamie shook her head in wonder, unable to keep the smile off her face as she mentally ran through what Rod had outlined.

'It's absolutely incredible. I can't see any flaws at all.'

'There aren't any, that's why. It's meant to be, Jamie. It's meant to be.' A little voice told Rod to exercise a modicum of caution. 'Obviously, I need to sort things out with Bella first. Make everything official and agree some sort of settlement. I can't go ahead and make plans otherwise. I don't want things to become messy. Not when we've waited this long.'

Jamie nodded in agreement, spreading another slice of toast with a layer of jam, realizing that she hadn't really eaten last night.

'When you've sorted everything out, then we can talk to Dad.'

'What do you think he'll say? About his daughter taking up with a Deacon?' teased Rod. 'Isn't that every father's worst nightmare?'

Jamie thumped him on the arm good-naturedly.

'Actually, I think he's quite a fan. He was certainly singing your praises when I was calling you every name under the sun the other week.'

When Jamie went in to fill up the teapot, Rod sat in the sunshine, trying to take in what was happening to him. It was just possible all of his dreams were coming true at once. Jamie, his beloved Jamie, who had never been far from his thoughts all these years, despite what he might have pretended to himself. And Bucklebury Farm ... his gaze wandered lazily round the garden. It was almost perfect as it was, even though there was the odd tell-tale sign of last night's revelry – cigarette butts in the flower beds, beer bottles tucked into peculiar places, heel marks in the lawn. He thought he might build a little summer house – somewhere they could have breakfast when it wasn't quite as warm as this, or shelter from the hot midday sun with a bottle of beer ...

Stop, he told himself sternly. He was going too fast. There were miles of red tape to sort out first. He had to find himself a decent lawyer for a start. He wasn't a vindictive or a spiteful man, so he wanted to be fair to Bella, but at the same time he had his own interests to protect. And if they were going to buy out Bucklebury from Jack, he'd got quite a bit of extra money to find. Without Bella's half of Owl's Nest (he was resigned to the fact she'd have to have half) and Pauline's contribution, he was going to have to scrape up another couple of hundred grand from somewhere. But it would be worth it. He'd have everything he'd ever wanted ...

26

As the church bells rang out across Ludlow indicating the end of the Sunday service, Christopher managed to extricate himself from Tiona's heavenly embrace and stagger back home in time for lunch. The boys were running round the garden with a hose, letting off steam after being frogmarched to church by their grandmother that morning. Rosemary was chopping up mint to go with the leg of lamb she'd put in the Aga a couple of hours earlier.

'Good party?' she asked.

'Fantastic,' replied Christopher carefully, and hastily offered to help peel the potatoes. He couldn't face actually lying to his mother about where he had stayed the night before. The chance of her corroborating his evidence with Jack or Jamie or any of the other guests was fairly slim, but he didn't want to risk it.

He spent the afternoon bowling for the boys so they could practise their cricket, a supreme act of self-sacrifice designed to assuage his guilt for he was secretly yearning to curl up on the sofa and relive the night before, like a lovesick teenager. He'd taken off the shirt he'd been wearing, but instead of dropping it into the laundry basket he hid it at the back of his wardrobe. Occasionally he nipped indoors for a surreptitious sniff of the scent that still clung to it, feeling like a total pervert but unable to resist as it transported him instantly back into Tiona's arms.

The phone rang twice during the afternoon and each time he nearly jumped out of his skin. He thought there was no way she would phone him at home, then reasoned if she was as desperate to hear his voice as he was to hear hers, she was clever enough to manufacture an excuse. And no one would think it was particularly odd if she phoned. She did work for him, after all.

But it wasn't her. The first time it was a friend of Hugo's, wanting to check up on some homework. And the second time it was Zoe, calling on her mobile. Her train was due in at six-thirty and she needed a lift back home. It was the reality check Christopher needed. He had his second shower of the day. The first had been scalding hot to wash away his sins. This one was cold, pinpricks of ice to sharpen his senses, to ensure he didn't make any of the careless mistakes that so often trip up the unfaithful.

The answerphone light was flashing furiously when Rod got home that afternoon. He'd deliberately turned his mobile off when he'd gone to Bucklebury Farm, as he didn't want any drunken prank calls from Foxy. But whoever was after him was persistent. It was probably a client moaning about something – for some reason people who were busy the rest of the week seemed to think Sundays were the best days for getting results out of other people. Rod made it a rule that anyone who hassled him on his day of rest got sent to the back of the queue.

Or it could be his mother on the warpath, having found out about Lee. It incensed her when her offspring fought amongst themselves, which inevitably they did from time to time. He really wasn't ready for a wigging.

Or it could be Bella, pleading for a fair trial. But he didn't want to think about her yet either. He wanted everything straight in his head when he next confronted her.

Whoever it was, he didn't want to know. He drifted upstairs in a dream and took a shower, steaming hot followed by an icy-cold blast. He went back into the bedroom with a towel round his waist and opened the chest of drawers to find some fresh clothes. The phone rang again. He let the answering machine click in downstairs while he got dressed. As he did up his jeans, it occurred to him that it might have been Jamie phoning.

He ran back down to the sitting room and rewound the machine. He'd have to listen to all the messages before he got to hers. He paced round the room, buttoning up his shirt. The first was from Foxy, very drunk the night before, telling him what a great night he was missing. He grinned and wound on to the next message.

'Rod? It's Pauline. I'm on my way to the hospital with Bella. She's taken an overdose. Get here as quickly as you can, for God's sake.'

His bowels froze. The message had been at gone midnight last night. He listened to the next one.

'Where are you? I'm at the hospital. They're just taking her into intensive care.'

The next message was Pauline, almost incoherent, sobbing.

'I'm still waiting to hear. Where are you?'

The next message was icy calm but incredibly weary.

'They think she's going to be all right. But they're

keeping her in. I'm going to stay here. She needs some-body with her ...' She didn't say any more, but the voice was dripping with reproach.

The last message was downright curt.

'Rod. It's Sunday morning and I'm on my way home to have a shower and get changed. Then I'm going back to the hospital. Bella's conscious, but not feeling too bright, obviously. I'd appreciate it if you could call me. *If* you get back in ...'

'End of messages,' the computerized voice informed him.

A psychiatric nurse came in to Bella that afternoon. She found it hard to believe that's what he was – he looked incredibly young, with spiky blond hair. More like a member of a boy band than anything. He told her his name was Dave, and that he needed to ask her a few questions. Despite his appearance, he was very reassuring and surprisingly gentle. He wanted to know all about how she'd been feeling lately. If she'd been depressed. If she'd meant to kill herself. If she still felt as if she wanted to die. If she knew what it was that was making her feel this way.

Bella didn't want to answer his questions at first. She felt dreadful, for a start. They'd put her on a drip, to re-hydrate her, but her head was still pounding. Her stomach and her chest felt flayed on the inside, raw from vomiting, and she ached all over. She lay in her bed listlessly. She couldn't summon up the strength to speak, only to let two big fat tears slide down her cheeks.

Dave persisted. 'The thing is, Bella, if we can get to the

bottom of this we can try and help you. You probably feel very alone at the moment, as if there's no answer.'

She took in a deep, juddering breath and wiped away her tears.

'It's stupid. I don't know where to start.'

'It's not stupid. It's important. And I'm not going to tell anyone what you tell me, if you don't want me to.'

His voice was soothing. Bella thought perhaps it wouldn't hurt to tell him.

She tried to explain. How her body had been her only currency. The one thing that had got her admiration. The one thing she had that no one else could match up to. All her life, she had clung on to the maintenance of her perfect proportions as her *raison d'être*. Without it, she'd be nothing. Invisible. Irrelevant. Women envied her. Men lusted after her. And she needed that adulation to feel worthy. That was all she was. A great pair of tits, a peach of an arse, a washboard stomach and fabulous legs.

Dancing had been the platform on which she showed off her assets. She remembered how she'd always been able to make her daddy smile when she danced for him. She'd put on one of her spangly dresses and show him her latest routine, and she'd soon be able to coax him out of his black mood. Often she remembered trying to distract him. Twirling and whirling desperately in the lounge, vying for his attention, anything to stop that horrible noise – the thumps she would hear upstairs, followed by her mother's muffled sobbing. Sometimes it worked. Sometimes it didn't.

She remembered the last time it didn't. She'd known somehow that this black rage was even darker than the rest. She'd pulled out her very best dress, the one with the blue and green sequins that made her look like a mermaid.

'Come and watch, Daddy. Come and see. I've got a new routine.'

She hadn't, but she thought she could make one up. He'd walked past her without looking. And she'd never seen him again ...

Bella found that once she'd started to explain things to Dave, she couldn't stop. Out it all came, the years of hang-ups and neuroses and self-doubt, and the incredible strain of keeping up appearances, the illusion of the happy, all-dancing, all-singing Bella, when really she felt dead inside. She told him everything, right up to her deception of Rod, the heinous crime that had made her realize what a terrible person she was, and how she felt she really didn't deserve to live after that.

And not once did Dave look shocked or disapproving, just nodded thoughtfully as Bella's darkest secrets spilled from her lips.

When Christopher pulled up in front of the station at half-six, Zoe was already waiting. He was surprised at how terrible she looked. As white as a sheet, with her hair cropped close to her head and dyed several different shades of what could only be called orange.

'You've had your hair done,' he said as she got in, keeping his tone deliberately bright yet noncommittal. He had learned long ago that this was the safest tactic, until you had a lead as to the wearer's opinion. Telling a woman her hair looked great when she thought it was an unmitigated disaster was suicide. As was not mentioning it at all.

'Don't look at it. I haven't had time to do it properly,' she replied wearily, flopping into the front seat.

'Good weekend?'

Zoe gave a grimace, accompanied by a shrug. Christopher felt a strong urge to fill the silence.

'The Wildings' party was great. I ended up having to stay over. Jack's punch was totally lethal. Especially on an empty stomach – I hadn't eaten all day. It was hectic in the office. I needed a few drinks to wind down, I can tell you. The kids were fine with Mum—'

He was keenly aware he was contravening the first rule of the guilty, which was to say as little as possible. Too much detail and you risked tripping yourself up. But it was neither here nor there, as Zoe didn't seem to be listening. She interrupted him in mid-flow.

'Christopher – can we stop off at the pub? We need to talk.'

Christopher felt a flicker of fear. This was the moment. She was going to tell him that things had to change, that she wanted to go back to London, that they were going to have to separate. So – how did he play his cards? It wasn't going to look too good if, in a few months' time, it came out that he'd been at it with Tiona before their separation. Christopher was an honourable sort of chap. He didn't believe in duplicity. He was already deeply uncomfortable with what he had done. He looked sideways at Zoe. She had her eyes closed, her face an expressionless mask. He wondered what was going through her head; if she was rehearsing what she had to say.

'Sure,' he said, the lightness of his tone belying the heavy dread he was feeling. It was all going too fast. He wasn't ready to make life-changing decisions. He didn't know what he wanted.

If you'd asked him yesterday what he wanted, he'd have been able to answer. He wanted the old Zoe back, the one he'd had in Shepherd's Bush, and he'd have done anything in his power to get her. But his torrid night of passion with Tiona had clouded his judgement. He wasn't sure how he felt about his wife at all.

Rod burst through the door of the hospital, feeling like a character out of *ER* as he looked wildly round for help.

'My wife. Bella Deacon. Where is she?' he barked at the receptionist, who looked through her records painfully slowly before directing him to the correct ward. He couldn't be bothered to wait for the lift. He bounded up the stairs and through the double doors that led to the upper corridor.

The first person he saw was Pauline, hovering by the coffee machine. He almost didn't recognize her, and he was shocked by her appearance. He'd never seen her looking anything other than perfectly turned out, but here she was without a scrap of make-up, hair flat and lifeless, in an old sweatshirt and jeans. She looked years older, battered and sunken, like some long-suffering middle-aged woman you saw on the back of the bus or at the cigarette kiosk in Kwik Save, buying a packet of fags and a Lucky Dip in the hope of a miraculous escape. As he hurried towards her, his heart contracted with fear.

Pauline felt a mixture of emotions as she spotted Rod coming down the corridor at long last. She wanted to be curt and frosty with him for staying out all night, for not being there for Bella. But why should he have been, after the way he'd been treated? Why should he be there even now? For Bella had told her what had happened, when Pauline had asked her why on earth she'd done such a terrible thing. And now Rod was there in front of her, she felt nothing but shame for what her daughter had put him through. She looked at him warily, expecting hostility.

She should have known that he wasn't one to bear a grudge, not in a situation like this. Rod was bigger than that. Instead, he held out his arms to her.

'Pauline – I'm so sorry I wasn't around. Are you OK?'

Pauline nodded wordlessly. Despite herself she allowed him to hug her to him, and to her surprise she enjoyed the comfort that his embrace brought her, the strength of his arms, the warmth of his chest. It had been a long time since Pauline had allowed herself to depend on someone else, and she realized at that moment just how alone she was in her life. No matter how strong, how independent you were, there were times when you needed other people. And although her knee-jerk reaction had been to berate Rod, to blame him for Bella's condition, because by doing that she would be exonerating herself, she knew now she needed his support more than she needed a scapegoat. Especially as she had a sneaking feeling that perhaps she was to blame for what had happened.

'Where is she? Is she all right? Can I see her?' Rod asked her anxiously.

Pauline nodded her head towards the nearby ward.

'She's through there. She's talking to the psychiatric nurse.'

Rod looked startled. Pauline felt her bottom lip tremble.

'She's a real mess, Rod. And I had no idea ... I'd never

have left her alone if I'd known what a state she was in. Why didn't you tell me what was going on? She could have died, for God's sake. She could have died!'

The full horror of the past twelve hours suddenly caught up with her. Resilient, stoical Pauline, Pauline the coper, had remained alert and resolute throughout the night in case her daughter had needed her. But now the reality hit her. The terrible image of Bella lying inert on the floor, surrounded by all those bottles; her fear that she had been dead; her fear throughout the journey to the hospital that she still might die; her fear, once she realized that she was going to pull through, that Bella might suffer some irreparable damage: all these memories suddenly closed in on her and she crumpled.

Rod held her as she sobbed. As he gazed at the sickly green wall over Pauline's head, he saw all the plans he'd made that morning slipping through his fingers, fluttering gently away and out of the nearest window.

At five to seven, Christopher pulled into the car park of the Royal Oak. It was a beautiful summer's evening and the pub was lounging rather smugly in the last of the golden sunshine, keenly aware that it looked utterly idyllic. Christopher thought it was a pity they weren't a happily married couple taking advantage of a few stolen moments away from the children to enjoy each other's company. Instead of an embittered and battle-weary couple about to meet their nemesis.

They commandeered one of the last tables in the garden. When Zoe asked for a mineral water, Christopher should have got the first indication that something was not quite right. Usually she would have leaped at the chance of the sun being over the yardarm to order a large white wine. He himself had a pint of Honeycote Ale, realizing with a guilty pang that the last time he'd been here he'd enjoyed the very same with Tiona.

They sat in silence with their drinks for a moment, basking in the warmth, before Zoe finally looked up. The glare of the evening sun made her squint, so Christopher couldn't read the expression in her eyes.

'I just want to say ... I'm really, really sorry.'

'What for?' Christopher's heart was hammering. He still didn't know what *he* was going to say, or how he was going to react.

'For being such a complete and utter miserable bitch. I don't know how you've put up with me. I've been selfish, self-centred and unbearable to live with for the past few months. And I've got no real excuse. So I want to apologize. And I don't expect you to forgive me.'

Christopher looked slightly flummoxed, not too sure where this was going.

'It's been difficult for you.'

'Not really. I've made it difficult. I can see that now. I didn't make any effort whatsoever. I didn't even try to like it here. Just sulked and spat my dummy out. And that wasn't fair on you. Things are tough enough without me bitching ...'

She fumbled in her bag for a cigarette. She didn't usually smoke, but she had a few left from the night before, and she needed some sort of crutch if she was going to go without a drink. Christopher put his hand out for one as well, though it was seven years since he'd given up, just before Hugo was born. The two of them lit their illicit fags, each grateful for the fact that the ritual bought them some time.

'So, I've come to a decision,' Zoe finally announced. Christopher nodded carefully. This was it. Should he too come clean? Zoe was looking at him rather defiantly, her chin tilted upwards as she spoke.

'I'm turning over a new leaf. I'm going to make the best of things. If I'm going to be stuck here for the rest of my life, I'm bloody well going to enjoy it. So I want to make a few changes.'

Christopher felt giddy. He wasn't sure if it was the un-expected shock of what Zoe was saving, or the unfamiliar hit from the nicotine.

'What changes?' he asked.

She lifted up her mineral water.

'First, I'm not going to drink. I don't seem to know when to stop, and it only makes me worse. Not that I'm an alcoholic or anything. I just don't think booze does me any favours.'

'Probably not,' said Christopher faintly, his mind racing.

'Second, I'm going to do something constructive. The boys are at school, so I've got plenty of free time on my hands. I'm going to get a part-time job or start a little business. Unless you want some help in the office?' She grinned ruefully. 'Might as well keep it in the family.'

Christopher groped round desperately for a get-out clause. That was the last thing he wanted! Zoe and Tiona working side by side. He needed to nip that one in the bud straight away.

'Um – I don't know if it would be a good idea. Us

working together. You'd probably hate it. You should try and find something you enjoy.'

'I thought maybe interior design or something.'

Christopher nodded what he hoped was encouragement. 'Good idea.'

'Finally, I'm going to learn to ride. I figured if you can't beat them, join them. And there's no point in those stables sitting empty.' She beamed triumphantly. 'The boys can learn too. Then we can all go out riding, as a family.'

Christopher was aware that his mouth was hanging open. Zoe was burrowing about in a large carrier bag she'd brought with her from the car.

'I went and bought this. Just to show you I mean business.'

She proudly held up a wax jacket. A designer wax jacket, of course – with a nubuck collar and cuffs and lined with bright pink quilted silk. Christopher caught sight of the price tag dangling off it and didn't like to mention she could have bought herself a decent horse for the same price.

He smiled weakly. It was typical Zoe. Worse, it was why he loved her. She was so guileless, so deliciously and shamelessly superficial. On the surface.

'Very good.'

He listened, numb with shock, as Zoe prattled on with her plans. And when she finally nipped inside for a wee, he collapsed with a groan, leaning his head on the warm wood of the picnic table.

What the hell was he supposed to do now? This wasn't the plan: a sudden reconciliation, a contented wife, happy families all round. He could hardly turn round and tell

Zoe it was too late and he was shagging the arse off Tiona. He no longer had any justification for an affair. Last night it had been all too easy for him to convince himself that any man would have done the same in his position. But now the goalposts had moved.

Common sense told Christopher he should take Tiona to one side, tell her last night was a silly mistake and insist that they put their relationship back on a professional footing for the sake of the company. He thought she would understand that. She was ambitious for Drace's, after all. He could use the lure of managing another office as a sweetener. He thought she would probably see sense.

But Tiona seeing sense wasn't the real problem.

Could *he* see sense?

He felt like some young Regency buck who'd been lured into an opium den against his better judgement, then become hooked on the all-consuming sweetness, powerless to resist its charms. He was defiled, corrupted. He couldn't just walk away. She was under his skin, in his very blood and bones.

Did he love her? he wondered. God knows.

All he knew was that the woman he once loved – still did, probably – the woman he was married to, the mother of his beloved children, had just offered him an enormous olive branch by way of immense self-sacrifice on her part. What sort of a bastard would he be to throw it back in her face? Not that he'd be capable of it, even if he wanted to. Christopher didn't do heartless bastard. At least, he never had up until now.

'Buggery bollocks,' muttered Christopher to himself in despair.

*

Eventually, the psychiatric nurse emerged from the ward, and took Rod and Pauline into a small, windowless room to talk to them.

'I've asked Bella's permission to tell you what she's told me,' he said gravely. 'I think it's important that you have the full picture straight away, so you can decide on the best thing to do.'

There was no hint of reproach in his voice as he spoke. He didn't point the finger of blame at anyone. Which somehow made it worse. Both Rod and Pauline felt sick with guilt and shame that it should have come to this. And that it could have been too late.

'We'll probably never know if this was a genuine attempt at suicide or just a cry for help,' concluded Dave. 'But Bella is going to need a lot of support from both of you if she's going to get better. She needs to have some sort of counselling, or therapy, so she can sort things out in her own mind and understand her condition. And she needs a lot of care and patience and love and understanding to help her through that. It's going to be a treacherous journey. She's lived with her disorder and her low self-esteem for most of her adult life. She's got a lot to unlearn, and the only way she's going to do that is if she knows she can depend on you both.'

Rod stared impassively at the wall behind Dave's head. It was sprinkled with posters for support groups and NHS helplines. Beside him, Pauline was weeping quietly. Automatically, he reached out for her hand and patted it.

'It's going to be all right. She's going to be OK.'

'Don't leave her, Rod. Promise me you'll look after her. I know she did a terrible thing ...'

Dave looked at Rod sympathetically.

'What you've got to appreciate is her fear of losing control is totally irrational.'

'I know. I realize that.'

Dave touched him on the shoulder in a gesture of male solidarity, as if to say he understood.

But he didn't understand. He didn't have a bloody clue. How was he to know that Rod had just fallen back into the arms of the woman he'd been waiting for all his life?

Jamie slumped in the hammock with a plate of baklava. She needed fat and sugar to restore her energy. As she licked the last flakes of syrupy pastry from her lips, she fell back on to the pillows and allowed herself a little daydream, a delicious fantasy to float away on. A wedding of Hollywood proportions, a mélange of white silk and blossom and rosebuds and ringlets and pealing bells and triumphant fanfares. Jack drove her to church in the Bugatti, then escorted her proudly up the aisle. All the little charges she'd ever looked after were there, rosy-cheeked moppets clutching her lace train in their pudgy little hands. And at the end of the aisle Lee Deacon stood proudly by his brother's side, forgiven for his perfidy all those years ago, because this was a tale that was going to end happily ever after...

Jamie wasn't used to such ridiculous self-indulgence. But she was determined to revel in this utter bliss for as long as possible. She realized she'd been starved of true romance, and that it had been of her own making. She'd had flings, of course she had. But she'd always backed away from any real commitment. She'd met people she admired, she'd met people she fancied, she'd met people who shared her values, but no one who had encapsulated everything. No one had ever been able to live up to Rod and because of that she'd pushed them away if things ever looked like getting serious. Her job had provided a built-in excuse; she'd always been able to move on, choose a far-flung destination for her next assignment in order to run away. She'd broken a couple of hearts, she felt sure she had. But she never felt guilty. Why should she have resigned herself to second best?

And she'd been right to hold out. Otherwise she wouldn't be lying here now, unable to wipe the smile off her face. It was bliss. She and Rod were wallowing in the unbridled passion of new love, but without the hideous agonies of insecurity and doubt that a new affair often brought, for they already knew they were right for each other. They'd done the hard bit.

And the icing on the cake was that they were going to be able to stay at Bucklebury. Not that this was a prime motivation – Jamie was sure she'd be happy with Rod in a mud hut. But there was a pleasing symmetry to the tale, as if things had gone full circle. She and Rod would be able to pick up the reins from Jack and Louisa, keep the legend alive. Of course there would have to be changes, but if Jamie had learned anything over the past few weeks it was that change was necessary and good.

Jamie finally let sleep wash over her, exhausted by the emotional rollercoaster of the past twenty-four hours, but completely and utterly contented.

Sick with self-reproach from what the nurse had told him, as well as the realization of what it meant to his future, Rod walked into the ward and over to Bella's bed like a condemned man walking to the gallows. He pulled back the thin pink and blue floral curtain and his heart turned over.

She was lying under a sheet that was drawn right up to her chin, her bluish-white skin threaded with veins of a darker blue that matched the bruised shadows under her eyes, like marbles under the paper-thin lids. She looked like a corpse being revealed for identification, as if the sheet had been drawn back by the pathologist for his inspection. He couldn't believe it was possible for someone to disintegrate in the space of just one week. She looked so tiny, so young, so pale. She exuded weakness and fragility. It was like seeing an injured kitten, victim of a hit and run, lying in the road. Only a monster could walk away.

If only he hadn't come to see her. If only he had ignored Pauline's messages, if only he had hardened his heart he would never have learned the truth. But after talking to the psychiatric nurse, he knew he was as responsible as anyone for the state she was in. If she'd been a child, he'd have been guilty of serious neglect.

As her husband, it was he who was honour-bound to protect her and heal her. She needed him more than anyone – his support, his approval, his protection – if she was going to survive. If he turned his back on her now, he would be responsible for her actions.

He stared at her closely, trying to find a vestige of the woman he'd married, the vibrant, glowing creature who had walked up the aisle to stand at his side. She'd been dressed in a sheath of white satin, as tall and slender as one of the lilies in the bouquet she was carrying. There were sighs of admiration and thinly disguised envy from the congregation, both the men and the women. And he'd felt proud that she was his. Little did he realize the torture she had been through to achieve her supposed perfection.

With the benefit of hindsight, Rod could now see that her avoidance of food was bordering on the obsessive. But he'd got used to it; assumed that most women were card-carrying calorie-dodgers who spent their lives snipping fat off their meat and left their potatoes, who recoiled in horror at the sight of the dessert trolley and could only be talked into a portion of fruit salad in order to be sociable. Common sense should have told him that she ate barely enough to survive.

He realized she was stirring. With a huge effort she lifted her lids. Her eyes stared straight at him. He heard her take in a sharp, ragged breath of panic, and put out a hand to reassure her.

'It's OK. You're going to be all right.'

Her eyes closed again, but this time it was to hold back her tears. He put a tentative hand out to touch her forehead. She felt surprisingly cold and clammy, as if there was no life-blood beneath the skin. He forced himself to stroke her, as you would a sick child, a tender gesture of comfort. Eventually, she opened her eyes again and looked at him dully.

'I'm sorry,' she whispered.

'There's nothing to be sorry for,' he reassured her, and saw the faintest trace of a smile on her lips, as if she knew better but was happy to go along with him.

'What do you want to do?' he asked gently.

He had to bend his head to catch her reply. Her voice was barely more than a whisper.

'I want to come home.'

She looked at him pleadingly, and in that moment

he knew she meant that home was Owl's Nest. Which meant undoubtedly that it was he who held the key to her recovery, that he wasn't going to be able to offload the responsibility. Obviously their marriage meant more to her than he had chosen to believe.

He could see her tense under the sheets, bracing herself for the steel-toe-capped boot of rejection. Rod knew that the decision he was about to make was the most important of his life, with momentous results for not just himself. He alone could make the choice...

Five minutes later, he walked back out of the ward to the corridor where Pauline was waiting.

'The sister says she can go, once the doctor's checked her over,' she told him. 'In about an hour, she reckons.'

Rod looked at his watch.

'There's just something I've got to do,' he said carefully. 'Then I'll come back and fetch her.'

Jamie heard the Audi coming down the drive in her sleep. Reluctantly, she wrenched herself out of her dreams and sat up. She smiled as she rubbed her eyes and jumped out of the hammock eagerly. They'd agreed not to see each other till the next day, but obviously Rod hadn't been able to wait, and she was glad. The prospect of an evening without him had been torture.

But as she walked towards the yard, somehow she could tell by the car's funereal speed that Rod was not the bearer of glad tidings. She could feel his dread from a hundred yards, and its cold tentacles insinuated their way into her heart.

She reached the car just as he was climbing out. His expression was grim; his features set hard.

'What is it?'

In a dull, lifeless monotone, he told her. And as he finished describing the events of the last couple of hours, he delivered the final blow.

'I've got to stand by her, Jamie. She's my wife. I've got to share the blame for what's happened; for what she did.'

Jamie nodded, not trusting herself to speak.

'If I leave her, God knows what she might do. I can't risk that.'

He grabbed her and held her tightly.

'I love you,' he said fiercely. 'But there's nothing I can do. Please say you understand.'

Jamie swallowed a huge lump that had risen in her throat.

'Of course I do,' she managed.

For a few moments they clung to each other. Silent tears poured down Jamie's cheeks. She wanted to scream at him to forget Bella, that she didn't deserve his loyalty. But she knew Rod was honourable. And that was, of course, why she loved him so much. So she didn't protest, didn't make it harder for him than it already was, but told him he was doing the right thing and that she understood. Because Jamie too was honourable. The very quality they both shared, the reason they should have been together, was what drove them apart.

She held on to him tightly, wanting to prolong the moment, the last time she would ever hold him, because they both knew that it had to be a clean break. There was no point in trying to compromise.

Eventually Rod disentangled himself from her.

'I've got to go ...'

He went to give her a final kiss, but Jamie jerked herself away, knowing that to feel his lips on hers would be the ultimate torture. Choking back her sobs she ran inside, wishing that she could have been calm and dignified if only to make it easier for him.

Rod watched her go in despair. For one wild second he was tempted to run after her. But then he imagined Bella, waiting for him in her hospital bed. Fragile, damaged, tortured Bella. He walked back to his car with a leaden heart.

He drove back down the drive at full speed, changing gear angrily, churning up the dust. As he reached the gateway he was tempted not to stop, to drive straight out on to the road regardless of whatever was coming. But he knew that was a stupid, childish gesture. He was more likely to hurt someone else than himself. Besides, the chances of anything coming were fairly remote and he'd just end up in the ditch on the other side of the road. So he slammed on the brakes at the last second. Futile attempts at suicide weren't going to help anyone.

Jamie would survive, he told himself. She was stronger than Bella. And she'd survived before.

And he? Would he survive? Rod supposed that didn't really come into it. He was trapped by his wedding vows whether he liked it or not.

27

In later years, Jamie would say that the week following the party was quite possibly the worst of her life, with the exception of the week her mother had died. To begin with, the phone had rung incessantly with people thanking her and Jack profusely for a wonderful party, and saying how sorry they were Bucklebury was to be sold: it marked the end of an era. Jamie forced herself to remain bright and cheerful throughout all these conversations, despite the fact that underneath her heart was breaking. If not, in fact, already broken.

To add insult to Jamie's injuries, Jack mooted the idea of his moving to Cape Town with Lettice. The more he thought about the idea, the more he liked it, but it played on his conscience. He didn't want to keep the proposition a secret from Jamie – after all, the last time he'd kept something from her, she'd disappeared for months. He wanted to be honest and open with her, no matter how difficult it was.

'I wouldn't be there all year round. Three months here, three months there, probably. And back here for Christmas, of course. Unless you wanted to come out for some sunshine.'

How could she protest, when she herself was going to

be away with work most of the time? Anyway, she had no fight left in her.

'Whatever makes you happy,' she said wearily.

'I want *you* to be happy about it,' protested Jack.

'I am. Honestly. I think it's a very good idea.' Jamie did her best to reassure him, feeling it would be churlish to spoil his excitement.

On Friday, Tiona came to value the farm. She hadn't been there five minutes before Jamie wanted to throttle her with her tape measure.

'Beautiful proportions. Beautiful,' Tiona pronounced. 'This could make a lovely family home. But there's a lot of work to be done if you want to get your best price.'

Jamie frowned. 'What sort of work?'

'Some of the decor is a little … shall we say eccentric? Pig wallpaper in the downstairs cloak isn't everyone's cup of tea.'

Jamie felt very defensive. She loved the pig wallpaper – it was quirky. And it had been there ever since she could remember.

'And you could really do with a good spring clean,' Tiona carried on, looking meaningfully at a thick cobweb lurking in the hallway. 'And perhaps a lick of magnolia paint everywhere, just to neutralize.'

Jamie glared at her.

'Personally, I love the aubergine in the drawing room,' Tiona went on smoothly. 'But despite all these make-over programmes, most people remain resolutely conservative when it comes to interior decor. Anything slightly out of the ordinary frightens them. And they haven't got the imagination to visualize what it could be like.'

'I see,' said Jamie icily. 'So what you're saying is fumigate the place and redecorate it from top to bottom?'

Tiona was used to having to soothe ruffled feathers after she'd given it to people straight. They never liked their taste being brought into question. But it was her job to make sure they got the best market price, so she had to be honest.

'Not at all,' she said. 'You just need a little bit of time and effort. Light and airy are the keywords,' she informed her helpfully. 'If I were you, I'd pop along to one of those cheap linen shops – buy a load of white bedding and towels for the bedrooms and bathrooms. Get a window cleaner. And de-clutter. People hate other people's clutter. They love their own, but when they look at a house with a view to purchase, they want a blank canvas. Just keep the odd carefully chosen ornament on show, so the whole thing doesn't feel too sterile. Otherwise, everything in cardboard boxes in the garage. You've got plenty of storage space, after all.'

Jamie had no intention of changing a thing. If people couldn't see the beauty of Bucklebury Farm as it was, they didn't deserve to buy it. But she bit her tongue, because Kif was selling Bucklebury for her at a reduced percentage, and if that meant putting up with Tiona's patronizing tone, then it was a small price to pay.

Just before lunchtime on Friday, knowing that Tiona was safely out measuring up Bucklebury Farm, Norma gathered up the information she'd carefully collated into date order, before tentatively asking Christopher if she could have a word. He looked a little bit wary, but could hardly refuse.

'Of course. Shall we pop into Tiona's office? It's a little more private.'

Ironic, thought Norma, as she followed him in. She felt a little dry-mouthed with nerves. She wasn't a vindictive woman, though she knew what she was about to do might make it look as if she was. What she was, more than anything, was loyal. She'd been loyal to Hamilton for over twenty years. Which meant that she was now loyal to Christopher, and she hated to see him being made a fool of. In more ways than one.

It had taken her all week to gather together the relevant paperwork. She'd had to wait for Christopher and Tiona to go out each day on their lunch break. It had been pathetic watching them this week, each of them making a great show of going out of the office separately when it was blindingly obvious they were meeting up at the pub down the road. Norma had been watching from the sidelines for some time as Christopher fell under Tiona's spell; the fact that Zoe had been away the weekend before, when Christopher had taken Tiona out for dinner, had not been lost on her. And now it seemed they were in the throes of an illicit affair. Norma disapproved thoroughly, but in the meantime had taken the opportunity to go through the files in Tiona's office. Tiona usually guarded them like a dragon, but love, or lust, or infatuation, or whatever it was, was making her careless.

She cleared her throat nervously. Christopher smiled at her, kindly.

'I think I know what this is about,' he said.

'No,' replied Norma. 'I don't think you do.'

Christopher looked startled.

'I've been suspicious for a long time,' she went on

400

carefully. 'I'm not one for making wild accusations. I've checked and double-checked my facts thoroughly. But I'm afraid there have been some … discrepancies in some of the sales that have passed through this office over the past year.'

'Discrepancies?'

Norma laid her evidence out on the desk.

'On all of these sales, the property has been quite seriously undervalued in the first instance. And then it hasn't actually gone on to the open market. No details have been written up, no board has gone up, there's been no advertising. And the vendor has accepted the first offer that has been made.' She paused. 'The only offer, in fact.'

Christopher was looking at her in horror. Norma felt quite distressed. He was such a gentleman, like his father – even if he had been hoodwinked by that little hussy. He would be mortified to think that Drace's had been caught up in such immoral dealings. If word got out, their reputation, the reputation that had been so sterling up until now, would be in shreds.

Norma carried on her litany.

'The purchaser hasn't always been the same. Not at first glance, anyway. But I've done a bit of research. Each of the purchasers has been connected in some way to Simon Lomax.'

She said the name as if it should mean something, but Christopher looked blank.

'I forgot – you probably won't have heard about him. He's a property developer from London. He pinpointed Ludlow as a hot spot about five years ago and started buying up houses by the handful. When prices shot up, he started selling them off at a huge profit. He's made a fortune. And he's still buying – at the right price. Most estate agents will have nothing to do with him. He's not exactly unscrupulous but … well, let's just say your father wouldn't deal with him.' She paused momentarily. 'But somebody from this office has been.'

'Do you know who?' asked Christopher, though he'd already guessed.

'Miss Tutton-Price,' answered Norma, allowing herself to enjoy the revelation for one glorious moment, even though it was obviously causing Christopher distress. 'I imagine that there was some sort of, well, shall we say incentive scheme?'

The word 'backhander' wasn't one that would trip lightly off Norma's tongue. Christopher just nodded gravely, leafing through the files she'd handed him.

'Norma, would you leave this with me?' he asked finally. 'I'm sure you realize just how sensitive this information is, and if word got out … well, Drace's would be ruined. I'm sure you don't want that any more than I do.'

'Absolutely not,' said Norma. 'That's why I brought it to your attention. You can't carry on this sort of thing indefinitely, not without somebody cottoning on in the end.'

'Well, let's just be very thankful that it was you that spotted it, and not a client.' Christopher smiled at her warmly, and Norma felt relieved that he wasn't the type to shoot the messenger. She scurried out to her desk and picked up her handbag. She was already late for her lunch; she didn't want the vegetable puffs to have sold out before she got to the bakery.

*

402

As soon as Norma left Tiona's office, Christopher felt an overwhelming desire to be sick. There was no denying it. The evidence was there in front of him, in black and white. Tiona had been on the bung. Looking back, it must have been easy. The office had been left in her care when Hamilton had first fallen ill. She had every opportunity to run things exactly as she wished. And when Christopher had taken over, he'd left an awful lot of the responsibility to her, leaving her free to carry on. She had carte blanche. If it hadn't been for the eagle-eyed Norma …

The burning question, however, had to be was she still at it? How treacherous was she? Christopher felt a trickle of cold sweat run down the back of his neck. He couldn't believe it of her. How could he have been so taken in? She was so beguiling, so convincing. What kind of sick and twisted mind did she have, to sleep with him knowing she was committing serious fraud in the name of Drace's? Every film about crazy women that he'd seen flipped through his mind. What, exactly, was her game? And how was he going to handle it?

There was, he supposed, just one small slim chance that, now she was in the throes of an affair with him, she regretted her past follies. Christopher looked through the files – the last transaction hadn't even exchanged yet. It was a small house on Silver Street, owned by a Mrs Turner. He wasn't sure what to do, whether it would be best to stop the sale before it went through in order to do the honourable thing and get Mrs Turner her best price – which was the estate agent's moral undertaking. But that might open a can of worms …

And what about Tiona? How would he go about confronting her? And what would her reaction be? Defiant or regretful? Christ, it was scary. It wasn't as if the dice were entirely loaded in his favour. He'd been sleeping with her. For God's sake, he was to all intents and purposes in love with her! They hadn't really had a chance to discuss where they stood with each other all week. They'd sneaked out at lunch, shared a few knee-trembling snogs in the secluded garden of a riverside pub, but they hadn't discussed their relationship properly. He'd meant to, of course, especially in the light of Zoe turning over a new leaf, but as each day dawned it was too tempting to carry on with things as they were: deliciously thrilling.

He was well and truly compromised. How could he go in with all guns blazing, when she could quite easily turn and call his bluff? Which he had no doubt she would. She was obviously totally unscrupulous. Looking back on it, he wondered whether Tiona had suspected Norma was on to her. That would explain why she was so anxious to be rid of her. Well, thank God he hadn't given in. He was, he suspected, going to be needing Norma more than ever in the near future.

He looked at his watch. Tiona would be back within the hour. He couldn't face her yet. He needed to sort through the implications of the situation with a clear head. Work out where he stood legally and morally. Work out what risks he could afford to take. If there was one thing, just one thing, that had to come out of this intact, it was his marriage.

He went back out into the office, where Norma was licking the last of the flaky pastry off her fingers, wiping her mouth with a paper napkin.

'I'm going out for the rest of the afternoon. I need to think very carefully about how to handle this. Can I trust you not to say anything to Tiona? I need to get my facts absolutely straight before I talk to her.'

'Of course,' said Norma. She wasn't going to say a word. She was going to relish sitting there all afternoon knowing that Tiona was for it.

On Friday afternoon, Jack and Olivier sneaked off to the garage in Lower Faviell, where the delivery they'd been awaiting had finally arrived. At the last minute they'd agreed to go halves on a new set of tyres, an extravagant luxury that neither of them could afford. The old set should have lasted another couple of outings, but they both felt that as the Corrigan Trophy was the pinnacle of the season, the one race Olivier really had a chance of winning, it was worth the expense. Jack had kept the purchase quiet from Jamie by having them delivered to the garage. It seemed wicked to spend several hundred pounds on something so frivolous when she was taking the sale of the house so hard. And she'd bitten both their heads off at breakfast when she'd found Olivier's racing overalls soaking in the sink and the washing-up not done. Yet again, she'd shouted, and they'd been aggrieved. They'd actually been very good about their domestic duties recently.

But she'd been in a black mood ever since the party. It wasn't just that she was tired; she seemed defeated in some way, as if the stuffing had been knocked out of her. Jack had seen her talking to Rod Deacon at the party – dancing with him at one point – and wondered if that was in some way cause for her mood. But he was frightened to probe; terrified of what he might unleash if he pressed her for the cause of her depression. So instead he laid low, keeping out of her way when he could.

The tyre change was completed swiftly at the garage, and he and Olivier returned the car to the barn, rolling it on to the trailer ready to leave for the racetrack at Sapersley at the crack of dawn the next morning.

'Any idea what's wrong with Jamie? She seems very down,' Jack asked Olivier casually.

'No,' said Olivier. 'Time of the month, maybe?'

Olivier hated himself for saying it. He didn't think he'd ever used that as an excuse for a woman's bad humour – to his mind it was a cheap get-out. But he had a better idea than Jack about her gloom. Even though he wasn't sure of the full story, he'd also seen Jamie with Rod Deacon the night of the party. And, unlike Jack, he was privy to the fact that they'd actually spent the night together, and that Deacon had been conspicuous by his absence ever since. The incident had brought home to him just how out of his reach Jamie was – she patently only saw him as at best a friend, at worst a nuisance – and it hurt. So he was burying himself in the preparations for the race, focusing on making it a glorious triumph that would overshadow his frustration.

At six o'clock, Jack went off with Lettice to a drinks party to celebrate the end of the Ludlow Festival. Jack wasn't entirely sure it was his scene, but Lettice loved mixing with the directors and actors and musicians who had contributed to this vital part of the town's culture. The annual Shakespeare play, held in the ruins of the castle, had done as much to bring life to the town as its reputation for gastronomy, and the festival had grown from modest beginnings to include a literary festival and a jazz spin-off. Lettice had tried to persuade Jamie to come too.

'You might meet a gorgeous hunky young actor,' she'd cajoled, but Jamie was in no mood for socializing. In fact, she was looking forward to some solitude in which to prod her emotional wounds. Her nerves were in shreds. Despite her agreement with Rod that it was best if they didn't contact each other, half of her, the half that believed in fairy tales and happy endings, had expected him to phone nevertheless and say he couldn't live without her.

It was Olivier who caught the brunt of her mood when he finally came in from the barn. He wanted to spend the evening relaxing, not thinking too much about the race the next day, getting an early night. He couldn't admit even to himself how important this race was. It was only Claudia's presence that was making him nervous. After her father's ridiculous proposal, he realized that her car would be kitted out with no expense spared, turning her into a formidable opponent. At the end of the day, if someone had enough cash they could put up serious competition, which was why in the end he'd agreed to blow the last of his savings on the tyres.

He found Jamie curled up in the leather chair in the living room, staring into space, looking thoroughly miserable.

'Come for a drink at the Royal Oak. I'll buy you scampi in a basket,' he offered.

Jamie shook her head, smiling wanly. 'No thanks.'

'Why not? It'll do you good to get out.'

'For God's sake, why can't people realize I want to be left alone?' snapped Jamie.

Olivier looked aggrieved. 'Sorry. I was just—'

'Yeah, well, *don't* just.'

Jamie knew she was being unreasonable, and put her

hands up to her face, pressing her fingers into her sockets to stop herself from crying. She shouldn't be beastly to Olivier; it wasn't his fault that she'd found the love of her life and lost him again in the space of twenty-four hours. It wasn't his fault that Tiona had been snotty about the farm. It wasn't his fault that her father was planning on swarming off to the other side of the world with Lettice, even if the old bat wasn't as bad as she'd first thought. Which meant she'd be left all on her own, with nowhere to live and no one to love. A ball of self-pity rose up in Jamie's throat and she choked back an enormous sob.

The next moment she could feel Olivier patting her on the shoulder awkwardly. The physical contact opened up the floodgates.

'It's so unfair,' she sobbed.

'What's the matter?'

'Everything! And bloody Dad's landed on his feet, as usual. Ducking out of his responsibilities. He didn't have to stand here while Tiona Tutton-Price looked down her nose at this place. And he's thinking of buggering off to Cape Town with Lettice. Mum hasn't even been gone a year. It's disrespectful.'

She looked at Olivier for support, but his face was stony.

'Don't you think it's out of order?' she persisted.

'No.' Olivier's tone was flat.

Jamie frowned. 'What do you mean?'

Olivier paused for a moment before looking at her defiantly.

'I think that if you knew the truth about his marriage, you'd say good for him.'

Jamie thought she'd misheard. Or misunderstood.

'What?'

'I think he deserves someone like Lettice, after putting up with your mother.'

'I think you'd better explain what you mean,' said Jamie indignantly.

She looked at Olivier and felt a tremor of fear. The look on his face was grim. His tone sent a shiver down her spine.

'It's about time someone put you in the picture about your precious, sainted mother.'

Jamie's hackles rose. 'What picture, exactly?'

'Your mother,' he explained carefully, 'ruined my parents' marriage. They were perfectly happy until she came along. We all were.'

Jamie laughed in relief.

'If your parents couldn't get on, it certainly wasn't Mum's fault—'

'Shut up,' he said fiercely. 'Shut up till I've finished.'

Something in his voice made Jamie obey him.

'That day we were called in from the pontoon? My mother had just found your mother and my father in bed together. And your mother laughed. She just shrugged and laughed. Said they were bound to get caught sooner or later. She didn't have an ounce of shame. She couldn't have cared less.'

Jamie was utterly outraged.

'You're sick—'

'I tell you what makes me sick. Your father having to take the rap all these years. Everyone called him the irresponsible one. He took the blame. Because he was loyal to your mother – God knows why. He didn't want your precious illusions about her shattered, even to this day.'

Jamie stood up, trembling.

'Why are you telling me this?'

'Because I had to suffer the truth. And the consequences. Thanks to your bloody mother, my mother almost had a nervous breakdown. I had to look after her. She was like a zombie doped up to the eyeballs on tranquillizers the doctor gave her to cope. And Dad was no better. Your mother had bewitched him. Every given opportunity, she gave him the come-on. Enticed him. Lured him. In the end he couldn't resist—'

Jamie snapped. She hurled herself at Olivier's chest, beating her fists against him.

'Shut up! Shut up, with your filthy stinking lies.'

He stood impassively as she railed at him, not flinching from the blows, until she eventually collapsed in a heap and fell back into her chair. He stood over her, defiant.

'I'm sorry it had to be me who told you. But I don't think it's fair on your father. The only thing he cared about was protecting you from the truth, even if it meant him getting the blame for everything. Even now! None of this is his fault, not really. It's all down to your mother and her selfish, self-centred—'

Jamie clamped her hands over her ears.

'Get out. Get out of this house. I don't ever want to see you again.'

Olivier gave a defeated shrug.

'You see, even now she's coming between people. Driving a wedge—'

'Just go!'

A moment later, he was gone.

*

Jamie slumped in her chair, shaken by the scene that had just unfolded. What on earth had come over Olivier? Where on earth had he got all that rubbish about Louisa? She tried to look at it rationally, from his point of view. She remembered from that summer that Olivier's relationship with his father had been an uneasy one, that he had been much closer to Isabelle. No doubt when the holiday had come to such an abrupt end, it had been natural for him to jump to conclusions and blame his father. And not want to believe his mother capable of any wrong. But Jamie had known better, had seen right through Isabelle and her come-hither, bedroom eyes. And she knew her father had no will-power, had never been able to resist temptation.

It was amazing how that single incident, so many years ago, should still be causing dissent. She felt a bit guilty that she'd sent Olivier packing like that, but he'd chosen the wrong moment to unload his misguided theories on to her, when she was feeling particularly vulnerable and defensive.

She went into the drinks cupboard and poured herself a hefty slug of brandy, to calm her nerves and take the edge off her emotions. Sleep, that's what she needed. A nice, deep, oblivious, healing sleep. She'd wake up tomorrow and start with a clean slate. Concentrate on sorting her life out, because it was becoming increasingly clear she was on her own.

Olivier stormed out into the stable yard, hurled open the doors of the barn and threw himself down on a bale of hay. He fumbled in his shirt pocket for his cigarettes, furious with himself. Why the hell did he have to open his mouth like that? It was the last thing poor Jamie wanted to hear, the horrible truth about her mother, even though Olivier wasn't entirely sure she'd believed him about what had really happened that summer.

He'd heard the story often enough, from his own mother, as she retold it over and over in her tranquillized stupor, as if sharing the horror with him could lessen the pain she was feeling...

Isabelle Templeton's Charles Jourdan heels had clacked along the cool marble corridor. It was too hot in the mid-afternoon to roast in the sun; Jack had suggested a walk along to a nearby bar, and she'd agreed. She wasn't one for a siesta like the others. It always left her with a heavy head for the rest of the afternoon, and then she could never get to sleep at night – she'd been dogged by insomnia for years. She and Jack usually stayed on the beach, to keep an eye on Jamie and Olivier, even though they were old enough to look after themselves, really. But you never knew. There had been an incident a couple of years ago, when a young teenager had over-indulged on his first beer and drowned. And Isabelle had a tendency to be neurotic.

She'd come back to the villa to get something to put on over her bikini. She twisted the heavy wrought-iron handle of her bedroom door and pushed it open. Then froze. For there in front of her, on the enormous double bed with its ornately carved headboard, was Eric, lying on his back with Louisa astride him, her chestnut hair falling wantonly over her creamy shoulders, rotating her slender hips sensuously.

Eric was totally oblivious to his wife in the doorway,

lost as he was in impending ecstasy, judging by the way he was groaning and urging her on. Louisa, however, had a clear view of Isabelle in the mirror that hung over the bed. She met her eyes boldly in the glass, and didn't stop in her stride for a moment.

Isabelle, being French, was used to the concept of affairs and mistresses. Normally, she might have turned a blind eye to her husband's indiscretion. But, somehow, Louisa's flagrant mockery of her presence enraged her. In two steps she had reached the bed, grabbing Louisa by her chestnut mane and pulling her firmly backwards.

She didn't lose her dignity. It didn't descend into a brawl. Eric cowered and gibbered excuses. Louisa just rolled her eyes.

'For God's sake, stop apologizing. It was only a quick bonk,' she drawled. 'This hot weather always makes me rampant in the afternoon, and Eric was the only one around. Think yourself lucky it wasn't Olivier.'

Isabelle ignored her, and pulled two large suitcases out of the sliding wardrobe.

'Get dressed,' she snapped to Eric. 'And take our things out to the car. We're going.' She turned to Louisa. 'You'd better go and pack yourself. You needn't think you're staying on here.'

Louisa shrugged.

'If you really want to spoil the holiday for everyone,' she said, and sauntered out of the room without a care in the world.

The embittered cold war that his parents subsequently embarked upon put Olivier off marriage for life. The antagonism between them lurked like a venomous snake

413

in every corner of the house; you never knew when it might strike and unleash its bitter poison. The atmosphere was constantly threatening; every now and then recriminations would lash out, spiteful barbed attacks that would leave open wounds for days. His mother was on the attack, his father on the defensive, each equally capable of inflicting pain and misery on the other.

Olivier found it unbearable. And he couldn't see the point. Why didn't they just split up and get a divorce? He knew his mother was Catholic, but as far as he knew not a practising one. Why did they carry on torturing themselves and each other?

One afternoon, he found his mother breaking up the dinner service they'd been given as a wedding present. She was slowly and deliberately dropping each plate on to the marble floor, where the delicate bone china shattered into a thousand pieces, her face totally impassive. It wasn't an impulsive reaction to a heated argument; it was a cold, calculated act that symbolized how she felt. When every last piece had been destroyed, she calmly walked out of the room and locked herself in the bathroom. Olivier swept it all up before his father could see it. He knew she was goading him by her actions, and Eric was capable of far worse than smashing a few plates. If he could hide the evidence, then it might be weeks before Eric noticed the service was missing, and immediate recriminations could be avoided. Olivier wrapped the shards carefully in newspaper, took them out to the bins, then went to pack.

He escaped as quickly as he could, hitching a lift to Dover, crossing over to France on the ferry, then working his way gradually over to the Alps, where he got a job as a barman in one of the lesser resorts in the Trois Vallées. He worked hard, played hard, and was particularly delighted that as Christmas was the resort's busiest week he needn't come home and suffer his parents' hideous snarling over the season of goodwill.

The only thing he learned from the experience was that the more you loved someone, the more you could hurt them – or be hurt by them. Thus he had danced round the issue of love for all of his adult life, and found that it suited him to avoid it. If he didn't get attached, no one could take him unawares by lulling him into a false sense of security and then hurting him.

There had been a couple of near misses, times when he had found himself becoming more fond of someone than he would like, which made him feel very exposed and vulnerable. And the subsequent evasive action he had to take left a very bad taste in his mouth, as he knew he was causing damage, and leaving his victims hurt and bewildered. There had been Imogen, golden-hearted, gung-ho and as mad about skiing as he was, who was a chalet maid in the resort where he had been coaching. They had clicked immediately, spending their days off skiing together and the nights, rather predictably, embroiled between the sheets. There had been one night, after a particularly hairy escapade on a black run when things could have turned very nasty indeed had the weather not been kind to them, when he had felt incredibly close to her, as if by flirting with death their souls had been welded together. And by the way she clung to him, he knew she felt the same and it had all gone too far. The next day he arranged for a transfer to another resort and left, leaving no forwarding address and no explanation. He hated himself for it; he never liked to dwell on how

Imogen must have reacted to his disappearance. But surely one short, sharp shock was better than years of mental anguish and torture and abuse that he would have learned courtesy of his parents?

As he lit another cigarette from the butt of the one he'd just finished, Olivier knew instinctively that his treatment of Jamie that evening was his usual defence mechanism kicking in. He should never have said that about her mother. But the only way to keep her at arm's length was to inflict pain upon her.

He was becoming far too attached.

The other night, after a couple of pints of Honeycote Ale, he had found himself slipping into a fantasy involving him and Jamie in Jack and Louisa's four-poster bed. It wasn't a sexual fantasy, far from it. No – what he saw was himself bearing a tray, with mugs of tea and a pile of toast and the papers, slipping back under the duvet with her for a cosy, lazy Sunday morning, the picture of contented, domestic bliss, Parsnip and Gumdrop at their feet. And it frightened him. It was definitely time for him to move on.

Adding to Olivier's discomfort was his shame at betraying Jack. When he'd arrived at Bucklebury, they'd had several heart-to-hearts, and Jack had made him promise never to reveal the truth about Louisa and her bedroom habits. And Olivier had sworn not to breathe a word, though time and again it had frustrated him to see Jack taking the flak. It had been all he could do to keep his mouth shut on several occasions. When he'd seen Jamie curled up in that chair, raging at the world, beside herself with sorrow and holding Jack responsible, he hadn't been able to keep quiet any longer. He'd wanted to see justice done. But it had backfired on him. Badly.

Olivier trod out his second cigarette with a heavy heart. There was no way he could race tomorrow now. He decided he would leave a note for Jack apologizing, and just go. He didn't know where, but that didn't matter at the moment. Just as long as he put enough distance between him and the Wildings. He'd buggered things up enough for them already. They'd probably both be glad to see the back of him.

As he scrabbled about the workshop for a piece of paper and pencil, he reflected with a wry smile that at least one person would be happy with the outcome. By pulling out of the race he'd be leaving the way clear for Claudia's victory. Ray would be made-up – not only would his daughter win the trophy, but he'd have saved himself a hundred grand in the process.

As he started to compose a letter of apology to Jack, the implications of this gradually filtered through to Olivier's brain. What was the point in him running off, leaving the field wide open for Claudia, when he could take Ray Sedgeley up on his offer, throw the race, clear a hundred grand. Which he could then use to assuage the guilt he felt for his betrayal of Jack, for he could buy his half of the car off him. With a hundred grand, Jack and Jamie could restore Bucklebury to its former glory. Everyone would be happy.

Olivier told himself not to be ridiculous. The plan went against everything he believed in. But then, he reasoned, he couldn't sink much lower than he already had. He'd betrayed Jack; Jack who'd treated him almost like his own son. Certainly treated him better than Eric had done. And he'd destroyed Jamie's illusions about her mother. Throwing the race might go against everything he stood for, but Jack and Jamie stood to benefit. And only he would ever know the truth about what he had done. Ray Sedgeley certainly wasn't going to tell anyone. And Olivier thought he could live with it on his conscience, if it meant that Bucklebury was saved for the Wildings.

Olivier weighed up the pros and cons one last time. If he walked away, everybody lost. If he threw the race, everybody won. Except him, of course. But that was all he deserved.

Before he could change his mind, he pulled out his mobile and rang Ray's number, praying that Claudia wouldn't be in close proximity when he answered.

'Sedgeley.'

'Mr Sedgeley. It's Olivier Templeton. Can you talk?'

There was a moment's silence.

'Yep.'

'The deal we discussed the other night. I'm just calling to tell you I want to take you up on it.'

There was a delighted chuckle.

'Good lad.' Ray sounded euphoric. 'And listen – I know how you feel about it, but it's the way of the world. Like I told you, if you don't do it, someone else will. You don't win in the long run by playing it straight.'

Olivier couldn't be bothered to argue. He was tired and he wanted to get away before Jack returned and found out what had gone on. He'd drive to Sapersley tonight; sleep in the car. Swiftly, he hooked up the trailer to the Land Rover and drove off down the drive for the very last time.

28

Olivier arrived at Sapersley in record time. For once the meandering country lanes that made up most of the route weren't clogged up by tractors chugging along at an infuriating pace, their drivers oblivious – or perhaps not – to the impatient drivers behind them. The track was set in the grounds of Sapersley Hall at the foot of the Clee Hills: the original owner of the house had been a racing enthusiast and had it built for his own amusement just before the war. Many vehicles had been tested here during the throes of their development; its proximity to the Midlands made it particularly convenient as a venue for putting new marques through their paces. Now it was in use as a private commercial venture, complete with a driving school, and its exquisite setting made it ideal for corporate days out as well as a popular venue for historic cars recreating the fierce competitions of yesteryear. Nowadays, of course, the races didn't represent the pinnacle of months of research and development and investment, they didn't make or break a car's future and reputation and commercial success, but to the individual competitor it was still one's pride and glory at stake.

He turned in through the gates and past the field that had been set aside for camping: people often came down the night before a race and made a weekend of it. The good weather meant it was peppered with tents and caravans, and there was an almost carnival atmosphere. Plumes of smoke from portable barbecues were wisping their way into the sky. The smell made him hungry. He wondered if he'd be able to crash in on someone, pinch a couple of sausages. They were a friendly bunch, on the whole, rivals only for the fifteen minutes or so it took to run a race.

He checked his paperwork to see where he had been allocated a space in the paddock. There were other people still unloading. Some fussed over their cars like anxious mothers with a newborn baby, running scrupulous checks and polishing and covering them with customized tarpaulins; others, like Olivier, had a more relaxed attitude, treating their cars with respect but not mollycoddling them.

He found his allotted space and started to undo the webbing ropes that lashed the car to the trailer.

'Want a hand?'

Olivier bent his head over a wheel arch, pretending not to have heard the teasingly provocative question. The last person he wanted to see at the moment was Claudia Sedgeley. He wanted to brood on his own, not engage in her inane chitter-chatter. She didn't take the hint, though. She started to help without being invited. And he had to hand it to her: she was very capable and didn't seem too worried about snagging a nail. With an extra pair of hands the job was over far more quickly.

'Thanks,' he said grudgingly, and went to turn his back again, to make it clear he was busy. But she wasn't put off that easily.

'Do you want to come and have something to eat? I was going to make a salad.'

Olivier shook his head.

'I'm fine.'

'Well, at least come and have a drink,' she persisted. 'You can't tell me you're not hot.'

Olivier sighed. He was going to have to be bloody rude – or give in. He looked at her. She was wearing a pair of white overalls; despite the bulky fabric and the unforgiving cut, her enviable figure was still discernible underneath. She'd rolled up the trouser legs to display smooth golden calves and was wearing eminently unsuitable pink trainers. Her hair was tied high up on her head with a bandanna; several tendrils had escaped and were sticking to her brow. Her cheeks were slightly pink from exertion; her hands were dirty. Olivier smiled to himself in approval. Dishevelment definitely suited her more than the designer fashion victim look of last week's party. In his opinion, anyway.

He hesitated. He could turn down her invitation and go and sulk somewhere; pick over his argument with Jamie and berate himself for his foolhardiness. Or he could succumb. Then a thought occurred to him.

'Where's your dad?' he asked casually.

He needed to exercise caution. He might have done a deal with Ray, but he didn't necessarily want to have to look him in the eye or spend more time with him than he had to.

'He's taken some clients out for dinner. He's brought them to watch me race tomorrow. They're all staying at the Rose and Crown.'

No wonder Ray had been so pleased when Olivier had

phoned. He could show off his clever daughter in front of his customers; puff himself up with pride as she went to collect her trophy. And Olivier would walk off with a hundred grand; a hundred grand with which to assuage his guilt before he started off on a new life.

He swatted the thought away like an annoying fly. He didn't really want to give it head space. After all, he'd never done anything like this before. And even though he told himself he wasn't going to be the one benefitting from the fix, it still went against the grain.

He realized he'd drifted off. Claudia was looking at him strangely.

'Hello? Are you coming or not? Because I'm starving and I need a drink.'

He relented. Why the hell not? Claudia might take his mind off what had happened. Better to spend the evening imagining what was underneath her overalls than torturing himself for his lack of morals.

'OK. Why not?'

He followed her across the ground and over the field to where her Winnebago was parked at a distance from everyone else. It was enormous; it couldn't do more than two miles to the gallon. Shiny, shiny black with 'Claudia Sedgeley' emblazoned on the side in pink italics, and a silhouette of a girl's head in a racing helmet with a ponytail flowing out of the back. Inside, it was snug but luxuriously kitted out, with sleek brown leather seating, a table, a streamlined kitchen and a single bed with storage underneath. Claudia flicked a switch and music oozed out of a discreetly hidden sound system.

She opened the drinks fridge. It was filled with mini

bottles of Moët, two bottles of Polish vodka and several cartons of tomato juice.

'There's not much choice, I'm afraid. Dad only drinks Bloody Marys. And I only drink champagne.'

Olivier raised his eyebrows. Claudia opened her eyes wide in arch self-defence.

'It's got fewer calories than anything else. I have to watch my weight very carefully, you know.'

She took them out a bottle each, popped them open and stuck in pink bendy straws. They flopped back on the leather seats and sucked contentedly. Claudia kicked off her trainers, stuck her long legs out in front of her and wiggled her toes luxuriously. Her feet were smooth and brown, the toenails painted with what Olivier knew from his mother was a French polish, pearly pink with white tips.

'The trouble with champagne,' declared Claudia, 'is it goes straight to my head no matter how much I practise.'

Olivier had to admit that he too felt light-headed, though in his case it was probably because he hadn't eaten since breakfast, so Claudia insisted on making them supper.

'I'm no great cook, I'm afraid, but I can open a packet,' she said, removing the ingredients for chicken Caesar salad from another fridge. Olivier watched as she sliced up some pre-cooked char-grilled chicken, shook ready-chopped lettuce out of a packet and sprinkled them with croutons and Parmesan, then slathered it all with creamy dressing.

They sat at the table to eat, mopping up the salad with part-baked ciabatta that she warmed in the oven. Soon Olivier found he was feeling better; the food restored his strength and the champagne had lightened his mood. And as they chatted, Olivier found himself intrigued by Claudia. On the surface, she was a product of her environment: people often put up a front that did them no favours, and with her flashy lifestyle, her pre-prepared, perfectly packaged existence, her unashamedly in-your-face clothing, Claudia was eminently dislikeable on first meeting. But underneath she was warm and funny. She didn't take herself at all seriously; she was happy to send herself up. Olivier was curious as to what made her tick.

'So,' said Olivier. 'What on earth got you into all this? I don't mean to be rude, but you're not your typical racing driver.'

Claudia grinned.

'Exactly,' she said. 'If there's anything I hate it's being predictable.' She took another swig out of her bottle and leaned forwards. 'Have you ever been to Birmingham?'

Olivier didn't think he had.

'Where I live, people are only interested in what you drive and how much money you have. I wanted a bit more than that. I didn't want to turn into my mother. Obsessed with charity lunches and who's who at the golf club.'

Claudia put an imaginary gun to her head and pulled the trigger.

'Not that I don't love my mother,' she added hastily. 'I just don't want to be her.'

'I know what you mean,' said Olivier darkly. 'If I thought I was going to end up like my father ...'

'Oh dear,' said Claudia. 'I sense issues. Would you like to lie on my couch?' She patted the leather bench seat, smiling. 'I'm good with issues. I've had shedloads of therapy.'

'No thanks,' Olivier assured her. 'We could be here all night.'

'That's OK,' she replied lightly. 'I'm not doing anything else.'

Their eyes locked for a moment, both recognizing a frisson of suggestion in her tone.

'Another drink?' Claudia offered, not taking her eyes off his.

Olivier shook his head regretfully, though what he really wanted to do was get well and truly paralytic.

'Not the night before a race.'

She smiled at him tauntingly.

'You're so controlled. Such will-power.' She walked over and stood in front of him, fingering the Velcro opening of her overalls with a minxy little smile. 'Does your abstinence extend to other things? Is it no sex before a race, like David Beckham before a match?'

Bloody hell, thought Olivier. She was a fast worker all right. She bent over and brought her face close to his, her eyes dancing with mischief.

'Personally I find it helps me get a good night's sleep. Otherwise I'm tossing and turning all night.'

Olivier looked at her for what seemed an eternity, mulling the prospect over in his mind. He could be uptight and po-faced, accept a cup of coffee and then go and sleep in the back of his car, freezing his balls off. Or he could accept Claudia's fairly blatant offer, and get a decent night's sleep in a comfortable bed into the bargain. If he turned her down, he knew he'd just go and stew over his argument with Jamie, and curse himself for breaking his promise to Jack never to tell her the truth. A night with Claudia would certainly take his mind off things.

A ripping sound broke his reverie. Claudia was sliding her finger down the entire length of the opening, a provocative grin on her face. Her overalls were now gaping open, and it was clear she had nothing on underneath. Olivier's eyes widened as she let the sleeves drop down her arms, then shimmied out of them altogether. She did have something on underneath – a G-string like he'd never seen before. A black satin waistband from which a string of freshwater pearls ran down between her legs. Decidedly uncomfortable, he thought – but then again, perhaps not? Perhaps it was the ultimate stimulation: pearl against pearl? It was certainly doing something for him. He couldn't have turned her down now, even if he'd wanted to.

He hooked a finger into her waistband and pulled her to him. She smelled divine. Castrol and Coco Chanel. Against his better judgement, he went to kiss her.

He didn't care if this was a mistake. Anyway, why was it a mistake? They were both consenting adults. Neither of them was being unfaithful to anyone. Maybe the mistake had been ignoring what was under his nose for so long? Perhaps he and Claudia were made for each other. It certainly felt right. Each time she touched him he shivered with the electricity. Just kissing her was better than the best sex he'd ever had – she was teasing him languorously with her tongue, running it lightly along the inside of his mouth in a gesture that was so sensual he felt himself go quite literally weak at the knees. Shedding his clothes hastily, he pulled her on to the bed, then groaned as she began a journey with her mouth, kissing his jawline, taking tiny, playful little bites on his neck, sucking on his nipples – he'd no idea he liked that.

She was sitting astride his chest. As he looked down he could see her pinkness, the string of pearls disappearing into forbidden territory. He couldn't wait much longer. She smiled and bent down to whisper in his ear. He could feel the softness of her hair tickling his face.

'Put your arms over your head,' she commanded, and he obeyed. He was totally in her thrall. She leaned over him, and he felt her full breasts in his face. He groaned with the sensation, and went to find a nipple with his mouth as she ran her nails lightly over each arm then stroked the inside of each wrist.

As he arched his back with the pleasure of all the sensations, he heard a soft click. Before he'd fully registered what was going on he heard another, then felt cold, hard metal against each wrist. Suddenly alarmed, he pulled on each hand, and a realization clutched at his heart. Handcuffs. The crazy, kinky bitch had handcuffed him to the headboard!

'What the hell are you playing at?' He wasn't sure whether to laugh or panic.

Claudia smiled and slithered off him. She was taking off her G-string. He gulped and swallowed, praying that this was the moment he'd been waiting for. She was trailing the pearls over his chest, snaking them down his body and then round the base of his achingly stiff penis. They were cold and hard, in total contrast to the warm softness he was hoping to feel.

Then he tried to sit up in alarm. She was tying them in a knot round it! Jesus, thought Olivier wildly. What perversion was she about to execute? Images of trussed-up

MPs with masks and oranges in unmentionable places came into his head.

She was hovering over him. He could smell her perfume. As she bent to kiss him, he wondered what was going to happen next.

'Goodnight, sleep tight,' she said simply, and as he began to struggle, she put a warning hand on his chest. 'Don't bother. The handcuffs are police issue, courtesy of a friend of mine. You'll never get out.'

She picked up her discarded overalls and climbed back into them.

'You should be warm enough. And don't bother shouting – that's why I parked so far up the hill. No one will hear you, and anyway, the place is soundproofed.'

She patted him affectionately.

'Sorry it had to come to this, but I can't risk losing that trophy tomorrow. I'm going to stay at the Rose and Crown with Dad. I'll come and let you out tomorrow afternoon, when it's all over. You can congratulate me then.'

As she walked out, she dropped the tiny key ostentatiously into the fruit bowl and gave him a little wave. Olivier looked down at his penis, still treacherously stiff, with its pearl collar, then flopped his head back on to the pillow and groaned.

He'd already sold his soul to the devil, and the devil's bloody daughter had gone and taken matters into her own hands.

As Claudia walked down the hill, she wasn't sure whether to laugh or panic. She just hadn't been able to resist it. She'd nursed Olivier's jibe in her heart all week, until it became a hard ball of resentment, urging her to take her revenge, make him feel as frustrated and powerless and worthless as she had when he'd mocked her for being a daddy's girl. She'd also proved to Olivier that he found her attractive – there'd been more than enough evidence of that, she mused.

Deep down, she knew that ritual humiliation, no matter how irresistible, wasn't really the way to get a man to love you. But Claudia was too impatient and too proud to take it slowly, to let nature take its course, to let Olivier unpeel the hard outer layers to discover her kitten-soft centre. After all, she'd spent her whole life proving herself and old habits died hard. She'd spent too long giving out the message that she wasn't to be messed with to roll over and have her tummy tickled.

Of course, she hadn't really meant to leave him there all night. She went to join her father for drinks at the Rose and Crown with his clients, to sparkle for them. Ray didn't have to point out that it was they who were paying indirectly for her indulgence: Claudia had grown up enough lately to know better than to bite the hand that fed her. And afterwards the thought of a comfy hotel bed was really just too tempting: much better than stumbling back to the Winnebago in the dark. She'd get up early and release him from his chains, she thought, as she drifted off into sleep.

29

Jack hadn't got back from his knees-up in Ludlow until late, so it was early Saturday morning before he realized that Olivier had already legged it to Sapersley the night before.

'When did he go?' he asked Jamie, aggrieved. She was spooning coffee into the cafetière, desperate for a caffeine kick-start after a rather sleepless night.

'Yesterday evening. We had a bit of a falling-out.'

'What about?' Jack was concerned. He hated it when people didn't get on, and there was enough tension in the house.

'Oh – nothing really. Leaving the kitchen in a mess when we've got people coming to view. That sort of thing. It's me, I'm afraid. I'm a bit uptight.'

She was rather vague, because she couldn't bring herself to reveal what Olivier had said about Louisa. She knew Jack would be hurt, and she didn't feel the need to stir things up unnecessarily. She was a great believer in least said, soonest mended. She'd just have to make sure Olivier got on his bloody bike as soon as possible.

Jack came over to hug her.

'I know things are tough, darling. Isn't there something I could do to cheer you up?'

Tears stung the back of Jamie's lids. If only there was. There always had been when she was little – Jack could always think of a way to bring sunshine into a rainy day. She wriggled out of his embrace before her tears betrayed her and she had to explain.

'I'll be fine,' she reassured him brightly. 'I'm going to pop over and visit Hamilton this morning. It's his birthday and poor Kif's tied up all day. I promised I'd drop in – I feel guilty enough I haven't been to see him before now. It must be awful ...'

'Yes,' agreed Jack, but seemed hasty to change the subject. 'I'd better get a move on if I'm going to be of any help to Olivier. Um ... I don't suppose you want to come along later? The Corrigan Trophy's at two.'

'No, thanks,' said Jamie, very definitely. She would, quite frankly, rather boil her head in oil.

Christopher was hiding in the little kitchen at the back of Drace's, alternately taking deep breaths to calm his nerves and gulping coffee. He watched the hands of the clock creeping round the face and prayed for divine intervention, because without it Tiona would come through the door bang on quarter to nine just as she did every morning. Flood, hurricane, biological warfare – he wasn't bothered, as long as it postponed the moment of reckoning.

He knew it was unlikely, though, so he ran through his rehearsed speech one more time. He had to plunge straight in with it. He couldn't beat around the bush exchanging pleasantries and would-you-like-a-cup-of-coffees. He had to get straight in there with 'Tiona, can I have a word?' Calm, authoritative and without emotion.

The treacherous long hand nudged towards nine. Ting – the clock struck quarter to. And as predicted, in she came through the door. Christopher imagined the air becoming rose-scented around her, and groaned. He put down his coffee cup, squared his shoulders and marched out into the office to greet her.

She smiled such a sweet smile, obviously delighted to see him. She looked more delicate than ever, a pale blue cashmere cardigan unbuttoned over a sundress, her hair falling loose to her shoulders.

Christopher faltered. There must be some mistake. She wasn't capable of such treachery. In five minutes' time, she'd explain everything to him, there would be some plausible explanation that he hadn't managed to hit upon – even though he'd been racking his brain for one ever since Norma brought him those wretched files yesterday. He would laugh with relief, and then he'd be able to feel those heaven-sent breasts, press his lips to her velvet flesh ...

'Morning, Christopher.' Her voice was low, drenched with honey.

'Tiona.' He took in a deep breath, steeled for confrontation, then quailed. 'Would you like a cup of coffee?'

Jamie arrived at Havelock House, a sprawling gentleman's residence screened by a rank of monkey-puzzle trees, and immediately felt filled with even more gloom. No matter how these places were dressed up, they were always depressing. No matter how elaborate the vase of flowers on the table in the hallway, no matter how gleaming white the tablecloths in the dining room for those capable of communal eating, there was no getting away from the fact that people rarely left here unless they were in a pine box.

She asked directions to Hamilton's room, and followed a care assistant down a maze of corridors, trying not to peer into other people's bedrooms en route, not wanting a glimpse into the dreary monotony of their lives. She caught sight of a little old lady refilling her budgie's bowl with seed, her wizened face alive with love for her only companion. Jamie could hardly bear it, wondering what would happen to the budgie when the old lady died.

The care assistant showed her Hamilton's door. It was slightly ajar, so she tapped gently and walked in. An old man was hunched up in a chair by the window, and for a moment she thought she'd got the wrong room. But then she saw by the few belongings on his dressing table – his monogrammed brushes and a photo of Rosemary – that this was Hamilton.

He'd been a tall man, not overly muscular but definitely fit, his shoulders broad enough for him to look imposing in the tweed suits he always wore. And he wasn't strictly handsome, but he was nice-looking, with his sandy hair swept back from his forehead just like Kif's. Now he looked like a shrunken little gnome. His face was gaunt and bony, his nose seemed huge, his eyes were hollow. He was wearing striped pyjamas, but his shoulders were hunched so that his head poked forwards, like a chicken about to peck the ground for food. He'd been shaved, but Jamie could see where they had missed the occasional tuft on his upper lip. And his hair could have done with cutting; the ends were straggling over his collar.

Jamie found her voice was stuck somewhere in the back of her throat. Somehow 'happy birthday' seemed like such a futile and ridiculous thing to say. What could possibly be happy about it? She looked down with shame at the tin of shortbread she'd bought from Hilly before she came. They'd both agreed that food was probably the only gift that would have any impact. What did someone in Ham's condition care for new socks or aftershave?

She cleared her throat and was surprised when her voice came out clear and true.

'Hello, Hamilton. It's Jamie. I've come to wish you happy birthday.'

Christopher found it hard to steady his hand as he dug a teaspoon into the catering-size tin of Nescafé and spooned coffee powder into Tiona's gold-rimmed Wedgwood mug, cursing himself for missing the window of opportunity. If he'd had any balls, the confrontation with Tiona would have been virtually over by now. Instead, here he was waiting for the kettle to boil again while she went through the post, unaware that there was a problem. Another ten minutes and Norma would be here. He'd wanted to get it out of the way before the rest of the staff arrived.

For God's sake, man, where are your balls? he asked himself. He knew he was making a fool of himself, but he felt bewitched. Tiona was the stuff of Greek legend, a siren luring him on to the rocks – the very rocks his marriage was veering towards. He forced himself to envisage the worst-case scenario. Zoe finding out about Tiona, and the Association of Estate Agents finding out about Tiona's fraud. Resulting in divorce, a messy investigation and the collapse of Drace's, not to mention the besmirching of the family name. Only by taking the bull by the horns and handling this situation firmly but sensitively could he save his marriage, his family business … and his face. Tempting though it was, he couldn't just let things slide.

He poured the water on to the coffee, added a splash of milk and carried it into the outer office.

Tiona dimpled at him as she took the cup.

'Thank you.'

'My pleasure. And … could I have a word before everyone gets here? In your office?'

He indicated the small room she still utilized. She twinkled at him, obviously thinking he was up for a quick grope before Norma arrived.

'Of course.'

He followed her inside, trying not to breathe in her intoxicating scent, and shut the door firmly.

Jack drove to Sapersley as quickly as he could, hoping that Jamie hadn't given Olivier too hard a time the night before. He knew his daughter could be quick-tempered and sharp-tongued, and he felt guilty that the lad had felt the need to escape. He'd find him and apologize on Jamie's behalf – she was under a great deal of strain at the moment. When today's race was over, Jack resolved to do something to ease the pressure she was feeling.

It was easy to park, as members of the public hadn't arrived yet – racing proper didn't start till after lunch, so they were likely to appear in dribs and drabs from midday onwards. He made his way through the autojumble stalls, some makeshift, some slick and businesslike, that sold car spares. Tables were crammed with gaskets and windscreens and entire engines that were picked over by enthusiasts looking for the elusive part that would transform their machine into the ultimate racing dream.

Other stalls sold flying jackets and racing goggles and baseball caps. The air was thick with the smell of frying donuts, organic sausages, crêpes and fresh coffee. There was a wide range of food to choose from, not like the old days when he and Eric had raced, when an old caravan served up greasy bacon sarnies and lukewarm tea. He felt a stab of nostalgia as he suddenly realized how very much he wanted Olivier to win the trophy today. Olivier hadn't said a lot, but it was obvious his relationship with his father was far from ideal. As far as Jack could see, Eric had treated him rather shabbily. In Jack's view, you didn't try and force children into something they didn't want. You had to let them be themselves, let them follow their own path and be supportive. Olivier hinted that he wasn't living up to his father's expectations, that he had let him down in some way. Jack's personal opinion was that your children couldn't let you down, only the other way round. Any suggestion that he was making up for what he considered to be Eric's failings he kept firmly at the back of his mind. His nurturing of Olivier had never been intended as some sort of elaborate point-scoring.

Jack didn't like to admit it, not even to himself, but he'd grown very fond of Olivier. He didn't quite look upon him as the son he'd never had, because he'd never felt the need for a son, but he'd enjoyed giving him the benefit of his experience and seeing him flourish under his tuition. As he approached the paddock, his heart thudding with the anticipation of the day ahead, he wished for about the millionth time that the clock could have been turned back, that their lives could have been lived differently, and that Eric could have been there with him to watch Olivier race.

Five minutes later, he was puzzled. He'd found the Bugatti and the Land Rover parked in their allocated space, but no sign of Olivier. It was half past nine, and the car hadn't been past the scrutineer yet. Practice was due to start at ten, and the Corrigan Trophy was second on the race card – they'd have to get a move on. He checked with the race organizers, but they hadn't received any notification of anything untoward, or Olivier withdrawing from the race.

Perhaps he'd forgotten something crucial, and someone had given him a lift to fetch it? But what? On closer investigation, Jack found Olivier's jacket in the Land Rover with his wallet in his pocket. Increasingly concerned, he asked around. A couple of people had seen him arrive the evening before, but hadn't seen him since.

The throaty purr of an engine behind him made him jump out of the way. He turned to see Claudia Sedgeley at the wheel of her Type 35, looking decidedly incongruous in a pink halter-neck top and minuscule hot pants.

'Hi, Mr Wilding,' she greeted him. 'Thanks for a fantastic party the other night.'

'Pleasure,' replied Jack.

'All set for the race?' she asked.

Jack frowned.

'No. I can't find Olivier.'

Claudia shrugged.

'Maybe he's gone to the loo? I know what nerves do to my stomach.'

'No. I mean he seems to have disappeared altogether. No one's seen him since last night.'

Claudia looked concerned. 'I saw him when he arrived. We had a quick drink. He said he was going to grab something to eat at the pub. I didn't see him after that – I got an early night.'

'And you haven't seen him this morning?'

She shook her head. 'Sorry. It's a bit of a mystery, isn't it? Maybe he got lucky and he's shacked up in someone's tent?'

Seemingly unperturbed, she flashed him a smile, released her handbrake and drove off.

Jack watched her go. Something in her body language had made him suspicious. She seemed a little too bright, a little too glib, a little too eager to meet his eye. As she drove away, he noticed Ray standing nearby, watching his daughter with a smile on his face. The cocky, self-satisfied smile of someone who thought they'd got it in the bag.

Christ, thought Jack. Surely they haven't bumped him off? The Corrigan Trophy was a nice little incentive for beginners, but surely it wasn't worth killing someone for a fairly hideous cut-glass bowl and a cheque for two hundred quid?

Claudia's heart was thumping. She needed a bloody Oscar for that performance. Underneath her cool, she was in a panic. She'd meant to get up at five, go and let Olivier out, apologize to him, massage his ego and maybe some other bits if he'd let her near him. But she'd overslept horribly – only waking up when her dad came looking for her at eight. And Ray had been on her tail since then. She'd had no opportunity to sneak off to the Winnebago on her own. And now time was slipping by – if she didn't get him out before long, it would be too late. And that had never been Claudia's intention. Even she could see there was no point in winning a race by eliminating your greatest threat. Leaving Olivier chained to her headboard stark-bollock naked wasn't going to prove she was the better driver, just a nasty little cheat.

Tiona sat on the edge of her desk, swinging her legs, looking for all the world like an innocent schoolgirl. She peered at Christopher in concern.

'You look very serious.'

'I am,' he said, trying to keep his voice level. 'There's no easy way of tackling this, Tiona—'

She raised her head in alarm.

'Zoe's found out,' she said flatly.

'No.'

'Then you're worried that she might?'

She jumped off the desk and moved over to him, slid her arms around his waist.

'There's no pressure, you know that. I don't want you to think I'm trying to back you into a corner. If you want to cool things off...' She traced his lips with her finger. 'I'm not a marriage wrecker. I've got no claims on you. Of course your wife and family come first. I understand that...'

Feather-light fingers caressed his brow. He swallowed. The urge to kiss her was unbearable. He could feel his body responding: his heart was pounding and there was a sweet ache in his groin that was crying out to be assuaged.

'It's nothing to do with us,' he said faintly. 'Not directly.' He lifted up the incriminating sheet of paper that Norma had typed out, detailing all the transactions. 'It's this.'

Tiona took it out of his hands and examined it. 'What is it?'

'It's a list of transactions. I want a few things clarified.'

'Like what?'

Her tone was faintly snappish. Christopher looked at her with interest: she looked slightly unsettled, a tiny tinge of pink on her cheeks. She mustered up a little smile.

'Is there some sort of problem?'

'They ... all seem to have been sold for under their market value.'

Tiona's eyebrows shot up. 'In whose opinion?' There was an edge to her voice, which she covered up with a light laugh. 'We all know a property is only worth what someone is prepared to pay.'

She sounded slightly defensive. Whether through guilt or innocence, Christopher couldn't be sure, but she was definitely rattled. It gave him the courage to go on the attack.

'Yes. But none of these actually went on to the open market. It seems *we*—' he couldn't resist a hint of sarcasm here '—were happy to accept the first offer that came along. No board, no advertising, no details even prepared.'

She studied the paper for a moment, a slight furrow between her brows, as if refreshing her memory. Was she acting? Christopher didn't take his gaze from her face, not wanting to miss any clue. Finally she put down the paper and sighed.

'OK,' she said. 'I know strictly speaking it's not the way we should be doing business.'

'Strictly speaking?' Christopher was incredulous. 'It goes against everything we stand for. Our role is to get the best price possible for our client—'

She put up a hand to stop him.

'If I hadn't done what I did, we wouldn't be standing

here now,' she said defiantly. 'We needed the money. You've heard of cash flow, I presume?' Christopher flinched at her patronizing tone, the flash of anger in her eyes. 'Well, six months ago there wasn't any cash flowing. Drace's coffers were empty. We couldn't afford two months, three months, five months to get these properties on to the market, get the offers in, then wait for the chains to complete before our commission came in.' She brandished the piece of paper at him. 'All these people wanted quick sales and that's what they got. Quick, cash sales, no questions asked, that went through in record time and gave *us* the money to pay the rent, the wages, our page in the paper, the phone bill ...'

She trailed off.

'I'm sorry if the way I operated didn't comply with your idea of how Drace's should be run. But I did what I could to save the company. Because I love it, and I want it to be a success. I want us to be the first agency people think of when they come to put their house on the market. And I really think we're getting there. You saw last month's figures ...'

Her voice wavered; her pretty little bottom lip trembled. Christopher crossed over to her. She looked up, her huge blue eyes swimming with tears.

'I'm sorry. I thought I was doing the right thing.'

Mortified that he could have suspected her of double-crossing them, when in fact she had brought them back from the brink of disaster, Christopher folded her in his arms and kissed the top of her head.

'It's OK. It's OK. I'm sorry,' he whispered, and relief flooded through him; relief that he could once more have his fill of her scent, her skin, her softness ... her.

Jamie had been with Hamilton for an agonizing half-hour. She prayed that when the time came for Jack to go it would be quick. How could people stand coming to visit their relatives, once so full of life, and now worse than dead, bereft of any dignity? She'd felt so foolish, prattling away to him, making a great ceremony of opening her card and the shortbread tin, her voice full of false enthusiasm, while he sat in a catatonic trance, totally oblivious. She couldn't bear it any longer. She got up from the slippery armchair that was provided for visitors.

'I've got to go now, I'm afraid. Have a lovely day, Ham. The others will be in to see you later, I'm sure.'

Could he hear her? Did he understand what she was saying? Did he care?

She walked over to him and bent to give him a kiss. He seemed to be dozing. She brushed her lips against his cheek gently. Suddenly his eyes snapped open and he lifted his head, staring straight at her. Disconcerted, she tried to smile.

'Goodbye, Ham. I'll come and see you again soon.'

She patted his hand, then started with shock as he grabbed her. The face that had been so devoid of emotion had come to life; the eyes that had been blank were filled with recognition, and with that recognition something else that Jamie couldn't quite identify. He seemed distressed, agitated. Perhaps he was having a fit? Or, more likely, whatever tranquillizer they gave patients to keep them under control had worn off.

'It's OK,' she said soothingly. 'I'll get someone to come and see you.'

But that clearly wasn't the right thing to say. His hands

were clawing at hers and she had to force herself not to recoil in horror. This was horrific! He was crying. Tears and snot were dribbling down his face. She wanted to pull away, find him a handkerchief, but he was plucking at her sleeve in desperation, clearly wanting to tell her something.

'What is it, Ham? Please – don't be upset.'

He was jabbering something.

'Wheezer. Wheezer.'

Shit. Was he asthmatic? Was he asking for some medication – a puffer or something? She reached for the buzzer to call the nurse, when a figure in the doorway caught her eye.

It was Rosemary. Rosemary, looking at Hamilton with an expression on her face that turned Jamie's insides to icy water. A grim mixture of loathing and disgust.

'What's he saying?'

Rosemary turned her eyes to Jamie, beholding her with the same disdain.

'He's calling for your mother,' she spat.

'What?'

'Louisa. He's saying Louisa. He thinks you're her. You look very alike – more than ever.'

Jamie was utterly confused.

'You have no idea, do you? Absolutely no idea, you poor little cow.'

Jamie blinked. Why on earth was the ladylike Rosemary calling her a poor little cow?

'Rosemary, what are you talking about?'

Rosemary took two paces forwards into the room. She was clutching Hamilton's present – a pair of striped Marks & Spencers pyjamas, which she hadn't bothered to wrap because there was no point – like a shield in front of her.

'Your mother ruined my life. My life and my marriage. Hamilton was besotted with her, completely besotted. Right up until the day she died. The day of your mother's funeral was the happiest day of my life. I thought perhaps I could have him to myself now, for the last few years we'd got left. But no – she even got to him in death. It finished him. He couldn't go on without her. I wasn't enough to keep him going. He gave up.'

With a trembling finger, she pointed at Hamilton, who'd dozed off in his chair.

'Look at him. She's done this to him, your mother. She's as good as killed him. And some days I wish he would die. Then maybe he'll get what he wants – he can be with her for ever and ever. And I can get on with my life. But instead I have to sit here and look at what she did to him. She's taunting me now, saying I still can't have him all to myself.'

Jamie felt a cold band of fear squeezing her heart. She tried to tell herself that Rosemary was upset, that the pressure of Hamilton's stroke was getting to her, that she was having some sort of breakdown and was becoming deluded. But something in the back of her mind was ringing alarm bells. The conversation she'd had with Olivier the night before made her wonder if there perhaps was something to what Rosemary was saying.

'Your mother was never happy unless every man in the world was in love with her,' Rosemary carried on, her voice high with emotion. 'She was relentless. If anyone tried to resist, she hounded them until they gave in. It was like an obsession. She couldn't bear the thought that any other woman in the world had more to offer than she did – that she wasn't quite the most irresistible creature that walked the earth. She might have been beautiful. But she was poison. Absolute poison. She ruined more marriages than she had hot dinners.'

'Rosemary – stop it. You don't know what you're saying!' Jamie was distressed at this transformation of Rosemary from meek and mild to a raging monster. Her colour was high, she was breathing hard and fast. Jamie was frightened she would have some sort of stroke herself.

Rosemary seemed to gather herself.

'If you don't believe me,' she said with dignity, 'then ask your father. He was under no illusions about Louisa. Not that it stopped him loving her. He absolutely adored her, even though she treated him like … like …'

She was searching for a word.

'Shit,' she said finally. 'She treated him like shit.'

Jamie was shocked. She felt sure that Rosemary had never used this word before in her life.

'He had to sit there while she flirted and cavorted for the benefit of whoever was her next victim. There was a hideous inevitability about it. She toyed with them, tortured them, reined them in until they were caught up in her web. Then, after a few weeks or months, she'd drop them like a hot potato, leave them to pick up whatever was left of their minds and their marriages. And she'd move on to her next victim.'

Rosemary paused for breath, then found she was talking to thin air. Jamie had fled the room. She supposed she wasn't surprised. She felt a little bit guilty that she had been so vicious. But then, why should she have to bear the brunt of Louisa's legacy all alone? And it wasn't as if

Jamie was a little girl any more. By the time Rosemary was her age, she'd already suffered eight years of torture, knowing she was married to a man who didn't love her, not really, not the way she wanted to be loved.

She looked over at the armchair where Hamilton was still fast asleep. Lucky him, he was able to retreat from the pain. His mind had finally found him a means of escape; shelter from the horrible truth. While she, Rosemary, of perfectly sound mind, had to endure the torture day after day. She put her hands to her face and wept, bitter, noisy, unashamed sobs of grief and self-pity and helplessness and hatred.

Convinced that the Sedgeleys had cooked up some evil plot between them, Jack had gone searching for clues. By ten o'clock, he could hear the clerk of the course announcing the imminent start of the warm-up laps. Time was running out.

Finally, someone admitted to seeing Claudia and Olivier head off towards her Winnebago the evening before. Jack set off determinedly across the field. Behind him, competitors were warming up their engines, reminding him that if he didn't track Olivier down in the next ten minutes, they'd be out of the running.

At last, he arrived at the Sedgeleys' trailer. The door was unlocked. He wasn't quite sure what he expected to find as he opened it tentatively, but it certainly wasn't a naked Olivier handcuffed to the bed with a G-string wrapped round his willy.

Olivier didn't think he had ever been so humiliated.

'In the fruit bowl. The keys are in the bloody fruit bowl.'

Jack groped amongst the satsumas and found the key.

He undid the handcuffs, finding it very hard not to laugh or make a facetious remark. As soon as he was freed, Olivier leaped off the bed and grabbed his clothes.

'Do you want to tell me ...?'

'Nope.'

'I thought the little monkey was up to something.'

'Little monkey?' Olivier was incandescent with fury. 'I'm going to bloody kill her. I'm going to pull her pink fingernails out one by one, then her toenails—'

Jack put a placatory hand on his arm.

'Do me a favour. Don't do that. At least, not until you've won the race.'

'Isn't it too late?'

'Not if you get your skates on.'

Olivier started pulling on his jeans. Moments later, he was fully dressed and flying out the door of the Winnebago, a bemused Jack in his wake. Beads of sweat were breaking out on his forehead as he reached the paddock. As he raced towards his car, he saw Claudia pulling on her racing slippers, lithe in her brand new shiny red quilted overalls. He tapped her sharply on the shoulder. She looked up, startled for a moment, but in a flash she had recovered her equilibrium.

'Oh – hello,' she said nonchalantly. 'Did you sleep well? I was just about to come and let you out.'

'Sure you were.'

Claudia widened her eyes.

'Of course I was. It wouldn't be a fair race otherwise, would it? I just wanted to teach you a lesson.' She narrowed her eyes and pushed her face towards him. Olivier thought she looked like a spiteful little snake. 'No one accuses me of buying my way in. If I get that trophy, it's because I'm a better driver than you.'

Olivier grabbed her wrist and looked at her watch. He had ten minutes to get his car past the scrutineer and lined up for the start of the practice race.

'We'll see.'

As he stalked over to his car, he saw Ray Sedgeley. He looked him boldly in the eye and received a conspiratorial smile in return. He was obviously still under the impression that their deal was on, totally oblivious to his daughter's own attempts to sabotage the race.

Olivier jumped into the driving seat and started up his engine. The rumble fired up his adrenalin as he edged the car carefully through the crowds to the scrutineer.

He was going to show those Sedgeleys how to win a race fair and square.

Nolly Deacon had worked part-time at Havelock House for the past five years. She pushed the tea trolley round, dishing out the cheap, synthetic cakes that the owner bought in bulk. She always had time for the patients, and would often stay on for an extra half-hour or so, painting fingernails or reading snippets of news from the paper, on the basis that she hoped someone would do the same for her one day. Not that she'd be able to afford a room at Havelock House. It was outrageous what they charged per week, considering what she was paid and the corners that she knew were cut. Little services that were added to the bill but whose benefits the patients rarely saw. Like charging them for newspapers, which they often only got on the days their relatives visited. Nolly knew there was no point in trying to draw anyone's attention to any of this, but she tried to do her little bit to brighten their lives.

She'd arrived for her shift that morning and had nearly been knocked flying by Jamie Wilding rushing out of the front entrance, tear-stained and wild-eyed. Nolly knew at once who Jamie had been visiting, and had gone to investigate. She found Rosemary lying in an exhausted heap on the floor at Hamilton's feet, while he slept the sleep of the blissfully unaware. Gently, she helped Rosemary up. The poor woman was still shuddering with dry sobs. Nolly wrapped her up in a comforting hug.

'There, there. I know.'

'No, you don't. You've got no idea. Nobody has,' wailed Rosemary.

'Yes, I have,' Nolly contradicted her. 'I know very well indeed.'

It was well over forty years since Nolly had first come face to face with John Deacon. She knew who he was, of course. The Deacon brothers were notorious. And in her opinion John was by far the most handsome. With dark, chiselled features and a powerful physique courtesy of his job as slaughterman at the local abattoir, he was quieter than the rest. His younger brothers had a tendency to show off and mouth off, but John had a brooding quality. Those who knew him best weren't fooled; John was a force to be reckoned with, as anyone who'd ever crossed his family could tell you.

When he came into Rashwood Brothers, Nolly was intrigued. What would a Deacon be doing in a gentleman's outfitters? She treated him with the same courtesy she would any other customer, and was touched by his self-conscious embarrassment as he asked to hire a dinner suit. Swiftly, she put him at his ease, measuring him up with the minimum of fuss, and kitted him out from top to bottom. When he stood before her in the changing room, she had to admit that he looked the part, his broad shoulders filling his jacket, the white of his shirt dazzling against his skin, dark from the recent haymaking on their farm. Impishly, she gave him her seal of approval, and was rewarded with a glimmer of a smile as he counted out his wages to pay for the hire.

By the end of the day, when three other customers had been in for various accessories, she surmised that he had been invited to the social event of the summer. Louisa Partridge, daughter of a local landowner, spoilt, beautiful and wild at heart, was to be eighteen that weekend, and was having a huge party in a marquee in the grounds of Bucklebury Farm. Nolly found it strange that John Deacon should be asked – the guests were largely made up of pillars of local society, and pillars of society the Deacons were not.

Curious, Nolly asked around her friends that evening and got her answer – the word was that Louisa and John were in the throes of a passionate affair, supposedly secret up until now but to be made public that very evening. Nolly couldn't help nursing a fear that it was all going to end in tears – the apparently black-hearted villain she'd dressed up to the nines had shown a vulnerability that touched her. She suspected that Louisa was toying with him – she'd seen the girl in town on several occasions and felt instant dislike, not through jealousy of the difference in their fortunes, but through feminine instinct that this was a creature who got what she wanted through means that were not always fair.

When John came back to Rashwood Brothers the following week to return his suit, the evening's events had already become local legend. No one quite knew how or why, but during the speeches the Deacon brothers had released their prize-winning Gloucester Old Spot sow into the marquee, with ensuing chaos. Lucky Pig had a very sweet tooth, and nothing was going to stand between her and Louisa's beautiful pink-iced birthday cake.

John had been the soul of discretion as he handed back his suit, his dark features completely inscrutable, but Nolly had sensed deep hurt under his bravado. It was the end of a long, hot day, and impulsively she asked him out for a drink down by the river. He surveyed her gravely for a few long moments before nodding his agreement.

That drink turned into a courtship that delighted both of them with its simplicity. Nolly and John were a perfect match: the handsome, taciturn slaughterman and the bubbly, vivacious shopgirl. Before six months were out they were engaged to be married. It was only a week before their wedding that Nolly finally managed to extricate the truth about Louisa's birthday party from her fiancé.

Louisa had begged and pleaded with him to come, and against his better judgement he had finally agreed, though the prospect filled him with dread. Despite Louisa's protestations, he knew he would stick out like a sore thumb, that people would be laughing at him behind his back. But he'd swallowed his pride to please her, because he'd thought he loved her. He'd turned up early, dressed in his hired finery, to meet her by prior agreement in the hayloft that had been their secret love nest for the past few months. Only to find Louisa, her bespoke pink silk ballgown pushed up round her waist, with Hamilton Drace between her legs. Hamilton Drace, whose engagement to Rosemary Cole had been announced in the local paper only the week before …

Now, Nolly Deacon remembered her husband's painful, faltering revelation as she stood gazing at the distraught Rosemary. She pressed her lips together. It was over forty years later, Louisa had been cold in her grave nearly a year, and she was still wreaking havoc and misery. The likes of John had had a lucky escape, though she knew the scars of humiliation were still buried deep inside him. Poor Rosemary had undergone a lifetime of suffering; her entire marriage had been undermined by the whims of the capricious Louisa.

She took Rosemary kindly but firmly by the arm.

'Come on. Come with me, love. I'll make you a cup of tea.'

She led Rosemary into the little room where matron saw relatives of the inmates, whenever she wanted a private chat about their antisocial habits or needed to add yet another costly service on to their bill. Nolly slipped her a couple of tablets, the ones they gave the patients when they became too obstreperous. They might not take away the pain, but they'd help her cope. Rosemary gulped them down gratefully, washing them down with a cup of tea.

'He did love me,' she said to Nolly defiantly. 'He always said he loved me in his own way. It was just that he loved her too. And it was the love he gave her that I wanted.

The passion. The excitement. The ... sex thing. He loved me like I love my dogs. Very much. But who wants to be treated like a faithful pet? Patted on the head, given an affectionate tummy rub every now and again.'

Nolly put a comforting hand on her shoulder, feeling it was best not to say anything, just listen. Rosemary sniffed. She seemed a little calmer now.

'His heart never leaped when I came into the room. I know it didn't. But whenever she was around ... you could see it in him. His eyes never left her.' Her pale blue eyes filled with tears again. Nolly was afraid the colour would be washed away for ever. 'And now look at him. Even after she died, she wouldn't let me have him. She's taken him with her.'

She sobbed quietly into her handkerchief for a few moments. Then she seemed to gather herself together. Gone was the hysterical, wronged wife, and in her place was the composed gentlewoman, stalwart of the WI and the PCC. She gave an apologetic smile.

'I'm so sorry. I ... quite forgot myself for a moment.'

'There's no need to apologize. It's what I'm here for,' Nolly reassured her.

'I'm sure it's not. But thank you anyway. You've been most understanding.'

Minutes later, Rosemary scurried away, still clutching Hamilton's pyjamas. Nolly followed at a safe distance, making sure she had got into her car and driven away, before she marched determinedly back to Hamilton's room and stood in front of him.

'Look at me, Hamilton. I want a word. I know what this is all about and I think it's about time you snapped out of it.'

Caught unawares, Hamilton looked up at her in surprise, and she knew she'd put her finger on it. For Nolly was firmly convinced that Hamilton hadn't had so much of a stroke as a breakdown, and that he could be brought back from the brink. His reaction told her he was salvageable. If he'd been beyond redemption, there would have been no response, just the usual catatonic stare. But he hadn't been able to hide his shock at her confrontation, which spurred her on.

'I know you've lost Louisa. I know life doesn't seem worth living without her. But as one of my sons is so fond of saying – get over it.' To punctuate what she was saying, Nolly plumped up two pillows and shoved them behind Hamilton's back. 'I don't know if you've realized it yet, but I'm afraid life isn't fair. Sometimes we get dealt cards that are out of our control. As another of my sons is fond of saying, shit happens.'

She tried to suppress a smile at the look on Hamilton's face. But it was a minor triumph. At least he was showing some emotion.

'But the rest of the time, when the shit isn't happening, we're in control,' she carried on. 'So – you can sit here and moulder in this home till the day you do die – which could be years, because you're a healthy bugger, despite all the efforts you go to to convince everyone otherwise. And by doing that, you'll cause distress to all those who love you. Not to mention waste a huge amount of money on the bills. It costs nearly five hundred quid a week to keep you in here. And I'm sure Christopher could think of better ways of spending that money. All you're doing by sitting in here sulking is lining the pockets of the smug, fat bastard who owns this place. Who incidentally pays me the princely sum of three pounds fifty an hour for wiping the dribble off your chin.'

Again, Hamilton looked shocked. Nolly moved in for the final kill.

'You should count your blessings. You've got a wife who loves you. A son who's struggling to keep his head above water because of the mess you've left him in. And two wonderful grandchildren who deserve to have happy memories of you. It's up to you.' She looked at him slyly. 'Of course, if you really want to end it all, and put everyone out of their misery, including yourself, I can arrange that too. I could, accidentally on purpose, leave a little bottle of something lying around. I'm sure you'd be more than capable of getting the lid off.'

She fixed him with an arch look, eyebrows raised, to show that she meant it. That should call the old bugger's bluff, she thought.

'Right, now. Elevenses. Flapjack or cherry slice?'

There was a moment's silence, which to Nolly seemed to go on for ever. Then he spoke.

'Flapjack, please,' said Hamilton, very meekly, his voice hoarse from lack of use. And as Nolly went to fetch his tea, she gave a little skip of triumph. She wasn't going to let Louisa Partridge get away with ruining yet another marriage from beyond the grave.

30

As usual before a race, Olivier couldn't face food. And judging by Jack's attitude towards him, he hadn't yet found out about his altercation with Jamie. He must have hotfooted it to Sapersley before Jamie was even up. But Olivier felt sure it was only a matter of time before Jack was party to the truth about his betrayal, and in the meantime he was eager to put as much distance between them as possible. He felt awkward in Jack's company, knowing what he had done, so he took himself off for a walk in the grounds to psych himself up before the start.

As he walked through the cool of the oak trees, Olivier looked again at the photo of Eric he'd found in the barn – hair swept back, laurels round his neck, laughing in victory as he held up the Corrigan Trophy he'd won all those years ago. He looked carefree, not the cynical old miser he had become. Olivier was determined to prove that he could do as well as his father, if only for himself.

He'd excelled himself during the practice laps. His car was running well, and he remembered the foibles of the circuit quite clearly from his outing earlier that year, so he'd found himself coming in first, earning him the honour of pole position. The practice had demonstrated there was no real competition out of the fifteen entries.

There was a magnificent Bentley whose power easily matched that of the Bugattis, but the driver was inexperienced and somewhat lacking in bottle. By contrast, a feisty little Morgan three-wheeler was being driven by a young go-karting champion with an intrepid determination and no fear, but the car didn't really have the power. The only real threat was Claudia. She'd come fourth in the practice, but Olivier suspected that perhaps this was tactical, that she'd worked out how easy it would be to catch him up once the race proper had started.

At last it was time for the race. Feeling like a total heel, Olivier let Jack think that his detachment was down to pre-race nerves, as his mentor talked him through his tactics and gripped his shoulder in a final gesture of support. As Olivier slid his car into place at the front of the grid, he had to resist looking back at Claudia in triumph. He might have the advantage at the moment, but he hadn't actually won yet. She was three places behind him, the Bentley and the Morgan in between them. Anything could happen. Otherwise there would be no point in racing.

As the rest of the cars lined up, big, fat drops of summer rain started to fall. Olivier looked up at the sky anxiously – there was plenty of blue amongst the clouds, so it was probably only a shower. They would have to wait a few minutes for it to pass before they started. He tutted to himself in irritation. The track would be wet and greasy, which put a whole new slant on the way he would be able to drive. Risks he had taken in the practice would have to be reconsidered. Swiftly, he reassessed his strategy, knowing that this was when the benefit of experience came into play, experience he didn't have. But then, this was a novice race. That was the whole point.

Behind him, Claudia cursed the impromptu rainfall. She thought she was going to explode with frustration. She just wanted the race under way, to be able to focus on what she was sure would be her victory. It was even more important to her now to win. Olivier had given a look of pure disdain earlier that had cut her to the quick. She wasn't going to go crawling to him. She'd rather die. The only way she could think to regain his respect was by winning fair and square, then embarking on some sort of damage limitation exercise.

She looked up at the sky. The rain seemed to be easing off as quickly as it started – one of those flirtatious summer showers whose only purpose was to annoy. The commentator was announcing the start of the race. She turned on her engine and the exhaust fumes hit her like a blast of amyl nitrate, giving her the sudden, mind-blowing rush of blood to the head she needed to focus.

Jamie pushed her way through the crowds, searching the seats for Jack, ignoring the strange looks she was getting. She knew she must look deranged, bedraggled from the shower, her face puffy and swollen from crying, but she didn't care. She had sobbed all the way from Havelock House, trying to come to terms with what Rosemary had said to her. Of course, she'd wanted to dismiss it as the ranting of a grieving woman, but combined with what Olivier had said the night before, a horrible picture of the woman she'd loved best in the world was emerging.

Time and again Jamie had told herself it wasn't true; that both Olivier and Rosemary had their reasons for being spiteful. But Jamie couldn't deny that little memories were emerging to substantiate their stories. Bitchy remarks that Louisa had made over the years; visions of her mother engaged in what she had thought was innocent flirtation; periods when Louisa had disappeared for days on end, or descended into a black gloom. All of these reminders combined to give Jamie good reason to doubt her mother's innocence. But she clung on to the hope that Jack would refute the slurs Olivier and Rosemary had made.

The commentator was burbling away, winding the spectators up for the start. It seemed as if the summer shower had gone as quickly as it had arrived; the sun had emerged apologetically from behind the clouds, and all around the circuit umbrellas were being shaken and folded up in relief.

At last she saw him, standing by the pit lane, his ancient Burberry mac over his shoulders, his eyes glued to the starting grid. The air was filled with the rich smell of fumes. As the Union Jack came down, and the cars surged forwards, she arrived at Jack's side. He looked startled to see her.

'Jamie! I didn't think you were coming.'

'I want to know the truth, Dad.' She was standing there, jaw clenched, fists in a tight ball.

'What about? What's happened?' Jack looked alarmed, as well he might.

'I want to know the truth about Mum.'

Jack looked nonplussed.

'What truth? What do you mean?'

'About her affairs. With Hamilton. And Olivier's dad. And whoever else. I want to know everything.'

All colour drained from Jack's face.

'Who's been talking to you?'

'Who hasn't?' said Jamie bitterly.

'Jamie – I don't think this is a good time. The race has just started—'

'Bugger the race. I don't care about the race!'

Jamie realized she was shouting, though the roar of the engines meant that she wasn't attracting as much attention as she might. All eyes were on the racetrack; people craned their necks to watch the cars' progress, not remotely interested in their domestic crisis. Nevertheless, Jack looked about him uncomfortably and put an arm round her.

'Ssh – calm down.'

He drew her away from the trackside, away from the noise, away from the spectators.

'I need to know!' Jamie persisted, not caring if the entire audience heard what she was saying. 'Did she have affairs with them? Hamilton and Eric?'

She was trembling with fury. And the fear of what she was about to discover. Jack sighed.

'Yes. Yes, she did. But you mustn't think ill of her, Jamie. It's just the way she was.'

'What do you mean – the way she was? You can't say that about Mum!'

'Jamie, I'm sorry. But it's the truth.'

'How many other people?'

Jack shrugged helplessly. Jamie persisted.

'Rosemary said there were lots of other people. That she did it all the time. Who?'

'I'm not going to stand here and name names. Not when she's not here to defend herself.'

'Why did you let her, Dad? I don't understand ...'

'It was the only way,' said Jack simply. 'I loved her. And

it was the only way I could keep her, to turn a blind eye. If I'd tightened the reins, she'd have been off. She always came back to me, because she knew I was the only one who could manage her. No one else would have put up with it.'

He paused, and the babble of the commentator rose to a higher level of excitement as the cars completed their first circuit. Jamie put her hand to her throbbing head, trying to take in what she'd been told. It was as if her whole life had been turned upside down: the two people she'd loved best in the world weren't who she thought they were, and she was struggling to make sense of it.

'I always thought it was you who played the field.' She said it almost accusingly, as if she wanted that to be the case. Which perhaps she did – she was used to the idea of Jack the lady-killer. Not Louisa the man-eater.

Jack gave a sad smile.

'Yes, well, there you go. I spent my life covering up for her, flirting with the wives so they would feel flattered and wouldn't notice what their husbands were up to.'

'Why didn't you ever tell me? All my life I've blamed you for things you weren't to blame for.'

'I didn't want to spoil your illusions about your mother. Because whatever her faults, she was a very special person. Our relationship was very complex, and hardly conventional. I would never have been able to make you understand.'

'Well, I don't,' said Jamie. 'I don't understand. It just seems so unfair.'

'What you've got to realize, Jamie, is that I was very happy with the way things were.' Jamie saw that her father was on the brink of tears himself. 'Fifty per cent of Louisa was better than nothing at all.'

461

Jamie looked at Jack with new eyes. All those years she'd thought he was weak. All those times she'd berated him for being spineless. When he'd had to be so strong. She thought of all the harsh things she'd said to him over the past weeks, how he took her criticism unflinchingly and never defended himself when he had every right.

'I'm sorry,' she whispered. 'I'm so sorry.'

'Don't be,' he said. 'If I hadn't liked it, I'd have walked away. And just remember, none of this changes how she felt about you. She was a wonderful mother to you. Don't let what you've found out spoil any of your memories.'

Jamie felt as if she needed to be hugged. Badly. And looking at Jack, she thought perhaps he did as well. He looked tired and drawn, as if the revelations about Louisa had taken it out of him. With a shudder, she thought how close she had come to rejecting him completely, how last night she had been so despondent about her life she would have packed up and left the country for two pins, leaving Jack all alone. If it hadn't been for Olivier...

Olivier! How appallingly she'd treated him too, accusing him of lying, banishing him from the house. She had to apologize, make it up to him.

'Olivier. I need to speak to him—'

Simultaneously, they both turned to look at the track. Three cars were leading the field – Claudia in front, followed by the little Morgan and then Olivier. As they approached the next bend, a gap opened up between Claudia and the Morgan. Olivier suddenly seemed to surge ahead, lining himself up to insinuate his way between them.

'Jesus!' said Jack. 'He's never going to make it. Not at that speed.'

Olivier's teeth were gritted; his fingers gripping the wheel like a vice, even though he kept telling himself to relax. He couldn't believe he'd let Claudia pass him – and the Morgan – but he'd been erring on the side of caution because of the wet track. Now he realized caution was not the way to win. They were approaching the bend known as the Devil's Elbow: he knew from Claudia's past performances that she didn't have the killer instinct on cornering; that it was her weak spot. He could get by her if he didn't let his nerve fail him; if the car gave him all she'd got. Which he knew she would ...

He dropped down a gear and put his foot down. He knew it was reckless, like the craziest game of chicken, but it would give the spectators something exciting to watch. They didn't want cars pootling sedately round the track. They wanted risks and drama and madcap foolhardiness, and that's what they were going to get.

After all, he reminded himself, he had nothing to lose.

He was past the Morgan. He could get past Claudia, if he could just summon up a few more miles per hour. Grinning like a maniac, Olivier pressed his foot right to the floor and lined himself up, hoping against hope that his eye was accurate. An inch either way at this speed and he'd be toast ...

Christopher sat in the pub. He and Tiona were having a late lunch. She'd gone into the main bar to order their prawn baguettes, and he was brooding over a glass of red wine. He didn't usually drink at lunch, but today he needed it.

For some reason, the euphoria of his discovery that

morning had worn off and he was starting to feel uneasy. After his confrontation with Tiona, he'd had a quiet word with Norma and assured her that everything was above board. The pitying look she'd given him had taken him aback rather. Then she'd said that, under the circumstances, she was going to have to consider her position at Drace's very carefully. Christopher had started to protest, and she'd cut him off quite abruptly.

'I hope you realize that whatever story she's given you is utter rubbish.' Her look was defiant, but Christopher could see she was upset. 'I'm sorry, but I don't like to see you being made to look a fool.'

At the time, Christopher had told himself that it was just office politics, that Norma was reacting like that because she didn't like Tiona pulling rank on her. But her words kept ringing in his ears. Had he been fobbed off?

Tiona's bag was lying on the floor by her seat. She'd taken her purse to pay for the lunch. Her tiny little mobile phone was visible. He stared at it, transfixed. Did he have the nerve to check up on her? Did he want to know the truth? He could, of course, carry on with what he was starting to suspect was a charade. He could be his usual ostrich-like self, pretending that nasty things weren't happening. Or he could take matters into his own hands for once. Prove he wasn't a gullible, suggestible fool whose libido was ruling his head. Christopher swallowed. He wasn't used to subterfuge and espionage. But he had enough sense to realize that there was rather a lot at stake here, and that he owed it to himself and his family to take control.

Tentatively, he reached out his hand for the phone, hoping fervently Tiona would be a few minutes yet. The pub was popular and busy with Saturday lunchers, so he'd probably got a bit of time.

Quickly, he flicked through the address book on her mobile. He stopped when he got to Lomax. That wasn't actually incriminating in itself, he supposed. His pulse was racing as he fumbled with the keys – he'd got out of the habit of texting since he'd left London. Eventually he managed to stab out a message.

'*Got hot prop for you. 140k. Go or no?*'

He wavered for a moment, casting an anxious look towards the bar. She could be back any second. He pressed 'send', then waited for the icon to indicate that the message had been sent before deleting it from her outbox.

Thirty seconds later the phone beeped. The reply had arrived. Christopher read it; a single word. '*Go.*'

His fingers raced over the keypad, sure and swift this time.

'*My fee has gone up. 3k upfront.*' He jabbed 'send' before he could have any second thoughts.

The next thirty seconds were agonizing. Two beeps told him that the answer that would decide his future had arrived. He pressed 'read'.

'*You're having a laugh. 2k on completion or forget it.*'

Christopher stared at the words, which branded themselves on his brain. He looked up. Tiona was standing there.

'That's my phone,' she said accusingly.

'Yes,' said Christopher, placing it on the table. 'I think you'd better sit down.'

He was surprised to find that he was icily calm. Tiona put out her hand to pick up the phone, but he snatched it out of her grasp. She looked at him, surprised.

'You've just had a text from your friend, Simon Lomax,' he said lightly.

'So?'

Christopher knew she was capable of bluffing it out. She had nerves of steel. But he was ready for the kill this time.

'You failed to mention he was paying you. When we had our little chat this morning.'

Christopher thought he now knew what it was like to corner a rat. Before his very eyes, Tiona turned from a vision of sweetness and light to a snarling creature with teeth bared and claws at the ready.

'It was there for the bloody taking,' she said viciously. 'Why shouldn't I make some money out of it? If I hadn't pushed those deals through you'd be bust. And I never got any thanks for it.'

'You were doing your job, Tiona,' Christopher pointed out quite reasonably. 'It's what you get paid for.'

'Not enough. I had to rip you off in order to survive.'

'Well, at least I know now. We can review the salary for your replacement: make sure they don't feel the need to sink so low.'

'Replacement?' Tiona's eyes glittered.

Christopher allowed himself the luxury of a laugh. It was strange, but he felt exhilarated and in control. He had nothing to lose by calling her bluff. He suspected his worst mistake now would be to play into her hands.

'You don't seriously think I'm going to carry on employing you?'

'But what about us?'

'I don't think our relationship comes into it any more.'

'Doesn't it?' Her tone was dangerously arch. 'I wonder what Zoe would have to say?'

Her meaning was abundantly clear. Christopher held her gaze firmly. He wasn't going to let her frighten him.

'Right,' he said decisively. 'This is what we do. You clear your desk. I'll write you a glowing reference. And that's the end of the matter. You say nothing and I won't prosecute.'

She sat back for a moment, then gave an imperceptible nod of agreement. Confident that she didn't hold any more cards, Christopher couldn't resist a little dig.

'On second thoughts, don't bother to clear your desk. I'll ask Norma to send on any of your personal possessions.'

He had the pleasure of seeing her lips tighten in annoyance. He knew bringing in Norma would goad her, but he felt vindictive.

A waitress appeared with their baguettes, standing by their table with a plate in each hand. Christopher stood up.

'I think I'll have mine to go.' He took one of the baguettes off its plate and gave the waitress a dazzling smile before walking out of the pub without a backward glance.

As Olivier left the road, he felt a split second of terror and then icy calm as he waited for the inevitable. Time went fast and slowly simultaneously: the crash came all too soon, yet it seemed to take a lifetime before the crumping sound reached his ears. He sat in the driver's seat for a moment, stunned. Then a voice inside his head told him to pull himself together – he knew he had to get out as quickly as he could, in case the car burst into flames. As he swung his legs over the side he could already see the fire and ambulance crews. He ran clear as a paramedic approached him. He waved him away.

'I'm fine.'

'I think we should check you over.'

'I'm *fine*.' Olivier couldn't hide the irritation in his voice. He didn't want any fuss. Behind him the fire truck was filling the car with water as a precautionary measure. Olivier wanted to tell them not to bother. As far as he was concerned, it didn't matter if the car went up in flames. It was beyond repair. He'd felt the chassis going, the engine had gone through the floor, every single panel was dented. That's what happened when you hit Armco at top speed.

Well, he thought bitterly. That tied everything up very neatly. Not only had he betrayed Jack's trust, but he'd trashed his most treasured possession. He looked around. Jack was bound to be on the scene any minute, and he didn't think he could bear to face him. Because he knew Jack. He wouldn't hold it against him. And Olivier didn't think he could bear his forgiveness, not when he'd already let him down so badly ...

As Claudia swept over the finishing line, an almost orgasmic thrill swept through her body. She'd done it! She'd bloody well done it! Grinning from ear to ear, she drew the car to a gradual halt. She turned to look behind her, to see who had come second. She could see the little Morgan, but after that ...

She frowned. Something wasn't quite right. The race seemed to have come to a halt behind her. She peered into the distance. Someone had come off the track, totalled their car. Pulling off her goggles and her helmet in order to see and hear better, she heard the concerned tones of the commentator.

'... Olivier Templeton, whose own father won this trophy over twenty years ago in this very same car. There doesn't look to be very much left of it ...'

A chill ran down Claudia's spine and, despite the heat of the day and the thickness of her overalls, she broke out into an ice-cold sweat.

Olivier was making his way towards the paddock when, out of the corner of his eye, he saw someone approaching him. He turned to snarl. It was Claudia, her face contorted with distress.

'Olivier!'

He surveyed her coldly. 'Well done.'

She ignored his congratulation. 'I'm so sorry ...'

'Really?' His reply was heavy with irony. 'I'm surprised. I'd have thought it was just what you wanted. Me out of the running for good. Leaves the road to glory nice and clear for you, doesn't it?'

'Olivier ...'

But he turned and walked away, the stiffness of his back telling her not to follow.

Claudia stifled a sob. He had looked at her with such contempt, showing just how little he thought of her. Why was she such a stupid cow? Why did she feel the need to prove herself all the time; have the upper hand? Why couldn't she embark on a relationship on equal terms, instead of playing elaborate games? She'd blown it this time. The first person in her life that she'd really wanted, and she'd played the most dangerous game of all. He could have died, and all because she'd thrown down the gauntlet, challenged him to a duel that meant he'd taken risks he shouldn't have.

A marshal approached her. They wanted her in the commentary box, so she could discuss her win.

'No comment,' she snapped, turning on her heel, and the marshal looked nonplussed. He thought maybe it was a good thing there weren't more women participating in the sport. They were never bloody happy.

Olivier was about to start up the Land Rover when someone tapped on the window. He flicked off the ignition in annoyance and wound it down. Ray Sedgeley was standing there. He looked a little shaken, rather grey round the gills, not his usual cocksure self.

'Are you OK?' he asked anxiously.

'I'm fine. Now why don't you just fuck off?' Olivier snarled.

'I've come to settle my debt. Though you needn't have gone that far. Jesus, I thought you were a goner.'

'What debt?'

'You threw the race, didn't you? I owe you a ton. I expect you want cash – don't want the Inland Revenue asking questions.' Ray managed a nervous smile.

Olivier looked at him coldly.

'I don't want your money.'

'Don't be stupid. A deal's a deal.'

'There was no deal.'

Ray started to panic, wondering if Olivier had decided to grass him up to the authorities. Even though he knew he could blag his way out of it, he didn't want Claudia's reputation muddied. He put an avuncular hand on Olivier's shoulder through the window.

'Now come on. A hundred grand. You're going to need it for repairs for a start—'

'There was no deal,' repeated Olivier. 'I didn't throw the race. I was trying to win it.'

He wound the window up viciously and Ray snatched his hand away just in time. The Land Rover started up, and he jumped out of the way as Olivier pulled off.

Ray stared after him in disbelief. If that was gentlemanly behaviour, he could keep it. What a complete and utter prat, turning down a sum like that in the name of honour.

Christopher sat on the terrace at Lydbrook that night feeling as if a great weight had been taken off his shoulders. He didn't mind admitting that he'd been frightened. Very frightened indeed. But he had stood his ground and remained calm, and in the end Tiona hadn't made a fuss.

At four o'clock he'd closed the office. If anyone wanted to buy or sell a house that badly, they could wait till Monday. He told Luke and Norma to go home early; Norma was clearly gagging to know what had happened, but he couldn't bring himself to relay the gory details – she'd have to spend the weekend in suspense. Then he'd gone home himself, and Sebastian and Hugo had leaped on him with glee, which was most gratifying. Zoe was ambling about the garden with a trug, happily filling it with the supper ingredients. She'd bought the *River Café Easy* cook book. Tonight was pasta with pancetta and fresh peas. He felt a surge of gratitude for her efforts.

Inside the house, he could hear the phone ringing. He got to his feet and went into the cool of the hall to answer it.

'Hello, Lydbrook.'

'Hello, Mr Drace. It's matron here, from Havelock House.'

Christopher felt his heart lurch and begin a terrifying descent to his boots. He hadn't been to see his father. It was his bloody birthday. And now – what? Was he dead? He wouldn't be able to cope with, the guilt—

'What is it?'

'Rather a nice surprise, I think. Your father's sitting up bright as a button, demanding to see you. I know it seems extraordinary but on the face of it – well, he seems to have made a remarkable recovery.'

It was a solemn Jack and Jamie who returned to Bucklebury Farm that evening. The remnants of the car had been loaded on to the trailer and Jack had arranged to have it towed to a specialist garage, though nobody held out much hope.

A quick inspection of his room revealed that Olivier had cleared out his few things and gone.

Jamie sighed.

'I shouldn't have been so vile to him. I told him to get out and never come back.'

'He probably feels bad about telling you,' said Jack. 'I made him swear never to breathe a word ...'

'Do you think he's gone back to his father?'

'I doubt it. He made it pretty clear their differences were irreconcilable.'

Jamie thought about Olivier's father,

'No wonder you didn't want to talk to Eric about the car,' she mused. 'Not after him and Mum.'

'No,' said Jack. 'In some ways it was even worse, being

shafted by my best mate. I'd come to expect it from Louisa, but I thought better of Eric.'

'He sounds horrible,' said Jamie. 'I think you're better off without his friendship.'

'He was all right in the old days. Reading between the lines, I think it was after his affair with your mother that he got all bitter and twisted. I think Isabelle gave him a pretty hard time.'

'So will you get in touch with him now? About the car, I mean? You'll have to split the insurance money – you can't keep that quiet.'

'Insurance money,' said Jack flatly.

'Yes.' Jamie felt a flutter of panic. 'Surely it was insured?'

'For on the road, yes.' Jack looked deeply uncomfortable. 'But not for racing.'

Jamie looked at him in disbelief.

'What?'

'Hardly anyone insures for racing.'

'But that's crazy!'

'It's prohibitively expensive.'

'So people go out there on the track in cars worth more than most people's houses and if they trash it – tough luck?'

'I'm afraid so.' Jack at least had the grace to look sheepish.

Jamie leaned her head against the back of the sofa and closed her eyes for a moment. On the face of it, when she looked, her life was a complete disaster. She was having to sell the family home. She'd lost her mother and the love of her life. She'd alienated her staunchest supporter, who'd subsequently trashed their one potential source of cash, which was now a mangled heap of useless metal.

Then she began to laugh.

'What's so funny?' demanded Jack, rather indignantly.

The one thing that had come out of all this mess was that she now knew the truth about her father. She thought back to Olivier's lecture, how he'd pointed out that Jack was the most important thing in her life, and realized how right he'd been.

She got up and crossed the room, throwing her arms around Jack and holding him tight, trying to pour as much love into him as she could, to make up for all the times she'd been exasperated with him in the past, all the times she'd blamed him for his irresponsibility and capriciousness. At least now she was going to get the chance to know the real Jack.

'I love you, Dad,' she said, squeezing him as tightly as she could.

31

It was late October, and Ludlow was bathed in a glorious golden light that set off the russets and ochres of the falling leaves. The streets and shops were busy with tourists, lured by the last of the crisp, bright sunshine before the gloom of November set in.

Rod and Bella came out of the travel agents and into the high street. They smiled at each other a little shamefacedly. It was, after all, an outrageous amount of money to spend on a holiday, but they both deserved it after the last couple of months, since Rod had brought Bella home from hospital. In a few days' time they would be on their way to Mauritius, to Le Touessrok, a spa hotel of such glamorous proportions that they almost couldn't believe they'd been allowed to book in. It seemed a just reward for the hell they'd each been through, though they hadn't actually voiced that to each other.

That was how their relationship worked these days. They skated over unpleasant issues, except when they actually had to face them. When Bella went to therapy, for example. Then they had to confront the ugliness face-on. The rest of the time they tried to make life as pleasant as possible. And be pleasant to each other. They'd both got rather good at it, considering.

She'd been going to counselling for two months. Sometimes Rod went with her, to support her and to learn why she'd become what she had. He'd been deeply shocked by what had been revealed during these sessions – her torrid childhood at the hands of a drunk and violent father who had, to confuse her further, been warm and affectionate and adoring when he wasn't in his cups. Rod's admiration for Pauline had grown in the face of what he had learned, as had his sympathy for Bella. Meanwhile, his relationship with her had moved on to another plane. He felt incredibly protective and was enormously patient, holding her when she cried, talking things through with her, reassuring her. She took up all of his spare time. Which was a good thing, because it stopped him thinking too much.

Now, as they walked through Ludlow back to the car park, Rod felt a sense of gloom descend upon him. He realized that, far from looking forward to the holiday, he was dreading it. There would be no work to distract him. Work was his saving grace. Work was what stopped him boiling over with the frustration of it all and throwing things at the wall. Work was the only thing that stopped his life being completely and utterly pointless. Deep down he knew that saving Bella was only done out of a sense of duty combined with guilt. He wasn't doing it because he loved her.

What the hell were he and Bella going to do, with only each other and a multi-million-pound spa to distract them? They couldn't enjoy the restaurant, because three nights out of five she freaked out about food and had to be calmed and cajoled into eating. They couldn't enjoy the sports facilities, because she would become obsessed with burning calories and sneak on to the scales and get her BMI measured in secret – then be ecstatic or despairing. She had a long way yet to go before any of these pleasures could be enjoyed. Added to which, every other female would be a potential threat, depending on how they measured up under her critical eye. But Rod couldn't bring himself to point any of this out.

And then there was the thorny question of bed. Or what they might do in it. They still hadn't had sex. It was a loaded bloody gun. It raised too many issues; there just wasn't any point. And what, thought Rod, was the point of a holiday without rampant sex at inappropriate times of the day?

They turned up a side street and Rod realized they were passing Drace's. Out of habit, he looked in the window. He was always on the lookout for the next restoration project; he'd been thinking recently that a move might help take their mind off things and give them each a common interest.

As soon as he looked he realized he shouldn't have. In the centre of the window was displayed the prime property. Bucklebury Farm. With five lavish photos demonstrating its not inconsiderable charms. And across the middle of the display, in blood-red letters, were splashed the words 'Under Offer'.

Rod turned, hooked his arm through Bella's and walked away very quickly, before his mind started torturing him about what might have been.

Twenty-eight people had been to see Bucklebury Farm since it had gone on the market in September. Kif had ended up doing block viewings while Jamie made herself scarce for the day: it was too painful for her to watch people traipsing through her beloved home discussing the changes they would make. He went to see Jamie when a firm cash offer came in from a local couple with two horse-mad daughters. He knew it would be traumatic; he knew she would be in a quandary about whether to accept – for Jack had left it up to her to deal with the sale. And he wanted to talk her through it objectively. Or as objectively as he could, for he was as loath to see the farm go as she was.

'They've offered thirty grand less than the asking price. But, as you know, we built that in, so in reality you're getting what you wanted.'

Jamie nodded. She still couldn't believe they were talking about over half a million. But prices in Shropshire had zoomed up, especially houses that were pretty but manageable with that dreaded word 'potential'.

'Fine,' she said wearily. 'I'm not going to quibble.'

'In that case,' said Kif, 'I'll call the Taylors this afternoon. Tell them you've accepted their offer.'

Jamie nodded, then burst into tears. At once, Kif was at her side, hugging her to him.

'I know it's horrible, darling. I know.'

'It's not that,' sobbed Jamie. 'I haven't talked to anyone about it since I found out. But I can't bear it any longer. It's Mum ...'

She sobbed even harder into his chest. Kif made more consoling noises.

'It's perfectly normal to still feel sad.'

'It's not about her dying,' said Jamie. 'It's about ... who she was. I'm finding it really hard to handle. And I can't talk to Dad, because he gets upset.'

Kif was mystified. Then quite horrified, when Jamie told him what she'd discovered about Louisa. Not the whole truth, of course. She left out the bit about Hamilton, because she wasn't going to blacken Kif's image of his own father, not when Hamilton was doing so well and he and Rosemary seemed so happy. But about Eric Templeton, and the other unidentified lovers.

'It's as if she wasn't the person I thought she was. The Mum I loved.'

Kif was silent for a moment as he digested the revelations.

'I don't know what to say, Jamie,' he said carefully. 'All I know is she was a wonderful person – at least that's how I remember her. Great fun, and kind, and generous. And talented. And she was brilliant to all of us when we were growing up. If she had a dark side, or if she went off the rails a bit every now and then … well, you don't know, do you? About people's marriages and what they're looking for or why they might feel insecure or need another person? It doesn't necessarily mean they don't love the one they're with …'

Kif trailed off. He didn't want to sound too understanding. After all, Jamie wasn't to know he was speaking from experience. It had been two months since Tiona had left and he hadn't heard a word from her since their confrontation in the pub. Her only taunt had been to put her house on the market with his biggest competitor.

Jamie looked at Kif, impressed. She hadn't expected such a lucid reassurance. She wondered whether to unburden the rest of her unhappiness on to him, then decided that the story wouldn't really elicit all that much sympathy. In bald terms, she'd shagged Rod Deacon twelve years after they'd first had sex and was upset he'd gone back to his wife. How could she convince Kif that she felt she'd lost the love of her life? He'd just tell her what she'd been telling herself for the past couple of months – pull yourself together and move on …

Ray Sedgeley was in despair.

Ever since the day of the Corrigan Trophy, Claudia had barely been out of her bedroom, let alone the house. The Bugatti was sitting in the garage. Barbara was tearing her hair out, insisting they should sell it, but Ray refused, clinging on to the hope that Claudia's interest would resuscitate itself.

Winning the trophy had been a hollow victory for both of them. But neither could reveal to the other why it left such a bitter taste in their mouth, why Olivier Templeton had left them both feeling ashamed and the glory tainted. The trophy itself hadn't been put on the mantelpiece. The cut-glass bowl had been shoved in a cupboard.

Ray thought he knew what was at the root of Claudia's depression. He didn't think it was just that she'd lost her bottle after Olivier's accident. There was more to it than that. She was actually pining, and it frightened Ray. He'd never known his daughter to fall under someone's spell, but he'd sensed her attraction to Olivier. He found the lad intriguing himself; he was still amazed that he'd walked away from his money like that. After all, Ray would have gladly paid out; would never have known that Olivier hadn't thrown the race.

Thus Ray was thoroughly impressed with Olivier's integrity. And he would jump through burning hoops to get his daughter what she wanted. And so one afternoon, when he'd failed to coax Claudia out of her self-imposed isolation, he picked up the phone and dialled through to one of his friends on the police force.

'Colin, mate. I wouldn't usually ask, you know I wouldn't, but I need you to do me a favour. I need you to track someone down for me ...'

Then he sat down in his office and dialled up the Internet.

By the end of the day he had all the information he needed.

'Thanks, Colin. You're a real pal,' he'd told his friend, before hitting the print button on his computer. He shuffled the pages into the correct order, took a deep breath and went up the stairs, pausing for a moment outside the door before bearding his little lioness in her den.

32

If this was the English Riviera, thought Claudia, then
you could bloody well keep it. It had been bright sunshine when she'd climbed on to the train in Birmingham.
Now, as she glided through Torquay in a taxi, she wished
she'd brought her fur-lined mac. She couldn't even see the
sea, the rain was so heavy.

The taxi pulled up outside the hotel. It might have four
stars, but the doorman wasn't breaking his neck to bring
her an umbrella. Holding the copy of *Vogue* she'd bought
to read on the train over her head, she splashed through
the puddles into the foyer.

Five minutes later she was having a stand-up row with
the receptionist.

'Why can't I have it?' she demanded. 'You've told me
it's vacant. What's the problem? I'll pay the going rate.'

'But you're not on your honeymoon,' protested the
receptionist. She was being deliberately stubborn. She'd
loathed Claudia on sight. She had the real version of the
fake Burberry bag she'd been so proud of. So she wasn't
going to let her have the honeymoon suite without a
battle.

'Details, details,' scoffed Claudia, and leaned over the
counter. 'I'll have you know my father collects hotels as a

hobby. One word from me and he'll snap this place up. And the first person he'll get rid of is you.'

The receptionist sighed and prodded at her computer with her false nails.

'Fine. Whatever. It's two ninety-five a night plus champagne. Do you want champagne?'

'Definitely,' said Claudia. 'And I'd like to book a lesson with your tennis professional.'

Two hours later, singularly unimpressed with the honeymoon suite but keenly aware she could do nothing about it, Claudia stomped on to the hotel tennis court. A watery sun had emerged and she could now see the sea in the distance, but she was no more enamoured of Torquay than she had been on her arrival.

A tall, rangy figure dressed in tennis whites stepped on to the court. From behind her sunglasses, she surveyed his long, brown legs. And his golden hair. She swallowed, then marched up to him, swinging the racket she'd rushed to buy the day before.

'I booked for three o'clock. You're late,' she announced.

Olivier surveyed her with the detached amusement that she'd expected.

'I need some help with my backhand,' she went on crisply.

He showed no surprise; she gave no further explanation. For the next hour Olivier ran Claudia ragged round the court, slamming balls across the net to her that sometimes she returned, sometimes she didn't. At the end she stood in front of him, dripping with sweat, breathless.

'What now?' she demanded.

'I think you probably need a shower,' he drawled, then relented. 'Tea on the terrace?'

Half an hour later Claudia was showered and wearing a white linen dress. She felt like a character from an Agatha Christie novel as she stepped out on to the terrace. Olivier was sitting at a table in front of a doily-lined, three-tier cake stand, clustered with cream-filled delicacies and cucumber sandwiches.

Olivier chivalrously poured her a cup of Earl Grey.

'So,' he said. 'Is your arrival here just a happy co-incidence?'

Claudia shook her head. 'No.'

'How did you find me?'

'Dad's got a friend in the Serious Crime Squad.'

Olivier looked alarmed.

'So what's my Serious Crime?'

'Leaving the scene of an accident,' she said lightly.

Olivier helped himself to a mini éclair. Claudia looked down at the sprigs on her bone china plate. She looked up defiantly.

'I came to apologize,' she blurted out. 'I'm really ashamed of how I behaved at Sapersley. I was a really bad sport. I can see that now. But I was so wound up at the time. I wanted to prove myself. But instead I just proved I was a bratty little princess. So I've come to say sorry. Because I wanted the chance ...'

She looked at Olivier. He was staring at her in amazement. The words she wanted to say stuck in her throat.

'I wanted the chance for us to be friends,' she finished lamely. 'Because I think we could be. And I'd rather be friends than enemies.'

She looked away, embarrassed by her outburst. Olivier was touched. He knew how much that must have cost her. Apologies didn't come easily to the likes of Claudia.

'Thank you,' he said softly. 'I really appreciate it. And to be honest, I wasn't very nice to you either. I know I wound you up. I shouldn't have said those things, about your dad buying you in. You're a good driver. You deserved to win.'

Claudia gave a little embarrassed shrug.

'Whatever.'

Olivier pushed the cake stand towards her.

'Come on. Eat some of this.'

Claudia took a *mille feuille* oozing with jam and cream.

'There is something else,' she announced. 'I've got a proposition.'

Olivier looked wary.

'I want to do the Mille Miglia next year.'

'Wow,' said Olivier. 'Who wouldn't?'

The Mille Miglia was infamous. A thousand-mile madcap race around Italy that took place every May, it started and ended in Brescia, taking in some of the most magnificent, breathtaking scenery the country had to offer. Glamorous and gruelling, only the cream of classic cars were allowed to enter, and were carefully chosen for their history and provenance.

'I reckon I've got a good chance of getting an entry,' said Claudia. 'But I need a co-driver.'

There was a little pause.

'Right,' said Olivier.

'I'd like it to be you,' said Claudia.

Olivier swallowed. He felt a flutter of excitement in his stomach. This was a wonderful opportunity. To take part in a slice of motoring history, to speed through Italy on streets lined with applauding crowds, in a race known as the most beautiful race in the world.

'What does your father think about it?' he said cautiously.

'Actually, it was his idea,' admitted Claudia. 'I expect he thinks I'd keep stopping to buy handbags.'

Olivier's mind was racing. It was the chance of a lifetime, but part of him still felt reticent about accepting. He wasn't sure where he stood with Claudia: how he felt about her, or how she felt about him. There was no doubt he found her attractive; he still cringed inwardly when he remembered their encounter in the Winnebago.

'I don't want any funny stuff,' he warned. 'No handcuffs.'

Claudia's face lit up.

'You'll do it, then?'

Olivier paused for a moment before nodding.

'I'd be mad not to, wouldn't I?'

Rod and Bella were sitting at the dining table in Owl's Nest. They'd spent the afternoon packing, as they were due to go off on their holiday the day after. Rod had made spaghetti carbonara and thought he had perfected it this time: the bacon was crisp, the eggs and cream still slightly runny. He'd grated a bowl of fresh Parmesan to sprinkle on top.

All Bella saw when she looked at it was a mass of fat and carbohydrates tangled up in a glutinous mess, taunting her. She longed to be able to pick up her fork and dig in with as much enthusiasm as Rod. But she knew if she did, she wouldn't savour the experience. She would be berating herself through every mouthful. And then she would spend the rest of the evening in torment, trying to suppress the urge to rush to the loo and spew it all up, thereby relieving herself of the guilt and the calories.

Her progress was slow. Some days she managed. But other days, like tonight, it was sheer torture. She put down her fork.

'I can't do this any more,' said Bella simply. 'I can't take the pressure.'

Rod looked at her sympathetically.

'We always knew it was going to take time.'

He watched as she stood up from the table and walked over to the window.

'I've been thinking,' she said. 'While I'm still with you, I constantly feel sick with guilt about what I did. How I betrayed you. And I feel under pressure to make up for it. But I don't think I can. Not yet.'

'Bella – you can take your time. I'm not putting you under any pressure.'

'No. I know you're not. And that makes it worse.'

She was looking out of the window, not at him. Rod admired her straight dancer's back, the way she stood with her feet slightly turned out, the curve of her neck.

'I can't go on holiday. It would be torture. I won't be able to eat. Or lie by the pool without looking at every other woman. Or put on a bikini without freaking out ...'

Rod couldn't look at her, knowing that he'd been thinking the very same – it would be admitting defeat, telling her she was a lost cause.

'I think we should call it a day.'

She spoke so softly he wasn't sure if he heard her right.

'What?'

She turned back round to face him.

'I think I could cope if I was on my own. Maybe one day I'll meet somebody new. And I'll make sure they know the deal right from the start. So they can decide whether they want to take me and my ...' she faltered for a moment, visibly upset '... my crazy fucked-up mind on board.'

'You're not crazy and fucked-up.'

'No? Then why am I seeing a shrink? And why did I try and kill myself? And why did I hurt you the way I did? I can't forgive myself, Rod. So I don't see how on earth you can forgive me. And I don't want to sentence you to a life of wondering whether I'll ever be normal again. Wondering if you dare broach the subject of sex.'

He couldn't deny any of what she was saying. He couldn't reassure her. And if anything, he loved her for knowing that. She walked back over to him.

'I know how much you want babies. So I'm giving you the chance to get out there. Go and find some normal girl who can't wait to be a mummy. It shouldn't take you long.'

She stroked his hair. He was surprised at how calm and composed she was.

'You're a wonderful man, Rod. I knew that when I married you. But I can't keep my side of the bargain.'

'You're just feeling a bit low. The therapist said you'd have ups and downs.'

It was a lame gesture of reassurance. She smiled her thanks nevertheless.

'I've been thinking about it over the past couple of days. To be honest, the thought of the relief ... not to be under pressure. To sort my head out in my own time.'

'Nobody expects you to do it all on your own, Bell.'

'I know.' She paused for a second. 'I'm going to move back in with Mum.'

'You've made up your mind, then?'

'Yes. I've made up my mind.'

That evening, Olivier and Claudia went into Torquay for dinner.

'I know a great little fish place,' Olivier had said. 'Award-winning. You'll love it. Can you be ready for eight?'

He was waiting in reception when she came down in a pink trouser suit and three-inch heels.

'For God's sake, go and get some jeans on,' he said, exasperated. And when they arrived at their destination Claudia realized why. She'd thought award-winning meant Michelin star.

'I can assure you, the Golden Chip award is far more prestigious,' said Olivier, presenting her with a huge white wrapper of fish and chips. Claudia looked dubious.

'I'm not having any princessy behaviour on the Mille Miglia,' he warned her.

Claudia relented. They sat on a bench on the quay, huddled up close together for warmth, and Claudia found she was ravenous. Ten minutes later her wrapper was empty and she licked the last of the salt from her fingers.

'Right,' she announced, as she dropped the papers into a bin. 'It's my part of the deal now. I've got a bottle of champagne chilling in my room. I think we should go and celebrate.'

*

Jamie was in the barn, where she'd made three piles. Tip, charity shop and storage. She'd spent the last month working her way through Bucklebury Farm, sorting out three lifetimes of possessions. It was a gargantuan task, but she was being utterly ruthless, and she had to admit it was quite therapeutic. The purchasers wanted vacant possession by the end of November; the solicitors were working their socks off trying to get the paperwork in order so they could exchange the following week in the hopes of completion a month later.

She looked at the towering pile of worn-out domestic appliances, old clothes, broken crockery, yellowing magazines and redundant paperwork. She heard a footstep behind her.

'We're going to need to borrow a horsebox or something to get this lot to the tip.'

'Why don't you get a skip? I can get hold of one for you.'

She whirled round. Rod was standing there. There was a look on his face. Excited. But a little unsure.

She swallowed.

'Hi.'

He smiled gingerly.

'Hello.'

For a moment, they just stared at each other. This was the moment Jamie had been dreading, coming face to face with Rod again. For the past two months, she had miraculously managed to avoid him. Every time she went into the post office she held her breath in case he came in. Every time she saw a pick-up or a sports car, she panicked, in case they had to slow down to pass each other in the narrow lanes. And now he was here in front of her, her worst fears were confirmed. She felt as much for him as she ever had. Her heart was pounding, her stomach fluttered, she could feel the heat on her cheeks as the blood rushed to her head. She took a deep breath to steady herself, and tried to look cool.

'What … can I do for you?' she asked, with the polite detachment of a shop assistant.

He was looking into her eyes. She backed away in self-defence – she wished he wouldn't do that! Whatever he wanted, why couldn't he just spit it out and leave her alone. She couldn't take this—

'Bella and I. We're separating.' Rod managed to blurt it out.

Jamie blinked.

'Oh.'

'It's amicable. We've talked it over and decided it's for the best.'

Jamie's mouth was dry. She could hardly speak.

'I see.'

'So …'

Rod felt rather awkward. He didn't quite know what to say next. What if Jamie wasn't interested? What if she'd moved on, found someone else, had realized he was just a silly infatuation, a mistake from the past.

'I don't know if it's too late. Or if you're still interested …'

'In what?' Jamie asked carefully.

Rod swallowed.

'In me.'

There was paperwork strewn all over Claudia's room: entry forms and maps of Italy and itineraries and photographs. The two of them spent hours talking excitedly about their plans, until they realized it was nearly midnight.

Claudia flopped back on to the bed.

'More champagne,' she demanded.

Olivier picked up the bottle and tipped it up. It was empty.

'Shall I call room service? Get them to send up another?'

Claudia grinned. 'Now who's being a princess?'

Olivier poked her playfully in the ribs.

'I'd be perfectly happy with a pint.'

Claudia rolled over and picked up the phone.

'Can I have another bottle of champagne, please? To the honeymoon suite.'

She hung up. Olivier looked at her.

'Honeymoon suite?'

'Oh yes,' said Claudia. 'You know me. Nothing but the best.'

Olivier rolled his eyes. Claudia turned over on to her side, and rested her head on her hand, looking at him.

'I know you said no funny stuff,' she said softly, 'but there's a Jacuzzi. And I'm aching all over from that tennis this afternoon ...'

Later that night, Jamie put in a call to Christopher. She winced when she heard his cheery tones.

'Jamie, hi.'

'Kif. Um – you are going to absolutely kill me. The sale of Bucklebury – we want to pull out.'

Jamie explained what had happened, inwardly cringing, knowing that Kif stood to lose a substantial commission. There was silence on the other end of the telephone. Was this an abuse of their friendship? She panicked.

'We'll pay the commission anyway. I know you did me a favour. We'll get the money together—' she babbled.

'Jamie. Shut up, will you?' commanded Christopher. 'I think it's the best news I've heard in ages.'

33

Jamie slopped her way across the yard in her wellingtons. February was living up to its nickname of February Filldyke – the rain hadn't stopped all week. Luckily they'd finished all the structural work on the stables just before the heavens opened. All that was left was the interiors; they could do the landscaping in a couple of months' time, when the weather was dry. Every day she hoped and prayed they would finish on time. The first lot of visitors was booked in for the Easter weekend in early April. She'd warned them that their holiday accommodation might be a little rough round the edges, but they hadn't seemed to mind, especially as she'd given them a substantial reduction in price in anticipation of teething problems.

The whole project had been staffed almost entirely by the Deacons. Between them they represented nearly every trade needed – brickies and plasterers and an electrician – and they'd been uncharacteristically reliable and conscientious. Jamie had learned not to ask where most of the building materials had come from.

She had to admit that she almost felt one of the family now. Once or twice a week she and Rod trooped over to Lower Faviell Farm for tea, grateful that after a hard day's work they didn't have to cook. You never knew how many

Deacons might be there, but Jamie had come to love the noisy camaraderie, the huge pies and stews that Nolly produced, supplemented by mounds of chips churned out by the deep-fat fryer. Jamie would sit down with a chilled alcopop solemnly brought to her by John from his illicitly stocked fridge, usually a child on each of her knees as they watched the latest pirate DVD on the massive television that thundered over the banter and arguments. She would fill Nolly in on the latest developments at the farm, while Rod went to the pub for a quick pint with however many of his brothers were around. Nolly had welcomed Jamie into the fold with a warmth and generosity that she could never repay. She would never be a replacement for Louisa – they were far too different – but Jamie cherished the easiness of their relationship.

She found Rod in the end cottage, fitting the final kitchen. They'd gone for a simple Shaker style, each finished in a different colour – apple green, teal blue and raspberry pink. The cottages were shaping up to be more stunning than any of them had hoped. Open-plan downstairs, with two cosy bedrooms and a bathroom in the roof space, they were fitted out to a high specification. Jamie was rushed off her feet sourcing materials to kit them out, from bedlinen, curtains and carpets right down to the vital corkscrew.

Rod had his head inside a cupboard, his electric screwdriver doing overtime. He emerged, looking hot and bothered.

'You'd better go and have a bath. They'll all be here in half an hour,' Jamie said.

Rod pulled a hanky out of his overalls and wiped his sweaty brow.

'Sure you don't need a hand in the kitchen?'

'No. It's all under control. You go and get cleaned up. Try and leave me some hot water – I'll jump in the shower after you've finished.'

Jamie hurried back to the kitchen and opened the Aga door to inspect the huge side of beef that was sizzling nicely. The roast potatoes were nearly done. She'd give them five more minutes then move them to the warming oven.

She opened the cutlery drawer to start laying the table. There would just be enough room; Hugo and Sebastian would have to squash up on stools. They could get down as soon as they were finished, then everyone could spread out a bit over cheese and coffee.

It was incredible to think who was going to be sitting round the table that lunchtime. A few months ago, Jamie wouldn't have believed it was possible. Herself and Rod for a start, ostensibly host and hostess. They were going through a complicated purchase of Bucklebury Farm from Jack – the solicitors were working out the most tax-efficient way of avoiding death duties and capital gains. Rod had sold Owl's Nest and paid off Bella, which had given him some cash to help fund the purchase. The conversion of the stables was being underwritten by Lettice: she had insisted, on the proviso that one of them would always be available to her and Jack whenever they came back from South Africa. For their relationship had blossomed from a friendship into a romance, and there was even the threat of wedding bells. Jamie was still surprised that the prospect of Lettice Harkaway as her stepmother was actually a pleasant one – she'd grown very fond of her over the past few months.

There were going to be six Draces at the table. Not least Zoe and Christopher, with the two boys. Having emerged from her Chardonnay-soaked crisis, Zoe had found her *métier* at last. Rod had taken out a lease on an empty shop at the bottom of Corve Street, and had opened a showroom, which Zoe was running. Though she was no great cook even now, Zoe knew that a fuck-off kitchen was an essential status symbol in this day and age even if you only ever paid homage to St Michael in it. And once she applied herself to it, she had a good eye. Rod trained her rigorously in the pitfalls and dangers of kitchen design, so she didn't go too far down the road selling something that was totally impractical. And she revelled in sourcing the accessories – tiles, table linen, Italian coffee machines, beautiful crystal. She liked to joke that she'd always been good at buying... And of course, once she had come down off her high horse and discarded the idea that everyone in Shropshire was a provincial oaf, she made friends. And didn't obsess quite so much about her roots and her shoes.

Even more heart-warming than Zoe and Christopher's presence at the lunch table was Rosemary and Hamilton's. No one knew quite what had brought about Hamilton's emergence from Havelock House, but his transformation was nothing short of a miracle. He had improved so much that he was actually able to go back to work at Drace's. Not full-time, just on a part-time consultancy basis, because he and Rosemary were spending quality time together. The resulting change in Rosemary was quite dramatic – from a shadow of her former self she had radiated into a sparkling stalwart of the hunt committee, the parish council and the gardening club.

497

Then there was Claudia and Olivier, the surprise love match. Though when everyone found out, it was obvious they were perfect for each other. It was Claudia who had forced Olivier to reunite with his father. Claudia who, despite being the trickiest daughter on the earth, actually had an incredibly strong sense of family and had demanded to meet Eric. And to Olivier's surprise, the two of them got on like a house on fire. Somehow, Claudia brought out the best in Eric – perhaps because she met him head on, rather than finding his ways irksome. And on seeing his showroom she had decided, with her ruthless streak underlined with practicality, that this was the answer to her and Olivier's prayers. After the Mille Miglia in May, they were going to take over the showroom. Claudia relished the prospect of being head of sales, while Olivier learned the nuts and bolts of buying from his father.

And although nobody else knew it, Eric had written Jack a letter of condolence mixed with apology for what he saw as his appalling behaviour all those years ago, a letter that made it clear that he never expected them to be friends again, but underlined his respect for Jack and his grief that his bad behaviour had cost him their friendship ...

'It would be only too easy to blame the heat of the midday sun and too much champagne,' he wrote in his sloping script. 'But it was a moment of selfish foolishness on both of our parts. There was never any danger that I would take Louisa away from you. She loved you, and I always envied you that love ...'

And as a final postscript, Eric offered to fund the repair of the totalled Bugatti. He looked forward, he said, to the prospect of him and Jack watching Olivier on the racetrack again next season.

Rod came through into the kitchen, washed and scrubbed and bearing two glasses of champagne. Jamie declined. If she started drinking now, lunch would never be served.

'You've got to,' insisted Rod. 'It's a bit special.'

Jamie was puzzled. Rod wasn't usually precious about his wines. Maybe he was more keyed up than usual because they had so many guests. But there was no one he had to impress. She shrugged and took the glass, taking a sip.

'Lovely,' she said, and went to put it down on the side when she realized Rod was grinning at her most peculiarly.

'What?' she demanded.

'Go on, have another sip.'

She rolled her eyes and took another slurp. As she tipped the glass, something slid up the side and she nearly swallowed it. She put the glass down hastily and peered inside. She poked a finger in and fished out ...

A ring. A gold ring with a pear-shaped diamond.

Rod suddenly looked nervous.

'I don't know,' he said, 'if you could bear the stigma of becoming a Deacon. I won't be in the least offended if you keep your own name. But I would like you to become my wife.'

Jamie smiled.

'I can't think of anything that would make me happier,' she said. 'And I've got no intention of keeping my own name. I've been practising writing Mrs Jamie Deacon for years.'

Being drenched in champagne, of course, the ring slid

on to the third finger of her left hand easily. And when Hugo and Sebastian hurtled through the door moments later, they were disgusted to find Rod and Jamie kissing in front of the Aga, and the roast potatoes burned to a crisp.